MW01140460

police man USA

novel

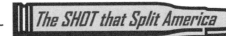

The SHOT that Split America

R. ANDERSON

authorHOUSE®

2nd edition, 2022

AuthorHouse™
1663 Liberty Drive
Bloomington, IN 47403
www.authorhouse.com
Phone: 833-262-8899

Published by AuthorHouse   04/06/2022

ISBN: 978-1-6655-3684-4 (sc)
ISBN: 978-1-6655-3686-8 (hc)
ISBN: 978-1-6655-3685-1 (e)

Library of Congress Control Number: 2021918187

Print information available on the last page.

Cover artwork R.ANDERSON

police man *USA*

R. ANDERSON

policemanUSA.com

CONTENTS

PROLOGUE

The man hurried along an alley behind a row of apartments, his eyes squinting looking for a specific unit.

Wearing running shoes and a ball cap, he turned the corner and walked down the inner courtyard lined with tall bushes. The exhaustion was catching up to him, but adrenaline kept his legs moving.

He breathed hard climbing up the stairs to reach the front porch. It appeared to be the one he was looking for, *1206-B*. For thirty-eight hours he hadn't eaten or slept but he was sure *1206-B* was the one. The tall lanky man rang the bell and forced a smile.

"Beth? You home?"

As his body arched forward to conceal any movements, his hand reached for the doorknob. A moment later, he ducked inside the modestly furnished condo.

"Beth?" He made sure to shut the door behind him, but not to lock it. "It's me."

He removed his hat and fixed his messy hair.

"I ran out of gas." He waited several seconds. "My car is just down the street."

The man slipped through the living room into the kitchen, then upstairs to the bedroom bureau, and lifted the lid off a jewelry box—a pearl pendant, gold and silver chains, two diamond rings—this was far better than any loose change.

He crammed his pockets with jewels until noticing a white cat watching from the bed— he froze, then smiled, but it was uninterested and looked away.

"Hello?" A sweet-sounding voice came from the downstairs foyer.

Silence hung in the air for a tense moment.

Next, he heard light footsteps from the young woman advancing up the staircase.

1

DIVIDED STATES OF AMERICA
2084

Detective James Merit sat in his office on the top floor of the Pilgrim State Police Department, an art-deco style building designed of steel, brick, and glass. Merit was twenty-nine, lean and muscular, with thick brown hair tightly combed to the side. His coffee-colored eyes looked out the window idly watching pigeons fly between buildings—biding his time, waiting for someone to die.

★★★

Like everyone in the state of Pilgrim, Merit had a job, went to church, carried a gun on his side, and obeyed the law. Some people didn't walk the straight and narrow, and their missteps kept the pigeon-watcher busy. Merit was a homicide investigator, just like his father before he'd retired. His dad had been a part of a dying breed of officers, someone who solved cold cases the old slow way, by following leads out in the field.

Merit, on the other hand, was a *hot* homicide detective. His job was to work a murder immediately after it was reported and solving it required solely watching recorded video footage from the station. With the department's extensive, state of the art video surveillance program and elite crime-solving technology, there was no longer a need for detectives to respond to a crime scene. In 2084, an investigator could solve crimes within hours as opposed to days, weeks, months, or years.

Crime had declined significantly over the years because the citizens of Pilgrim followed the same philosophy— a philosophy quite important since America was divided into two giant states a half-century earlier: The state of *Pilgrim* and the state of *Frontier*.

Pilgrim was created from twenty-two of America's former states, previously referred to as the *Middle States* and the *Bible Belt,* some to include Nebraska, Kansas, Iowa, Arkansas, Texas, Mississippi, Kentucky, Tennessee, and Florida.

Frontier was forged from the remaining twenty-eight named border and coastal states of Arizona and California, running north to Washington then east across North Dakota, Minnesota, Wisconsin, Michigan. It connected with additional northeastern states being New York and New Hampshire to name a few.

Even though the state names were removed the names of the cities, towns, mountains, lakes, and rivers remained the same.

Merit lived in the city of Tulsa and growing up learned that T-Town—the oil capital of the world, once belonged to the defunct state of *Oklahoma,* but it didn't mean a lot to him. He had his opinions and convictions, but he wasn't interested in the specifics that had split the nation over fifty years earlier. Merit was not an introspective man. He kept his life simple, his desk organized and his conscience clear.

A green light blinked on the console to the side of him. He looked at the glass offices adjacent to his, but he didn't see any other detectives or officers. Perhaps they were on lunch break, having meetings, or in training.

Officers no longer patrolled the streets of Pilgrim. Police patrols were replaced by thousands of mini-drones, equipped with onboard micro-cameras that drifted across Pilgrim's skies. The cameras filmed twenty-four hours a day and relayed their recordings to massive data storage banks. If a crime was reported in progress, uniformed officers were dispatched to the scene. If any follow-up investigation was needed, detectives remained in the stations and solved crimes by studying the recorded footage. Capturing a suspect on video as they arrived at the scene, committed a crime, or fled was the quickest, most reliable method for an investigator to make a case. People who contemplated committing a crime knew they would be caught on film, which proved to be a major deterrent in criminal activity.

The green light was still blinking—Merit pressed the RECEIVE button.

"Pilgrim P.D. This is Detective Merit." The voice on the other end sounded distant and electronic.

"Detective Merit," said a male voice, "We found new evidence in a murder case and are turning it over to you."

"Who is this?" Merit strained to hear him.

"The Frontier Police Department."

Merit had little interest in speaking to officers from Frontier P.D. From what he'd heard their society was lazy, disrespectful, and out of control. "Oh." Merit changed to a monotone voice. "What case?"

"The Soldier Quinn case."

"Soldier Quinn." Merit thought for a moment. "Never heard of him. How old's the case?"

"Sixty years."

"Sixty?" Merit wasn't sure he'd heard the voice correctly. "The number six zero?"

"Yes. Are you going to take it?"

Merit suppressed a laugh. "No. I only work *hot* homicides."

There was a pause on the other end. "The U.S. Resolution statutes mandated that Pilgrim P.D. work all old unsolved homicides from Frontier."

"Yeah, I don't know about all of that, but I'll transfer you down to our Cold Case Unit." Merit pushed another button, sending the call to the unit located in the basement.

Besides initially being drawn to law enforcement because his father was a cold case detective, Merit mostly appreciated police work because of its practicality. There was some discretion required in the decision-making process, but in his expertise, a video recording spoke for itself. His decisions didn't rely on what he wished were true or how he felt in his heart or what he hoped had happened. He functioned by a logical code when studying footage and drawing a conclusion which was often summarized by a familiar axiom: The camera never lies.

Two minutes later, Merit noticed that the green light was still blinking.

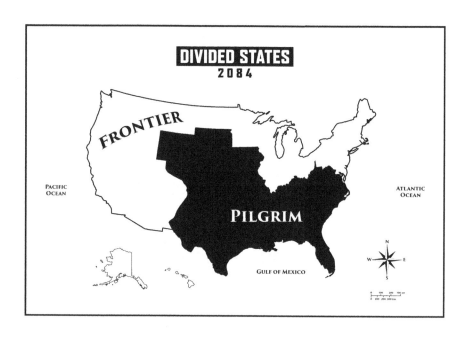

DIVIDED STATES
2084

FRONTIER

PILGRIM

PACIFIC
OCEAN

ATLANTIC
OCEAN

GULF OF MEXICO

2

A handsome African American pole vaulter and an attractive sprinter met in 1980 at The Drake Relays for a collegiate track meet and married three months later. The Quinn's had premature twins, a baby girl, and a boy. The girl died shortly after birth and when the infant boy bravely fought to survive, they aptly named him Soldier. At two, they sensed something was different about him. He was late to walk and talk, and his motor skills were weak. At daycare, he played alone. Soldier had subtle fixations, pushing a toy car back and forth obsessively. He was diagnosed with mild autism. His dad was determined not to allow him to grow up to be treated differently. Their condo backed up to a private golf course and every evening he snuck Soldier onto the green to practice putting to improve his hand-eye coordination. Soldier held the club awkwardly and clumsily slapped the ball. A "natural" he was not.

—Charles Harris, *sports@bostontimes.com*

PHONE CALL

The basement where the Cold Case Unit was located looked dingy, and some of the overhead light panels flickered or were dark. Merit made his way down the office's main aisle flanked by cubicles normally manned by cold case detectives. Most of the desks were vacated—only a few cops were still assigned to the division—the rest of them were littered with stacks of papers and coffee cups. What Merit noticed more than anything was the dead silence in the basement. No wonder the call he forwarded from Frontier hadn't been answered.

Merit took a left at the end of the aisle, walked a few paces, and saw a white grease board with a few cold case stats scribbled in black magic marker.

2081 – 15 unsolved homicides
2082 – 9 unsolved homicides
2083 – 6 unsolved homicides
2084 – 2 unsolved homicides

Noting they'd only had *two* cold case murders in the current year, Merit shook his head. What did they do all day? And they had computers, so why the old grease board, stacks of papers, sticky notes, and opened evidence cartons?

"Anyone here?" Merit knocked three times on the top of an empty desktop.

Merit advanced to a cubicle occupied by a man in his late fifties with thinning hair and a paunch over his belt. The plaque on the outside of his cubicle said DET. HUBBARD.

"I transferred a phone call down here a few minutes ago, did you hear it?"

Hubbard continued looking ahead and never turned from his desk to make eye contact. "No, I didn't hear it down here." He pronounced the word "down" with noticeable sarcasm.

Merit dropped the number from Frontier P.D. on Hubbard's cluttered desk. "Here."

"Why didn't *you* answer the call?" Hubbard shook his head and sneered. "Instead of pawning it off on me?"

"No. Frontier P.D. called and said they had some new evidence about an *old* homicide they want to give *you*."

"What evidence?" Det. Hubbard barely turned his head to the right, using only peripheral vision to see Merit.

"I didn't ask."

"Why not?"

"Screw Frontier P.D. and plus, I don't work cold cases."

Hubbard blew off Merit's comment. "Yeah, you work your famous hot homicides in your little crystal ball." He waved his fingers over the computer as if he were casting a magic spell.

"Yeah, I solve them, if that's what you mean."

Hubbard swiveled around in his squeaky chair, faced Merit, and with a gruff voice said, "Why don't you call them back? Talk to them— Go see them in person. See what it's like to get out and follow-up."

"Because that's your job." Merit forced himself to look directly back into Hubbard's eyes.

Five alert tones sounded from the speaker on the wall. Merit glanced at the sign, a touch of adrenaline fired through his bloodstream. A sign in red flashed the words HOT HOMICIDE.

3

By the age of five, Soldier had evolved into an unusually accurate putter. The repetitive swinging of the putter club gave him the internal stimulation he craved to soothe his mildly autistic symptoms while simultaneously grooving his stroke. His dad moved him on to ball striking. The club's golf pro noticed Soldier and his dad trespassing but appreciated the boy's persistence and improved skills and looked the other way. He even delayed the sprinkler system at night, buying Soldier extra minutes of practice time. Over the next several years, the Pro gave him free lessons, and by age eight Soldier parred the course's back nine. A disgruntled member reported the Pro's improprieties, though, and the board fired him. Soldier suddenly had no instructor, no place to practice, and his future as a golfer was in jeopardy.

— Brook Lyons, *www.GolfingWorldMagazine*

THE HOMISCOPE

Merit was at his best when hot homicides came in. He'd worked hundreds, and it was a comforting feeling knowing that nothing would surprise him.

He rode the lift to the fifth floor, where he was met by Sergeant Tom Travers. The even-keeled, fit supervisor walked briskly, then slowed to match Merit's calm stride as they proceeded down a long white corridor with tile walls so clean that it looked like the antiseptic interior of an operating room at a hospital. Officers emerged from half a dozen rooms, donning tactical gear and heading for the roof where they would strap on drones to fly to the crime scene and the surrounding neighborhood.

The control center was receiving a barrage of updates from medics, officers, detectives, crime scene techs, and other personnel responding to the crime scene. Their dialogue was converted to a computerized voice that emanated from speakers throughout headquarters.

"It appears to be a female white in her early twenties with blonde hair," the mechanical voice said over the loudspeaker. "From the town of Joplin, located one-hundred and twelve miles northeast of Pilgrim P.D., population of approximately seventy-five-thousand. The victim was found deceased in her condo, *1206-B* by a coworker when she didn't show up for work today. She was discovered partially clothed. Said coworker stated that the front door was unlocked when she arrived, and the victim appeared to be raped and possibly stabbed due to the presence of blood."

"You need anything, Merit?" Sergeant Travers said.

Ahead was a door with a sign attached that read HOMISCOPE ROOM.

"No. I'm good, Sarge." Merit secured a wraparound headset that contained speakers for both ears as well as a microphone so that he could send and receive communication to Sgt. Travers and officers in the field.

"This will be your one-hundredth hot homicide for the year, and it's only May." Travers stepped aside as Merit opened the oval hatch leading to the homiscope.

Sergeant Travers returned to the Control Center. He always made sure that surveillance cameras and drones were fully operational so that he could feed Merit all the information he needed. Meanwhile, like an astronaut stepping into a space capsule for a mission to Mars, Merit vanished through the hatch.

★★★

Merit entered the shell of the darkened spherical homiscope, which had a diameter of thirty feet. He strode confidently across a slender catwalk and sat in the orange leather chair in the center of the room. The catwalk retracting into the wall behind him, Merit strapped himself into the ergonomic seat that resembled a compact dentist's chair suspended in midair by powerful magnets. His feet rested on foot pedals, his hands grasping joysticks with several buttons. The assembly at the center of the homiscope was known as The Nucleus because it had as many controls along its surface as the most sophisticated fighter jet cockpits. He pulled back the right joystick, and the chair tilted up at an angle of twenty degrees. He then depressed the left foot pedal, and the cockpit angled down ten degrees and swiveled to the left by fifteen degrees.

Everything checked out as hundreds of flat screens that comprised the concaved circular wall around him flickered to life, all having been activated by Sergeant Travers in the Control Center.

"Ready Sarge." Merit made the homiscope sling swivel 360 degrees. He then tapped his miniature wrist computer to start its stopwatch function.

"Got it. Live feeds coming to you, Merit. The victim was a nurse at Sacred Cross Hospital. Beth Honeywell. Age twenty-two. Other vital statistics being sent to your screens as they come in."

Tiny solar-powered drones randomly patrolled all cities and towns in Pilgrim and could be manipulated to congregate near a crime scene when programmed to do so. No larger than a cup coaster and light as a leaf, each drone was equipped with a high-powered lens and a sensing device to gauge temperature, distance, speed, wind, and other environmental factors. The unmanned, semi-transparent drones undulated up and down in the air, like translucent jellyfish gracefully pulsating in the ocean. Many were now outside of Nurse Honeywell's residence feeding information to the homiscope.

Merit saw Nurse Honeywell's address to his lower left and immediately called up digital recordings of a two-mile area surrounding her condo made over the past seventy-two hours, so he could get a feel for the general vicinity. More screens appeared on the interior walls of the homiscope, with the cockpit tilting to give Merit a view of each new screen as it appeared. Some recordings he saved and moved to the right of his chair on a master timeline, while others were moved to the left for repeat viewing. Still, others were discarded as irrelevant. Screens popped on and off like fireworks on New Year's Eve as he sought to create a master timeline.

He listened to the comments of neighbors, as they spoke to officers outside the scene.

"She was such a hardworking young girl. She graduated from nursing school this spring."

"Who would do such a thing?"

"She had a boyfriend. He came over a lot for dinner but always left before ten o'clock. Had a key and would let himself in."

"I have a search warrant signed by the district judge," Travers said to Merit. A photo of the warrant popped on one of the homiscope's screens a second later. "You can send in the safety drone." The remote-controlled drone, fitted with several sorts of cameras, always preceded an officer's entry into a crime scene in case the suspect was still hiding inside.

The Nucleus faced forward and remained stationary as Merit depressed the third button on his left joystick, edging the hovering drone into the residence of Beth Honeywell. A delicate hand was critical to carefully navigate the drone through the scene, and its digital imagery would be crucial for later documentation, so he pressed the RECORD button. The drone sent him a live feed as he paused at the front door and observed no signs of forced entry.

He hedged the mini-drone viewfinder through the door's threshold to avoid contaminating the scene. This phase of the video crime-solving process provided him the biggest rush—entering the unknown for the first time, like a pioneer into a new world. Even though he'd done it countless times over the last eight years, he still had to steady his nerves by slowing his breathing, like a doctor before performing an intricate surgery.

Just inside the entryway, he noticed the victim's purse and set of keys on the stand. She hadn't been ambushed, and he saw the naked shape of the victim on the floor of the foyer, torn black panties strewn nearby.

★★★

Sitting inside the homiscope's cockpit Merit agilely guided the drone to hover only twenty inches above the young nurse's bare feet, and first noted her toes were clenched shut. He then smoothly piloted the drone level up past her knees and observed blood smeared on her inner thighs, with several drops on the carpet between her legs. It looked like dried blood, not spatter, which would have indicated that some sort of sharp instrument had caused the blood loss. There were no puncture marks, slashes, or lacerations on the front of her body, which would have been consistent with someone using a cutting instrument to inflict the damage.

He scanned the drone further along past her hips and torso, filming her exposed chest, and noticed a black sheer bra was tightly wrapped around her neck, appearing to be the weapon used to strangle her. He steadied the camera over her head, photographing the look on her terrified face, mouth open and forming the shape of an "O," her eyes stricken with fear and fixed on the ceiling as the rookie nurse took her last breath.

He forwarded the photos of the crime scene to the medical examiner's investigator, who had just arrived on the scene to provide a preliminary evaluation.

No one, not the police nor any authority figure, was permitted to view live or recorded drone footage. Only trained, certified detectives could do so, and that was only after a crime was reported. To prevent detectives from wrongly viewing any public footage, all citizens, including persons in the media, were randomly chosen—much like a jury—to man police stations, ensuring the video system was not being compromised or abused. After ten days of storage, the video was deleted, guaranteeing the public that all images had been permanently erased.

The people of Pilgrim didn't object to being filmed twenty-four hours a day by cameras if they weren't constantly being monitored by Big Brother. Those who chose to reside in Pilgrim during the state's inception fifty years earlier had consented to live in a society where cameras would be used to combat crime to ensure it was a safer place. It wasn't the perfect system to eradicate all crime, but it was extremely efficient, as well as fast, fair, and reliable.

At first, the swarms of mini-drones populating the airspace of Pilgrim felt intrusive to its citizens, but in time the people quickly became immune to the tiny translucent flying saucers and the constant buzzing sound they emitted. With the significant drop in crime, accompanied by a super-speedy trial, followed up with swift and severe punishment for the perpetrator, the residents quickly came to embrace the advanced techniques of law enforcement and a progressive, updated judicial system.

Working inside the homiscope Merit captained the drone into the kitchen and saw open drawers and cabinets. The perpetrator had been looking for something, probably money, drugs, or a gun. He checked the back door and all windows and observed no signs of a forced entry. Someone either had a key, was inside when she had left for work or had followed her in. He eliminated the idea of someone waiting for her inside since a roommate or boyfriend wouldn't rummage through drawers and leave them open.

Next, he maneuvered the drone up the wooden staircase, noting a small piece of silver jewelry on a step. At the top of the steps, Merit abruptly paused the drone midair, a pair of round golden eyes belonging to a white cat, stared back into his line of sight. He elevated over the reach of the curious feline and into Honeywell's bedroom. A rectangular imprint was visible on the dresser because of a light coating of dust on the wooden surface around the spot where the box had rested. Pink-colored hospital scrubs lay bunched on the floor. In the bathroom, the shower curtain had been shoved to the left, and both hot and cold valve handles were in the on position, water was spraying from the shower spigot.

Merit assumed Sgt. Travers was watching from the Control Room like he normally did. His sergeant had told him how he studied Merit's methods and was fascinated by how he worked. Travers had calculated Merit's average time for solving murders using the homiscope at just under forty-eight minutes; the next closest detective's average time was three days. His talent was well-respected throughout the law enforcement community, and his peers marveled at his proficiency and one-hundred percent clearance rate.

Merit began piecing together what he saw to formulate a working hypothesis of how the crime had gone down.

"Check to see if a key on her key ring unlocks the front door," he said to a crime scene tech, who was at the scene decked out in antiseptic all-white coveralls.

Merit performed one swift second sweep of the condo and pulled the drone out with a single press of a button on his right-hand joystick.

Who *was* this suspect?

4

Soldier's father told him, the greatest golfer of all time is Vic Jackson. Soldier promised his dad one day he would beat Jackson and be the best. On Soldier's ninth birthday, his father bought him his first set of clubs. While driving home to celebrate, his dad fell asleep at the wheel, struck a tree, and was instantly killed. Soldier became despondent and stopped talking and playing golf. Several months later, Soldier's mother took a gamble. She invested her late husband's pension into Soldier's future. She tracked down the fired golf pro and offered him a full-time job coaching Soldier. The thirty-seven-year-old, ex-tour player agreed to mentor Soldier. Every day he picked Soldier up from school and scrambled to different public courses, driving ranges, or any open spaces to practice.

—Timothy Rands, *Biography of Soldier Quinn*

A KNACK

The computerized voice provided constant updates in Merit's earpieces. "One of Nurse Honeywell's coworkers stated that she was working the seven-to-three shift yesterday. On nice mornings, she rode her bike to and from the hospital for exercise." The updates were being gathered by one of several Pilgrim cops that had responded to the hospital and other locations she frequented.

Tilting the homiscope's cockpit up, Merit called up a schematic of routes between her condo and the hospital. To make the one-way trip by bike would have taken approximately thirty to forty minutes. He looked at the digital captures of the previous morning—Thursday, between 6:00 and 7:00. They showed the young nurse arriving at work on her bike in the morning at 6:35. It was now Friday at 1:30 p.m. The call had come into headquarters at 1:18.

A window of opportunity of thirty hours and forty-three minutes had existed for someone to break into the apartment, but Merit knew that the window could be narrowed considerably since he theorized that Beth Honeywell had been startled, meaning that the intruder had gotten into the condo shortly before the victim got home. Burglars didn't break in and wait long periods of time. They get in and out—unless they were surprised in the act.

Okay, that meant she would be expected to arrive home the previous day around 3:40 p.m., forty minutes after her shift was over at 3:00 p.m., give or take depending on how long it took her to get to her bike and whether she had encountered traffic or stopped along the way.

The external report of the Medical Examiner's investigator was one of the many sounds that popped into Merit's ear: "Urine discharge, slight bruising on the neck, red marks around the eyes, petechiae, no sign of trauma to the front or back of her body. Possible sexual assault. Probable cause of death, suffocation caused by strangulation. Manner of death, murder."

"Thanks," Merit said. "And make sure to bag her hands and feet."

Merit decided to look at surveillance in her neighborhood taken four hours before Honeywell arrived home on her bike. He saw kids running along the sidewalk, tossing a ball back and forth. He deleted a woman walking a dog before retreating inside her home.

He studied a flurry of images flickering on the panels of the homiscope wall. He looked ahead, to the sides, above, behind, and beneath him, and grabbed clips that could assist him in creating a timeline of images while he dismissed hundreds of others.

Two hours before the deceased got home, several people could be seen walking in a one-mile perimeter of her condo, the mailman, the recycle pickup truck worker, but it was mostly random vehicles that passed through the frames. The detective quickly saved the footage on the screen to his left labeled STORAGE BIN to see if their faces or vehicles would appear later.

Twelve minutes elapsed since he'd entered the homiscope, but he remained cool and calm. His goal was to put one piece on the timeline, then work backward or forwards. It would come to him—it always had. *Happy birthday,* he said under his breath. It was a verbal cue he used when starting a homicide as a reminder to *hear* the visual clue.

Merit spun and looked again at the scene of Honeywell crossing a street on her bike near the hospital when she arrived in the morning. The bike rack was located on the edge of the parking lot, which Merit scanned right to left. He quickly pushed the right foot pedal while moving the right joystick to the side, so he could again see the cars driving in the established perimeter of the condo.

Then, in some masterful, unexplainable process of elimination, he added, switched, and interchanged video clips faster and faster, gradually accelerating to a remarkable speed.

A second officer at the hospital cut in. "Merit, the nurse's supervisor advised Nurse Honeywell left a half-hour early yesterday due to a female-related issue." *Ah.* That explained why Merit couldn't find the nurse biking on any of the streets past 3 p.m.

Before he searched for her on the bike, Merit plucked a piece of footage from inside her condo's upstairs bedroom and zoomed in tightly on the pink scrubs bunched on the floor. He detected dark red spotting in the crotch of her pink scrub bottoms, corroborating her supervisor's account and explaining the dried blood on her thighs and drips on the floor he'd earlier noted.

Quickly rewinding to 2:20 p.m., he tracked the caregiver pedaling south on Iris Street before she moved out of the frame. He then estimated her time of arrival at the condo as 2:50 p.m., not 3:30. The hovering drone had been positioned too far away to depict any of her facial details, but the neon pink scrubs she wore—the pair he'd seen in her condo—were enough to confirm it was her. Yes! She was alive at that time, and after eighteen minutes and forty-five seconds in the homiscope, he added his first clip to start the master timeline.

★★★

In milliseconds, Pilgrim's top Hot Homicide investigator Detective Merit spun in the gyroscope-like cockpit, clicking, tapping, and double-tapping different keys, as well as flipping switches and levers as video snippets, flashed on a myriad of screens. He scanned to see if anyone followed her but saw no one. He surfed monitors without any rhyme or reason that anyone who'd ever watched from the Control Room, most notably his sergeant, could figure. At the twenty-four-minute mark, Merit's timeline began to grow, and as a piece of artwork with gaps being filled in, the sequence of events started to be recognizable.

Merit quickly tapped the left foot pedal while moving the left joystick to the side so he could again see the vehicles coming and going from the general vicinity of the nurse's condo. He determined there had been no drones circulating within several blocks of her condo when he estimated she would have arrived, so he surveyed footage from the flock of drone cameras within a two-mile radius.

His trained eye scouted for anything that appeared odd, and that *odd* could take shape in an unfathomable number of subtle ways. Merit focused on a car parked a mile from the Honeywell's condo. He turned a dial on the cockpit's dashboard, homing in on a two-door dirty black passenger vehicle parked in the back lot of a fast-food joint on Thursday at 2 p.m. He then determined that the same black vehicle, from another drone's vantage point, was absent from the parking space an hour and fifteen minutes later. It was just one of the hundreds of vehicles that he clicked in a span of seconds, but Merit dragged the segment to a storage bin.

The homiscope cockpit spun in a frenzy as the hot homicide detective viewed new displays every second, working backward and forwards in time, moving with such speed that he was as animated as a man conducting an orchestra, assimilating bits of information concurrently.

In a matter of seconds, he'd accessed bank accounts, retrieved driver's licenses, service station receipts, yearbook photos, dated pawn tickets, employee applications for persons possibly owning numerous vehicles in question as well as various models of similar bikes. Just as rapidly, he viewed abstract images: the angle of a shadow cast on the ground from the sun, pieces of jewelry, reflections off windows, and interpreted sound waves and audio frequencies caused by moving vehicles, voices, animal sounds, and general movement.

That's how Merit surpassed other detectives on the Pilgrim Police investigative unit. He possessed an unexplainable knack—a sixth sense of sorts for absorbing an onslaught of video images. By quickly establishing patterns, scrutinizing movements, and anatomizing data, he had the talent to detect one tiny, intricate flaw or uncover the ever-so-minute inconsistency that he discerned as useful in solving a crime.

While devouring visual stimuli, Merit was inundated with a hail of incoming audio information. Officers, detectives, neighbors, witnesses, and other officials fed him a slew of facts, figures, tips, statistics, and data through his headset requiring his brain to quickly compare, contrast, match, measure, verify, process and eliminate then respond with the questions necessary to drive the investigation forward.

The interchange transpired so fast that the dialog sounded like a foreign language, colorful snapshots looked like a nonsensical dream, and he was picking up even more speed. Things were starting to come together when Merit hit the stopwatch button on his high-tech computerized wristwatch.

★★★

The homiscope's spinning motion began to lose momentum, like a ride winding down at an amusement park. When it came to a complete stop, Merit was in the same upright position as when he started.

The mental energy he spent analyzing the mass of information combined with the rapid gyration his body underwent in the cockpit, gave him the sensation that he had traveled through space and time. After the several seconds it required to find his bearings, Merit eyed the time flashing on his computer watch and saw that he had solved the current year's one-hundredth homicide in thirty-eight minutes and twelve seconds. A personal best.

I got him.

5

Soldier used his father's death as motivation and spent countless hours practicing golf. What psychologists would have considered deficiencies stemming from mild autism—social isolation, an abnormal compulsion duplicating one movement— "Tunnel vision" proved to be ideal attributes for developing a golfer. Soldier entered his first tournament at age thirteen—and won it! Over the next several years, the Pro hauled Soldier to compete in local, sectional, and, by the time he was sixteen, national tournaments. On car trips, they discussed how to handle the stressful conditions of tournament play, adjust to different types of courses and tactics to get an edge. By seventeen, his mother's investment had paid off, as Soldier accepted a scholarship to The University of Texas. As a freshman, he unexpectedly won the NCAA golf title. The Pro asked his prized pupil if he wanted to turn professional, but Soldier replied, "I'm not ready."

—Brian Mills, *Soldier: Life and Death on the Green*

A THOUSAND WORDS

"You got the killer?" Sgt. Travers intercepted Merit walking down the hall outside of the Homiscope Room. "I leave for five minutes, and you get him."

They shook hands, Merit nodding with a slight smile.

"That's amazing," Travers said. "Who killed her?"

"A nurse." Merit tilted his high-tech watch at the wall where it projected an enlarged driver's license with a photo featuring a middle-aged male white in his forties with medium-length brown hair.

Travers removed his glasses. "John L. Parsons. Who is he?"

"Nurse Parsons. He worked at the same hospital as Honeywell but in a different unit, and their shifts overlapped."

"How'd he do it?"

"Yesterday he left work, parked his car in the back of a restaurant, and changed clothes in his car. He walked the back alleys, cut through the courtyard, entered her front door, went upstairs, and started to steal her stuff. She was at work but for personal reasons left early. When she got home, she went upstairs to take a shower, where he was hiding behind the curtain."

"He panicked." Sergeant Travers interrupted Merit. "She ran down the stairs, he chased her, dropped a piece of jewelry, and to keep her quiet he strangled her to death." He glanced to the side for a moment, then looked back with a follow-up question. "There was no forced entry, and I heard the tech tell you that the key to her front door was on her key ring. So, how did he get in her place?"

"Yesterday at work, I located him on the hospital's key tracking log entering the employee's break room. I figured he went through her purse and removed her house key, then on his break, went to her condo. After he killed her, he put the key back on her key ring, hiked to his car, changed back into his scrubs, and returned to work. I got him on film dumping his clothes in the trash can at a car wash on his way home. A tech is there now, collecting them."

"Where was her gun?"

"In her purse, by the front door."

"She almost got to it." Travers sounded disappointed. "That's good work." He offered him a fist bump, and Merit reciprocated. "And the blood on her thighs?" Travers said.

"It was from her period. There was no trauma to the body. She suffocated."

"And we won't know if he raped her until after the autopsy," Travers said.

Merit nodded. "I'll type up the murder warrant then give it to you to get a commissioner to sign."

He returned to the Homiscope Room to finalize his work, which consisted of producing a two-minute video clip, including the most pertinent scenes, before editing and splicing it with establishing shots, crime scene photos, graphics with names, dates and time stamps, security footage, evidence collected, and any other records. When the piece was finalized, it would play like a crisply edited, information-packed, two-minute movie with a beginning, middle, climactic ending, and a backstory. The fact-based film would be overwhelmingly convincing, proving to anyone watching—a judge, jury, the public, and most importantly the defendant—that he was, beyond a reasonable doubt, guilty of the murder of Beth Honeywell.

When a detective was subpoenaed to testify in court, the video was submitted as evidence, and once it was played, it was virtually impossible for any attorney to defend against. "A picture is worth a thousand words" was always the prosecutor's closing statement at a trial.

Hours later, having finished completing the two-minute portion augmented by a voice-over chronicling the chain of events that led to naming John Parson as the perpetrator, Merit tilted his head back and closed his eyes.

There was always a sense of accomplishment after solving a case, but this one felt a little different. He didn't know why but didn't give it any more thought.

6

Sports talk-show hosts scrutinized Soldier's collegiate success, debating that he was too immature and his frame too weak to compete on the adult tour. The daily grind would eat him alive. Soldier heard the negative commentary and called his Pro to tell him he had made a big decision: He was going to quit college and turn professional. By winning the NCAA tournament, Soldier entered his first major by special exemption. He surprised everyone when at eighteen he won the 1998 PGA Championship, capturing his first major. Soldier followed it up with a string of tour wins, but critics questioned whether he would succumb to the new pressures. At the next major, Soldier didn't even make the cut. The naysayers had a field day—a 'one-hit wonder', but over the next two years, the high-functioning autistic athlete got the last word when he won four of the next eight majors. Still, he faced a road of unknown hazards ahead.

—author unknown, *Clubhouse Journal vol. XLVI*

CAPTURED ON FILM

Murder suspect John Parsons arrived home with a bag of groceries thirty miles from the condo of Nurse Beth Honeywell. He saw a small, flat computer screen attached to his front door and froze, the bag of groceries slipping from his arm. The screen read MR. JOHN L. PARSON: PRESS PLAY. He'd been caught. His heart started to race. He peered into the darkness and saw no one but assumed officers were crouching in the shadows with their rifles pointed at him and ready to chase if he tried to escape.

Parsons faced forward and touched the illuminated PLAY button. The two-minute movie Merit had edited started. When the digital recording reached its end, an automated voice from the computer spoke without emotion as the words appeared on the screen: GUILTY or NOT GUILTY. Parson's face was pale, for he knew what was coming—he was about to hear what all murderers heard once they'd been captured.

The voice explained that he could surrender, plead *guilty*, and automatically receive life in prison. This was the way of justice in Pilgrim, eliminating lengthy and costly trials that the public would have to pay for. If he chose *not guilty*, went to trial, and lost, however, he would receive an automatic death sentence, *execution by firing squad* carried out by civilians within twenty-five days of a guilty verdict.

Back in the old America's judicial system, when it was comprised of fifty states, the criminal court's standard for determining guilt and innocence fell under the formulation of English jurist William Blackstone: "It is better that ten guilty men escape prison than one innocent man suffer." But that principle no longer aligned with modern-day Pilgrim's ultra-conservative doctrine, which erred less on the side of caution. Its methodology refused to allow ten guilty dangerous criminals to roam the streets for the sake of mistakenly accusing one man. It made sense to Merit, and over-examining the idea led to "paralysis by analysis."

John Parsons raised his arm: GUILTY or NOT GUILTY, his trembling finger pointed at the computer screen as he prepared to make his choice.

7

In Soldier's first five years competing on the tour, he rose to the ranks of number one and racked up an amazing eight majors. Soldier drew many comparisons to the great Vic Jackson, yet he and the Pro agreed on what his father once professed: "To be the best player of all time, he must beat the best." Vic, nicknamed the "Autumn Fox" because of his fiery red hair and cagey demeanor on the course, had retired from the game forty years prior. Vic had taken more than thirty years to accomplish his record-setting twenty-two major titles. But after Soldier's amazing start, fans and the media pushed for him to catch the sly fox's seemingly untouchable record. Each year, the pressure mounted to accomplish what many people once thought was impossible.

—Francis C. Mehring, *TheSportingFactor@aol.com*

THOU SHALT NOT KILL

Having left the homiscope, Merit received pats on the back, high-fives, and handshakes from a dozen officers, fellow detectives, and supervisors, as he walked down the hall to his office. He was private by nature and merely grinned and gave a perfunctory "Thanks," as he passed his admirers, making sure to humbly add, "Thanks for your help." It was his job, one he did well, but standing in the limelight wasn't his style.

Back in his office, he sat at his desk and filled out the necessary casework on his computer. It always took him longer to document the details of what he'd done than to solve a case. And besides filling out long forms to be stored in the police database, he had to assemble a much longer video documenting the more important drone feeds he had used to bring John Parsons to justice.

His console showed that Nurse Beth Honeywell's family was calling to thank him, but closing the case came first, besides what could he say other than, "I'm sorry for your loss." At some point, he would recite these words to her family, but not yet. He always felt funny after solving a murder because he'd never experienced any sympathy for the victims—a detail he kept to himself. He justified his lack of empathy as a reason why he excelled at his job. He would have to muster up some solace when he finally spoke to the family.

By the time Merit finished making his case log, he looked up and saw that the sun had set. He'd been at his desk for hours and decided to call Ruth to tell her goodnight.

"You're on the news again James," Ruth said. "I'm glad you caught him."

"Thanks. I did it in under thirty-eight minutes."

Only his girlfriend Ruth, his mother, and father called him by his first name James, most everyone else referred to him by his last name, and he also referred to himself as Merit.

"Is it true, James—that she didn't really know him, but at work one time she felt sorry for him and lent him money so he could make his rent? And then he went and killed her for her jewelry, so he could sell it to buy drugs?"

"Drugs make you do bad things. And I don't know all the rest, I didn't talk to him."

"That's what the news said. Well, I hope he'll be shot."

"He won't be. He hit the guilty button." Merit changed the subject. "How was your day?"

"The usual. Are we still going to the ranch on Saturday, James?"

"For sure." He sounded enthusiastic. "You gotta meet my folks." He transferred the phone to his other hand and placed it on the other side of the head. "Where are you now?"

"I'm in bed."

Merit swiveled his desk chair to the computer on the metal shelf behind him and tapped a few keys on his phone, sending a hologram to his girlfriend of eight months. After he checked to see if the office cubicles were empty, he knelt by his desk, flattened his hands together by his chest, and said, "Love you. God loves you. Sweet dreams." His projected shape appeared instantly in Ruth's bedroom, kneeling, and mouthing the same words as he kissed her on the forehead.

"Goodnight," she said. "I love you. Wish you would come by later."

"Me too. After we're married. We gotta stick to the plan, right?"

There was silence from Ruth's end. There was no living together out of wedlock—one of the many moral codes citizens had to abide by in the ultra-conservative State of Pilgrim.

The hologram dissolved into thin air.

★★★

Merit rode the lift to the property room on the seventh floor. He approached a horizontal pneumatic tube and spoke. "Request voice identification for Detective James Merit."

"Authenticated," came an automated male voice as a cylinder slid through the transparent tube and stopped in front of the detective.

He put the thumb drive on which his video and case log were stored into the cylinder and spoke. "Case 2084-295476. Murder. Bethany Honeywell. May 28, 2084. Defendant John Parsons apprehended. Case closed."

Merit screwed the tube shut and watched the cylinder speed away to the rear of the property room, where robotic arms would catalog the thumb drive and store it as evidence.

Merit was tired but decided to take a quick look at the nine o'clock news on one of the floor-to-ceiling wall monitors stationed on every floor of the building. He normally didn't watch the news because he believed that the way it was reported fed off people's emotions and those facts became irrelevant.

Prisoner Parsons was already en route via police helicopter to a retired Caribbean cruise ship anchored thirty miles off the coast of Galveston, Texas, to serve a life sentence. The ninety-two-year-old vessel had been painted over in various shades of military green. There were two hundred such floating prisons anchored throughout the Gulf. The retired, recycled ships were cheaper than building new prisons, and the long swim to shore was a major hindrance for any convict contemplating a breakout. The former luxury liner, having been converted to a floating prison, had been stripped of all amenities, and a foreboding sign on the hull read: STATE OF PILGRIM PRISON SHIP # 62

The news showed Parsons, clad in a jumpsuit, hopping from a chopper onto the stern helipad. It was Merit's first time seeing him other than examining the headshot on his driver's license. Merit read his lips: "I didn't do it." The wild-eyed, drug-using convict was led away by four guards into the depths of the ship to be processed to live out the remainder of his life.

Yeah— you did, or you wouldn't have pressed the guilty button Merit thought as he sealed the remaining video evidence in a tamper-resistant, transparent, pressurized box. Like Ruth expressed, he too wished that the nurse's murderer would've faced the firing squad. If you illegally killed someone, it made sense that *you* should be killed too. That way you couldn't kill again—it was common sense. Pilgrim's law of logic trumped The Bible's Sixth Commandment.

Suddenly, a hand slapped him on the shoulder from behind. He wheeled around, startled to see Sergeant Travers. Only a skeleton crew was working the night shift, and Merit had assumed his sergeant had long since left the building.

Travers was impressed with his detective's work. "Merit, you eaten yet?"

"No, I'm starved though. I just got to wrap up a few more things."

"Let's go eat when you're done—my treat. I want to tell you something."

Merit frowned. Sgt. Traver's was easy-going but always direct, and saying he had something to him tell later, was out of character.

"Is something wrong?"

8

Soldier, the African American golfer, became an extremely popular sports figure, but off the course, just like as a boy back in daycare, he had trouble making friends. He tried to connect with players on the tour, but his one-dimensional interest in golf made him appear shallow to others. He had no real relationships, so he filled the void of loneliness by practicing. Despite his immense success, the game didn't come easy for Soldier. He spent an extraordinary amount of time refining every stroke and swing to obtain a fine balance of touch, timing, and power. With his dedication and ability to focus, by age thirty-three he had won three British Opens, two Master's, the PGA Championship, and U.S. Open title, giving him fifteen majors. But could an unexpected encounter on an airline flight derail his drive?

—Timothy Rands, *Biography of Soldier Quinn*

RED FLAGS

Merit accompanied Sgt. Travers as they strode along a sidewalk in Pilgrim's downtown district toward their regular eating spot, a twenty-four-hour diner. It was a weeknight, so the streets weren't too busy, and stretching his legs felt good after sitting so much.

"Nope. Nothing's wrong Merit." Sgt. Travers cackled. "By the way, how's your father doing?"

"He's doing good— thanks. Me and Ruth are gonna go see him after church on Saturday."

"Tell him that we could use him. I got a couple of cold cases going nowhere." He winked. "We should bring him out of retirement."

"He probably would, if you asked him," Merit said.

They both chuckled, Travers nodding in agreement. The sergeant skipped a couple of steps ahead and held the door open for the prized detective to enter the lobby of the restaurant. "Is your dad still working those horses a lot, or is he gettin' too old?" He smiled.

"No. He's in real good shape for his age." Merit exhibited a child-like exuberance when he spoke of a visit to his parent's ranch. "In fact, he and I will ride them this weekend."

★★★

Seated in a window booth of a restaurant three blocks from headquarters, the two investigators were approached by a waitress who told them that dinner was *on the house.*

"Really?" Merit raised his head from studying the menu.

"Just look around," the hostess turned her head toward the customers seated about.

Patrons were looking at the detective who'd solved the murder of Nurse Honeywell. Heads turned every few seconds to see the man who'd been featured on the evening news, someone who consistently brought swift justice to the Pilgrim State and its citizens. Drones and guns were all well and good, but a man like Detective Merit represented what Pilgrim was all about—law and order and quick justice that translated to security, stability, and peace of mind.

After ordering a couple of slabs of thick grilled steaks, a ritual they celebrated together after Merit solved a murder, Travers looked his companion in the eye. "We've got a homicide."

"Let's go," Merit started to get up without giving it a second thought.

"No. Not a hot one." Travers laughed as he gestured for Merit to take his seat again. "It's a cold case."

"No thanks then." Merit sat and straightened the linen napkin back on his lap.

"It's about the death of a famous person a long time ago."

"From this afternoon?" Merit looked up. "I took that call from Frontier P.D. and gave it to Hubbard down in Cold Case. It's *sixty* years old."

"Yeah. It involves the case of a great golfer named Soldier Quinn. He was killed because he was African American."

"Why would they kill him because of his race?"

"You don't know much about old America's past, do you?"

Merit shook his head one time.

"It's why we have the Divided States of America. It's why they split America into two giant states. It's why there's a Pilgrim and a Frontier. Some say it started because of his death."

"Yeah, I knew it was something like that, but I'm not a big history buff," Merit said. "What was so great about him?"

"Golf was a sport where they hit a tiny white ball really far into in a small hole in fewer hits than their opponents." His sergeant cupped his hands together to form the shape of a circular hole. "It used to be a really popular sport."

"I've seen some old footage of it." Merit stared at Travers blankly. "It didn't look like much of a sport to me." He turned around to see his food being delivered, then turned back to the sergeant and crossed his arms. "So, what's the big deal with him?"

"The big deal is he was murdered over sixty years ago, and no one has ever been able to solve it." The sergeant took a swig of a carbonated drink. "Have you ever been there?"

"To Frontier?" Merit scowled. "No. Never will, either. Everyone knows that they don't have rules or laws, and they don't respect the police. And apparently, they're too lazy to even investigate their own murders."

"Yeah, but that was the agreement. The statute mandated that Pilgrim P.D. investigates any new evidence found on old murders that took place in Frontier."

"Why can't *they* do it, Sarge?"

"Over the past fifty years, Frontier's been slowly phasing out law enforcement and doesn't have the sophisticated equipment we've developed to solve cases. I'll have Hubbard or someone in The Cold Case Unit work it."

"Good. They don't have much to do anyway." Merit cut his medium-rare, cooked steak into smaller bites, and didn't look up. "What evidence did they find?"

"Somebody there just found the gun that was used to kill Soldier." Travers raised his head slightly as he speared a piece of steak with his fork, to spy Merit's reaction.

Merit could sense his sergeant was trying to tempt him into taking the case by mentioning its difficulty, a cat-and-mouse mind game of sorts. Merit talked with a mouthful. "That was ancient history. Whoever did it is dead and long gone, so what's it matter now? I mean, Sarge, would *you* go to Frontier?" He pronounced "Frontier" with contempt. "Would you travel all that way to where there are weird people who don't have any laws, who don't like the police and try to solve some sixty-year-old unsolvable crime of some has-been golfer?"

Travers finished chewing before answering. "No, I wouldn't. I wouldn't go either."

"Then why would I wanna go try?" Merit shoved a piece of steak into his mouth.

Travers wiped his lips with a napkin, looked into Merit's eyes. "Because your father tried."

9

Soldier never had a serious girlfriend, so he caught everyone off guard when he announced that he'd gotten married to a flight attendant. They made a good couple. Shortly after, they conceived their only child, a boy. Many detractors believed that with a wife and new child, Soldier's endless hours spent practicing would be curtailed, hurting his chances of breaking Vic's record. But Soldier again defied his critics, the "family man" tacked on three more majors, amassing eighteen in all. His wife preferred being a stay-at-home mom, but she hadn't foreseen Soldier traveling so much, and being alone took its toll. Three years after their child's birth, she filed for divorce. With Soldier's hectic schedule, his only son spent his adolescent years raised mostly by his mother.

—Leslie Dale, *"Holes of Gold": A Documentary Film*

LITTLE COCOON

Merit got into his car in the parking lot behind Pilgrim Police Department. It was late, and he was full and exhausted. He was about to hit the ignition button when someone tapped on the driver's-side window. It startled him, and he flinched, instinctively drawing his sidearm.

"Crap, Hubbard!" Merit cracked his window open with his left hand while holstering the gun with his right. "What are you doing here this late?"

"Working." The weathered-looking cold case detective rested his hands on the car's window ledge. "So, you solved your one-hundredth hot homicide this year, eh? Congrats, super- detective."

"Yeah, I guess." Merit was suspicious of Hubbard's agenda.

"Why'd he do it?"

"I dunno why." Merit eyes looked away then darted back. "He did it, I caught him, and he's in prison."

"You didn't ask him?"

Merit shook his head. It was a waste of time to ask *why*.

Detective Hubbard counted on his fingers belittling Merit's efforts. "You didn't go to the crime scene, didn't view the body, search for evidence, canvass the area, interview witnesses, attend the autopsy, or even interview the killer. And you probably didn't speak to the victim's family, did you? Or did you have Sarge do it for you again?"

Merit stared blankly. "I had a long day." He touched the ignition button.

"Poor detective. Spent half a day solving a case." He clapped, in a patronizing manner.

"I saw your numbers downstairs." Merit indicated toward the precinct. "You've had two homicides all year."

Hubbard nodded, conceding the fact. "Heard you turned down the golfer murder case too."

"Why do you care?" Merit started to roll up the window. "I'm leaving."

"Your father didn't turn it down."

Merit had had enough. He elbowed open the car door to get out, pressing it against Hubbard's waist, trying to control his anger. "Shut up, Hubbard! You don't even know my dad." He was breathing fast. Hubbard used the girth of his wide hips and shoved the door shut to prevent Merit from exiting.

"Your dad trained me," he sneered. "Your dad not only solved cases but took the time to find out why. He cared." Hubbard backed away but stopped. "You've never *really* worked. You've never really cared. You only care about how quick you can solve it."

Merit opened his car door and shot back. "How do *you* know? You don't know me." Merit knew Detective Hubbard was right. He had never poured his heart and soul into a case. He never needed to, and it was true, too, that he liked to solve them quickly, faster than anyone else, but he wasn't going to admit that fact to him.

"You've solved a lot of cases..." Hubbard nodded several times in approval. "...but you're scared—scared to put yourself out there. It's easy to spin around inside your little homiscope cocoon, watch TV screens and pick out the bad guy and then have everyone say how great you are."

"If it's so easy, why don't you do it?" Merit shot back. "Go worry about your own cases. All *two* of them." He chuckled nervously. "And I'll take care of my one hundred." Merit had never been challenged about his work ethic and felt uneasy having to defend himself.

Hubbard turned and walked to his car. "I can walk away right now and live with myself knowing, I've been there." He pointed to nowhere. "I've seen it, smelled it, touched it, felt it. Felt it *here*." Hubbard faced back towards Merit and pounded his chest with his fist. "Can you? — you can't. Because you know deep down that you're cheating yourself." He motioned to the world beyond the parking lot with a sweeping gesture of his hand. Hubbard opened the door to his car. "You don't have passion. You're not a real cop, just a fake detective."

Merit had heard enough. He'd never had any serious arguments with anyone in the department, but Hubbard had this coming. He stormed towards Hubbard's car.

"What does *that* mean?" He mimicked Hubbard's sweeping gesture of his hand. "Oh, you're a real detective because you care about your two victims?" As Hubbard crouched in his old sedan, Merit's voice rose, "You say all that and walk away? —*You're* the one who's scared." He grabbed the passenger side handle of Hubbard's car and yanked on it, but it was locked, so he yelled through the glass. "You're jealous. You're jealous of me. I've solved thousands more than you ever could. You don't do dick." He slapped the trunk of Hubbard's car as it pulled away.

Hubbard's clunker came to an abrupt stop. He leaned out and with arrogance about him said, "Hey Merit, now *that's* passion," then drove off into the night.

10

Soldier was caught off guard when his coach of twenty-six years, the Pro, was investigated by the IRS for tax fraud, evasion and skimming off the top of Soldier's earnings. Soldier's only friend and "father figure" had betrayed him, yet out of allegiance, he forgave him. The Pro was sentenced to six years in a federal penitentiary and Soldier was alone again. He tested out a handful of swing coaches to replace the Pro, but none were a good fit. Soldier concluded it was time for him to go at it alone. Soldier had close guidance on his game ever since he was a boy, and pundits believed going solo at this late stage in his career would be a huge mistake and risk his chances of breaking the record held by 'The Fox'.
—Larry Farrell, *Athletes and Business blogwizard*

PHOBIA

Merit had the following day off and wanted to forget the harsh jabs of Detective Hubbard, so he went to the sports complex on the edge of the city. He was mostly mad at himself for losing his composure to some fat man he didn't even know.

Merit was athletic, a frequenter at the gym. He spent the first hour playing a relatively new sport called sleitis. Two players batted a lightweight oblong-shaped ball across a net of laser beams at a torrid pace.

When he finished his match, he was sweating profusely, and his legs felt like rubber. However, he couldn't get his mind off the words of Detective Hubbard, words that kept accusing him of being less than he could be as a police officer.

It's easy to spin around in your little cocoon, watch TV and pick out the bad guy.

"What a prick." Hubbard's words had impugned his abilities, his very profession.

He decided to let out his frustrations on the obstacle course after forty minutes of weightlifting. He loved to dodge the falling boulders and swinging pins of different sizes. He raced across shifting stones in a pond, swung from bars that moved unpredictably left and right, and climbed a rock cliff where the footholds might be retracted at any moment. At the end of the course was the hologram room, where he had to navigate a half-mile of simulated weather hazards: lightning strikes, snow blizzards, tornados, intense heat, and driving rain. When he was finished, he emerged from the room, perspiring and out of breath.

"Hey, Merit," said a fellow detective. "We're going swimming. Wanna come?"

"No, I'm good. I just finished." Merit grinned faintly.

"A little water won't kill you."

Merit stared at the pool's swirling water. His breathing became short, his heart raced, and a sensation of panic boiled on his skin. He wasn't scared of the water, but he was petrified of putting his head under the surface, a fear he'd had since a young boy. It was an embarrassment to his manhood that he'd managed to conceal. "I'm late for church. See ya."

The fellow detective made no reply, but performed a can-opener, clutching one knee to his chest, as he leaned back and jumped off the edge of the pool. His splash created a booming sound and a mushroom of water, as Merit ducked for cover.

11

Soldier again proved his detractors wrong. At the age of thirty-nine, without a coach, he racked up three majors in two years, tying Vic's record. Sports fans, the media, and even casual viewers were ecstatic. The world anticipated watching Soldier break Vic's record at the upcoming Master's, but two weeks before, he unexpectedly withdrew. He'd been having trouble walking the course and was diagnosed with degenerative ankle joints. His fans were worried. Over the next several years, Soldier tried everything to heal his arthritic joints, from therapy to acupuncture, from blood spinning to microscopic surgery, but nothing worked. As each major passed without Soldier in the draw, a new crop of players garnered major titles—most notably, a young, brash North Korean golfer, who had snagged four majors and boasted that he was better than Soldier.

—K. Frank, *golferspage18.com*

TODAY'S SERMON

Merit and Ruth attended church four times a week. He pulled his vehicle into the parking lot of the mega-church, the Temple of Divine Guidance.

The pastor was a well-known motivational speaker, a middle-aged suntanned man who wore expensive three-piece suits, and his services were streamed throughout Pilgrim. Merit was especially fond of the preacher since he timed his sermons so that each one was exactly thirty-minutes long. That kind of precision appealed to a detective who valued the same sense of timing and efficiency in his own work.

Merit and Ruth seated themselves and listened as Pastor Powell took the stage in the large church that was home to his congregation. A billboard-sized map of the State of Pilgrim glowed behind him with the symbols of the cross and a gun illuminated on either side. The theme of the sermon was on the importance of pain, struggle and fighting their antithesis, which was laziness. The majority of the minister's sermons made a lasting impression on Merit, and many times he felt as if the preacher was speaking just to him, but laziness wasn't one of the themes he could relate to. Merit didn't have a lazy bone in his body. He was no slacker. He'd always kept busy, worked hard, and attacked life's problems with self-discipline.

The pastor raised his hand. "And we rise to challenges every day by going to our jobs and trying to perform better than we did the day before." Pastor Powell smiled, as he walked around the stage to make sure he connected with all members of his congregation.

"But *really* challenging yourself is painful..." He looked out over the massive congregation. "...and pain should be a part of your life." The spiritual leader cracked open the well-worn book *The Road Less Traveled* he picked up off the podium and recited from a passage, "And laziness is not defined as doing nothing, but rather as spending time on the *wrong* thing. Avoiding the challenge that we most *need* to tackle, is laziness."

Merit winced at the concept.

The man of the cloth continued. "The more pain one can endure, the more growth one will experience. So, when the time comes to face the challenge you most *need* to tackle, the searing pain you'll feel trying to tackle it, is the fear being squeezed out of you." He closed the book and dabbed his sweaty neck with a hanky. "The Bible tells us the path to salvation runs through a narrow gate and down a hard road, but wonders await us at the end of that road if we have the courage to make the journey."

The pastor recounted other examples of hard work in the remaining fifteen minutes of his sermon, and they all made Merit feel unsettled. He'd never questioned himself before. He'd put in the time to obtain his position of respect. He rarely felt pain or discomfort in his life, at work, or in relationships, and he never pushed past his pain threshold except when he was exercising or competing. The words of Detective Hubbard, arrogant prick that he was, gnawed at his soul: "You don't have passion . . . You're just a fake detective."

As the service ended, Ruth rose and noticed her normally reliable mate had remained seated with a glazed look on his face. "James." She lightly kicked his foot so no one would notice.

Merit shot up, nodded, forced a smile, and took her hand as they made their way down the aisle toward the front doors. Ruth, whenever in Merit's presence, always looked proud, sat tall, and he liked that about her. She moved gracefully, spoke properly, practiced good morals, and was courteous to those around her, but she wasn't much for humor. Sometimes she acted a bit too old for her age, but it didn't matter, people said they looked like a good couple and most importantly, she'd told him she respected his line of work. He politely pushed his way through the crowd, members of which wanted to shake his hand to congratulate him. Ruth excused herself to freshen up in the little ladies' room and whispered that she'd meet him at the car. Merit had always deflected adulation, but for the first time decided to accept. Instead of moving through the crowd like he normally did, he mingled, shook hands, nodded, and allowed his admirers to pat him as if he were a movie star.

Merit then spotted the preacher making his way through the congregation, apparently also wanting to congratulate him. This was the first time he would meet the holy man face-to-face. If only Ruth hadn't stepped away, she could have witnessed someone as important as Pastor Powell tell him how much he appreciated his service in making the state of Pilgrim safe.

"Detective Merit." The minister mouthed his name, lifting a left hand in the air signaling.

Merit couldn't stop from grinning. "Yes, sir. You can call me Merit."

"Merit, I need to tell you something."

Merit extended his hand first to shake the pastors. "No, sir. You don't have to tell me anything. Thank you—I'm glad he's in jail too." He squeezed the pastor's big, tanned hand firmly.

The clergyman placed his other hand on Merit's left shoulder. "I am glad, but I do need to tell you something." With a solemn look on his face, he leaned in toward Merit's ear. "I was just informed, your father has passed away."

12

Several years passed as Soldier sat alone on his huge estate off the Gulf of Texas. It appeared he would remain tied with Vic's record. With no golf, no family, no friends or interests, he became clinically depressed. And with no exercise, he packed on unwanted pounds. A paparazzi photographer using a telephoto lens secretly captured Soldier on his secluded boat dock using a cane. They plastered the unflattering photo of him shirtless, his large gut exposed, receding gray hairline and sagging jowls across tabloid magazines. People were shocked to see how out of shape and old he appeared. At age forty-three, Soldier Quinn quietly announced his retirement on Twitter and slipped into life as a recluse.

—Herb Sutherland, *Master Golfing Network*

FATHER TIME

A couple of days after Merit's father's funeral, he and Ruth drove out to the family ranch, where they helped Merit's mother pack up clothing and box other things she'd decided to give away.

Mrs. Merit was a determined woman who never procrastinated. His whole life, Merit had watched his mother deal with the inevitable head-on. The sadness of her husband's passing was an obstacle that needed to be overcome, and she'd already begun sorting through her husband's belongings.

After three hours of work, Merit and his mother took a break and walked onto the back porch, where they watched the family's several horses in the corral twenty yards from the house.

"Mom, what did dad think of me?"

"He loved you very much. He just wanted you to reach your full potential, be passionate about your work, and find a girl you could love and spend the rest of your life with. Ruth seems like a lovely person."

"I know. We have a lot in common, and I really wanted him to meet her." He pursed his lips, and waited a moment, "Mom, what did dad think of me?" He sat across from her. "What I really mean is, what did he think of me as a detective—as a *hot* homicide detective."

"He talked about you all the time. He was very proud." She raised her eyebrows as if she wasn't sure how else to answer the question.

"But he worked *cold cases*." Merit pressed for an honest answer.

"He did most of the time. There were no hopscotch-a-scopes when he joined the force."

He politely reminded her. "Homiscope, Mom. It's a homiscope."

"He caught people quickly sometimes, but more often than not he worked long hours," she said. "Being out in the field is what he called it. Knocking on doors, shaking the trees, beating the bushes, and talking to people and such. He'd sometimes be gone for days. He said that what motivated him most, was thinking about the victim's family—the wife, or husband, the parents, or children—having to spend every day in limbo, and the pain they felt from not knowing who killed someone they loved so they could have closure."

"Did you know Dad worked a really old murder of a famous golfer?"

She sat forward, uncrossed her right leg, and slowly crossed the left leg back over the right. "That was a long time ago." Her eyes drifted to the wooden planked floors, "It took its toll on him." She paused, "On us. Not solving it. It's why he didn't have many friends." She looked up and touched her son's shoulder. "He was a lot like you in that respect. Maybe it's time for you to settle down and start a family. I worry sometimes that you live too solitary an existence."

Merit took in his mother's words and stared out the window at the horses and sighed.

"James?" She said.

"Huh?" He looked over at his mother, whom he loved, "Yes, ma'am."

"Do you want to ride them one last time?"

Merit forced a slight smile and then looked at two horses in particular. His smile faded, and his vision became blurry. His father's death was sinking in. All the time he'd spent with him as a boy, learning to shoot a gun, riding horses together across the open range were over. It hurt, there would never be someone to replace his father. He bit his lip to stop more emotion from flowing. He could feel his mother's eyes on him.

"I can't take care of them," she said, "and you live too far away, so I've offered them to a neighbor down the road. They have a little girl."

Merit swallowed and continued staring so she wouldn't see his tears forming.

"Is that all right?" She placed her hand on his shoulder.

Merit nodded.

She rejoined Ruth and went back to packing.

★★★

In the late afternoon, Merit stepped to the front door window and parted the blinds with his index finger. Several horse trailers had pulled up to the barn so that the noble animals could be loaded and driven to their new home. His sadness returned. His father had been buried at the cemetery behind the church, but it felt as if he were being taken away a second time. For the first time, he experienced emptiness, the loneliness of what a family member of a crime victim might feel. His father died naturally and peacefully, not violently at the hands of some unknown criminal.

His only real friend, the one he confided in, joked with, and shared his feelings—had been his father, and now he was gone, and soon would be the horses that brought them together.

13

At forty-five years of age, Soldier hobbled through his mansion with a walker. He couldn't exercise, had no hobbies, and couldn't turn his mind off with alcohol since he didn't drink. He rehashed how hard he had worked since a kid and how close he had come to winning it all. He'd never really cared about money or fame; his only desire was to fulfill the promise he'd made to his father to be the best golfer. After overcoming every obstacle in his career, had he come all this way to fall one major short? He figured the golf gods were teasing him, but deep in his heart he knew he was being punished, he was to blame for the choice he had made. The selfish choice to chase a dream instead of fulfilling an obligation to his family; namely raising his son. Insane thoughts swirled in his head, driving him almost mad.

—Ella Malovic, *Soldier-A Short Story audiobook*

OUT THERE

Merit sat in the center cockpit of the homiscope sphere, floating in the semi-darkness as if he were in outer space. No hot homicides had been called in, but he needed to be alone to think. He remembered his mother referring to the homiscope as the hopscotch-a-scope and chuckled to himself. It was the first time he recalled laughing or even smiling since the pastor delivered the bad news. He looked around at the sterile white screens of what Detective Hubbard degradingly called "the cocoon." With no crime scene investigation in progress, there were no screens to display, and only the curving surface of the inner sphere could be seen. He felt comfortable there—too comfortable maybe. For the first time, he realized how insulated he was from the world around him. No voices sounded in his ear, and his contoured seat was stationary.

"Hello?" he said.

The echo returned to his ear for the next several seconds.

He spoke in a softer voice. "Dad?"

His dad and guys like Detective Hubbard had tracked down leads for years out in the streets. Merit had scoffed at the grease board down in the basement, where the meager cold case statistics were recorded, but they had never solved a hundred cases in a single year. In the old days, solving a case or two a year was the norm. It was challenging work, but maybe that's what made it so rewarding for them.

Pastor Powell seemed to think that such work was the path to salvation, but what stuck with him most was the pastor's adage that avoiding the challenge we most *needed* to tackle was defined as laziness. The idea that he was lazy was a hard pill to swallow.

His mother had been right; he was uncomfortable around people. He'd rarely spent more than five minutes with the family members of a victim. He'd never sat around and watched sports and downed beers with the guys, and other than his father he never had the bonds that most men shared. He hadn't kissed a girl until he was eighteen, and that girl kissed *him* first. Ruth was the first woman he'd dated seriously.

He was seated erect in the nucleus chair, but something was off kilter inside him. Merit looked at the white wall again. When he was working a hot homicide, he watched videos of crime scenes, officers, victims, and witnesses, all of them out there in the world.

Out there.

★★★

Sergeant Travers looked up from his office desk at Merit. "Say that again?"

"I'm taking the case." Merit said.

"What case?" Travers had a puzzled look on his face.

"The golfer guy." He looked at him with impatience.

"The Soldier Quinn murder? You can't. I already gave it to Fredricks down in Cold Case. He's reviewed the file and has been briefed."

Sgt. Travers glanced at his computer watch. "And he leaves tonight at midnight."

"What's the big rush?"

"Frontier's closing its evidence storage building in thirty days. All of the evidence will be gone."

Merit bowed his head, then raised it sharply. "Then brief me now."

"I think you need some time." Travers hesitated for a moment. "You know—time to grieve." He leaned far back in his chair. "Don't you think so, too?"

Merit glanced out the window into the dark at the thousands of tiny lights blinking from the camera drones floating in space then glared back at Travers with a possessed look.

Travers glanced at his computer screen, and then back at Merit before shaking his head. "You don't know anything about the case, you don't think golf's a sport, and you hate the State of Frontier."

Merit inched closer and took in a deep breath, then let it out. "Sergeant, I want to go to Frontier and work the Soldier Quinn murder case."

"Why now? You've never worked one cold case."

"Why?" Merit stood firm. "Because I want to solve it."

Travers cocked his head and scrunched his mouth. "Really? Merit, why do you *really* want to go?"

"I need to prove something to myself." He knew in his heart, no matter how many hot homicides he solved, he would never feel complete as a detective unless he worked this cold case—the one his father worked. Merit looked even deeper into his superior's eyes, "It's something very important to me. Okay?"

The sergeant rubbed his hands over his face. Merit could tell he'd put his boss in a tough spot, letting him go away so soon after a loss of a family member, even though he was the one who suggested the challenge in the first place. Merit held his ground. "I've never asked you for anything—Never complained. I've solved over five hundred murders. I'm almost twenty-nine, and this could be my only big chance to prove something." He tested the boundaries of his friendship with his superior, "And you owe me."

"I don't have time to brief you. There's too much." The sergeant hesitantly leaned over and reached into a file box that contained the case. "Tell you what. I'll load the information about Soldier Quinn onto your helmet visor. It includes old articles, interviews about him from different magazines, books, some police reports, news clips, podcasts, and some video documentaries about the history of golf. You can watch it on your way there."

Yes! —He had his sergeant's okay. He'd stuck his neck out and accepted the challenge that he most needed to tackle, but he didn't want to exhibit too much exuberance. "Okay, sarge." He looked flatly at Travers. "Anything I should know before I go?"

"Do you remember a female detective named Derry Darrins?"

Merit shook his head.

"She went over to Frontier about ten years ago and tried to solve it. She was good. But she never came back." He opened the envelope and pulled out a stock photograph of Detective Darrins, the official picture of the cadet, fresh out of the academy. She was dressed in the formal class A's patrol uniform, complete with a garrison cap, tie, and the Pilgrim flag draped behind her.

"What happened to her?" The tall, buffed officer's hair was pulled back tight in a bun and her face was makeup-free. To toughen her look, even more, she lifted her chin and jutted her jaw, but he could tell she was an attractive young officer with smooth tight skin and blue eyes.

"No one knows. We sent units over there, but they couldn't find her. She just disappeared. We figured she was killed." Travers stared at her likeness.

An officer under his watch was presumably dead, and Merit knew he took it personally. He returned the photo to the file and stood behind the desk. "It's turned into a strange world over there. Watch your back. You can't trust anyone. *That's* what you should know."

★★★

With Travers by his side, Merit carried the file box out of the office and down the hall, a noticeable spring in his step.

"Remember that you only have thirty days to solve this thing." Sgt. Travers said.

'Got it. Thirty days to solve it." Merit nodded. "God's on my side."

The sergeant handed him two extra boxes of ammunition; even with God's help, extra rounds couldn't hurt in case he encountered a shootout. He glanced up at the digital wall clock. "You leave in five hours. Got someone you need to tell?"

"Yeah, that's right. Ruth." Merit appeared confused for a second. "Did I tell you? When I get back home, I'm gonna ask her to marry me."

"Sounds like a plan," Travers then shook Merit's hand. "You picked out a ring?"

Merit's face tightened, then he chuckled at himself, "I gotta do that, and quick."

At the end of the long corridor, a tall man with a towel draped over his head was being hustled into an office by several officers. Long straggly hair hung from beneath the towel.

It looked strange to Merit, "What's that guy all about?" The door was shut quickly behind them as they entered.

"Who? Him? I think he's a confidential informant. He was working on some counterfeiting ring case. The Fraud Unit had to bring him in."

"Well, I guess I'll go home now, pack a few things, and be back after dinner." Merit left to break the news to Ruth. "Sarge." Merit turned and faced him. "You gotta tell Fredericks I'm taking the case."

"Who? Oh, right. I'll tell him. Thanks." Traver's pointed at him, turned, and walked away. It didn't matter, there had never been a Fredericks on the Cold Case Unit.

14

Late one night, Soldier decided that instead of allowing his feelings to fester, he would let them out. He grabbed a mini-tape recorder and voiced his most private thoughts. He began with memories from his early years—his father, his tragic death, his mother, the Pro, junior golf, his college year. He then expounded about turning pro, winning and losing, the praise, money, the record, the media, marriage, divorce, and the thing that tormented him most to discuss, his son and the guilt he felt for chasing the record over spending time with him. He knew how it felt to grow up fatherless, and he went and did the same thing. After a two-month, verbal purging, he was done. He sealed the twenty micro tapes in an empty tee box and addressed it, "To my son, love Dad." But what if his son, who he hadn't seen in years, hated him? He stowed the box in his golf bag. He would give it to him in three years, he decided, when he turned eighteen.

—Kraig Chase, *UK News and Entertainment*

SEXUAL URGES

"I don't like it, James." Ruth was hand-drying the dishes. "Why didn't you tell me you were going?" She folded her arms defensively, staring at him with cold eyes.

"I told you, Sarge just asked me today when I was at work." he fibbed.

"And you couldn't have told him no?"

He sidestepped the question. "Remember what Pastor Powell said? We need to accept challenges."

"Not this kind. You've never traveled before, especially very far. I want you to reconsider." She was getting ramped up. "When do you think you'll leave?"

Merit paused from assembling articles in his backpack on the kitchen table. "Tonight."

"Tonight!"

"Detectives have to do this sometimes. Go out in the field. They all do it."

"That's not fair to me," Ruth placed her hands defiantly on her hips. "Maybe we should just call things off. You made a commitment to me. Frontier is not a nice place. I've heard stories, seen pictures. It's different. It's bad. Anything goes—drugs, sex, and they don't believe in God." She hesitated. "And I don't think you can handle your urges."

"What?" Merit's jaw dropped. "Where did that come from?"

Ruth was quiet for a moment, looking unsure whether she should continue, then turned around, "Your mom."

Merit scowled.

"Yes, James, your mom. Last weekend at the wake, she told me you've never had a serious girlfriend, and you've probably never had . . . sex."

"Okay, and—"

"And I probably shouldn't tell you this, but she told me your dad cheated on her over the years and said you might not be able to control your sexual urges either."

Merit scowled, shaking his head back and forth. "That can't be. You misunderstood her."

"Now you don't believe me." Ruth spun around and began to put away the plates, slamming them to make a racket. "Just leave me alone then."

"We've never argued, and I don't want us to fight right before I go."

Ruth moved around the kitchen, avoiding eye contact, and Merit followed her as she clanked pots and pans while shoving them in the under cabinets.

"First, you know that I'm very disciplined. I can control myself. Other girls don't interest me. I won't cheat on you. Trust me." Merit took Ruth's hand in his. "Nothing's gonna happen when I get back, we'll set a date."

"*If* you come back."

Merit thought of Derry Darrins and knew it would be better not to mention the missing female detective. Smiling warmly, Merit took Ruth in his arms and squeezed her tightly.

"So, what were you saying about setting a date?" Ruth said.

"I'm saying we're getting engaged."

Ruth kissed Merit, then leaned her head on his shoulder, "James, please don't tell your mom I told you. She told me in confidence."

Even though he was floored by Ruth's revelation about his father's indiscretions and rush to judgment, especially since he'd never given her any reason to doubt his faithfulness, he passed off her knee-jerk reaction as a symptom of a *new couple insecurities,* an issue they'd been counseled on to be aware of in the pre-marriage classes they'd attended at church.

To smooth over their first major flap, he nodded to keep her request confidential.

15

Soldier felt renewed after his emotional inner purging, but not so good about his outer self. In a mirror, he examined his receding hairline, bags under his eyes and became disgusted when he pinched his bloated gut. He had lifted weights, ate healthily, and made his shoulders broader than his waist, but now that was all gone. In a burst of rage, he punched the mirror. He scoured cabinets and closets for bandages and discovered crates of golf memorabilia. He thumbed through his college's golf program and spotted the team photo. He found his freshman picture and stared, wishing he could go back to when things were simpler. He skimmed his biography noticing his height at 6'3 and weight listed at 179 lbs. He fished out the scale and weighed himself at 239 lbs! While maybe he couldn't get back his hair, fresh face or innocence, he could get his weight back down.

—Billy Simpson, *The Golf Bum* (Pre-US Open Interview with Soldier)

MAJOR PROBLEM

"**W**hich is it, Merit?" Detective Hubbard pitched it in a voice that bordered on amusement. "First you turned down the golfer murder case, and now I heard you took it. Which is it?"

Merit spun around as he carried his drones and streamline backpack down a windowless hall that led to the rooftop helipad. It was where he would launch so that Pilgrim P.D. could monitor him for the first few miles with its telemetry. Merit tilted his head back. He didn't really want to see Hubbard.

"You shouldn't go," Hubbard said.

"Because it's too dangerous?"

"No. Because you're not qualified." Hubbard didn't mince words.

Merit felt slighted.

Hubbard patted the outside of his worn tweed jacket before locating a soft pack of cigarettes from the inside pocket. "Sorry about your father." He added, then lit a cigarette.

Merit slightly nodded. He had never seen any officer light up since practically no one smoked in Pilgrim, so when he exhaled, Merit couldn't help his eyes from watching the smoke escape between his lips.

"You're good in that homiscope. It's impressive. I watched you the other day. I guess it takes skill."

"I guess," Merit said.

"I couldn't do it." Hubbard shook his head, causing his cheeks to shake.

Merit regarded Hubbard with skepticism. Why had his entire demeanor changed since their last encounter? "I'm sorry that I, uh, got upset the other day outside your car. I gotta get going." He motioned to the helipad.

"Want a tip before you go, Merit?"

"Now? *Now* you want to help me? I really have to go and—"

Detective Hubbard continued to look at him.

"Okay." Merit's droopy body language suggested he was doing Hubbard a favor, "Go ahead tell it."

"Here's the tip." He looked sincerely in Merit's eyes. "Open your umbrella in the rain." Amused at his attempt at a lame joke, he burst out with an obnoxious laugh.

"You *are* a prick." Merit started to walk in the other direction.

Hubbard walked about in a circle, as he brushed his hand through his dirty hair with one hand, rubbing his chin with the other, as if deep in thought. "You know anything about golf?"

Merit stopped. "No. I'll learn as I go."

Hubbard pretended to laugh. "Great. He's working the murder of the greatest golfer of all time but doesn't know *anything* about golf."

"So what."

"Can you name even *one* of the four majors in golf?"

Merit about-faced and started to walk toward the door that exited to the helipad.

"Don't turn your back on me." Hubbard had the look of fire in his eyes. "I've done this for thirty-one years, and you can at the least give me the fucking common courtesy to act like you're interested in what I'm saying."

Merit could feel the stare of Detective Hubbard on the back of his head. Merit slowly pivoted, as he had an ingrained sense of right and wrong, and respecting an elder was the right thing to do his father had taught him.

"Here's your *problem*, caterpillar."

"Go ahead. What's my problem?" Merit faced him, crossed his arms, and gave him a blank look.

Hubbard laid into him. "You've spun around in your little white cocoon upstairs for eight years, solving murders, and you think you can solve a cold case, too, but it's the real world out there, and you're not qualified worth dick." He matter-of-factly walked back toward him. Merit didn't know if he was going to punch him or hug him. But Hubbard's tone shifted. "Don't go. It ain't worth it. You got nothing to prove."

Merit listened, but his pride wouldn't allow him to quit, and he *did* have something to prove. "No, I'm going, and I'm gonna solve it."

Hubbard grabbed Merit's shoulder and stood in front of him, blocking him from leaving. "Good—now listen." His demeanor turned on a dime. "Working a cold case is a lot like playing the game of golf. It's a grind." His tone focused. "You have a starting point—the tee. There are eighteen tee boxes."

Merit was extremely uncomfortable with Hubbard so close, speaking with such enthusiasm about the game of golf.

"But then you have the entire layout of the hole. The fairway may be straight, or a dogleg left or right. You have to take that into account when you make your club selection." He hesitated, a glimmer in his usually tired eyes. "Club selection—very important." He held up his index finger for emphasis. "The club you choose determines the lift you give a ball and how far it will carry. With me so far?"

Merit nodded, but most went in one ear and out the other and he rested his shoulder against the wall.

"Good. Then you have to watch for sand traps—called bunkers sometimes—and water hazards. Sometimes you hit around them, sometimes over, and sometimes you have to work out of them. Then there's the rough on the side of the fairways. That's tall grass. Got it?"

Hubbard spent a good twenty minutes giving Merit an overview about the game of golf—how to play it, the rules, the objective of the game, and sportsmanship. He was animated in his instruction, demonstrating how to swing off the tee, chip from medium distances, and putt by using his extended baton as a pretend club. He spewed golf terms, courses, tour events, and the four most important tournaments of the year, called the majors. He described the rules and etiquette and quizzed Merit every so often. He drew comparisons between the mental and physical challenges required to play golf at a high level to those essential to working a cold case, every minute or so eliciting, "Got it?"

"Right. Got it." Merit clasped his hands together. "That it?"

Hubbard nodded. "Yeah, that's it." He was breathing hard. "I've studied it. It looked like a challenging sport." He took a last drag and exhaled. "I'd like to see golf come back someday."

16

The morning after seeing his freshman photo of a trimmer self, Soldier started his comeback. He ate only one healthy meal a day. For rehab, he returned to the methods the training staff in college once used to heal his sore shoulder. He iced his swollen ankles ten times per day, ingested handfuls of anti-inflammatory pills and elevated his legs for blood flow to heal. To get his feel back, yet avoid pressure on his ankles, he putted from a seated position. He worked up to a thousand sit-ups per day. Each week he shed pounds, he slowly putted from a standing position for short stints and took full shadow swings. He theorized that the drastic loss of upper-body mass and constant icing and meds would reduce swelling in his ankles, allowing him to compete in one last major. What else did he have to do?
—Leslie Dale, *"Holes of Gold": A Documentary Film*

TOP-FLIGHT

At midnight, Merit rose into the sky beneath a crescent moon, his feet leaving the security of the rooftop below. Round drones were attached to the bottom of his feet, his butt, and behind his elbows. The flying apparatus allowed him to sit forward, as if riding a motorcycle, with the option to tilt back into a recumbent position to work the controls. He used slim, handheld joysticks to control the drones and adjust guidance, altitude, and thrust.

Glancing backward, he saw Hubbard's silhouette on the rooftop's edge, an orange dot that lit the tip of a fresh cigarette. The old cold case detective then turned sideways, as if lining up over an imaginary tee and made the motion of driving a golf ball. He drew his hands back, made a grand swinging motion holding his follow-through, and watched his make-believe ball, which was Merit, sail away high into the starry night, not knowing where it would land.

The mixed messages had been a most unexpected send-off from the grizzled cold-case detective. He wasn't sure, but it was only then that Merit realized that Hubbard wished that *he* was going. But he was too old, overweight, and close to retirement. Instead, the young hot homicide detective had drawn the plum assignment. Hubbard was jealous of Merit, who was on his way to solving the greatest cold case of all time.

Merit headed west, cruising smoothly at an altitude of a quarter of a mile, sure to stay clear of the array of mini-camera drones hovering beneath him. The flight was level, and his hand and foot controls were not that different from those in the homiscope, giving Merit complete mobility, as he glided effortlessly over the terrain below.

The moonlight made the landscape, mostly flat, glow with an unnatural beauty. Occasionally he passed over lights representing a Pilgrim town or a power grid, but the farther he flew, the more he saw large tracts of uninhabited land. He felt optimistic, glad that he'd accepted such a difficult assignment.

He had too much adrenaline in his system to fall asleep, plus he needed to watch the videos that Sergeant Travers had given him on Soldier's career and facts about the murder investigation. He put the drones on automatic pilot, it was, he thought, time to go to school.

★★★

The visor of Merit's helmet not only protected his face from the oncoming 60-70 mile an hour headwind, but three small screens could be activated on the inside of the clear shield so that he could view videos or get readouts of his surroundings—altitude, temperature, and time, as well as the operational status of his five drones. To keep his body temperature warm when flying at night or higher altitudes, he wore a lightweight hypothermic-resistant bodysuit.

First, he watched three hours on the game of golf, although he didn't know who any of the players were. It was old flat footage compared to modern Z-3 dimensional images, but it was easy enough to follow what the people in the frame were doing. Most professional players managed to hit the ball from tee to green—and into the hole—in three to five hits, properly known as strokes, with someone called a caddy carrying a bag with the player's twelve golf clubs—two drivers, eight clubs called irons, a pitching wedge, and a putter. But the ball didn't always land where the player wanted it to, and some of the players were visibly angered when a shot went awry. Their mixed reactions were amusing to watch.

He swapped videos and viewed an hour and fifteen minutes on the history of Soldier Quinn, compiled from various sources, who'd started swinging a club at the age of three. By age eighteen, he'd won his first major, which meant that a golfer had won one of the four biggest tournaments on the tour: The Masters, The U.S. Open, The British Open, or the PGA Championship.

Merit paused the recording and shook his head. Was it truly a sport? These not so athletic-looking men strolled around landscaped courses, chatted to their caddies, and stood endlessly over the ball just staring at it. As he watched, he felt the urge to scream, "Just hit the ball!"

Merit resumed watching the recording. By the time Soldier was thirty-nine, he'd won twenty-two majors, tying the record of the most famous golfer of all time. In 2026, Soldier was on his way to getting his twenty-third major, which would break all records and cause him to be heralded as the greatest golfer of all time and that's when the unspeakable event happened—The video developed static, causing Merit to curse under his breath, as the audio became garbled.

Merit briefly looked ahead to see where he was, although proximity alarms would have sounded if he were near any obstacle. The path ahead was straight, and overhead he could see a galaxy of stars that sparkled like diamonds. Maybe he'd be able to find Ruth a large diamond sometime soon to formalize their engagement. He was grateful to God he'd left her on a positive note.

The next video segment he watched was brief but described the aftereffects of Soldier's murder. Since the country demanded answers for the killing of the beloved sports figure, a commission was formed to investigate the high-profile murder. After two years, an inquiry declared that the murder was racially motivated. Someone armed with a gun had made sure that Soldier, a minority of African American descent, would not break the record of a Caucasian.

Frustrated citizens demanding justice deemed golf as socially divisive. They staged nationwide boycotts of golfing tour events and committed acts of vandalism that led to the demise of the sport.

Soldier's murder carried out by the use of a firearm also spurned massive political protests. Pro and anti-gun control rallies turned violent and the debate over law and order inevitably spilled into politics. Political polarization reached an all-time high. Soldier's murder had been the catalyst for pent-up ideological frustration. Tensions ran so high that skirmishes erupted along the borders between several neighboring states: A general east-west and north-south rift were developing, causing disruptions in trucking, commerce, the flow of oil, and the energy grid.

With the United States fracturing, political leaders were forced to take drastic measures. The fifty states of America were divided into two large states, Frontier and Pilgrim, each adopting opposite philosophical doctrines.

Merit could hardly believe what he was seeing and hearing. He had no idea of the complex situation surrounding the creation of the Divided States of America. Back in high school, he didn't pay much attention to class subjects such as history, social studies, or geography; his interests mostly were in sports and looking at girls, and a little in math and the sciences, so he did just enough work to pass. That gap of knowledge explained his vague recollections of the past and how it related to political matters that shaped the society where he presently existed. He continued watching the video.

By 2034, the border separating the two new states ran north from the Rio Grande, with states including Texas, Oklahoma, Kansas, Nebraska, Wyoming, South Dakota, and the states moving east and southeast Kansas, Iowa, Missouri, Indiana, Kentucky, Tennessee, Arkansas, Louisiana, Mississippi, Alabama, Georgia, Florida, the Carolinas, and West Virginia, respectively came to be called the Pilgrim State, even though the names of individual states would no longer be used. New Mexico, Arizona, California, Nevada, Oregon, Washington, Wyoming, North Dakota, Minnesota, Wisconsin, Illinois, Michigan, Ohio, New York, Maryland, and northeastern states Virginia, New York, Massachusetts, Maryland were heaped together to form one large state named Frontier.

When the segment ended, Merit looked up and stared out of his face shield, far out into the distance. Even though he found the documentary program vague in its presentation and parts he felt that needed further explanation, he did begin to feel a sense of the enormity of the event.

He had assimilated the facts well enough, although the idea of racism that had existed earlier in the century, was a concept he found difficult to grasp. All the references in the videos related to race; racism, prejudices, discrimination, biases, minorities, profiling, and bigotry were outdated terms and confusing to Merit.

When the U.S. divided in the mid-2030s, every citizen could freely choose to reside in either one of the two states that conformed best to their ideological, political, and religious beliefs. Once the moves were completed everyone was relieved, and the nationwide tension subsided. The states of Frontier and Pilgrim had clean slates to implement their own new identities, philosophies, and policies, but all their problems didn't go away. Both states still experienced crime, engaged in arguments over laws and enforcement, had disagreements over environmental concerns, government spending, health care, and other societal matters, but race, creed, age, or gender dissipated as a motive for committing a crime or cause for discrimination in their state of choice. With the option to pick one's ideal state, the public got what they wanted and with nothing to fight against or protest, racism, sexism, and bigotry organically vanished as a polarizing issue.

Merit believed Pilgrim operated smoothly based on the values enumerated by Pastor Powell and many other religious figures in their sermons. In his own life, he had never known anything but peace and prosperity in a land that was run with discipline and respect for the rule of law. It was beyond comprehension that Frontier could become so promiscuous and lawless. Even more staggering was the presumption that everything had stemmed from the single act of Soldier Quinn's murder and the subsequent contentious debate over the silly game of golf.

What had he gotten himself into? What could he expect when he arrived in Frontier? He didn't know, but he assumed that he would be allowed to do his job because he was a law enforcement officer, a courtesy honored between police departments. Merit looked at his visor and saw a glimmer of gold on the far horizon behind him. Even though he was traveling west, he wasn't moving so fast that daybreak wouldn't catch up with him in a couple of hours. He shut his eyes and fell asleep, as he made his way toward the Wild Wild West.

★★★

Several hours later, a sudden thrust of turbulence jarred Merit awake. He looked ahead, the entire sky before him an ominous wall of brown, and figured it was a dust storm. Dawn was breaking, and according to readouts on his visor, the swirling sands and dust particles blew harder. He hadn't received an alert regarding the storm but being reared on the plains and seeing firsthand how the meteorological phenomenon could actualize without warning, explained why.

He scanned left to right, but the storm was miles wide, and there would be no going around it. Going over it was out of the question because drones were restricted in altitude. The grit was thicker in some places than others, and the sand moved north to south. Merit was already close enough to the maelstrom to be pushed in a southerly direction.

He visualized himself as that imaginary ball that Detective Hubbard had launched from the tee off the precinct's rooftop. He was headed toward his first hazard, a sand trap, a massive wall hurling toward him over the mesa below. He recalled Hubbard saying that a player could hopefully avoid a bunker or else try to hit out of it, but now wished he'd listened closer to his advice.

17

By month six of Soldier's comeback, he had dropped twenty-nine pounds, halfway to his goal. He looked up locations for the year's upcoming majors. He schemed which course catered to his strengths and gave him the greatest probability of winning. He narrowed his choice to the U.S. Open held at Shinnecock Hills Golf Club in New York State. He planned to show up mid-June using an exemption and catch everyone off guard. To avoid being spotted practicing in public, at night he cracked long drives into the bay from his rooftop. Soldier's plan was working; he was injury-free, and his swing was improving, but with two months remaining, there was one thing he'd forgotten—a caddie. He contacted his lifelong caddie and asked him to help on one last run. He said he wished he could, but since he hadn't heard from Soldier had committed to another pro. Another relationship Soldier had neglected.

—G.L. Garden, *Airline and Travel Monthly*

PULL UP

What lay ahead was like an obstacle course, except this was real, and he would have to draw upon his training to somehow maneuver through the dust storm. He aimed for the less dense concentrations of sand and was two minutes into the storm when a strong wind gust sent him hurtling to the south as the sand pelted him. Merit tumbled head over heels, losing all visibility until he adjusted the drones' controls and righted himself.

Thinking quickly, he surveyed the columns of dust up ahead. He realized that the storm was no longer traveling north to south but rather northwest to southeast. He decided to play a hunch and ride directly into the heaviest concentration of dark brown sand in the hope of surfing the wind currents to move in a westerly direction. Fighting the storm would be useless. He would utilize the wind's energy as an ally to help him escape.

His hands and feet worked the drone controls, adjusting his pitch and yaw to compensate for the movement of the wind, but for the most part, the strong steering current he'd tapped into carried him quickly to the west. Gradually, visibility increased so that Merit felt he was looking through thin gauze fabric toward daylight. Glancing back to the southeast, he saw that he'd cleared the dust storm.

The ride was smooth and level again as Merit flew into the clear, sunny, late-morning skies. After several hours of cruising over miles and miles of monotonous brown desert scenery, and after being up most of the night, Merit's eyelids fluttered and he felt that loopy sensation. He decided he'd better get some shut-eye while he had the chance, as the weather forecast looked good ahead. He placed the drones on autopilot and set the alarm to roust him in six hours.

★★★

The temperature in the late afternoon had warmed to a crispy ninety-four degrees when Merit awoke. He immediately shed the bodysuit that had him sweating profusely, rolled it into a tiny ball, and stowed it away. Below him were lines of symmetrically straight green treetops dotted with orange flecks. He was gliding directly above an expansive orange grove, which he found quite beautiful, and as he gazed down, they appeared to him as some type of mathematical grid. The repeated pattern appealed to Merit's inner sense of order. He'd recognized its presence in other forms in nature, like beehives, snowflakes, spiderwebs, tree rings, and he'd always been drawn to them.

His head was thrown to the side as an orange flew up from the earth below, clocking him just beneath the helmet's visor, in the neck. The impact spun him around like a top. Another densely juice-packed orange caught him on his helmet, causing him to momentarily lose control. Yet another hit one of his shins.

"Fuck you, drone man!" a shout came from far below.

"No drones here!" another male voice shouted.

Regaining consciousness from the sucker punch, Merit raised his visor and saw what looked to be a long aluminum tube, a larger and more sophisticated version of a spud gun. This was more like a spud *cannon*, which shot the pieces of fruit with the force of highly compressed air. Two adolescents were pumping the handle of their homemade weapon to discharge another round of baseball-sized fruit.

Merit tried to gain altitude, but an orange grenade zoomed up and lodged itself in the carbon-steel propellers of the replacement foot drone.

"Don't shoot! I'm a cop!"

Merit's plea only hyped the two teens more as they quickly loaded five oranges, aimed, and fired in rapid succession.

"He's a PP. Let kill him!"

Suddenly *whoosh-whoosh-whoosh*—three projected oranges whizzed past his head, a fourth striking his gut and knocking the wind from him.

Since one drone was disabled, he would plummet to his death, probably never to be found. Merit had the presence of mind to draw his weapon and point it, but the citrus juice from the pulverized orange stung his eyes, and he couldn't focus on the blurry figures below to squeeze off a good round.

The threat of his gun forced the pranksters to bail from their post, but it was too late for Merit. The final orange nailed him in the jaw and rendered him temporarily unconscious. He was now flying inverted at a forty-five-degree angle and headed for the green treetop foliage below.

Whoop-Whoop. The drone's ground proximity voice system warned, "*Pull-up. Pull-up.*" until his limp body crashed atop the tree's leaves. His frame ripped through the heart of the tropical tree, cutting branches in half, cushioning his descent before he landed at the trunk's base with a *thud*.

★★★

Beneath the shady forest of fruit, Merit felt groggy, as he unstrapped the damaged drones and rose to his feet. After walking in circles like a drunken sailor for several minutes, he was able to regain his balance, take a deep breath, and stand erect. He checked his body, which was scratched badly from the branches, but they were mostly superficial wounds, and he had no broken bones.

His foot drones were damaged, but he thought he might be able to repair them if he had enough time and the right tools. Of even greater concern was the fact that his gun wasn't in his holster. It must have been thrown clear when he took the hit in the air. Panic set in as he felt vulnerable without his sidearm.

He began to search on the other side of the tree when a sudden noise to his right caught his attention, and he wheeled to the side to see a dozen darker-skinned workers standing quietly several yards away. Some of the men and women, all dressed in brightly colored smocks and hats, held baskets of fruit and stared at him as if he were from another world.

"It's okay." Merit held out his hands in a gesture of peace. "I'm a Pilgrim police officer. I won't hurt you."

He took a tentative step forward, but the workers backpedaled, afraid of the stranger in a tight-fitting, dark blue police uniform who'd fallen from the heavens. Glancing at the ground between him and the workers, he was relieved to see his pistol lying in the dirt.

He hadn't been in Frontier long, but he could already tell that having a gun would be paramount to conducting any kind of investigation. He cautiously inched forward, but the pickers glanced repeatedly from Merit to the gun. The cat and mouse situation reminded him of playing capture the flag as a boy with his cousins. Who would make the first move?

As the group retreated, Merit stooped over to pick up his trusty weapon, assuring them by enunciating each word in a steady voice. "It is okay. I am a cop. I am not here to hurt you. I'm trying to get to Frontier." A blur then appeared before his eyes. A small, brown-skinned boy, no more than eight or nine, darted past and scooped up the gun in one swift motion.

Merit pursued the boy, who was surprisingly fast, as his bony arms and legs flailed. The child ran in a serpentine motion through the seemingly endless rows of trees while Merit tried to keep the scrawny runt in his sight as he weaved in and out of the tree trunks like a downhill slalom snow skier. If he lost him, he might never get his gun back, an idea that terrified him.

"Stop! Stop—kid!"

The boy suddenly disappeared. Merit halted, only hearing the sound of his own panting breaths. "Keep looking," Merit said to himself over and over, but the little thief was gone. Merit then looked around to gather his bearings. He realized he was no longer under the canopy of trees but had been lured into an open space—a dusty pasture—and the juvenile was gone. So was his gun.

A high-pitched whistle blurted behind him. He whirled around, blocking the sun's bright glare with his hand to spot the boy standing a safe distance away, atop a barren hill. The boy pointed to a spilled basket of fruit near Merit's feet, one that contained his gun. Merit sighed as he checked it to see if it was loaded before he holstered it. The kid then pointed west at snow-capped mountains in the distance.

"*La Frontera!*" The boy extended the palm of his hand and moved it in an arching motion as if to indicate an overland direction. "Montaña. La Frontera." He seemed to be communicating that there was a city on the other side of the mountains.

Merit had never seen in person such a site as the majestic mountain range before him. Seeing the mammoth landform rising from the level of the earth made him feel as if he was on another planet. He looked back and flashed the honest youngster a thumbs up to say thanks, only to see that the youngster had vanished.

★★★

As Merit walked away, he compared the matrix of the orange grove where he'd landed, to the tall grass that Detective Hubbard described as deep rough that lined most golf course fairways. Hubbard had instructed that a golfer's objective was to stay clear of the rough, but if he found himself in the thick of it, he'd have to work himself out, and that is what he'd done.

Now it was onto the next tee box, with a monster obstacle ahead, a 12,012-foot snow-capped mountain range that there was no going around or working out of it or avoiding.

Without his drones, Merit would have to hike over the range, so he returned his weapon to its holster and secured the contents of his backpack before heading for the northwest part of the range. He wouldn't attempt to crest any of the high peaks since he didn't have enough provisions. He would keep to the ravines and lower hills to find the city that the young lad had pointed to. His welcome crossing the border to Frontier had not been particularly auspicious, but he had a murder to solve.

He trudged toward the base of the mountains passing a small sign that read: PALMS SPRINGS 24 miles, with an arrow pointed north of the westerly direction he was headed. The giant mountains appeared to grow even taller with every step he took, making them look more and more ominous to climb, but he would take one step at a time. This also seemed to be the logical approach to working his cold case since solving it wasn't going to come easy—not like anything he did in the homiscope. He would think of working the case as if it were the game he was learning —namely golf. One shot at a time, one hole at a time, one step at a time to reach his peak.

His trek finally landed him at the mountain range's base and looking up at the east side of the massive rock facade, he realized climbing it was going to be a much tougher task than he thought. A grind.

18

Three of the four golf majors were played on American soil. It was an honor to have your course selected to host a major. Years in advance, course owners politicked with PGA leaders, lobbied corporate sponsors, and hobnobbed with people of influence for the opportunity to secure a major. South Hampton's Shinnecock Hills was chosen to anchor the year's Open, but when officials pre-inspected the site, they found the grounds were not up to strict standards. With little time to bid out another, the committee opted for a course located on the opposite coast named Orange Golf Club in Southern California. The course wasn't historic or well-known but had a solid reputation among the golfing community, was well-maintained, and possessed a unique factor. But was it available on short notice?

Jerry Flair—www.golflinks.com

WELCOME TO FRONTIER

Forty-eight hours later, Merit's thighs burned, but not from scaling the mountain range as he initially planned, but from walking on a mostly level untraveled road. He learned a dam had been erected years earlier on the other side of mountains allowing the use of the old, once flooded interstate pass that bisected the San Jacinto and San Bernadino Mountain ranges, previously referred to as the I-10. As he stood on the summit of one of the lower peaks of what his mini-watch band computer told him was the San Bernardino Mountain Range, was a wide, breathtaking vista, one that the detective was unaccustomed to since the former state of Oklahoma was flat prairie land.

To the northwest was a sprawling city—that was his destination if the orange grove kid was to be believed—and to the front and left was miles of water dotted with hundreds of large and small islands that stretched far into the distance. He was weak from the climb, and he half walked, half slid down the rough incline of weeds, wild grass, and small stones until he stood at the base of the mountain.

He was lucky to have hitched a ride for a part of the trip on the back of a sluggish moving solar-powered vehicle, which allowed him to save a significant amount of time and energy. But he still had miles to walk before reaching the edge of the city, and he lifted his water bottle to his lips, noting that they were dry.

★★★

Five hours later, Merit was tired, thirsty, and hot after making his way through the suburbs of the metropolis that was heralded by a faded sign that read: *Capital City – Welcome to the Home of Frontier.* Some of the neighborhoods were rundown, while others were luxurious, harboring palatial mansions bigger than any homes he'd ever seen.

The edge of the central business district was a stretch of mostly rectangularly shaped, boldly colored architecture, resembling what reminded Merit of Lego building blocks, while others were worn stucco structures that were dirty and seemed to sag under their weight. Some were adorned with graffiti and had broken windows.

The common theme that graced many of the buildings, whether commercial or residential, was a variety of large, colorful murals painted on their walls. At first glance, the paintings consisted mostly of men, women, and children. Some had flowers and others had inanimate objects that appeared to be beautifully painted, but upon closer inspection Merit noticed that much of the *artwork* was sexually graphic, with male and female nudes engaged in different sex acts, something Merit didn't particularly want to see.

He realized quickly that he was somewhat of an oddity to pedestrians, who were dressed in shorts and T-shirts. The women were scantily clad for the most part, and some even walked about bare-breasted. Both men and women had tattoos and wore jewelry, many having full-body tattoos of every shade and color. The hair of most men and women was long—some had spiked hair or were bald—and they paraded around barefoot or with different styles of tennis shoes, flip flops, or open-toed sandals. Merit stood in stark contrast to the citizens of the city because of his clean, streamlined, navy-blue police uniform.

A scraggily looking man, who Merit was about to pass, walked for several yards by his side as if they were friends. Merit dismissed the disheveled character as either homeless or mentally ill and continued past him toward his destination.

Three people rushed to the man and showered him with coins, paper currency, and food. All looked suspiciously at the well-dressed and well-groomed detective as he resumed obliviously past. One man shouted in Merit's direction, "Hey, mister! You can't do that!"

Merit looked back, not sure who the man was addressing, and disregarded his comments as nonsense. There were no homeless people allowed on the streets in Pilgrim, being homeless was a crime. If a person was occasionally found to be wanting or needing money or a home, he or she wasn't allowed to panhandle in public. By force of volunteer citizens, transients were placed on cruise liners at designated stops along the Mississippi waterway— Dubuque, St. Louis, Natchez, Memphis, Baton Rouge, and New Orleans.

Aboard the '*dry*' vessels they attended daily drug, alcohol, and religious workshops, received treatment from psychotherapists and doctors, and were taught a useful skill or trade. After a forty-five-day therapy excursion around the Gulf of Mexico—which demanded passing stringent drug tests, numerous psychological and physical screenings, then convincing a panel of professional life coaches they were *ready* to contribute back to society, they were returned up the mighty river and dropped at pre-determined work sites. The rehab program wasn't flawless, many were repeat passengers, others never left the ship, and some drowned trying to flee, but in the end, it worked and kept the destitute off the streets of Pilgrim.

Frontier was indeed a different place, just as he'd been warned.

Six blocks farther on, Merit paused in front of two geometrically-shaped buildings fused to make a single structure. The triangular-shaped form was made of concrete, and the cubed part was constructed with large, square glass windows with a lower attached building that featured a slanted, flat roof. On the edifice, barely visible was the words *Los Angeles Police Department*. The structure hadn't been sandblasted or pressure-washed for years. A careful study of the letters indicated that they'd been removed altogether and what he was reading was a stain.

Many glass windows of the cubed facility were boarded up with sheets of plywood. Merit opened a reinforced security door before stepping into a wide, spacious lobby. The air was stale, and the floor was dusty and littered with stacked chairs, desks, and walls of disassembled cubicles. A woman stood behind a long hard surfaced counter protected by bulletproof glass that look as though it had sustained many blows from a sledgehammer. She was the only individual in a space that Merit theorized had once seen the bustling foot traffic of several dozen people. It was strange, he thought, that the police department of such a large city was almost deserted.

"May I help you?" The woman appeared as if she were afraid to speak. She was in her thirties and was as slender as most of the women in the street. Her hair was dyed right down the middle. Half was blonde, half was jet black. She wore a red T-shirt and faded blue jeans. It was hardly, Merit thought, the attire of a professional.

"I'm Detective Merit." His voice echoed in the great chamber for several seconds.

The young woman made no response as she stepped back and surveyed the stranger.

Merit produced his badge and credentials. "I'm a police officer from Pilgrim."

She held out the flat palm of her hand as if to indicate that he should be quiet. "We don't say that around here."

"You don't say *what*, ma'am?"

She lowered her voice. "The word 'police.' It's offensive."

"What do you call yourselves?" It was too late. She'd disappeared through a door behind the counter. "Offensive?" Merit began to poke around the lobby and noticed the walls riddled with bullet holes, exposed rebar in parts of crumbling concrete and sections charred by fire.

Five minutes later, two burly men appeared wearing clown masks that covered their entire faces. Merit assumed it was a practical joke that a fellow cop would play on another as some sort of initiation, but he found out that the two cops weren't kidding when they grabbed him under his armpits and lifting him from the floor, carried him through a doorway at the end of the counter.

This was not the welcome he expected.

19

Orange Golf Club sat halfway between L.A. and San Diego on a nature conservatory strip off the Pacific Coast Highway. The club had hosted numerous tournaments and several pro-celebrity events, but never a PGA event. Celebrities in the 1960s, 1970s, and 80s— Rock Hudson, Elizabeth Montgomery, Huey Lewis—used to escape busy L.A. and trek south along the P.C.H. to play a round of golf. People were drawn to the course because of its unusual configuration. The terrain from the ocean's reef climbed steeply, and the course was beautifully perched high on a plateau. It wasn't the typical, overly manicured course; it exhibited a more artistic, natural flair. The landscape was dotted with indigenous trees and native plants, with splashes of colorful wildflowers and large smooth rocks that jutted up from the earth. With the choppy, up and down geography, it was not the ideal site for Soldier to attempt a comeback.

—Roberto Reyes, *Rio De Janeiro Jornal de Opiniao*

GUN CITY

Merit was forcibly escorted down a long hallway, still not sure if he was the butt of a bad joke, to a small area labeled Interrogation Room 2. The clown masked men finally spoke through a voice scrambler in their mouths.

"Sit down," the first man motioned to a gray, metal, straight-back chair.

The second man took Merit's badge, wallet, gun, and backpack. "Do you have any other guns?"

"No."

"We're going to confiscate your sidearm. All of Frontier is gun-free. No drones here either, it's virgin air."

"This is a joke, right? I'm a police officer—"

The first man spoke again. "Welcome to the Frontier Servile Department."

"Servile?" Merit said.

"We're Frontier serviles. We don't use the word *police*."

"You're undercover officers—I mean serviles." Merit corrected himself.

Both men laughed in a mechanical voice. "There's no such thing. No uniforms, no guns."

"How do you serviles protect yourselves?"

Neither answered as one rummaged through his wallet, pulling out cards, I.D.s, and other contents as if it were a shakedown or a drug bust Merit used to see on television documentaries.

"All I know is that I was told to come here to find out who killed Soldier Quinn." Merit had hoped dropping the name could give him some credibility. His intuition was right.

The two men exchanged glances. The second man cocked his head. "Soldier Quinn?"

"Yeah." Merit shifted his eyes back and forth to both of them.

They led Merit through a dozen rooms cluttered with desks, unused for years. They walked past archaic SWAT gear and broken pictures of white helmeted cops on old BMW motorcycles. The offices were littered with trash and open file cabinets crammed with manila folders, coffee cups, and empty holsters, old bulletproof vests, and piles of uniforms. A closet on the right side of the hallway was dedicated to costumes, like the clown masks the two serviles who were dragging him wore, he caught a glimpse of all sorts of other colorful masks, hair wigs and capes. They finally arrived at an unmarked office.

The room was bigger and cleaner than most he'd seen, but it was far from modern. The nameplate on the desk read Servile Chief Reed.

He doubted that working on cold cases in Pilgrim, as difficult as they might be, entailed meeting this level of resistance. Frontier was known for embracing different values, but that was an understatement. Merit realized he was in unchartered territory, and thus far the only flicker of hope he'd had was the reaction of the two serviles to the name "Soldier."

The door to the office opened, and a man walked confidently in, sat down behind on the desk, clasped his hands, and sighed. He was in his early sixties and dressed about as messy as the others, although he wore no uniform. His wispy hair was slicked back but uncombed, and he had brown eyes and a five o'clock shadow that was hiding a bad case of acne on his chin and cheeks.

"Who are you?" He spoke with an air of self-importance.

"You have my badge and ID." Merit motioned to his wallet on the chief's desk.

The methodical moving chief with thick eyebrows flipped through his wallet, unclipped his badge and weighed the dense metal shiny shield in his hand.

Merit sat up. "I was called here to investigate the Soldier Quinn case."

"I'm not aware of anyone calling."

"Frontier P.D. phoned Pilgrim P.D. a week ago. I answered the call myself." Merit looked back at the men in masks then back at the chief. "A man on the phone said he had new evidence in the Soldier Quinn case and wanted me to come here and investigate."

"Did you get the man's name?"

Merit nodded no.

"Did you guys call?" The chief looked past Merit at the serviles disguised in silly clown masks.

Both shook their heads dumbly.

"They didn't call, and I didn't call, so, I guess you can go back, Detective James Merit." He read the name from Merit's identification card before flipping his badge-less wallet to Merit.

Merit could tell this bunch wasn't going to ante up any information and he'd have to force the direction of the conversation. "He said a gun was found."

"A gun?" The chief turned his back to Merit and walked to a tall filing cabinet with a tray on top filled with papers. "Oh, I think I remember what you're talking about now. A rifle. The rifle found on a beach." He dug through a messy stack of papers. "Yes, we do have that."

"Great. A rifle." Merit perked up. "If I can get the serial number off it, I can run it and see who it was registered to. It could be the killer—and I'd be out of here." Merit stood and approached the chief. "Can I see it?" Merit's eyes located the box on the form where the serial number was to be recorded, but the number had been redacted with a bold, black stripe. Merit had a bad feeling—but he kept his composure. "Does it say where they found it?"

"A beach. I just remember reading it was found by children digging on a beach." The chief sat down and folded his hands behind his head. "How long are you here?"

"I hope not long." There was an awkward pause before Merit broke the silence. "Is there someone who can help me?"

The chief burst out laughing. Not the kind of laugh one makes when they find something was actually funny. He scratched his knuckles on one hand, then the other. "Investigations aren't our specialty. I have evidence from over ten decades stored away, and we don't place a great deal of importance on cold cases."

"May I have my gun back now, sir?" Merit nodded toward his duty weapon resting on the chief's meaty thigh.

The chief looked down at the weapon then back up at him blankly. "Can't have a gun here. You were told that." He slowly slid the firearm out of its holster. Merit braced his body and held his breath. The chief of serviles inspected it, holding it up in the light to better see its details. He nodded his approval. "If you want your gun back now, you'll be escorted back to the Frontier Pilgrim border, and it will be returned to you."

Merit wanted to take the chief up on his offer, liking nothing better than to return to a state where the law meant something, a state where police officers were professionals who worked cases and solved them instead of collecting evidence for no purpose but to store it.

"No, I'll stay, chief."

The chief seemed unfazed, and he forced a wide smile. "I hoped you would."

Merit knew that was bullshit.

The chief inserted Merit's gun back in the holster and tucked it under the belt in his paunch for safekeeping.

"Where is the rifle stored?" Merit asked. "I need to get it."

"It's in our Property and Evidence Warehouse." He got up and exited the room abruptly.

Merit had a feeling that he would never see his gun again. "Okay, where's that?"

The door shut.

The men in masks threw a hood over Merit's head and roughly escorted Merit out of the room, like bouncers removing a drunken patron from a rowdy beer tavern.

20

Soldier's late entry into the U.S. Open sent shockwaves across the world. Media, fans, even non-golf enthusiasts, scrambled to book flights to witness history possibly being made. Hotels, motels, B & B's, and campsites were snatched up for miles around the cozy beach town. Soldier had not been seen in public in over four years. His "fat" photo was the public's last impression of him, so his appearance on the practice greens before the tournament's start, had everyone concerned. He looked emaciated and his face gaunt. Rumors suggested he had cancer and that this was his swan song. At his press conference, he dispelled the rumors and claimed to be injury-free. Afterward, there was a flurry of excitement, but critics doubted that Soldier, absent from golf for years, could withstand the demands required to survive four pressure-packed days of a major.

—Pro Sports Prod Inc. > 3 minutes ago

HOP ON

Within thirty seconds, Merit found himself seated outside on the steps of the old LAPD police station, the doors behind him locked by the two masked serviles, as soon as he cleared their threshold.

Merit was furious, as the hood had been ripped off his head on his release. The serviles had disrespected his status, and no one cared about the rifle that had prompted the request that he journey to Frontier. The chief had been marginally politer than the others, but he wasn't going to assist Merit. He needed that rifle––specifically the serial number off it. The idea that he could solve this huge case quickly and without too much hassle convinced him he'd have to find The Property and Evidence storage warehouse on his own.

He started to walk down the steps that led to the Commons in front of servile headquarters but stopped. A small crowd was forming, and they were giving dirty looks to the stranger dressed in blue.

"That's him." A man with purple and brown tattoos pointed up at Merit. He was bald except for a shock of blue hair growing from the top of his head.

"I saw him do it too." A young woman dressed in a two-piece bathing suit waved the others over. "Didn't give him anything."

Merit wasn't aware that anyone had taken notice of his brief encounter with the homeless man on his way into the city.

"He looks like a PP." An older man holding a crowbar advanced two steps toward Merit and slapped the iron bar in his hand as if he wished to use it on the stranger.

Merit turned around and tugged on the locked doors in futility.

The woman in the red T-shirt peered from a window several yards away. She, too, was not going to offer any help. She was a servile herself and wasn't going to chance opening the doors for a Pilgrim cop. Looking closer through the window, Merit saw the Chief and the backs of several serviles shuffling out the side door, the chief throwing on a fake beard, wig, and a hat.

Merit's mouth was dry as cotton as the crowd moved higher on the steps. He decided that if he got away, he'd return home as soon as possible. A detective had to have *something* to work with—a lead, a piece of evidence, an informant—even a hunch that represented a starting point.

There was one thing the serviles neglected to confiscate. Merit pulled out his cell phone to call for help, but there was no service. Even if the device had worked, he wondered, who would he have called? Certainly not the local serviles.

A man wearing a black bandana over the bottom of his face, and another over the top of his head, stepped out from behind an art sculpture, and grabbed Merit by the arm, pulling him sharply to the side. He was slender but muscular, and long, blond, wavy hair stuck out from his scarf.

"Come with me." Only a set of steely blue eyes were visible on the man.

Merit followed the mysterious figure along the portico and down the side steps, the crowd of eight in pursuit. He had no other choice but to trust him at this point. The man mounted a blue pedal-driven scooter and motioned for Merit to climb on its twin a few feet away.

Merit hesitated and glanced at the crowd, which was only twenty yards away and closing.

The man on the scooter grabbed the collar of Merit's shirt. "Hop on. Now!"

Merit stepped onto the scooter and inserted his feet into the pedal sockets. The man sped away, with Merit close behind as the angry mob chanted "PP! PP!"

★★★

The mysterious man swerved off the main drag and detoured under a building's alcove a mile away.

He braked to a stop and stepped off the two-wheeler. "I suggest you lose your uniform."

"What do I wear?" Merit looked down at his clothing then up at the man's attire.

"Take it off. Hurry."

Merit, who took pride in his upper torso, removed his streamlined-fit blue shirt. The man clamped his teeth down on the sleeve of Merit's shirt and yanked it back and forth—*Grrr* like a dog, causing a slight tear, and with both hands, he ripped the sleeve off. He repeated the process on the other sleeve and the collar, turned it inside out, and tossed it back to Merit. "Put it on."

Merit followed his instructions. "Who are you?" He then waited while the man tied the torn collar piece of his shirt around Merit's head to form a headband for his answer.

The man peeled off his handkerchiefs. "I'm a servile. Servile Beck." His face was tan and smooth, and although his hair was wavy, it was combed and looked neat. Merit wondered if he could trust him but looked around and quickly realized he had no other choice.

Merit took out his cell phone again. Maybe it would work in a different location, although he still wasn't sure who he could connect with. It was an act of desperation.

"It's not working?" The servile reached for the phone. "Let me see it."

Merit handed him the phone, which the man promptly spiked on the pavement, smashing it to bits.

Merit threw up his hands. "What are you doing!"

The man was composed, as he spoke to Merit while looking over his shoulders to see if they were being followed. "Cell towers were destroyed long ago, and satellites that carried mobile signals haven't been monitored for decades. If these people see that you have a phone, they'll know you're not from here." He tapped his temple with his index finger. "Technology equals Big Brother." He winked. "Now let's get out of here."

Servile Beck swung his leg over the scooter and peeled off. Merit followed suit, the warm wind blew against his face. "Where are we going?"

"To the property and evidence building." Servile Beck then popped a baby-wheelie, as if the green flagged had dropped at the start of a drag race, then jumped the curb onto the street and accelerated ahead, with Merit following his lead.

21

Soldier narrowly survived the U.S. Open's first day cut, providing rabid fans the slimmest of hopes. Over the next two days, he got his competitive legs beneath him. With birdies on Saturday's last three holes, he climbed into the top ten, delighting the fans who howled "bull's-eye" when he sunk the final putt. Back in his hotel room, while icing his aching ankles, Soldier was informed that his fill-in caddie had come down with the stomach flu and would miss Sunday's final round. If he had any chance of catching the leader, he needed someone that knew his game, but more importantly, someone he could trust. He looked in his phone contacts for a replacement, but no one could get there on such short notice.

—Michael J. Flemming, *The Dallas Star*

TEA TIME

The day was sunny and bright, and the patrons of an outdoor café—as most of them were—seemed unconcerned with the arrival of a man-powered scooter. The servile Beck had asked Merit earlier if he was hungry, and realizing he'd been in Frontier for over forty-eight hours without food, he told him he was starved. Merit was eager to get to the Property and Evidence warehouse to get the rifle, but with six to seven more miles to go, he took the break.

They ate, talked and laughed, as if they didn't have a care in the world. The two law enforcement officers, one from each of the divided states, sat at a table under horizontal wooden beams wrapped with green ivy. Maybe all the serviles here weren't so bad as the Chief and the two clown officers that roughly tossed him out of headquarters. Merit downed his third hot cup of tea.

"It's feeling a little better." Merit tenderly massaged his jaw with his fingers, testing its soreness by opening his mouth slightly and then closing it. "I think this hot tea's helping my jaw. Thanks. The pain's going away."

"Good, man. What happened to it?"

Merit was embarrassed to give the true answer. "I, uh, got hit by an orange."

The servile nodded as if it happened all the time, and he continued sipping his drink. His movements were slow and deliberate. He had movie-star qualities and looks. His blue eyes, with longer than normal lashes, casually surveyed the surroundings every few seconds to see if the two were being watched. The pores of his face were almost invisible, and he had no stubble. Merit figured him to be in his early forties. He seemed nice and had a pleasant, confident demeanor about him. Merit could see them being friends in different circumstances.

Merit decided to solicit an answer. "I'm curious Beck, why are you helping me?"

"I dunno." He added in a playful smile, "There's nothing else to do."

"What about policing the streets or investigating crimes?"

Beck put a finger to his lips. "Shh." A reminder to Merit to avoid using the word "police." He leaned closer. "We don't really have any crime, so citizens don't want us to say that word." He indicated the people lounging in the café.

Merit opened his jaw several times, and each time he was able to stretch it wider. "Yeah. It's feeling a lot better."

"It should. It has *loose* in it."

Merit shook his head not quite comprehending what Beck was saying.

"The tea has pot," Beck said.

"Right." Merit held up the cup and savored a hot sip. "It's a teapot?"

"No. There's pot in the tea. You know—spliff, bud, hay, loose . . .*marijuana*."

Merit spewed the remaining mouthful back into the cup and angrily said, "Why didn't you tell me?" He snatched a glass of water and rinsed his mouth.

"Marijuana's not illegal. It's in every drink. Even in the water."

Merit set the water glass down on the table and pushed it to the middle. "I'm drug-tested. I could lose job my over this."

Beck continued matter-of-factly. "All drugs are legal, and nobody eats meat. That's why that waitress gave you that look when you asked to have that cooked medium-rare." He nodded at Merit's sandwich. "People live off fresh food. There's no killing animals or owning pets either."

That explained why Merit had seen so many stray dogs alongside the roads, as well as hordes of cats as his eyes looked up to see many sprawled out on the exposed beams of the cafe.

"So what's this I'm eating?" Merit held up what he thought was a cheeseburger.

"You really wanna know?"

Merit cringed. "No, I guess not. But there are no drugs in it, right?"

Beck shrugged. "There's loose in everything. It's why you're feeling better, man." He indicated the other patrons seated about. "It's why everyone's loose."

Merit set the half-eaten sandwich made of an unknown substance on the plate, and rummaged through his backpack, finding a stash of beef jerky. "I'll eat these."

Beck seemed comfortable as he sat, exchanging pleasantries with other patrons. He was especially relaxed with women and had a confidence around them that Merit had always lacked.

Merit admittedly felt a little mellow and leaned back and breathed in the clean, crisp ocean air he was experiencing for the first time, the warm sun toasting his cheeks.

"You're loose." Beck stood, "Loose feels good." He picked up the dirty dishes and walked them toward the counter.

In the meantime, Merit decided to check out the scenery, the other patrons.

Like others Merit had seen, the women were scantily clad, and Merit again noticed some were without tops. He couldn't resist allowing his eyes to wander. Their breasts were not the typical round-shaped breasts naturally bestowed on the women of Pilgrim. These tiny and full-figured Frontier gals possessed firmer breasts in a variety of shapes, sizes, and configurations that was beyond his imagination.

One young lady stood, and before she turned around and walked away, shot him a seductive look. He couldn't help noticing that she boasted a set of thinner and longer— missile-shaped breasts that bizarrely extended out *and* pointed slightly upward. They reminded him of the cucumbers or zucchini he'd plucked from his ranch vegetable garden as a kid. Her freakish body didn't correlate with anything he'd ever seen, but he couldn't take his eyes off them.

"Go get some of that?" Beck had appeared over his left shoulder.

"What?" Merit nervously wrung his hands together as though washing them.

"Go get it." Beck motioned to the bullet-breasted young lady.

"Get what? —That? No, that's too weird." Merit was stammering. "I'm not interested. I have a girlfriend." He abruptly stood. "What I need is to get to the property and evidence building."

As Beck led him to the exit, Merit felt a sense of shame for lusting after the young woman with breasts that pointed out and slightly up. He scolded himself, thinking he should have acted more professionally since he represented Pilgrim P.D.

As they were leaving, he commented that a majority of customers and staff had tattoos, and Beck explained that the color and design of the tattoos signified people's beliefs, social expressions, and spiritual aspirations.

"Spiritual?" Merit, thinking maybe he'd been misinformed about Frontier and its atheistic beliefs, livened up. "So, you *are* believers here?"

"Yeah. You can believe whatever you want here, but there are no religions."

"No, there are. On my way in, I saw lines of people coming and going out from a bunch of different churches."

"Yeah, we have churches. That's where you get drugs. They got any kind you want—Bump, bennies, coke, circles, speed, uppers, downers, planks, zanies," Beck said. "And angels and Bibles and heaven and hell and Adam and Eve are all silly ancient bullshit. Nobody buys into that witchcraft anymore."

Merit strapped on his backpack, wincing at Beck's sacrilegious statement. He was disturbed to learn that the Lord's house had been converted into drug houses. He wanted to confront Beck but opted to bite his tongue for now as he needed his help. "What do you believe in?" Merit said, as they mounted their scooters and took off alongside each other down the sidewalk.

Beck reflected for a moment, then shot him a look. "Sex."

22

The Security Director for the U.S. Open grossly underestimated the number of safety personnel needed to man the golf spectacle. When scheduling officers weeks prior, he hadn't anticipated Soldier's late entry. On the last day of the event, Sunday, the venue was over capacity and was growing by the minute. The stands and fairways were packed. People stood crammed shoulder to shoulder, back-to-back. The day before, the director had requested local sheriff's departments to send officers to help with crowd control on Sunday. He was told that most were working a triathlon on Sunday, but when the race was completed, they would assist. A line of fans wound around outside the entrance. After three holes of play, the director locked the gates, but the rowdy—many intoxicated spectators refused to go.

—ryan.cash@PGAsecurity/fraud.net

CRIME AND PUNISHMENT

Merit and Beck weaved on their scooters in and out of street traffic, which was comprised of bizarre-looking people, panhandlers, dogs, goats, rats, and merchants selling items from pushcarts, many smoking weed and sharing drugs. Merit had no choice but to trust that Servile Beck was leading him to the Property and Evidence warehouse so he could retrieve the murder weapon, the rifle that killed Soldier.

"Servile." Merit pulled up even to him. "That's a weird name for cops."

"Yeah. It started a long time ago, back when Frontier first began. People didn't trust cops and complained, so the police started accommodating them. Once you start giving in to people's demands, that's going down a black hole, you know."

Merit nodded. At least he and Beck agreed on something.

"How much farther to the warehouse?"

"About three miles. It's out on a big peninsula. Twenty-five more minutes."

There was less traffic, and they coasted beside each other and carried on a conversation.

"At first some claimed the word 'police' conjured up hate, so they replaced it with the word 'warriors.' We were warriors for a while until some felt the word was offensive, so they changed it to 'guardians.' Later some said the word 'guard' in guardians made citizens feel as if they were being watched, like prisoners, so they changed our name to serviles."

"What's it mean—servile?"

"It means acting in a submissive fashion. Many believed that giving serviles any name at all was providing them with a title and having a title could cause us to feel entitled or powerful and led to an abuse of power. So about ten years ago they decided to get rid of the name 'servile.' Then, they just decided to get rid of the police in general. Not just the names—but actual serviles. And they've been phasing us out ever since. Soon they'll be none of us."

Merit listened to the entire spiel without responding, his mouth agape, almost physically sick at hearing the irrational line of reasoning. "No police. That's some scary shit."

"You know, no matter what good we do, the people will never like us."

"They like us back in Pilgrim." Merit felt inclined to defend the people of his state. "Who's gonna protect the public from the criminals?"

"We don't have any more crime."

"Bullshit. You can move crime, you can deter it, but you can't stop it." Merit knew that fact from the criminal justice courses he'd taken back in college. "It's human nature."

"You'll see."

Merit was miffed at the line of reasoning. "How can you stand being a cop here?"

"They definitely hate us, and want us gone, but you get used to it."

"That's why you wear masks, huh?"

"Yeah. But you know—if you think about it . . . I can kind of agree with what they're saying about not needing the police to watch over them. People have been playing pickup basketball games forever without using referees, and it worked out fine. Right? If people can referee themselves, why can't people police themselves?"

"Calling a foul on yourself for slapping your opponent's hand and admitting you stabbed someone in the gut is totally different. I don't believe it will work."

"It's working. Look at me, man. I'm living proof. I got nothing to do." Beck grinned.

"What are you gonna do if it happens?"

"It's already happening now, man."

They turned the corner and Beck braked, skidding to a stop—Merit halting next to him.

"There it is." Beck pointed his finger up to the top of a tall building that was visible over a clump of mature palm trees.

The twelve-story warehouse was an eyesore. It was a massive-sized intimidating structure with only a few windows, all of which were painted tar black.

Beck looked back at Merit. "What's wrong?"

Merit was licking his lips making a sour look on his pale face. With no warning, he bent over, opened his mouth, and vomited a stream of a brownish-green chunky substance between two bushes.

23

On the final Sunday, Soldier's shots were not coming easy. Still, by the ninth hole, he clawed to within five shots of the North Korean phenom who sat atop the leader board. Players who had finished hovered in the clubhouse to watch. They were astonished at the enormity of the event. Soldier and the North Korean were the final pairings on the course. People around the world were glued to their devices. There was a hint of fear in the announcer's voice when he warned viewers "not to venture to the site…the gates are closed, you'll be turned away," but the warnings fell on deaf ears. Number crunching analysts estimated the people in attendance at over four hundred thousand, adding to a heightened sense of danger.
                                            —Hunter, C., NEWSWORTH *Today*

a•cop•a•lypse

After Merit spit the residual bad taste out of his mouth from puking, he told Beck he felt better and was *ready to go,* ready to enter the Property Room.

"You sure?" Beck looked in Merit's eyes the way a referee checked a glassy-eyed boxer who'd been knocked out to determine if he had his wits about him.

Meri took in a long breath, exhaled, and nodded.

Beck replaced his bandanas around his face and head to conceal his identity. They ditched their scooters and walked towards the Police Evidence Building that was a block away.

The combination of the marijuana—*loose* spiked tea and the faux-meat sandwich sloshing around in Merit's stomach during the one-hour scooter ride, was a mixed-cocktail that didn't agree with his system.

Marijuana or *any* kind of illegal drug or alcohol had never entered his untainted body and his system rejected it. He couldn't remember the last time he'd hurled, at least several years when he ate burritos and played a game of sleitis before letting it digest. He'd forgotten what a violent act throwing up inflicted on his entire body, but he was glad it happened, he felt much better.

No cars, palm trees, or landscaping adorned the flat ground surrounding the old evidence building's perimeter. SERVILES SUCK was spray-painted on the side of the bleak gray complex, causing the building to stand in stark contrast to others in the vicinity, which were modern and clean. The front doors were locked, with a heavy metal chain threaded through two iron handles.

"Let me have the key." Beck put out his hand.

"I don't have one." Merit displayed the open palms of his hands as empty.

"Didn't chief give you one?"

"No, and he also took my gun." Merit scoffed. "You have a key though, don't you?"

Beck shook his head.

"How do you get in to get your evidence for court and stuff?" Merit asked.

"There's no more court, so I don't need a key."

"I gotta get in there to get that gun." Merit tugged violently on the chain.

Beck produced a metal file from his key chain, unfolded it and began to pick the lock, manipulating the tool back and forth like a professional cat burglar.

"What about the guys in jail now?" Merit said. "What's going to happen to them?"

"Only the most serious violent offenders—murderers, rapists, and robbers—are locked up. They've been in prison for years while waiting to go to court."

"Frontier's not going to prosecute them?" Merit scowled. "They're just going to release them back into society?"

"Yup."

"That's insane!" Merit was stunned. "What about the victims?"

"Remember Frontier's motto: Individuality, Equality, and Forgiveness. The victims forgave them."

Merit looked at him, dumbfounded. "That's the stupidest thing I've ever heard. How does a dead person forgive his killer?"

"A family member can give it. And we don't really have murders anymore." The file Beck was using snapped in two. He slammed the heavy chain against the steel door in frustration. "Let's check around the back." Beck again led the way, snooping around the base of the one-block circumference of the sturdily built fortress.

"So, when are they letting these jack-off prisoners out?" Merit said.

"Same time they're destroying this building. In twenty-seven days. On the Fourth of July." Beck paused, "Acopalypse Day."

Merit scrunched his nose as he pronounced the word. "Acopalypse?"

"Yeah. The end of cops. No more policing. That's what they're calling it. It's gonna be a huge day in Frontier. Everybody's coming to celebrate. They're demolishing this building with the evidence inside."

Every ten or so yards, they passed a solid steel exterior door with no handle to pull. Beck wedged his fingers in the cracks to pull them open but found each one was shut tight. Their eyes scanned up along the row of second-story windows to locate some type of opening but saw there were grates welded over them. The historic old Evidence Building was sealed tight as a drum. Beck salvaged a rusted steel rod from the weeds and pried it between a door and its frame. He leaned against it, hoping to use his body as leverage to jimmy it open.

"What if you need the evidence later to convict those guys in jail?" Merit leaned his body to the back of Beck, who was pushing the pole sideways, for some added muscle.

"That's their whole point. With the evidence destroyed, they'll never be able to prove anything to convict them, and they'll be free as a bird." They worked the metal bar, grunting, back and forth in rhythm. "Police work as we know it is coming to end, my friend."

"Not as *I* know it." Merit poked his thumb at his own chest.

The heavy-duty door without warning sprung open, making a crashing noise, sending them to the hard ground of gray dirt mixed with broken glass and grits of sparkling sand.

24

Tiny prop planes flew slowly over the course's coastline, dragging banners that read: "Good Luck Soldier" and "Break Vic's record". Commercial blimps circled high above like vultures. Their bird's-eye camera view captured the multitudes of fans, scurrying like ants determined to witness history. People abandoned their cars on roads and freeways, stumbled down mountainsides, and hoofed it to the course, only to be locked out. Others camped out on hillsides and watched through binoculars. Hundreds of boats, kayaks, and jet skis sailed to the club's cove to be part of the spectacle. Boaters blasted music, danced, and got drunk on their decks. Guys and gals in bikinis paddle boarded or swam to shore, then streaked drenched across fairways to the final holes. The officers, feeling powerless, looked the other way. It was absolute chaos.

—Arata Lindsley, *The Greater Tokyo Chronicle*

BELLY OF THE WHALE

Inside, the property and evidence warehouse's halls were darker and dirtier than the lobby at the Capital City Police Department. Beck flipped a series of industrial light switches on a panel, but there was no electricity. Merit produced a slim police flashlight, with the name Pilgrim Police Department embossed on the end, from his backpack. Several large rats and a family of black-masked raccoons scurried from the corner to the center of the floor and paused before retreating into a hole in the wall.

Beck explained the layout of each floor, referencing a dusty placard on the wall. "Each floor contains evidence from an entire decade. What year did your murder happen?" His words echoed.

Merit never liked to release information about a case he was working but realizing the huge amount of evidence that was stored, he decided to make an exception. "It was 2026. It happened in 2026."

"That's old. That stuff would be several flights down in the basement."

They went into an area beyond the lobby and saw dozens of rows of steel-frame shelves extending far into the gloom. Most shelves contained sooty cardboard cartons labeled EVIDENCE in faded red letters. Many containers lay overturned, apparently vandalized, their contents having been spilled on the floor.

"I can't believe they're destroying all this—all the hard work officers did to collect it."

Merit sneezed several times from the dust in his nostrils.

The two of them started winding their way down the stairwell into the building's guts, hanging onto the aluminum railings to prevent tripping. One floor's shelving stacked thousands of obsolete red, white and blue American flags and California Republic State flags sequestered from public and private schools, universities, federal buildings, and government offices during the first years of Frontier's inception. Another entire floor was dedicated to confiscated religious artifacts. Bibles, hymnals, figurines, statues of Jesus on the cross, priests' robes, nuns' habits and other objects of worship from all denominations lined the floor and walls.

"It's not a bad system here Merit. It organically polices itself. Yeah, maybe somewhere, some person may commit what used to be considered a crime, but with no laws—well, with no laws, there's no crime to commit."

"So instead of holding people accountable after they did something wrong, you back-doored it," Merit said, "You legalized everything at the front end to avoid punishment."

"Not me—they. At first, what your State of Pilgrim classifies as property crimes, like theft, shoplifting, burglary, or vandalism, were legalized here in Frontier. They asked people here not to steal, but if they did, it wasn't a crime."

"What about the victims and their belongings, Beck?"

"There are no victims here. Just 'forgiveness.' People learn from a young age that if someone takes something of yours, it's something you didn't really need anyway. It's a piece of plastic or metal that can be replaced."

"What about personal crimes, like rape, robbery, and murder? People aren't made of plastic." Merit said.

"Same thing."

"So, you let these idiots go around raping and robbing people all day."

"No. It's like this. Citizens voluntarily contribute money to a public fund. People who don't have much money can use it as they may, no questions asked. With free money, they no longer need to rob, and they can pay for sex, so nobody gets raped."

"Are you sure you're still a cop?" Merit shot him a look, raising one eyebrow slightly, in jest.

Beck stopped on a landing, "The people here pay upfront instead of paying for it at all on the back end like Pilgrim does after they break one of your thousands of laws. And by the time you pay for all your cops, their equipment, drones, district attorneys, defense attorneys, judges, costly trials, prisons, medical costs, and so on, you end up paying more at the back end and raise your taxes to cover it. Not here. It's all part of Frontier's philosophy, and it works."

Merit had always embraced the purity of Pilgrim's full-proof formula for solving the problem of crime—*If a bad guy's in jail or dead, he can't commit a crime*—and he didn't want to admit it, but Frontier's equation—*if there are no laws to break, there are no crimes to commit*—though radically different, in a twisted kind of way, in theory made sense; however, he still had his doubts. "You have a lower crime rate because you've done away with laws, not the crimes."

"Frontier will do away with prosecuting all crimes on July Fourth when this building is professionally imploded." Beck made an explosion sound—*kapow!*—with his mouth.

"Acopalypse Day." Merit smirked and shook his head. "It won't work. The threat and fear of punishment and following through on it is the real deterrent. People inherently crave boundaries, limits, direction, order. Without it, they slide down into slovenliness and sin."

"It's like the resistance theory," Beck said. "Remove the temptation to do something illegal—and a person loses interest in doing what is harmful. See? With each new generation, the philosophy takes hold with more and more of the population. In fact, they're pretty much there. People are content. There's no need to lock people up like animals."

The ideas Frontier believed were idealistic and nonsensical, and he started to think that solving Soldier's murder would make no difference to anyone in Frontier, which is why Chief Reed at the LAPD building had expressed no interest in helping him, even though it was the most well-known unsolved homicide in history.

Merit had never encountered such off-the-wall thinking back in Pilgrim, but he liked Beck, and for fear of biting the hand that was feeding him, he'd agree for now. "Yeah, I can see what you're saying. Now let's find the boxes where the evidence I need is stored."

Beck asked. "What's your victim's name?"

If Merit had any chance at solving this case by finding the rifle, he couldn't hold his cards so close to the vest. "Soldier Quinn."

Beck stopped in his tracks, and turned back to address him, "Soldier Quinn?"

"Yeah." Merit stopped four steps up behind him.

"You're working Soldier's murder?" He looked squarely into Merit's eyes. "That's big. The biggest. You must be good—*real* good. Everybody's tried to solve it. He was the greatest golfer."

★★★

Merit followed Beck down a dark aisle farther into the building's bowels of evidence for several steps before the servile stopped and pointed to a long row of dilapidated cartons.

"Everything is stored chronologically," Beck said. "June 18, 2026. The date of Soldier's death. Here, Merit. Case 2026-018943. Soldier Quinn. Homicide/Murder."

"How'd you know that date?" Merit asked.

"*Everybody* pretty much knows it. It's a big date in Frontier's history."

Merit was impressed with Beck's knowledge. If the date Soldier was killed was such an important date in Frontier's history, which essentially forced the division of the old America into two separate states, then it must have been an important date in Pilgrim's history, too, but he wasn't aware of it. Sergeant Travers was right about him, he didn't know his history very well.

Merit and Beck removed four rectangular cartons and opened the lids. Inside the first box was a pile of DVDs and cell phones. Another held crime scene photographs, interviews, and police reports. A third held more papers and several boxes of golf balls. A fourth long carton held Soldier's golf clubs, which were stored horizontally in a leather and canvas golf bag.

"Wow!" Beck was excited. "These are the clubs Soldier Quinn, *the* Soldier Quinn, used at the U.S. Open." He stood the bag up, leaned it against the shelf, took out the putter, and started tapping balls down the long narrow concrete floor between the tall racks of shelves.

Aggravated at Beck's desire to putt balls instead of digging through evidence, Merit sifted through a box of various police reports. On the top, as if it had recently been placed in the carton, was a receipt for the rifle.

"This is what I came for!" He held it up. "The original evidence receipt for the gun."

"What kind of gun was it?" Beck looked over his shoulder.

"I'm not exactly sure." Merit's eyes carefully studied it, as his index finger scanned back and forth and from top to bottom of the form to ensure he didn't skip over it. "Here. It's a rifle. It's got the complete make and model, M24 (SWS) Sniper Weapons System, although the serial number has been blotted out again. Shit! The actual gun should be around here somewhere. Your chief said so." There was a sense of anticipation and urgency as Merit tore open shelf after shelf of boxes. "Help me look."

Five minutes later, Merit stood in the middle of a pile of opened boxes with his hands on his hips. "Where is the gun? I need the actual, physical rifle." He was getting angry but didn't want to lose his cool in front of Beck.

Beck looked up from his putting. "They probably destroyed it."

"No. Your chief said it was here. They found the gun used to kill Soldier. That's why I rushed here from Pilgrim." He was starting to think the chief had sent him on a wild goose chase. Merit also pieced together why Sgt. Travers said he had thirty days to solve it, Frontier was destroying all the evidence on July 4th.

"I'm guessing that whoever found the gun down here, took it for the money." Beck's attention drifted back to the clubs. "Look at these. They called them woods. And these, I think they called these clubs irons—"

Beck swung a driver wildly, his backswing nearly clobbering Merit in the face. Merit grabbed it from his hands, "Careful, this could kill somebody," and laid it high on the end shelf out of reach, like a parent with a child's toy—who wasn't playing nicely. "What's that big book in that carton?" Merit pointed.

Beck knelt and paged through the thick manual titled *MMI*. "There must be a thousand pages in here. Maybe it's a rule book?" He flipped through several. "Boring," he concluded, as he tossed it to the side. "So, he was shot with a rifle. That's important. Most people always figured that, but there's never been any proof of it."

"Some kids dug it up by accident on some beach."

"Merit, do you know a lot about the murder?"

"No. I've only read a few articles, and I've watched some videos about him. I just know he was a big golfer, was African American, and someone didn't want him breaking some golf record. I don't know if he was killed in his house, on the street, during the day or at night . . ."

"You don't know how he was shot? Really? He was playing golf. It was a beautiful June day, and he was playing at the U.S. Open here and . . ." Beck paused and remained very still, thinking he might have heard something.

"And?" Merit was intrigued.

"And you're right, Soldier was about to break the record for majors held by a white golfer and all these people there were watching, and then on the last hole, that's when it happened—"

"What happened?" Merit stopped unpacking the box.

"Shhh." Beck put his index finger to his lips, and his other hand on Merit's shoulder.

The sound of voices drifted down from the floors above them.

Beck softened his voice, "Did you shut the door we came in?"

"I don't remember. Shit. Sorry."

"Don't worry about it, man. It's probably vigilantes." Beck listened intently. "It sounds like they're in the lobby. Let's wait and hope they don't come down the stairs."

"Vigilantes?"

Beck frowned as if his explanation wouldn't make sense to someone who didn't understand the ways of Frontier. "Vigilantes. Frontier citizens who hunt down cops, so we'd better get out of here. Pick up what you need because it may not be here tomorrow."

Merit hastily stuffed papers, file folders photographs, a box of tees, a glove, stacks of DVDs, and electronic equipment into the golf bag that was empty thanks to Beck's examination of Soldier's clubs. The muffled voices of the possible vigilantes were getting louder. The vigilantes, if that's who they were, were carrying on indistinguishable banter with intermittent bursts of laughs and curse words.

Merit listened to their unintelligible muttering and believed there to be at least three, maybe four or five. There were loud sounds and bangs, items crashing down, reverberating through the stairwells. As the voices grew louder, Merit instinctively reached for his sidearm and had a sinking feeling when he felt nothing there. "How we gonna get out of here?"

"Listen Merit..." Even though Beck was laid back, he had a natural intensity when he spoke, and when it was time to act, he was clear and concise. "...we can't go up until they come down or we'll run into them. Just wait here, and if they start to come down our aisle, I'll tug on your sleeve, and we'll double back and go up the steps. Be quiet. Remember that it's three flights up to the lobby. Okay? Then find the door we came in. That's the only way out. Stay with me." Beck pulled the bandana over his mouth and nose.

Merit gave him a thumbs-up. As he stood upright and looped the cylinder-shaped golf bag's strap over his shoulder, his flashlight slipped from his hand and rolled under the raised bottom of the shelf to his right. Here he was, a great detective sent here to solve the biggest case in history, and he not only forgot to shut the door but dropped his light, giving away their location. The beam pointed forward so that there was enough illumination a few feet ahead.

"I need my light."

"No time." Beck dragged Merit by the arm. "We gotta get out of here."

The two officers made their way quickly down the aisle, hands extended in front of them as they blindly stumbled over debris and cartons that had fallen from the shelves. Merit glanced over his shoulder to see tall, large shadows on the wall behind him. His sense of hearing grew sharp in the darkness, and he quickened his pace as he heard the footsteps of what sounded like two men walking at the other end of the room.

Merit and Beck turned right, moving down an aisle that cut across the others at a right angle, but the vigilantes had obviously found the flashlight and then split up. One now stood several yards away, although Merit couldn't see his face because of the glare produced by the strong beam.

"Fuckin' serviles!" the man with the light yelled.

Beck said into Merit's ear, "Run!"

25

In hopes of catching a glimpse of Soldier, a sea of fans lined not only both sides of the fairway in play but adjacent fairways as well. Some held their cell phones blindly over their heads to record the action. Those further back sat on each other's shoulders, while more desperate ones climbed trees and hung precariously from limbs to get a view. After Soldier struck the ball, they migrated like a powerful ocean torrent to see his next shot. Other fans staked their claim several holes ahead, waiting to get just one look. When Soldier smacked his ball off the fourteenth tee, rambunctious fans shouted "Bull's-eye," blew whistles, waved signs, punched beach balls in the air and took another swig of liquor. It felt more like an outdoor rock concert than a golf match.

—Jay and Ian, *Sports Talkcast 100*

BRANDED MAN

Merit ran straight ahead inside the property room to escape the vigilantes' pursuit, falling to his knees when his right foot caught the edge of a box on the floor. Scrambling to his feet, he darted through the darkness, but he no longer heard the footfalls of Beck. He and the servile had gotten separated.

Three flights up, weak light directly ahead indicated that he'd left the side door open. Beck obviously knew his way around the property building and had used the exit, which had an interior handle. Outside, squinting from the blinding daylight, he softly shut the door and walked as quickly as he could, hugging the wall for concealment, the weight of the golf bag pulling on his right shoulder. Beck was nowhere to be seen.

Merit's scooter was at the front side of the building, but he didn't have the luxury of circling back to find it, plus he wasn't sure it would still be there if the vigilantes had spotted it. He decided his best course of action was to aim for an alley across the street and disappear as quickly as possible.

Five minutes later, he wandered alone down streets with pedestrians staring at him, as he carried a leather bag that most people wouldn't recognize. So much for blending in, he thought, as he ducked down several more alleys to make sure the vigilantes wouldn't be able to track his movements. Though he'd been hidden away in the homiscope, pulled from patrolling the streets years earlier in Pilgrim, it felt foreign not chasing others—feeling as if *he* were being pursued and having to look over his shoulder.

Merit found himself in an open-air market and borrowed a green-colored visor cap from one of many zip pockets on Soldier's bag to conceal his short hair. He nervously approached a middle-aged man and asked him if he knew of a hotel where he could stay. The man, who didn't appear to regard Merit as an outsider, scribbled down an address on a sheet of paper.

"You found that bag here at the market?" the friendly man said. "Nice antique. That's from the late . . . 1990s maybe early 2000s." He eyed the bag enviously. "It's extremely rare."

"Yeah." Merit forced a smile. "Guess it was my lucky day."

Merit breathed a sigh of relief, but as he did so, he saw a young Hispanic woman, sultry and flirtatious, staring at him, mouthing words, as she slowly drifted away from his location. She was tiny and thin, no more than five feet tall. She had long straw-like blonde hair and was messy as if she'd just woken up. He gravitated toward her, wondering what she might be trying to tell him. Did she know who he was? Was she a friend of the servile Beck?

He was still ten feet away from her when he bumped into a large muscular man. The male figure looming over him was easily six foot six inches and looked like a wrestler on steroids.

"Sorry," Merit's eye still lingered on the seductive woman.

The hulking-sized man blocked his path. Looking around him, Merit saw that he was loosely surrounded by a group that he figured were vigilantes.

"Is this your flashlight?" The tallest guy shined a beam in Merit's face, causing him to reel backward. They were all well-built, except for one who was big but fat, regarded Merit with menacing stares. He figured they had noticed the name Pilgrim P.D. stamped on the wand's handle.

The detective shook his head and moved back two paces, but another muscle-bound stud—short and stocky, stood behind him blocking his path.

"I asked you a question." Vigilante One raised his gravelly voice, as he held the beam closer to Merit's face. He was a brute of a man with a square jaw and dark brown eyes. His skin was tanned from constant sun exposure. He wore long cut-off blue jeans and a hoodie vest made of lightweight T-shirt material, but there was no shirt underneath.

Merit shifted his eyes to the left. Spying a basket of fruit, he picked up a handful of peaches and shoved them into the face of the vigilante in front of him, forcing the soft, fleshy produce into the man's eyes, temporarily blinding him. He then pushed over the entire table upon which the basket rested, slipped around him, and ran.

He'd only traveled a few yards when he surveyed the market and saw a total of six men—he'd been able to count them rapidly and saw that three had broken into a run as they pursued him. Three others used skateboards to parallel his progress. He toppled another table amidst cries from shoppers to block three of them to his rear. He then sprinted down a narrow street and angled left into an alley clothed in shadow.

When he reached the end of the concrete path, he descended the stairs and moved quickly through a small neighborhood park. Two vigilantes managed to track his escape, so Merit jumped a fence, lifting the golf bag up and over the slatted fence after he'd cleared the obstacle, and once again broke into a run.

He lumbered up an overpass, down the other side, and took a sharp left. He was breathing hard from the exertion, but because of his workouts at the obstacle course and his weightlifting, he still had the energy to power through his attempted escape. He ran straight ahead and then stopped dead in his tracks.

Unfamiliar with the layout of any part of Capital City, he'd mistakenly arrived back at the open-air market, having come full circle.

He decided to speed walk through the center of the market, which was still in chaos because of the overturned tables.

He'd gone only five feet when he took a header, the golf bag flying from his shoulder, and came to rest under a long wooden table, before taking a sharp blow to his head that knocked him out.

★★★

Merit awakened and saw that he was in a storage room of what appeared to be a larger stockroom. Because its door was open, he saw that he'd been dragged down a long alley, away from any pedestrians. He'd been stripped to his underwear and was getting kicked in his ribs by the man who'd stood behind him at the market, Vigilante Two.

"Where's your gun?" Vigilante One with dark, beady eyes and an intimidating coarse voice demanded.

"I don't have one." Merit looked up at him from a vulnerable position.

"Bullshit."

Vigilante One took a knee and leaned over Merit's body, his face inches from the detective's.

"I don't have it anymore," Merit said. "They took it."

"Who are you here after?"

"I'm not here after anyone."

"PPs don't come here except to get someone."

This was the third time he'd been referred to as a PP, the first time by the orange fruit gunners, the second by hecklers outside the LAPD headquarters, and the term didn't register.

Merit saw that two of the vigilantes were sorting through the contents of the golf bag. "Looks like worthless shit," the fat goon said. "I'm not even sure what it is. Old computer equipment shit, a box of balls, box of tees and papers and shit. No gun."

"What's a PP?"

Vigilante Two, the only one with his hair fashioned like a Mohawk, kicked Merit in the ribs again, causing him to wince.

"You wanna know?" Vigilante Four hovered over Merit's prostrate form.

Vigilante One held out his arm, motioning for the others to step back as their cohort extracted a slender rod of iron from a steel drum on the side of the room. The metal rod had been resting in red-hot coals, its tip forming the reversed letters PP. Vigilante Two stepped toward Merit and got down on one knee as three others restrained him. Slowly, the Mohawk-headed vigilante brought the brand against the thin skin on the backside of Merit's neck and pressed.

The lead vigilante said, "Now you'll never forget."

Merit clenched his teeth in agony, internalizing the pain, as the red-hot initials seared his flesh. His body convulsed as he shut his eyes tightly and drifted in and out of consciousness.

★★★

The beer-bellied Vigilante took Merit's shirt from his backpack, rolled it tightly until it resembled the length of thick rope, and cinched it around his torso just beneath his armpits. After looping an old American flag with thirteen stripes and fifty stars around his neck, a symbol of repression in Frontier, they dragged Merit out of the room, down the alley, and stopped in front of a black steel light pole in a park across the street.

Hoisting his limp body into the air, they hung Merit by hooking the rolled-up shirt onto two prongs at the top of the pole, his feet suspended two feet above the ground. He was an example to any other cop from Pilgrim infiltrating Frontier.

26

By the twelfth hole, Soldier was only four shots off the lead when a group of men from security muscled through the crowd. They escorted a party of nine close to the tee box, including the bow tie-wearing portly club owner, his trim tanned wife, several of their attractive guests, and three men in business suits. They were privileged enough to get front-row seats to watch the last seven holes of history possibly in the making. At the event's conclusion, the men in suits would congratulate the winner, compliment the runner-up, and give a shout out to 'The Fox', Vic Jackson. On Saturday, the event's public relations planner had called the great Mr. Vic Jackson and asked him to be on stand-by in case Soldier was in contention on Sunday. To avoid the perception of being a poor sport, Vic agreed.

—Kent Gaines, *Men's Focus Journal*

HOUSE OF ILL REPUTE

Merit awoke to find himself lying on a rollout couch in a spacious loft. He lifted his head—his neck was very sore—to see sunlight reflected on the crests of blue waves in the distance. He touched his neck with his right hand and discovered that a bulky bandage had been applied to the spot. The pain of the wound brought back the memory of running in the open market and being abducted by the vigilantes. What had happened to Beck?

A woman entered the room wearing white painter's overalls cut off high up on her thin thighs and a peach-colored tube top that exposed the sides of her midriff and sun-kissed shoulders. As he looked at the contrast between her thick hair and tan skin, he realized that this was the Hispanic woman from the market.

He threw his legs over the side of the rollaway bed and tried to stand, but his ribs were sore, and he fell back onto the mattress.

Merit felt the back of his sore neck with his hand. "I remember you."

"I don't think so."

"Yeah. You were in the market, right before those thugs chased me, I think."

"Those thugs were vigilantes. They want to know who you're here after."

"I'm not after anyone—I told them that. I'm here to work."

The woman eyed him suspiciously. Was she second-guessing her decision to rescue him?

"How long have I been here?" Merit tried to roll over, but the slightest movement caused him discomfort.

"Three hours."

"Three? I gotta get to work." He looked around frantically. "Hey, where's that bag?"

"That old brown smelly thing? I threw it out."

"What! Why would you do that? That was mine!"

The woman disappeared into another room and reappeared seconds later, lugging the worn, cracked, leather and canvass golf club bag. "I'm kidding. Lighten up." She held the bulky bag at arm's length with two hands. "What kind of bag is it?"

Merit felt embarrassed for his childish fit. "It's a golf bag."

She became quiet and stared at him with a judgmental scowl. She dropped it on the floor as if were contaminated. "I don't want *that* in my house."

"Why? It's not mine. I'm using it to hold stuff for the work I'm doing. The bag is from a sport a long time ago."

"An ugly sport. A part of old America's past that we don't want any part of. Just keep it out of sight." She disappeared into the bathroom and washed her hands. "What kind of work are you doing?"

She grabbed some ointment and bandages, climbed onto the bed, and straddled Merit's bruised body. "This will help with some of the scrapes and cuts you sustained." She then applied salve to various portions of his body, after which she put dressings over areas where his skin was especially red and raw.

Merit could hardly believe that a woman—a virtual stranger—a beautiful young woman was hovering over his body, but he couldn't move. Despite his unease, he found her touch to be seductive and pleasing as her palms moved sensuously across his arms and chest.

Merit, in serious pain, fell back asleep.

★★★

The young Hispanic woman stood in the middle of the loft, leaning to the side, as she placed one hand on her angled hip. She bit her lip and looked at him lying on the rollout bed. "Listen, I don't like serviles—but mostly I don't like Pilgrim cops, their laws, their guns, their attitudes, or anything about them."

Merit was suddenly alert and lifted his head from the soft pillow. "If you don't like the police, why did you help me?" He was confused. The young woman in her early twenties was no longer treating him with compassion.

"I don't like to see anyone get hurt."

"Yeah. And how did you, all by yourself, stop *all* of those vigilantes?"

"I gave each of them pleasure." She showed no emotion.

Merit felt conflicted. He wasn't sure how he should react. He was grateful that his life had been spared, but he was repulsed by what the woman had done for him.

"You're a prostitute."

"I'm a pleasure attendant."

Merit nodded, "A call girl."

She didn't respond and continued looking down at him with a raised eyebrow.

He glanced again at his surroundings and the layout of her home, stylish yet modestly furnished, with colorful art prints on the walls, a series of large butterfly impressions done with lithographs, acrylics, and other art mediums. "How'd you know I was a cop from Pilgrim?"

"Go look in the mirror."

He grimaced as he stood from the soreness of his rib cage and hobbled into the bathroom, bracing his arm against the wall. He was hurt worse than he had originally believed.

Looking in the mirror, he tilted his head slightly and carefully peeled off the homemade bandage she had applied. The sticky tape tugged the blistered tissue that surrounded the scalded skin on his neck, causing him excruciating pain, but to prove his manhood, he didn't flinch. Once the temporary bandage was removed, he observed the two one-inch-tall letters singed into his skin and said, "PP."

"Pilgrim Pig." She had poked her head in, and spoke to his reflection in the mirror, "That's what PP stands for." She described with no inflection.

Merit, not wearing a shirt, leaned closer, pressing the side of his face against the mirror for a closer inspection. He squinted as he examined the crudely branded letters.

"That's what you people in Pilgrim do to their cattle." She glanced callously into his eyes. "Stick them with a hot poker, so if they stray, they can be identified. That's what they do to *pigs* here." She then backed away from the mirror's reflection.

For someone who claimed she didn't *like to see anyone get hurt*, Merit thought that she didn't come across as the sympathetic type. Lightly dabbing the area with his fingers and testing for pain sensitivity, Merit said, "Motherfuckers. They branded me." He replaced the bandage, covering up the mark seared on his neck. "I'm gonna kill'em." Wincing with pain, he limped out of the bathroom into her spacious loft.

"How are you gonna kill 'em? You said you don't have a gun."

"I don't." Merit plopped down on the edge of a deep, U-shaped sectional couch, with a coffee table in the center. "And if guns are so bad, why does everyone here want mine?"

"Guns are worth a lot."

"I got a bunch of them back home." He cracked a smile. "If you want more?"

"I hate guns." She kept a straight face. "They're ugly. They only bring destruction and death. Guns are wrong."

"Having sex for money is wrong." Merit stared back at her.

She ignored his comment. "Guns are worth a lot because they're melted down. Melted down and reused for something of beauty—jewelry."

The young gal lifted her arm and jiggled her wrist. A bracelet of small shiny metal beads to jingle. "My boyfriends pay me with these instead of money." She delicately held a thin necklace, strung around her taught, brown-skinned throat, rubbing one round metal bead between her thumb and slender finger, putting Merit in a temporary trance. She then stood by a table, picked up a plastic bottle, and popped several small blue pills.

"What's that for?" Merit asked.

"It makes me feel better. It helps me forget."

"Forget what?"

"Anything that happened, any event that occurred over the past hour or so. Take two and it erases even more." She swallowed four pills.

Merit figured she took the drugs to forget the sexual favors she had provided the vigilantes. "You won't remember *anything* that happened over the past few hours?"

"That's right. Blocks out negative memories. So, no bad feelings." She handed him the pill bottle. "You could use a couple."

He shook his head. He didn't want to forget the Vigilante's faces and what they had done to him. "I thought it was your profession and that it's legal here."

"It's *my* body, it's my life, and I can do what I want with it. Don't you do things to make you feel better?"

"Yes, but I don't do drugs to escape reality. I play sports, listen to music and uh, I like to ride horses."

"You like to torture animals." She glared at him.

"Are you serious? They like it."

"How do you know? —Are you part horse?" She got up from the chair and stood tall.

"Because I ride them."

"No one's ridden horses here in over thirty years."

"Thought you said you didn't have any laws here."

"I never said it was illegal. We don't need a law for every little thing we do, like you. Any person can see animals aren't meant to be broken, ridden, and forced to obey. It's cruel. Horses are meant to be wild, not owned like slaves."

She turned and walked to the bedroom with the ointments and bandages. "You'll need some clothes if you're going to do your *cop-thing,* or you'll end up killed by vigilantes again." She stomped back in and tossed a set of clothes across the room.

"Whose are these?" He held the used clothes up and inspected them with skepticism.

"A boyfriend left them." She left the room.

Merit inched his body to the edge of the couch and peered into the golf bag. It appeared that the materials he'd taken from the cartons in the property room were still in the bag. He was interrupted by a knock on the door, however. Merit looked up with alarm, dropped to the floor, and crouched behind a couch. "Who's that?"

"Calm down." She peeked through blinds. "He's a boyfriend."

A middle-aged, average-looking man entered and disappeared into a back room.

"Get some rest—Detective Merit." She stepped inside the door.

"Psst. Hey." Merit lifted his chin, tilting his head back slightly, "What's your name?"

"Starla. My name is Starla." She closed the door and then she was gone.

Merit smiled slightly. Okay, Starla. He deduced that *Starla* must have sifted through his wallet and found his ID to know his name and he was a Pilgrim officer. He had been knocked out for three hours, and he needed to get started, so he sorted through the change of men's clothing she'd left him. He cringed as he thought of what people back in Pilgrim might think of him if they could see where he was.

Especially Ruth.

27

On Sunday afternoon, when Soldier started his run, Vic Jackson was summoned by helicopter to the site. An officer transported the legend in an unmarked van near the eighteenth hole and slipped him into a private tent. The Autumn Fox signed autographs and posed for pictures with a few high-paying private members while he anxiously awaited the last holes to play out. The planner briefed Vic on his role. If Soldier were to win, Vic was to make a surprise appearance and present the trophy to Soldier—a passing of the torch, so to speak. Vic rehearsed the right things to say, cliché lines like, "Soldier's a great ambassador to the sport…records were meant to be broken." Vic put on a good face, but his body language suggested another. He'd worked hard to secure his twenty-two major golf titles. It would be a tough record to surrender.

—Michael McCarthy, *InterviewMag.Download*

PLAY DRESS-UP

Merit felt uncomfortable wearing a pair of baggy short pants with slits cut up the side held up by a belt made of macramé string. He didn't want to think of what an ex-boyfriend of Starla's had previously worn given her occupation, but after his run-ins with vigilantes and unruly crowds, he accepted the fact that he would have to dress the part of a Frontier citizen so as not to be identified as . . . a servile. He could hardly bring himself to pronounce the word since he was a police officer and nothing less. He was sorting through the evidence in Soldier's golf bag as Starla entered the room.

"Working on your case?" She stood in front of him.

Merit looked up from the evidence and was again struck by Starla's alluring green eyes and natural beauty. He looked more closely at her slender arms and saw partial tattoos on her upper chest that he hadn't noticed before.

"You like them?" She pivoted her arms back and forth flaunting the tattoos on her biceps, which looked like the inverted letters Y and the cursive letter W inscribed within ovals.

Merit knew better than to offer his true feelings. She was nice enough to let him stay, and he had nowhere else to go, so he looked at the tattoos and gave her a tight smile.

She looked down her nose at him. "These are probably *against the law* where you're from."

Tattoos were not illegal in Pilgrim, but Merit had wished they were, as he wasn't a fan of them. They desecrated the body, which was made in the image of God. He believed it was a sign of weakness to have one. Tattoos on a female were a clear indicator that she was damaged goods, typically a result of some type of sexual abuse in her past. "No, they're not *illegal* where I'm from, but I wouldn't get one."

Starla started walking toward him, "Which is why I'm going to give you one."

Merit stood and slowly hobbled to the nearest corner of the room. "Oh no, you're not."

"They're temporary." Starla broke into unexpected laughter. "Don't be such a tight ass. You can't go out looking like that, and I don't want you sitting in here all day."

Merit liked the sound of her lilting voice and the way she laughed even though he was being criticized. She moved closer, and he could smell her perfume, which was sweet yet subtle, not flowery like Ruth's.

She sat him outside on the deck in the shade and pressed pieces of paper—all with designs on their flip sides—against his skin, blotting them with a damp sponge. "There." After thirty minutes of listing to his whining and claiming torture, she stood back and admired her work. "You're starting to look normal." The tattoos were a bright red serpent, a purple pine tree, and psychedelic-colored symbols. When she'd finished, she restyled his short hair to look less perfectly combed, then added a small tattoo of a comet to his face and a large origami-shaped bluebird across his upper back.

Merit backed away to look in the mirror, although he also wanted to put some distance between them. He didn't want to feel attracted to her. He recalled Beck's easy interaction with the opposite sex at the outdoor café, but that wasn't him. Besides, he'd promised his heart to someone else.

"Yeah, well, thanks." He scrunched his nose showing his disproval and matted his hair she'd fluffed up, back down to lay flat.

Starla tossed him a shirt vest, open in the front, with colorful designs on it. "Did you find anything helpful in that pile of evidence?"

"There are lots of thumb drives. We have those in Pilgrim, although these are really old. But the rest of this? I'm not sure what most of it is. What are those small round silver disks?"

"DVDs." She picked up one of the razor-thin saucers and looked at both sides. "There's probably information stored somehow on them. They were used in very old computers. I'll take you to a flea market tomorrow. We might be able to find one."

Merit glanced at himself again in the mirror. Stupid. The image that stared back at him wasn't the disciplined clean-cut figure of a Pilgrim police detective.

28

When the Autumn Fox drank too much, he sometimes voiced his true feelings about the current state of golf. The players of his generation, he said, were more competitive and savvier. Today's golfers were soft, spoiled by big money purses and huge dollar endorsements, and they were intimidated by Soldier. Vic, inside the tent, overheard the officer's radio squawk in between the deafening roars from the gallery. There was a sense of distress in the officer's voice when he radioed the dispatcher, asking "When's the back-up coming?" and she replied, "They weren't." The extra officers expected to assist in crowd control after the triathlon were trapped on freeways that were basically parking lots. The extra security personnel working the event were not sworn officers and weren't equipped with radios, mace, or guns to protect themselves—many felt scared. They ditched their placards and blended in with the crowd or fled to safety.

—Michael McCarthy, *Interview download part II*

WRONG FINGER

The flea market was unlike anything Merit had ever seen. He hoped they could find an old computer to play his disks. Starla promised that he would fit in better with the people of Frontier with the tattoos, but he was very self-conscious about the designs on his body. It brought back the embarrassing feelings he'd experienced as a teen when an unsightly pimple surfaced on his puberty-stricken cheeks or nose.

Starla took him to an enormous structure, which she said was a former stadium where a sport called football had once been played. The seats had been ripped out, she explained, so merchants could set up their stalls. Beneath the area where seating had been, restaurants, stores, and medical clinics had been built.

She argued that the defunct game of football had glorified war and functioned similarly to the military in the way that it preyed on poor young minorities by brainwashing kids at a young age into thinking violence was a way out of poverty. She was glad that lawsuits eventually forced the corrupt league to fold. Merit, on the other hand, told her that he had seen old footage of professional tackle football and loved watching how a team of men in cool uniforms and helmets ran fast and crashed into each other. The game looked like a blast to play and wished he could have tried it. Trying to hit anything—a ball, a puck, a person as fast and as hard as you could—a hockey player firing a slap shot, a baseball player cracking a double, a sleitis player smacking a serve—was a sport. Waiting an *hour* for your turn to stand as still as possible then tap a tiny white ball as *softly* as you could into a small hole then walk twenty feet to the next tee clearly was *not* a sport.

Merit gawked at the vendors and shoppers, none of whom dressed with propriety or professionalism. Almost everyone—young and old, male and female—had tattoos. He also saw many over-the-top public displays of affection, which never happened in Pilgrim, "Show some respect," Merit said under his breath as a couple he passed engaged in an act of sex.

Starla bought a stick of raw cucumber and handed it to Merit. "Here. Something to munch on—and stop staring at everyone. They'll peg you for a servile and tell the vigilantes." Merit, having not eaten much of Frontier's vegan rabbit food with his sore jaw, could tell by the way his pants had sagged on his waist; he'd dropped several pounds in the first couple of days.

Starla took his hand and led him through the crowded market, and he felt the warmth of the petite guide's fingers curled around his own.

After buying Merit a pair of mirrored sunglasses so that people wouldn't notice his stares, he wandered to a jewelry booth. Some of the pieces were avant-garde, and one sign read PIERCINGS. Most of the jewelry appeared to have been made from pieces of inexpensive scrap metal, shells, and smooth stones.

"I want to look around for a few minutes," he said.

"What for?

Merit looked exasperated. "I need to get a ring."

She threw him a funny look. "You don't look like the jewelry-wearing type."

"It's for my girlfriend. We're getting engaged." Merit wanted to get it out in the open, not as much to let her know he was off the market, but more as a reminder to himself to stay faithful.

"What's *getting engaged*?"

Merit couldn't tell if she was being serious. "It's what you do before you get married. As for marriage, a man and a woman who are in love exchange vows before God and spend their lives together. At the wedding ceremony, they exchange rings as a symbol of their commitment."

Starla looked shocked. "Forever? They live their whole lives together, forever?"

"Yeah. What do you do here?"

Starla shook her head. "There are no weddings. Love's not limited to just one person. Marriage is man-made and unnatural. Just because someone or some culture invented it a long time ago didn't mean it was right. There are no contracts. It's just another law or rule to break."

"It holds people accountable." There was an awkward silence. "Was that your boyfriend?" He didn't mean to blurt that out.

"Who? —Where?" She rose on her tiptoes and looked around the crowd.

"That man who came to your house today. You called him your boyfriend."

"Yeah, I have a lot of friends that are boys."

"So the guys you provide pleasure—as a pleasure attendant, you call your boyfriends?"

"Yeah. But they don't live with me." She sounded repulsed. "Living with one person seems—I could *never* live with one person my whole life." Starla then spotted a jade ring. "Hey, here's a cool one." It was a simple circular quarter-inch wide band of green stone with tiny specs of brown. She slipped it on the index finger of her right hand and modeled it by sticking her hand in the air.

The jewelry vendor elaborated on the ring's history. "It's jadeite. It's a very dense stone from Guatemala. It was treasured by the ancient Mesoamerican cultures hundreds of years ago."

"Look at me." She giggled as she held her finger in the air. "I'm *married*."

Merit admired how the sea-green gemstone looked on her slender, brown fingers. The slick, polished jadeite closely matched her liquid green eyes, but he was bothered by her belittling of the sacred institution of marriage.

A few customers close by laughed with her.

"You're wearing it wrong." He was getting impatient and grabbed her hand as he removed it.

"Then show me how."

"No. Besides, an engagement ring is supposed to be a diamond set in a gold band."

"Sick! No one wears gold or diamonds. Mining rapes Mother Earth and destroys the environment."

"I'll get her a gold one when I get back home then." You can't win with this girl, Merit thought, frustrated that she'd gotten under his skin.

"We need to hurry Merit, I have an acting audition in a little while."

"Acting. You want to be an actress?" Merit stopped, his mouth hanging open. "What kind of acting? The theater or film?"

"I don't know exactly. It's a long-shot dream. I just know I want to be in front of the camera. It's where I feel really myself and forget about everything and escape."

"I hope it works out. It would get you out of your line of work." He said it out of the corner of his mouth.

"My profession has made me very wealthy. Most women here are wealthy from being pleasure attendants, more than the men, and that would be difficult to give up. So maybe I won't become an actress." She grabbed his hand and pulled him through the crowd. "Come on. Let's find your computers."

To Merit, Starla was a riddle. She was kind—most of the time—but she had a sharp edge to her, a vulnerable spot that required caution when speaking to her.

They found a booth that sold old fashion computers which looked to be fifty to seventy-years old. Merit was about to ask Starla which one would be right for his needs, but she had already moved away, saying, "Show the owners your disks and they'll help you. I gotta run."

"What do you mean?" Merit opened the palms of his hands to the sky. "Where are you going?"

"Remember?" While backpedaling she explained, "I have that acting audition."

After she disappeared in the crowd, he realized he probably sounded a tad desperate. He was suddenly alone, and a middle-aged man with gray hair combed straight back and falling on his shoulders looked up at his latest customer. He smiled, revealing that he was missing two front teeth.

★★★

"See anything you like?" The squirrelly-looking antique dealer with long, dirty fingernails said to Merit.

Merit showed the man the thumb drives and disks that he needed to use with a computer.

"Hmmm." The man stroked his stringy goatee. "I know where the small thumb drives go, but I'm not sure about those disks. Let me look at my inventory."

He looked at the antique monitors and towers on the tables around him as Merit picked up computer cables and examined them. He'd never seen such cords since every computer in Pilgrim was wireless.

"Hey, be careful with those!" the seller said. "They're really old. They'll crack. Without those, none of these machines will work."

Merit carefully laid the cables on the table and put his hands behind his back.

"Let's see." The vendor moved about the booth. "Got one over here . . . and then another there that might be . . . ah, no, here's the one you need. Got a laptop and everything. I'll let you have it for seven hundred." He squinted at his customer.

Merit took out some paper money that Starla had given him before they'd left her apartment. "I'm afraid that's too much for me."

"I gotcha. Let me show you this." The vendor raised a makeshift board that was used to bar people from entering his booth. "Come on back."

Merit stooped beneath the board and was led into a pop-up tent where he saw more electronics stacked on a folding table. "Okay, sir, what do you want to show me?" Merit turned around, only to see the gapped-toothed computer dealer on his knees, reaching up to unsnap the buttons on Merit's shorts. Merit, repulsed by the thought of a nasty old man—or any man for that matter—putting his hands near his crotch, instinctively kneed the perverted old man under the chin, sending him violently onto his rear end. Adjacent vendors, hearing the commotion as the man crashed into the table of computers, rushed into his tent to assist their fellow antique picker's cry for help.

"Did you fall?" A lady with big loop earrings approached. "Did you hurt yourself?"

Another vendor gave the old man a hand up. Blood streaming from his mouth, he was angry and pointed at Merit. "Who are you? You're not from here."

Merit backed out of the booth, threw up his arms, and acted as if he had no idea why the man was screaming at him.

"Get out!" Blood dripped from his frail, chapped lips.

The other vendors edged toward Merit, suspecting violence was afoot, circling him like wolves around their prey.

29

Soldier birdied the fourteenth and his game was peaking, while the North Korean was tensing and bogeyed his second hole in a row. Soldier was three shots off the lead with four holes to play. The humungous crowd surrounded Soldier, like the winds of a hurricane that could have crushed him, yet he played unaffected, protected inside the tiny eye of the storm. The only way the crowd hysteria didn't turn into a revolt was if the fans could control themselves. Loyal, civil golf fans respected the elite sport and held their emotions in check and applauded only when appropriate. These weren't your typical golf spectators with the same appreciation of the gentleman's game. They acted like animals at a Third World soccer match. How would the fans react if Soldier won? Even more disconcerting, how would they react if he lost?

—Roger Barrons, *Sydney Headlines Herald*

SEX SELLS

Leaving the giant coliseum empty-handed and peaking over his shoulder to make sure he wasn't being chased, Merit realized that he had nowhere to go. He needed Starla's guidance if he were to survive the culture shock and stand any chance at solving the case, so he made his way back to her apartment.

Not surprisingly, the door was unlocked. He had determined on his walk home, embarrassed by the unwanted sexual encounter, that Starla would be mad at him for reacting with violence, and he decided to keep the episode with the antique dealer to himself. He turned the knob and opened it a couple of inches and called out. "Starla?" You home?"

There was no answer, and he realized that she had only left for her audition two hours earlier. He decided to sit on her front stoop. He closed his eyes and soaked up the warm sun on his face. While waiting on her, he wondered why she was giving him, an outsider, free room and board. Even though she could be blunt and moody, she couldn't hide her soft side. He figured her to be the type of person who'd pull over to rescue a deer hit by a car or get mad if you stepped on an ant or take in a stray dog found on her doorstep. He didn't know why she'd allowed him to stay, but for now, he'd milk it for what it's worth.

He'd only been seated for a few minutes when a nice-looking couple passed by and dropped some paper money and three tiny silver balls that resembled pellets, he fired from a BB gun as a kid. Then he remembered the beads on Starla's bracelet and how they were a form of currency in Frontier. He tried to return them, but the couple had moved on. Sadly, he'd blended into the point of looking down and out and they were obligated to pay him.

Starla arrived home two long hours later holding a rectangular, wrapped package and a takeout dinner.

Merit stood and stretched. "A few of your *boyfriends* showed up while you were gone," he said, even though it hadn't been the case.

"I hope you were nice to them."

"I was. I told them you got married." A reference back to her mocking of weddings.

"No Merit, you didn't!" She shot him a stern look, then after detecting a smirk on his face, she entered the house with the bags and set them on a triangular-shaped dining room table. "Did you get the computer you needed?" She had moved to the kitchen and called out.

"What?" He tried to avoid the subject of his assault of the collector. "The computer? Did I get it? No, I told him it cost too much."

"Uh-oh." She beelined it into the loft where Merit was looking out the backdoor sliding window. "Is that how you said it? You said it 'costs too much.'" She grimaced while holding her breath.

"Something like that." Starla stared at him as if she knew he was hiding something, and he cracked under the pressure. "The pervert got down on his knees and tried to, you know."

She finished his sentence. "Suck you off."

He turned and faced her, "I was going to say, *tactfully*, perform oral sex."

"Yeah, I'm sorry—so sorry. I forgot to tell you." She nervously clicked her fingernails. "If you tell someone something *costs too much*, it's a signal—a nonverbal understanding agreeing to exchange the item you want for sex. It's normal. So, what did you do?"

"I barely touched the guy, and people got mad. I had to pretty much make a run for it."

She put her hands over her mouth and nose. "Phew. So, nothing else happened?" She exhaled in relief. "It's not that bad. A lot of guys get them."

"Yeah, guys get b-j's back in Pilgrim too, but probably not from some chapped lipped, ol' nasty sex offender in the back of his sour-smelling camping tent."

When she was done laughing, which made Merit feel good, she said, "So no computer, huh? You can't watch your evidence. So, what are you gonna do?"

Merit had no answer.

★★★

While Starla laid out the takeout dinner and utensils on the table, Merit went into the bathroom, removed his clothes, and took a shower, scrubbing away the tattoos and washing a bit of dye she'd dabbed onto his hair. He felt dirty after being around the crowds at the market, many of whom had smelled quite bad. He wondered if they knew what antiperspirant was?

Starla opened the glazed shower door to announce that the food was ready. Embarrassed, Merit turned and covered himself with his hands. "Hey, what are you doing?"

"Don't be a prude." She undressed, tossed her clothes in the corner, and put on a loose-fitting dress with no bra beneath it. He didn't see her chest but could tell she was rather flat-chested. Merit turned his head in her direction, unable to resist the temptation to peek at the taut backside of the toned body of his hostess.

He stepped from the shower, toweled off, and put on clean clothes as he watched Starla apply scented oil to her wrist and neck.

"Feel better?" she said.

"Cleaner, but not better about my work. I've been here five days, and I have no computer to watch the golf footage and interviews. I'm stuck."

Merit ate voraciously as he sat opposite Starla at the table. He drank two glasses of fresh-squeezed, drug-free grapefruit juice and looked up, realizing that he'd scarfed down his meal in just a few minutes. He then called attention to the seven, floor-to-ceiling tall, unique butterfly prints mounted on the wall behind Starla. "You like butterflies."

She swung her feet around the bench and looked back. "Those are moths."

"Oh. Aren't moths dirty?"

"No. I think they're unappreciated. And misunderstood." Her face had a look of rapture and reflection as her eyes panned over each painting. "Oh yeah. I uh, got something for you." She reached behind a chair and unveiled a wrapped package with a bow on top that she'd brought home along with dinner.

Merit blushed. "For me?" He hadn't gotten a present in years, the last he could recall was a high school graduation gift from his parents, and he'd forgotten what that was. He tore it open and was pleasantly surprised to find a laptop computer from the swap meet—the exact one he needed. "I don't know what to say?"

"Try 'thank you' …*tactfully.*" She winked.

"Thank you. That's a big help. I can get started now." As he carefully cracked the clamshell laptop ajar, he stopped and said, "Hold on. You didn't, you know, with that weird computer man to get it, did you?"

"No, I wasn't his pleasure attendant. I paid him though. I thought he was a sweet man."

"Sweet's the right word." Merit said.

He was about to utter a word of extra gratitude when someone knocked on the door. He frowned, clearly disappointed by the arrival of Starla's next *boyfriend.* For the first time since arriving in Frontier Merit was relaxed, and the moment had been spoiled. He figured it was time to get to work, so he dismissed the situation and plugged in the laptop.

He opened it but couldn't get it to boot. The investigator started hitting keys at random, and after forty-five minutes he stared at a blue

WELCOME screen. Merit picked up the first of many DVDs and didn't know what to do with them. He lifted the laptop over his head and turned it around, but he saw no place where the disk would fit. Wanting to slam the computer shut, he restrained himself and closed his eyes. No progress had been made by the first-time cold case detective in solving the murder of Soldier Quinn.

Starla appeared after her boyfriend left and stood above her guest.

"I don't know how to use this piece of junk," He pounded his fist on the tabletop.

"I'll help you, but later. Let's go for a walk." She tugged at his chair. "Get some fresh night air."

"I can't, I gotta figure this out." He squeezed his fingers in a tight ball. "Frustrating!"

30

By 4 P.M. on U.S. Open golf Sunday, all major television, cable, and radio stations had cut from their scheduled programming, like done during political debates, and aired the last several holes of the U.S. Open live. Professional baseball, soccer games, ATP tennis matches that were in progress were suspended while they cast the action on giant stadium Jumbo-Tron screens. The players, referees, coaches, managers, and fans sat in the dugouts on the fields or court and watched the action mesmerized. The only other event that matched this live televised spectacle was the O.J. Simpson—Ford Bronco, a slow-speed police chase across Southern California's freeways that occurred thirty years earlier, but this was streamed worldwide.

—Tomas Guferstan, De Standaard.be

METAL SOUP

Merit consented to Starla's request to go for a walk to calm down, trying to grasp how to log in and operate the antiquated laptop had frazzled his nerves. They strolled outside, side-by-side, under a clear night sky as a warm pleasant breeze blew off the calm bay. The weather there, he recognized, felt consistently warm, but never humid and sticky like back in old Oklahoma.

As they walked, Merit spied a fire in the distance, yellow flames illuminating what appeared to be a gathering crowd.

"What's that? A bonfire?"

"A melting." She clasped her hands together. "I love meltings. We're just in time."

They neared the melting and stood at the rear of a crowd of approximately one hundred people that was swelling by the second.

Kids sat on their parents' laps or shoulders. Several citizens stood on a raised platform, including the head honcho, Chief Reed.

The Capital City servile chief raised a handgun in the air to show it to his audience, announcing that it was a Colt 45 before handing it to a man standing on the ground. His assistant below, wearing a different clown mask and using industrial tongs, theatrically dipped the revolver into a cast-iron vat that was suspended over glowing coals. People applauded, sang, and hugged one another.

A tall woman to the chief's left, wearing a short see-through blouse, recited a poem about how much violence and the murder rate had drastically declined since gun meltings had begun. She then made a speech explaining how the melting of the weapon was a transformation and that the gun's metal alloys would be reborn when poured into a mold in the shape of a dove.

There were very few guns left in Frontier. Very rarely one would turn up in an old safe or under a house, and the finder would turn it in for a large payout, a financial reward that one could live off for a lifetime. The enormous reward was the backbone of the philosophy at Frontier's founding to motivate people to turn in guns until they were exorcised for good.

Chief Reed then called a citizen up to the platform, explaining that she'd found the gun behind a rafter in a condominium that was being renovated. He handed her a stack of Frontier dollars, reminding everyone that it was possible to become wealthy if one turned in just one gun.

"The tiny metal dove will be on display for several weeks," Starla said.

"Great. I'll make sure to see it."

Starla continued as if she didn't hear his sarcastic barb. "It will be melted down again and turned into the kind of BB pellets I showed you." She jingled her bracelet annoyingly next to his ear as a reminder.

Chief Reed spoke again, as he was handed another gun, raising it over his head so people could see the rifle that he claimed had been turned in by yet another lucky conscientious citizen.

Merit instantly recognized the long gun. It looked like the same make and model as the rifle listed on the receipt he'd seen in the property and evidence building—the matte black finished gun that in all probability was the very same gun used to kill golfer Soldier Quinn. The chief had lied to him. Merit seethed with anger as he saw the most valuable piece of evidence in his cold case—with the crucial serial number intact—about to be liquefied and lost forever.

"Hey, stop!" Merit waved his arms over his head. "Don't do that! It's—"

Starla yanked him away by the collar before he could finish his sentence, as she raised her voice in support of melting the rifle, cheering with the others as the chief handed the gun to his assistant to be melted in a larger vat. People turned and looked suspiciously at Merit, but Starla smiled and waved a dismissive hand. The chief glared especially hard into the shadows. It was unheard of to protest a melting.

"He's just high," Starla motioned to the crowd. "Sorry folks, mushrooms — bad trip," directing him away from the ceremony. She stumbled about to give the impression she was drunk and that they were harmless. "Yippee!"

Those standing nearby were placated and turned back to watch the gun's transformation.

Starla pushed him around a corner, shoved his back against a wall, pointed her finger in his face, and scolded him. "What were you thinking? You could have gotten us into big trouble."

"That gun's the reason I'm here." Merit was defiant.

"Okay, but no more yelling. You can watch, but don't do anything stupid or they'll know you're *not* from here."

Merit swatted her hand out of his face and nodded to her demands. They both peeked their heads around the corner and spied the melting ceremony. Merit cursed under his breath as he saw the chief dip the barrel into the glowing pot of molten metal until the slender sniper rifle, scope and stock dissolved into a shiny broth. The people watched, mesmerized with joy, some shed tears as if they were watching the birth of their first child.

Three thousand silver biodegradable balloons pinned under a mesh net were set free. Their release into the skies would symbolize to citizens across Capital City that a firearm's death and rebirth had occurred and signal surrounding towns to release their balloons—alerting other towns further out to follow suit, a domino effect. Over the next week, persons across the western part of the massive state could experience a sense of relief, purpose, and joy at the sight of seeing one drift high overhead.

"Shit." Merit watched the whopping-sized jiggling blob of balloons lift off like a U.F.O. then turned and walked away, shaking his head.

Starla skipped to catch up with him. "I'm sorry."

Merit refused to look at her. He could tell by the sassy way she said it that she wasn't sorry at all, and he turned and walked in a different direction.

The barefooted Starla hurried ahead of Merit, then walked backward and spoke as if he were being unreasonable. "It's gone. Get over it. Guns are bad anyway."

"That gun was my whole case." Merit snagged a tiny flowerpot from a windowsill and heaved it overhand as hard as he could, smashing it against the side of a wall.

31

The TV announcers articulated to viewers the implausible feat Soldier was on the verge of accomplishing. They marveled at what an achievement it would be to top the 'Fox's' seemingly "untouchable" record. But nobody, not the announcers, not the media, not other players, ever mentioned what was glaringly obvious to even the average viewer—The elephant in the room. It was more than just a golf record that could have been broken on that day. There was something much deeper to be broken—a race barrier. Vic was white, and the record was threatened by a minority. Today's duel wasn't as simple as who could hit the ball in the cup. It was steeped with layers of social complexity. What was at stake wasn't so much golf but power—who had it and who stood to lose it.

—Barbara Hatcher, *Florida Sun Sentinel*

COURSE STUDY

Merit occupied himself for the next thirty-six hours by going over the evidence more carefully, and Starla had bought six additional laptops since the detective had so many disks and drives to examine. Together, they figured out where to insert the DVDs and external drives and how to connect the many cell phones to the hard drives using various thin cables.

"I don't want to hear any more whining about how the *big cheese* melted that pistol," she said.

"Rifle. Remember? I explained. The long one's a rifle, the short one's a pistol. *P* for puny." Merit extended his hands out the sides to indicate the approximate length.

She looked back at him with a blank stare as if she didn't care.

Merit felt better when she was next to him and jealous when she was with her boyfriends. He knew he shouldn't be harboring such sentiments and tried to think about Ruth and how she was a much better fit than Starla.

He now had seven days of stubble on his face as he tinkered with the computers and ate occasionally from a platter of fresh and dried vegetables, fruits and nuts that Starla left for him to snack on. The pain from the brand on his neck had lessened, and he drank no tea to remain sharp, confining his liquid intake to freshly squeezed fruit juice. He was ready to dive into the video footage, but he eyed the stack of folders and reports, which he had arranged in neat piles. He knew that looking through crime reports is what cold case detectives did. Reluctantly, he picked up a folder on the top of the first heap of papers and began to read.

Merit learned that law enforcement had collected hundreds of cell phones from fans at the U.S. Open, some of which were probably right in front of him. Most of the footage from the phones had been transferred to thumb drives, and he had those as well. Of additional interest was the lengthy list of suspects that the law enforcement investigators from the police, the FBI, and a special investigation inquiry had compiled.

Merit looked up from the report. All the people had been plausible suspects, but they were dead now. They may have had motives, but Merit still believed that finding the killer was his paramount concern. Motives were secondary to him and finding a motive sixty years after the fact might prove to be a near-impossible task anyway. Maybe he'd look at the list of suspects later.

Starla walked from the bathroom wearing only purple panties and a cherry red V-neck tee with rolled-up sleeves. Merit respectfully turned his eyes away, *Man!* He thought to himself. *Can she make it any more difficult?*

"Merit, I have to run some errands." She slipped on a loose, pearl white-colored blouse and a tight skirt with a slit up the leg. "There's food in the kitchen. Keep working hard."

Working hard was the correct phrase, a Freudian slip Merit thought as he readjusted his legs. Reading more dossiers prepared by the FBI, he saw that the agency had later recovered a bullet from the day Soldier was killed. Merit didn't recall seeing a projectile in the evidence building, but there were a lot of boxes and sealed envelopes to go through and his visit was cut short by the Vigilantes. But no thanks to the chief, there would be no test conducted to determine if that projectile was fired through the recovered rifle he'd seen with his own eyes, an old military or police sniper rifle with a telescopic scope, the long gun was metal soup.

Golf courses, he now knew from watching the old video clips, were expansive pieces of real estate, and the gunman could have been almost anywhere. Merit looked at the footage of the tournament and the events leading up to his murder. His murder must have had a bigger impact than he first believed if Beck and the people of Frontier knew its details. Merit, however, was out of touch with his state's historical past.

Soldier on the final day of the four-day U.S. Open tournament, teed off on the first hole, paired with a young North Korean player, a rising star who already had collected four majors.

Merit decided to fast-forward through most of the final round and watch the last holes that Soldier played, according to what Beck had begun to tell him while in the basement of the evidence warehouse before Soldier was shot. His North Korean opponent had had a good round and was leading the tournament, with Soldier a few strokes back as he approached the 16th tee.

The course was packed, and the gallery was beyond the normal number of spectators allowed to witness a tournament, the police having been unable to stop people from hopping fences and trespassing onto the course.

With trees and scaffolding festooned with bodies, Soldier and the North Korean had walked to each hole as if they weren't aware of the throng to concentrate on their game. By the time Soldier had reached the 18th tee, the crowd knew they were possibly watching history in the making. Soldier was only one stroke off the lead, a deficit he could only make up if he played it aggressively.

The final hole was a par five, with five-hundred-and-seventy yards between tee and cup.

32

It was like a movie. Soldier was the hero, a warrior, who had fought and survived each obstacle, sand trap, water hazard, physical pain, and Father Time. The audience had witnessed a final battle scene with the enemy, the young North Korean. But he wasn't the real villain: it was Vic's record and America's dark past of racial discrimination. Soldier lined up over his final tee shot. With the slimmer frame, he looked different. He gazed down the long daunting fairway, the familiar green visor shielded his mysterious eyes like a cowboy in a Western. The bill of his cap concealed his receding hairline and coupled with the setting sun's glow that masked his flaws, he looked like the Soldier of his twenties. It was eerily magical. He'd turned back the hands of time and anyone watching felt young again, too. He cracked the tee shot. The ball cut up through the air, like an arrow to slay down a mighty giant. 'He may just win this thing!' blurted the commentator. Soldier then strode tall down the fairway as the crowd fell in, like a herd of sheep, behind their trusted shepherd, staff in hand.

—Marty Caddle, *The BCG News Channel*

U.S. OPEN SHOT

Merit needed to take a bathroom break, but he couldn't move. He was glued to his seat watching the U.S. Open golf dual between Soldier and the North Korean on his computer screen. Soldier's tee shot off the 18th landed and rolled near the center of the fairway, and the obvious club selection for his second shot would be a three-iron so he could lay up. He could then chip the ball with an eight or a nine iron onto the green and putt. But he had to gain two strokes to win and playing it safe wouldn't give him the U.S. Open title if the North Korean made par.

Soldier's caddie, a kid who looked to be in his mid-teens, took a driver out of the bag. Drivers were almost always used off the tee, rarely off the fairway—and he winced as he reluctantly accepted the club. But the caddy shot him a look and mouthed the words *Go for it*.

His time was running out. This was the last hole to catch the leader. There was no playing it safe if he wanted to win the tournament and beat Vic Jackson's record of career Grand Slams. After taking time to line up the shot and position himself over the ball, Soldier crushed it, sending it high into the air, hoping that he could get it close enough to the green—maybe even on the green itself.

The ball soared into the late-evening sky, already orange just above the horizon, but as it crested and began its descent, the ball drifted right toward a thick hedgerow to the side of the green, causing Soldier's face to curl into a grimace. He contorted his body hard left and under his breath, he whispered, "Sit! Sit!" Merit had read that this was a term golfers used when they wanted a ball to acquire backspin and roll in the direction they'd intended to hit it.

Instead of landing in the tall hedgerow of thickets guaranteeing a loss, the ball, fortunately, hit a large boulder protruding from the ground on the right of the fairway—nicknamed *Whales Breach Rock* due to its shape similar to the Humpback's tail. The white ball bounced left and forward and an additional thirty yards, where it clipped an edge of the concrete base of a cast-iron drinking fountain.

From there the ball careened left and forward another twenty yards, having now angled a full forty-five degrees left. With the force of its topspin, allowed it to crawl up the high, right backside of the sloping 18th green. The ball crested the back-right side of the green, where it met the hard-packed zoysia grass before it rolled right to left and funneled backward in the direction where Soldier had stuck the shot. It came to a stop twelve feet from the pin.

As the network TV host rightly described the most fortunate shot, the two ricochets, in addition to the right to left, back to front slope in the green, caused the "miracle ball" to travel in the shape of a question mark—by drawing the mark starting from the bottom and moving upward.

It was an amazingly lucky shot that had never been seen before, and when the ball came to a rest the crowd exploded with applause and yelled with uninhibited jubilation, creating a deafening roar sound, as if a formation of fighter jets had strafed fifty feet overhead.

Soldier had had the tenacity to use a driver, and victory was now within his grasp if he could make one last very do-able putt, the kind he'd made since a boy.

Merit was fascinated with what he was watching, with a game that he'd ridiculed, declining to call it a sport. He now viewed the shot with as much suspense as those in attendance over sixty years earlier. Indeed, he had said, "Stop! Stop" as the ball sailed right and bounced, his breath suspended in his chest until the ball came to rest on the green.

In one stroke, Soldier had leapfrogged the North Korean and was looking at a most probable win. If he made the putt, he'd score an eagle on the hole—two under par—and beat his opponent by one stroke. Soldier bowed his head and held out his arms wide in a Y position, a triumphant pose of humbled victory. He seemed to know that the great Vic Jackson's achievement was about to be surpassed and he'd accomplish the feat he'd promised his father as a boy.

As he relaxed his arms, he started to bring his left hand to his neck, as if to swat a bee. Had he been stung, Merit wondered? No, and what followed in a matter of seconds was gruesome.

The right side of Soldier's head exploded outward like a candy-filled piñata struck with a bat, its contents spewing over twenty-five feet onto the ecstatic faces of the unsuspecting crowd.

Soldier Quinn had been shot.

33

Most fans at the U.S. Open course couldn't see what had happened to Soldier, but they sensed something was terribly wrong. The term "active shooter" spread like wildfire, and panic set in. Sections of crowds stampeded back and forth like herds of spooked buffalo. Frantic fans leaped from trees, others tripped or were shoved into ponds. Some got tangled in the ropes used to cordon off portions of the course and were dragged like lassoed livestock. Vic, still in the tent, heard the crowd's turbulent roar, and his heart sank, believing his record had been shattered. He next heard the screams and felt the ground trembling beneath him, but being a native Californian, assumed it was a tremor. Before Vic could react, the plainclothes officer roughly whisked him out and into the back of the police van and tore out.

—A. Houston, *U.S.N. Today* 06.18.26 *updated* 23:24

PANDAMONIUM

Soldier Quinn had been shot.

Pinkish blood and white-hued chunks of brain matter splattered to the right in a cone shape, and the right side of Soldier's head caved in like a rotten pumpkin, creating a distorted look on what remained of his face, as the great American golfer's body collapsed on itself, causing his upper torso to crumple on the top of folded legs.

The crowd was in disarray while still others close to Soldier stared at the deflated body. They were frozen and unable to assimilate what had happened to their hero. The North Korean's caddy had rushed his player to a sand trap, tackled him down into the bunker and buried him in case a lunatic shooter was out to kill other golfers as well. "Hold on, something's happened," the television golf announcer famously phrased, "Soldier's fallen to the earth."

Soldier's young caddie stood immobile for three seconds and then stepped forward. His hand extended down, a look of horror and disbelief written across his young, blood-spattered features before he was pushed aside by the tidal movement of the crowd. Before his open hand touched Soldier, three uniformed police officers rushed forward, bowled him over, and scooped up Soldier's mortally wounded limp body and golf club. They swiftly carried him horizontally in their arms up the embankment, cutting through the crowd as if the dead body were little more than a battering ram.

A mass of fans parted forming a narrow passage for the officer's harrowing escape. Unwary spectators deep in the audience caught a glimpse of Soldier's gory gaping head wound cradled in the officer's arms, as dark blood leaked a steady trail of glistening droplets like dew on the green grass. Some fans instinctively dove to the ground and scooped up the red blades into their cupped hands, at the moment thinking somehow preserving the red extract could help.

Merit looked at the scene, almost as stunned as the onlookers at the U.S. Open and touched the PAUSE button. This was the crime he'd been sent to investigate. Previously, it had been described only as a cold case, a conundrum that needed to be solved. A murder had been committed, and he was there to find who did it. He was a detective, and he would discover who the killer was and return to Pilgrim, perhaps as a hero.

But watching the shooting had been unlike anything he'd ever experienced. He had watched the incident unfold second by second, and it had a profound effect on him, his left hand gripped a juice glass so tightly it could have cracked.

Merit rewound the video and looked at it in super slow motion. Even in the homiscope, he didn't usually see the actual offense being committed. He was used to viewing the aftermath. The bullet hadn't caught Soldier in the neck, however. His left-hand movement had simply been an involuntary reflex. The bullet had struck him in his left jaw, traveled through his head, and exited the opposite side above his right ear. The impact of the bullet, when it exited, ripped off the front right side of Soldier's face, leaving his nose and left eye intact.

★★★

After watching the horrific scene many times and the bedlam that followed, Merit focused on other angles that had been recorded by spectators' cell phones. Merit was back in his element, watching videos and looking for anything odd. When other detectives back in Pilgrim had asked him how he performed his magic, he would try to explain, but it was too difficult to convey something so abstract.

Over time, he narrowed down his explanation to a simple analogy he called "Happy Birthday." He expounded his reasoning in the following manner: "You may not know any musical chords, know how to play an instrument, or be able to sing on key, but if someone played the very familiar song 'Happy Birthday' to you, and played just *one* note differently, you could tell them exactly where it sounded wrong." That was the short version he used to describe his ability to spot inconsistencies when he viewed video footage.

When inside the homiscope, after viewing videos repeatedly and comparing them to other footage over and over, the slightest inkling of discrepancy would eventually present itself. The irregularity didn't necessarily solve the murder, but it was something to add to the right or left of a crime timeline.

Merit spliced together a single video using several others that he'd used to see everything that had happened on the 18th hole, including the actual murder. Sitting back and watching his edited version, he decided that the shooter most likely had to have been stationed somewhere to the north or west of Soldier's location since the golfer had been partially facing the 18th green.

He'd been hit on the left side of his face, and that meant that the bullet had to have come from either the front or side of where Soldier had stood. But that still left a lot of territory to examine using very old and incomplete snippets of flat footage.

The crowd following Soldier had been considerable in size. The killer could have been any one of a thousand spectators spread across the end of the course. There had been people on the fairway near Soldier stretching all the way to the 18th green and the clubhouse beyond, as well as sitting on fan bleachers set up behind the green.

He knew his work was far from done.

★★★

Merit had worked all day. He stretched and looked at the ocean through the large windows of the loft. The waves far below were beautiful, with rays of the evening sun catching their crests.

There was a knock on the door, which Merit assumed was a boyfriend of Starla's.

She answered it to the sound of a gruff voice, "Hey. Sorry to bother, but uh, have you seen any PP's around here?" It was a vigilante.

"What's he look like?"

Starla was quick on her feet, Merit thought, and her act was convincing. "He's got short brown hair, about my height, a hundred and eighty pounds, in pretty good shape, and he came here to take one of ours back to Pilgrim. He has a gun."

"A gun?" Her jaw dropped. "A pistol or a rifle?" She extended her hands out to her sides.

Slightly taken aback by her question, he shrugged, "I don't know."

"*P* is for pistol, the puny one." She smiled proudly.

The barbarian Vigilante scowled as he tugged at the crotch of his shorts and adjusted his privates, like a baseball player about to bat.

Merit closed his eyes and buried his head in his hands.

"Oh well, you got to get him! Who's he after?" She stepped out the door and shut it behind her. Merit could hear them talking, but it was muffled. He wondered if she was secretly signaling to the vigilante that he was hiding inside her home. He, therefore, looked for his most accessible escape route if the vigilante came busting in. Merit stealthily made his way to the window near them to eavesdrop and had an angle to see them both.

"We're not sure who he's after. It could be you. We figure he's hiding somewhere. Let us know if you see him."

Starla had her arms folded and nodded in appreciation of his warning. Merit recognized the vigilante with the Mohawk, the one who had inflicted the most pain on him in the alley—and took the most pleasure in doing so. The man started to leave, then turned back to her and cocked his head as if indicating he recognized her. Had she attended him sex for Merit's release? Maybe, but she looked different since her hair was slicked back after an afternoon dip in her heated pool.

"Do we know each other?"

She looked him up and down and shook her head.

He opened a money pouch. "Can you take a boyfriend right now?"

"Yeah—no, but sorry," she said. "I can't, I'm booked up."

"I'll come in and wait." He started to push the door open.

She stepped in his path. "I have two inside right now, an hour each."

The vigilante was like a lion in the African plains stalking a baby antelope he was about to devour. The vigilante towered over her, gawking down in a dominating way as if he were going to forcibly take her.

Merit, not hearing any noise or movement, altered his voice, a higher-pitched crackling sound to scare him off, "Let's go honey-child. Hurry up." There was more silence, and he began to worry. Honey-child? That was stupid. Was that the best name he could come up with?

He looked around for an object he could use as a weapon to clobber the guy if he came in, but there was nothing within reach.

Starla closed the door, and the vigilante finally strutted away.

Merit breathed a sigh of relief. It was a close call, a reminder that they were actively looking for him. Perhaps it was only a matter of time before they tracked him down. The last thing he needed was to have some *roid*-raged, muscle-head pull him away from the case now that he was finally making some headway.

Starla walked past him, crouched in a corner, and scowled down at him while mouthing the word, "Honey child."

34

Wave after wave of frightened spectators pushed outward from the epicenter of the shooting, setting off a chain of events. Tents, tables, concession stands, porta-johns and trailers were leveled. Announcers and cameramen, fifty feet in the air, leaped to the ground as metal towers crashed down. Some in the stands were crushed in the aisles, while others jumped off like passengers leaping from a sinking ship. Many scattered toward the course's perimeter ten-foot-high chain-link fence and scaled it like inmates in a prison riot. In the parking lots, cars speeding out crashed, creating gridlock. Some spectators lingered on the course in disbelief, while a few opportunistic professional photographers filmed the tragedy. Thousands sprinted the length of several fairways toward the shore, swimming madly toward boaters to be rescued.

—Jans Soles, *QADCRadio104 FM*

'G' WORD

Merit continued to look at cell footage that spectators had taken. Many scenes showed little but the backs of people's heads or a brief shaky glimpse of Soldier, his North Korean opponent, or the fairway and greens beyond them. He stored these on a spare thumb drive for later viewing since he never knew what detail he might be looking for in the future.

He then examined more files and crime reports before returning to the videos. He looked at the holes played earlier on the last day of the tournament to see if anyone in the gallery appeared suspicious. Maybe he could see someone lurking in the shadows or bushes, something— anything the investigators missed, that he could flush out.

He noted that several men wearing sunglasses never applauded a good shot and always stayed in the background. This seemed odd in that most people would have been expected to get as close to the famous golfer as possible. Many people held up portable periscopes made of cardboard and mirrors or cell phones on a selfie stick to see over the heads of spectators standing in front of them.

Merit stored videos of these men standing in the distance in a separate file labeled BACKGROUND so he could examine their movements when he had more time. They were curiosities at present, persons of interest, but not suspects.

The entire day passed, and Merit kept snacking on bland-tasting crackers and grain cakes with a pasty grit substance made of leaves spread onto it.

Starla, wearing an apricot-colored fitted nightgown, stood in the doorway of her bedroom. "Why don't you come and get some rest? You're gonna wear yourself out."

Merit's breaths increased, but he fought the urges, the weakness to succumb to the flesh Ruth claimed his father had genetically passed down to him. He hardly knew her even though they had become friends of sorts, and he needed to continue his work between power naps.

"Thanks," Merit took a deep breath and looked at his computers, "but I gotta keep working. This is going to take a lot of time. I'd usually have it solved by now."

"How is that possible?" She stepped into the large foyer.

"Well, back home I use this thing called a homiscope, it's a really highly advanced machine that allows me to—"

Starla didn't appear to be listening, as she diced vegetables to add to the late-night snack platter.

Merit switched topics. He told Starla how phenomenal Soldier Quinn had been and how he'd started playing golf as a young boy and had accumulated twenty-two majors.

"I'm not watching that." She shielded her eyes. "Golf is racist—and we shouldn't be saying *that* word.

"Nobody's here to hear you say it." Merit looked up at her for a moment and asked innocently, "Why is golf racist?"

"It is—–It was. The *G-word* was really bad back then. That's what I heard. Only white people played it." She brushed her thick hair and moved toward her room. "I'm going to bed. If you change your mind, we can share it."

"Thanks." Her answer was simple enough, and as Merit began to look at new footage, he started to see Starla was right. He couldn't help noticing that, besides Soldier, most of the other players he saw were white and almost all the spectators and announcers were also white. Then why were they all cheering for him?

An hour later, he rose and walked to the threshold of her room. He wasn't going to sleep in her bed, but he couldn't resist the temptation to look at her slumbering body. She was fast asleep, and he draped a lemon-colored comforter over her motionless body before closing the door and returning to work.

35

The police van that sped away with Vic, by chance, intersected the officers carrying Soldier. They flung Soldier's body, and themselves inside, as the van accelerated away. Soldier's bloody corpse was draped across Vic's unsuspecting lap. A slush of brains and Soldier's remaining eye stared up at Vic. The officers stripped Soldier of his shirt to use a bandage as if they were Marines saving a comrade in a war zone. They shouted, "Gotta stop the bleeding! Hold his head together!" It was too much information for Vic to absorb. The greatest golfer in history, with the reputation as unflappable in pressure moments, looked away from the unimaginable. For the next several hours, sheer pandemonium was unleashed on and around the course, the surrounding streets, town, and freeways. People watching the mayhem on TV felt dazed, sad, and powerless.

—J. Kings, https://calbreakingnews.com

PIXELATED SPOTS

By 10:30 P.M., Merit had watched the murder scene enough, and he recalled the first crime reports when he returned to work.

A rifle. Soldier had been a long-range target. Someone trained with that rifle and scope could have shot a human, standing stationary, easily from four to six hundred yards away.

If the kill shot had come from the north or west, he reasoned, then that's where he should look. He loaded footage showing the crowd near the clubhouse and adjacent fairways to the left or west, choosing to look at every inch of the course that had been recorded, from the water hazard to the other holes Soldier had played at the end of the round: the 16th, 17th, and 18th holes.

Maybe he didn't need the actual weapon. Perhaps it was enough to know that the rifle was a very accurate high-powered weapon used to shoot at long range. Anyone holding such a weapon would not have been standing close to Soldier. He or she would have stood out and would have needed space to hold the gun and aim. The spectators wearing sunglasses could be ruled out.

Merit, therefore, concentrated his attention on the final three holes of the course. He sat in a swivel chair and began looking at shots across the trees and lakes on his seven screens spread in a semicircle, pivoting back and forth rapidly, as if Starla's living space had become his private homiscope.

The 16th hole, from tee to green, ran south to north, with the lake on its immediate left boarded by clusters of mature trees. The seventeenth hole was adjacent to it and ran back from north to south. The 18th hole was next to seventeen and ran south to north, with the green very close to the clubhouse. There was a gentle down slope across all three holes, from the 18th fairway across the other two holes and down to the water hazards and trees.

"Okay," Merit had a determination in his voice. He roughly sketched it on a piece of paper. "I have the layout of the course and know the terrain. The killer most logically had to have been someplace near the end of the course, very likely on one of the adjacent 16th or 17th fairways."

Merit searched more footage of the area, starting with a tree line behind a water hazard, even further west of the 16th fairway. He consulted the television recording of the tournament, but its cameras only had a few brief shots of the lake and trees, and these seemed to have been damaged due to age. A few dark spots could be seen on and near the lake, some of them moving.

He switched to a different screen and saw that someone's cell phone had unintentionally captured a better, longer view of the water hazard. The same dots appeared, and it was the same for all footage he called up of the hazard, which had a beautiful fountain near its north end. He zoomed in from 100% to 200% and saw that the dark spots before the screen pixilated were birds—ducks or geese, was his guess.

"Hmm." Talking aloud to himself would sometimes give him more clarity and help him concentrate better, especially late at night. "Not that unusual for geese to be near water. They can fly and swim. And those tree limbs that hung over the water...was there a correlation between the water and trees?"

He'd read where many of the investigators had strongly theorized the shooter fired from cover inside a tree's outer layer of leaves and hopped down and blended in with the fleeing crowd. He watched a few of the birds landing on the water and then taking off later. Some had taken flight shortly after Soldier had been killed. He knew by this time that the crowd was expected to be very quiet so that the players could concentrate on their games. Indeed, tournament officials followed each player from hole to hole, at times holding up tall, slender signs that read: QUIET PLEASE.

Geese would normally scatter if they heard a loud noise or if there was a commotion of some kind nearby, and Merit figured that some of them had flown away because of the roar of applause from the crowd after the ball came to a rest or the sound of a shot being fired. Whether it had been the sound of the rifle discharging or simply the spectator's sudden ovation was of secondary importance to the fact that something had spooked at least some of the geese. Either way, they had been startled by sound or movement at the approximate time that Soldier's body collapsed on itself.

He looked at the videos many more times. Geese landed, Soldier was killed, and some geese flew away behind the trees. Merit's eye was drawn to these events over and over, but he didn't know why. Like the sound of one discordant note in the "Happy Birthday" song, something didn't look right. He replayed it over and over and over.

36

*During the mass exit hysteria, the police lost contact with the helicopter that
had airlifted Soldier's body. Twenty-two minutes after the shooting, the chopper
landed atop L.A. County Hospital's rooftop tarmac. A new, naïve medical
examiner investigator – the more experienced ones were off on the weekends –
performed an external, visual autopsy on Soldier. Eager to make a name for
himself, he ignored the protocol of first notifying law enforcement of his findings
and agreed to conduct an impromptu briefing with several local reporters. He read
from his notes, overwhelmed by the moment, his voice cracked, "Mr. Soldier
Quinn, the U.S. golfer, on June 18th at 6:42 P.M. Pacific Coast Time was
pronounced dead upon arrival…"*

—Internal Affairs Div., *Response and Procedure Review*

ODD BIRD

At nine in the morning, Starla approached the sleeping ball of Merit in
the swivel chair, his knees tucked up to his chest. Merit had decided to
work through the night with no distractions.

Papers with sketches, drawings, lists of times, some scratched out,
were strewn about. She glanced at his homemade workstation and saw a
screensaver, three screens frozen on a particular scene, and one playing
a continuous loop of Soldier walking down a fairway.

"Wow, this guy has been working really hard," she said.

Merit was roused from slumber and sat up straight, "Drop it!" He
reached for the nonexistent gun at his side. "Don't move!"

"Hey, it's me—Starla." She playfully raised both hands in the air,
indicating *you got me.*

"Huh? Oh, sorry." He sat up wiping the sleep from his eyes.

"That vigilante was right," she scowled. "You did come to get me." She then smiled.

"Nah, weird dream . . .anyway, good morning." He twisted left and right, stretching out his tight lower back.

"He's unusual looking." She was looking at a picture of Soldier on one of the monitors. "What was he?" She used the mouse and clicked on Soldier, enlarging his image several times. "His skin was darker than mine, and has really high cheekbones, jet-black hair, cut tight on the sides, with blue eyes. Was he a Pacific Islander?"

"He was African American. Very tall and slender. I'm learning about him. His parents were track and field stars. His father was from a state back then called Alabama, and his mom from a state named Ohio. His dad died when he was real young."

"He was very unusual looking. And that's why they killed him because his parents were runners?"

He looked into her eyes. "You're not joking. You don't know why either, do you?"

"No, but I've heard his name a lot. All of the people like him here. And I know he had something to do with the old United States, and he helped create Frontier, but that's it."

"Finally," Merit said.

"What do you mean?"

"Finally, we have *something* in common. You don't know *your* state's history either."

She smiled, amused by his realization.

Merit refocused his attention on the case. "What I've learned is he was about to break a golf record that was held by a *white* golfer, and that's why someone killed him."

"He was killed because of the color of his skin? That's so sad. I told you——that's what they did back then. And that's why you're here—to find out who?" She sounded impressed.

"Yes, but let me show you what I've found so far." He grabbed a pencil and sketchpad.

Quickly, Merit's pencil moved across the large white sheet of paper as he outlined the last three holes of the course and the water hazard.

He then showed Starla the video of Soldier playing the 18th hole and the scenes of his subsequent murder.

Starla turned her head away sharply. "No! I can't watch it. Is he gonna get it? You know, I don't like to see people get hurt."

"Okay but let me show you this lake where the big water fountain is. Watch closely."

Merit queued up the video that showed Soldier on the 16th fairway and the large water hazard to the west.

"See. There's the water spraying up from the fountain––there are three geese swimming close together on the lake," Merit pointed the eraser's end of a pencil against the screen. "Notice that by the time Soldier is standing on the 17th fairway, I found a different camera angle shot showing eight more geese flying in to join the three. There are now eleven geese. You see?"

"Yes, I can count. But those aren't geese." She slid the pencil out of his fingers and referenced the three birds frozen on the computer screen. "They're swans."

"How do you know about birds?"

"Waterfowl. They're all over the place. I've watched them. Then I look them up in this book. Those are trumpeter swans." From the shelf, she pulled a book titled *Ornithology: Marine birds of the Pacific Coast* and flipped through the bookmarked pages. "All-white body, long slender neck, and it's distinguished by a black bill. It's the largest species of waterfowl, second to the condor in size. See? The trumpeter swan." Her finger indicated a photo of the elegant bird in the book.

"Okay, now look at the lake from this other person's camera when Soldier is standing on the 18th fairway. There are twelve geese." He counted aloud, tapping the screen with his finger.

"Swans. Twelve swans." She said. "So, what's the problem? Another swan flew in––Or perhaps the twelfth swan was out of camera view or flew up inside that tree." She pointed to a clump of eucalyptus trees.

"Maybe, but nobody's cell phone captured that happening, and there were a lot of people recording Soldier's every move and the surrounding area. I figured someone's phone would have photographed it swooping in from some direction, but I can't find it."

"So now what?" She returned the book to the shelf.

Merit fast-forwarded one video to a point nine seconds after Soldier had been hit. "Three swans flew away immediately after the shot or applause. You can see from this person's phone camera angle that it picked up those three flying about fifty yards away in the distance. The others flapped their wings, disturbed by the noise of the crowd or a gunshot." He paused the camera footage. "Now on *this* screen, you see Soldier is shot and on the ground. If you look at this person's camera for a split second, it captures part of the lake." He forwarded one screen to align time frames and then froze it. "Now there are only eight swans left on the lake south of the water fountain. There should be nine."

She looked intently. "True, but maybe swan number twelve swam out of camera range. How much time is there between twelve swans in the frame and then eight?"

Merit by rewinding, fast-forwarding, and subtracting on his fingers calculated the answer. "Um, just over ten seconds."

Starla clicked her tongue, making a doubting sound. "Hmm. Ten seconds." She counted aloud ten seconds . . . "Ten seconds. That's a long time. It could have flown away." She backed away from the screens. "So, what's it mean?"

"Nothing. I'm saying something seems off." He looked closely at the beautiful long-necked birds in flight and mumbled so that she couldn't hear him say, "Happy Birthday."

Starla tilted her head as she looked at the laptop and scratched her head, then gushed excitedly, "I think I know who did it."

Merit looked over wide-eyed and all ears, "Who?"

"The goose shot him!" She pointed at the monitor screen with a straight face.

Merit, detecting she was trying to be funny, struck back, "No—It was a swan you dummy—Quack-quack, and I'm gonna shoot you!" He light-heartedly tackled her over the back of the couch onto the cushions, administered several playful punches to her midsection and a karate chop to the neck. He somersaulted over her and ended up on the stained concrete floor. Looking up at her out of breath, he stated, "I only have twenty-two days left. I need to get to that course."

Starla looked at the floor, where her houseguest had fashioned a large map of the entire course and its location sixty years earlier using household items. Seashells, drinking glasses and cups used as figurines were placed strategically across the floor, several of her large rugs were folded and layered on top of the others to emulate the course terrain.

"That won't be easy," she bent over. "It's just north of Laguna."

"So, I'll just bike there." He noted the relatively short distance on the map between their location and Laguna Beach.

"No, you won't." She fixed her hair that had fallen over her face during the roughhousing. "You can't. I'll show you why."

37

In the aftermath of Soldier's shooting, cell towers across Southern California were inundated with calls and crashed. Most off-duty detectives didn't receive texts requesting they respond to the crime scene. The few off-duty detectives alerted by word of mouth couldn't navigate against the deluge of cars and people fleeing the course. Some investigators ditched their vehicles and jogged several miles to reach the site. The first detectives that arrived found everything in disarray. Officers handed them scraps of papers with the scribbled names and numbers of witnesses who wouldn't wait. Their priority was to locate and lock down the scene. They then set up a command center in the clubhouse player's room where they later learned of Soldier's mortal condition on breaking news from the television.

—Internal Accountability Div., *Response and Procedure Review cont.*

WATER HAZARD

Late in the afternoon, Merit and Starla walked up the gentle slope of a hill with a canyon on their right. She had pulled him outside of her home to show him the difficulty he would have in trying to reach the course where Soldier was killed. To their left was shrubbery, but beyond it was the ocean bay. Starla paused and laid Merit's map on a wooden picnic table.

"This is really outdated," she said. "This is not what the area looks like anymore. It used to be called Southern Cal., as you can tell by some of the names on the map."

She pointed to a grid on the lower left. "Around the year 2035, a series of earthquakes and tsunamis hit the West Coast, and they changed the landscape of old Southern Cal forever."

Starla knelt by the table and formed a ridge of dirt with the angled palm of her hand. She then pushed the soil over to indicate that tidal waves had forced large volumes of water over parts of the high coastline then flowed down inland and covered the basin. When the water leveled off in the basin it formed a shallow bay and the higher parts of land on the basin formed hundreds of islands. "All of the lower-lying areas that are underwater was a big bowl that used to be called Orange County. That basin became a big bay of ocean water filled with tiny islands where there was higher ground. It's now called Orange Bay."

The pair hiked higher to a historic lookout point near the high foothills of the San Bernardino Mountain range that looked down over the Orange Bay and further west past the many islands to the Pacific Ocean.

"I've never seen anything like this," Merit stood in awe, the sun a large reddish-pink ball setting into the horizon. "My hometown is nowhere near the water. We have ponds and waterholes. This is amazing." He could still feel the warmth of the sunlight as it appeared to sink into the calm Pacific Ocean. "It looks like a giant cookie being dipped in a glass of milk."

Starla smiled. He reached his hand out and pretended to hold the top of the sun as if it were a cookie and was dunking it in the milk.

She took his hand and pulled it to her mouth, pretending to gobble up the treat. "Yum-yum sun cookie." She rubbed her hand over her tummy. "If you lived here, you could see this every day." She glanced at him for a moment, then looked down over the bay of many islands.

For a fleeting moment, Merit considered the idea of living in Frontier, then looked over and studied the left side of her profile. He noticed she wasn't wearing any makeup, fresh from swimming. He saw some dark brown freckles on her face he hadn't noticed before, and at that moment he was tempted to reach up and brush her cheek with the back of his hand but resisted.

Starla turned and dropped some old U.S. currency nickels in an old brass coin-operated telescope that was still in working order and showed Merit nine of the larger islands.

"See the biggest island way out to the left? That's San Clemente Island. Now move the viewer a tad to the right and find the next eight big islands."

Merit peered through the eyeglasses and, with his hands on the levers, steered the bulky instrument. He scanned from one tiny island, left to right, to another. "There's tons of them."

Starla assisted by manipulating the scope slightly north and tilting it upwards several degrees. "The next big island to the right is San Juan Capistrano, then Dana Point Island. See?"

He counted to the right and finally focused on the largest island, which was the farthest away. "Got it! The tallest island with rocks and cliffs covered with lots of greenery. What island is that?"

"That's where your golfer man was killed."

Merit removed his eyes from the scope. "That can't be. The golf course wasn't on an island. It was on the mainland, right on the coast of old Southern California."

"It might have been back then, but as I explained, the earthquakes and tsunamis changed that over fifty years ago, probably shortly after the golf man was killed. That's why I brought you here."

He stooped, squinting harder to have a second look, and adjusted a dial to get a clearer focus. In the thirty seconds since he'd last seen it, a low misty fog had formed, obstructing a clear view of the mysterious island that could hold the clues to solving the sixty-year-old murder of golf great Soldier Quinn.

"The island you're interested in is farther away than it appears," Starla said.

His mouth began salivating in anticipation of setting foot on the golf course and investigating. The view through the lenses suddenly blacked out, like an eclipse of the sun, indicating that time was up on the three minutes of allotted viewing for a single coin. He let go of the telescope and stood up.

"You're right. I can't fly and I can't ride a bike there. I'll rent a speedboat. I could get there in no time."

Starla shook her head as if her companion had still not assimilated the basics of Frontier culture. "Remember—no vehicles here are motorized because they use fossil fuels." By way of explanation, she pointed to hundreds of people at the base of the cliff far below them. "You'll have to get there another way." She dropped another coin in the slot, buying an additional three minutes of viewing time.

Merit gazed through the telescope and noted that people down towards the base of the canyon top looked like thousands of ants crowded together, or runners standing at the starting line of a marathon. "What are they doing?"

"Waiting for just the right time to take advantage of low tide," Starla looked at Merit's watch. "They'll have a short window of opportunity to island-hop. They'll use paddleboards, kayaks, inner tubes, bikes, surfboards, skateboards—whatever it takes to move across the land and water to get to their island before the tide comes back in. It can be dangerous if you don't know the tides and you get caught out there."

A loud grating sound could be heard as the water receded over rocks, pebbles, and shells. As some dry land appeared, Merit could see the landscape of what Southern California's Orange County basin had formerly been, the flat rooftops of abandoned buildings, eroded freeways, barnacle-infested billboards, highway signs, fast food restaurants, lamp posts, and other features of the infrastructure for a city that had been home to millions.

As more and more land appeared, people ventured forth with their devices, many on all-terrain solar vehicles and scooters, while others carried their flotation devices, boards and boats until they reached the waterline in the distance.

"It's about forty to fifty miles from here to that golf island." Starla looked over at him. "Hope you're a good swimmer."

Merit shuddered as his eyes looked down at the ocean below. "I'm not a big fan of the water." That same paralyzing sensation he had at the gym pool back in Pilgrim rushed through his body again, locking up his arms and legs. "Is there some other way?"

Starla laughed at the remark. "I gotcha. I'm afraid of heights too. Why do you think I stand way back here?" She inched backward even further from the edge.

"What kind of boat is that?" Merit pointed out in the distance.

"That? He's windsurfing."

Merit noted the windsurfer's head was high *above* the water. "I could handle that."

"Okay. Good. I know just the right person who can teach you."

Merit stepped back from the telescope to survey the vista before him in the final moments of golden twilight. As he did so, Starla stuck out her foot and tripped the detective. Laughing, he got up and chased her as she ran down the hill.

"Hey, do you want to go out and get some dinner?" He was surprised by the boldness of his impromptu invitation.

"Sure."

They strolled along, their shoulders touching every several steps, as the sun was no more than a sliver above the distant rim of the world. A breeze swept through the shrubbery, blowing Starla's hair to the side. They were just inches apart, and Merit's heart was racing, hoping that they would kiss as the rays of the dying sunlight painted their faces with a soft radiance.

Starla drew closer to Merit, her supple lips inches away from touching his when he was distracted by the sound of a snap of a twig. Merit, instead of kissing Starla, sharply turned his head in the direction of the noise and stared into the brush to see if there was any movement.

★★★

When Merit determined the noise was inconsequential, he turned back and realized their moment had passed, the distance between them grew. "Probably a squirrel or something."

"Yeah, probably." There was a melancholic note in her voice. "So, when will you go?"

"Tomorrow."

There was more silence. She was shocked by the short notice. "Oh." She uttered and turned to continue down the path.

Merit attempted to soften the blow. "But thanks for letting me stay at your place."

"When are you coming back?"

"I don't know. However long it takes to solve the case."

Starla steadied her eyes forward. She began nervously rambling, making Merit feel uncomfortable. "You should go— you need to. If you stay any longer, the vigilantes might find you—it's probably for the best," she said, which Merit didn't buy. "Yeah—that's good, you should go tomorrow."

"I don't want them knowing you helped me." Merit lethargically kicked a rock with his foot, disappointed at his failed opportunity. "Besides, you have your acting and more auditions."

"You should go back now so you can pack. And let's skip dinner," Starla's eyes turned to the ocean. "I'm not really that hungry anyway."

In silence, they plodded down the windy trail through the darkness. The excitement he experienced with her on the way up an hour earlier, when they were clicking so well, now seemed like it occurred years ago. She walked several steps in front of him when he noticed her discreetly pop one of her blue pills. It bothered him that the memory of the last hour they'd spent together would be wiped clean.

★★★

As Merit lay on Starla's sectional couch in the dark, he saw the light beneath the crack of Starla's door disappear and knew she was going to sleep. He convinced himself he had done the right thing by avoiding the kiss. When he'd told her earlier that he didn't know how long it would take to solve the crime, he knew that he was skirting the issue of when he would see her again. The truth was that he wouldn't.

He recalled Detective Hubbard's parting words: *Sometimes on the course, you don't know or see what lies ahead, such as a dogleg or a row of trees. You have to make your best decision with the information you have and deal with the outcome later.* He had gotten what he needed from Starla and was intrigued by her, but his gut said it was time to cut bait and move on. He didn't have to make these tough decisions in the safety of the homiscope. After a case, he always got in his car and simply drove home to the comfort of his own bed.

He knew in the morning that he would face another challenge, something he feared most, a major water hazard in the form of an expansive ocean bay that stood between him and the U.S. Open island course, the crime scene. Negative thoughts and doubts swirled in his head about learning to ride a windsurfer and reaching the mystic golf island.

Merit eventually fell asleep and had a pleasant dream of floating effortlessly on the warm surface of the still blue water under the sun he'd seen dipping into the water with Starla. But the clear ocean turned black as oil—his dream shifted. The giant setting sun was the underbelly of a monster-size prisoner cruise ship, and he was trapped beneath the keel as it pushed him—his head, despite his resistance, underwater.

He tossed and turned in his bed, causing his arms and legs to get twisted in the sheets. He slipped below the surface and began taking in water. A man's hand appeared to pull him up, but Merit's arms were bound in the linens and couldn't extend to grab a hold. A set of tiny hands latched onto his ankles— kicking convulsively he looked down to see the terrified face of rookie Nurse Beth Honeywell in pink scrubs, her eyes stricken with fear and mouth exaggeratedly enlarged, gasping for her last breath—tugging him down into the fossil-fueled abyss.

38

In the dark, with only one good flashlight, three detectives canvassed the course for clues. Their homicide lieutenant arrived and ordered them to stop out of fear that evidence could be destroyed. Fellow detectives, specialized units, crime scene techs, and canine units trickled in throughout Sunday evening. The remaining uniformed officers were stationed outside the perimeter fence to guard the eighty-five-acre course. Just before midnight, a chopper with the Coast Guard spotlighted the grounds looking for suspects, other victims—anything unusual. At midnight, an L.A. County doctor confirmed a second victim was treated for a gunshot wound but was out of surgery and his condition was non-life-threatening. The press reported that the bullet-grazed 'bystander' was a sixty-six-year-old white male.
— Marilyn Willis, *LAW and JUSTICE* vol. 2.2120

BEACH BODY

The following morning, Merit went to a boardwalk next to a lagoon to meet his windsurfing instructor.

He got up before the sun appeared to get an early start, but truthfully to avoid the awkwardness of having to say goodbye to Starla. He reminded himself that the relationship was a sand trap he had gotten out of before he had sunk too deep into it. He was moving on to the next tee box. Forget about the last shot and focus on the next; that's what the TV golf analysts had said that Soldier and the North Korean needed to do after a bad shot, and the ones who could do it best rose to the top. His body felt lethargic as he walked along the beachside concrete path.

The beach was empty except for a couple he saw holding hands strolling along the soft surf, reaching down every so often to inspect a shell. He ditched his flip-flops by the path's edge. He'd gotten accustomed to wearing the slides everywhere, like Beck did, which prompted him to wonder where the servile was. He missed Servile Beck's chilled-out demeanor but didn't have time to dwell on him. Besides, there was no way to know where he lived or how to get in touch with him.

He spied a slim young Asian woman with long sun-streaked hair that was wrapped above her head like a beehive. She had an extremely large bust, a skinny waist, and wore a two-piece bathing suit, or so Merit thought until he looked closer and saw that the bikini top was nothing more than a permanent tattoo that curved around the instructor's voluptuous body.

"Are you one of Starla's boyfriends who wants to windsurf?" She eyed him up and down.

"I'm not her boyfriend, but yeah, I'm here to learn."

"Whatever. You know Starla. I'm Nami." She turned and waded into the water.

Three hours later, after fighting off several panic attacks, Merit stood with his instructor waist-deep in the cove's water and climbed onto her board. Nami mounted the small craft and stood behind him so that she could grasp both of his hands and guide him through a few simple turns. He felt the firmness of her breasts, which momentarily took his mind away from the growing fear that he would fall head-first into the water. She then grabbed his hips and turned his body slightly, after which she ran her hand along his thigh and then bent his knees to give him more flexibility. They caught some wind and quickly gained speed.

"You're doing better, but you're too rigid," she instructed, as they cut across the lagoon. "Let the wind guide you as much as possible. Loosen up or you're going to topple."

Nami slid off the back so that Merit could get his sea legs, as he performed a few lazy circles in the shallow water and then zigzagged boldly around the cove before returning to his hot instructor. His confidence increased with every successful turn he made without dumping the craft into the lagoon water.

"Nice job," she clapped. "Go again, but faster."

He grasped the horizontal steering bar and sailed around the lagoon, challenging himself each time to go faster and jump higher waves, aligning the sail as he arched his body or stood tall, positioning himself to maintain balance as he went through his maneuvers.

Merit could tell Nami was impressed with his aptitude at picking up windsurfing so quickly. She'd told him he had exceptional upper body strength and with his balance and motivation was a natural. More truthfully, it wasn't so much his talent that kept him upright, but his deep fear from falling and going headfirst underwater that drove him.

She waved for him to bring it in.

Before he had a chance to slide off the board, Merit heard boisterous male voices coming from a point twenty yards down the boardwalk. He was able to discern from their dress that they were vigilantes, so he aimed the board for the shore and dove under the board's sail, as it tipped over, submerging his body in the shallow water, his head on the sand. The voices of the vigilantes were loud, and their speech was crude and vulgar.

"Hey, Nami baby," said Vigilante One. "How's the water?" Always in command of any situation, the tall man surveyed the area carefully and tugged at his hoodie vest when he was satisfied that he saw nothing out of place.

Nami stepped from the water's edge and walked toward them wearing platform-high flip-flops. Deflecting the inquiry, she merely said, "What's up, bad boys?"

Vigilante Two walked in her direction and checked out her rock-hard, cosmetically built super body. "We're looking for a PP."

"What's he look like?" She moved to the side of the dune opposite from where Merit was hiding.

"Tall guy. Short hair. Well built."

"With dark hair and abs like yours?" She toyed with them, stroking Vigilante Two's washboard abs with her long fingernails.

"Yeah." The lead Vigilante looked at the other, then back to her. "We had him tied up, but somehow he got away."

"I saw him about thirty minutes ago—he was cute. He went that way." She pointed in the direction they were headed.

The two men stood only feet away from the board beneath which Merit was hiding.

"Go get his PP ass." She pressed her rock-hard breasts against the leader's chest and opened her mouth seductively. "Find him and I'll give you bad boys a freebie."

It was the motivation the two men needed. They moved away, jogging quickly and kicking up sand as they headed in the direction the instructor had indicated.

Nami looked over her shoulder in Merit's direction. "They're gone."

Merit lifted his head from the sand and crawled from the shallow water. "How did you know who I was?" He spit out a mouthful of gritty sand.

"Starla told me. She trusts me. She's a great chick."

She reached down and hauled him out of the water as he rolled over in the sand. "Did she tell you?"

"What?" Merit propped himself up with his arms to hear her better.

"When she was a little girl, her dad was killed while in jail. She blames the serviles who put him there for stealing food to feed his family. She doesn't trust serviles or men. She was also raped. Did she tell you that she was raped too?"

"Yeah, she told me." Even though she hadn't, he was bothered to hear of Starla's troubled background. It confirmed his suspicion, from the studies he'd read, the chest of tattoos was a sign of sexual abuse in the past.

"Where are you headed in such a hurry?"

Merit stood up and, while brushing sand stuck to his body like granules off a sugar donut, peered out over the Orange Bay. The islands looked much different from ground level than from high atop the lookout. He counted them left to right starting with San Clemente Island and pointed to it.

"That one?" She looked down his arm like she was staring down the barrel of a gun. "That one's off-limits to the public."

"That's where I got to go."

"Okay, but that's too far to go straight there on this." She indicated the board she was applying wax from a tin to make it glide more efficiently through the water. "You'll be exhausted. You'll have to island-hop and rest along the way."

"Why is it off-limits?"

"It's dangerous. Creepy things over there, like sea monsters." There was trepidation in her voice.

Merit didn't know what to make of Nami's reference but figured it had probably started as a wives' tale. Not placing any credence on the idea, he changed the conversation. "Those vigilantes think I'm here to get somebody and take him back, but I'm not," Merit said, sticking his head up above the dune to see if they were out of sight.

"Yeah, but that's not all they do," Nami said.

Merit perked up. He could tell by her body language that she was about to unload something she didn't look comfortable revealing. He'd attended several classes in interrogation in college; however, was never able to put it to use working in the solitude of the homiscope but could spot nonverbal cues when a suspect was about to "give it up." It was usually some sensitive bit of information—a secret that made them feel uneasy, and with just the right amount of prodding and backing off, it could be extracted.

Suppressing the truth, his college criminal justice professor had instructed him, was like a splinter. It had a natural way of working itself out of one's body at some point. Even serial rapists or career killers couldn't stop themselves from bragging to fellow cellmates.

Merit quickly sensed the opportunity to try his hand at it, "It's okay Nami. You can tell me. What else do the vigilantes do?"

She paused and took in a breath. "I shouldn't tell you this." She looked around and lowered her head before softly stating, "They're paid to—" She stopped and looked over both shoulders to ensure no one could hear her. "I better not say, cutie."

She leaned in, put one hand on his shoulders, the other on his lower stomach and gave Merit a long, open-mouthed kiss, sending a tingling sensation up through his inner thighs. It came as a surprise to him, but he didn't resist. "You better go before they return. They're not so nice."

39

As dawn broke, detectives got their first look at the layout of the site of the U.S. Open. Trampled clumps of sod, cups, umbrellas, tables, bags, food, beer cans, wine bottles and clothing littered the course. Several giant scaffolding towers, the stands, rows of porta-johns, lay toppled as if a tornado had touched down. The beach town's detective unit pinpointed where Soldier was shot and expanded the scene to include the entire course. Deputies from surrounding municipalities responded to relieve tired patrol officers from their posts. All day, police rounded up witnesses around local hotels, restaurants, airports and streets but learned most had returned home. Others reported seeing the shooting, but amazingly, nobody saw a shooter. No one could definitively say which direction the shots came from or how or even if they'd heard shots. Detectives banked on at least one of the network's cameras had captured the shooter, but they were nowhere on site.
—correspondent Van Stone, *'Harrison' Edition News*

ORANGE BAY

It was late afternoon, and the sun had been eclipsed by a thick fog as Merit traveled west by windsurfing over the choppy ocean. He'd only fallen a few times, always managing to keep his head above water by flailing his arms and clutching the board. He wished he'd worn gloves as Nami had suggested. His hands were blistered and bleeding from holding onto the fiberglass steering bar, and his feet were cut and bloody from positioning his heels over the edge of the board to give him greater maneuverability in steering a course for his destination.

He had done as Nami had urged him to do—stop and rest on each of the eight bigger islands, and he even paused on two of the hundred or so minor ones, some no bigger than the size of a rooftop, protruding above the sea.

If his flying into the sandstorm had been a bunker, and if landing in the orange grove was the tall rough, he had to work himself out of, then the salty ocean was a major water hazard he needed to clear if he wanted to land safely on the green island and not be penalized a stroke.

The wind died down, and Merit was forced to sit on his board, his feet dangling in the gray water. The board drifted slowly to the west, and soon Merit saw a large outcropping of rocks rising from the ocean. Minutes later, more land came into view, spreading far to the north and south. It was U.S. Open Island.

He decided to carefully slip into the water to rinse away the blood and sweat from his body while he waited for the next wind which, he calculated, would be enough to propel him the final five hundred yards so he could make landfall. Something smooth brushed against his left leg, something moving very quickly beneath the surface of the water.

Merit froze, not daring to breathe. Looking around by pivoting his head slowly, he saw a gray fin cutting through the wavelets. His blood had attracted a shark. He climbed onto the board and lay flat on his belly.

"No way," he said aloud without moving his lips, hoping that the fin would recede into the distance.

Moments later, however, two more fins appeared, all circling the board. Occasionally, one of the sharks would break its circular pattern and glide past him, nudging the board sideways, as if testing its potential prey.

"Please forgive my lust, Lord," Merit looked up to the heavens. "If you get me out of this, I promise to walk in your ways. Forgive me for wanting to kiss Starla and letting Nami kiss me. And I'll stop cussing, and I'll be faithful to Ruth and marry her when I get home."

A slight wind came from the east, and Merit stood and hoisted the waterlogged, bright red and yellow sail from the water, positioning himself for what he hoped would be the final push to the island. "Thank you, Lord." He was doing five knots, but the sharks were easily keeping up with the board, and one was outpacing it, swimming rings around the slow-moving windsurfer.

Merit arched his back as the wind grew stronger, and he was doing ten knots, then fifteen. The board flew across the wave crests, and the land ahead loomed larger. He became optimistic as to his chances of reaching the coast, but a grayish-white snout poked the side of the windsurfer, knocking Merit into the water. He scrambled back onto the board, like it was hot coals, and resumed his course, but not before one of the predators snapped at his left heel, missing by inches.

He continued to gain speed and was up to twenty knots, occasionally riding air as the sailboard jumped tall waves. Still, the three fins followed the board in a triangular formation. Glancing over his left shoulder, Merit saw that one shark was directly aft of the board, and both its dorsal and pectoral fins could be seen, enabling him to estimate that the shark was at least fifteen feet in length.

He was only fifty yards from the island when the shark opened its maw, revealing three rows of jagged, serrated brown teeth. It lurched forward and bit down on the back of the board, just inches from Merit's left foot, its black, lifeless eyes regarding its prey with no emotion.

The gray shark bit cleanly through Merit's board, taking off two feet of the rear platform. The board was now unbalanced, sending Merit headfirst into the surf breaking onto the coast of U.S. Open Island. By intentionally belly-flopping and clasping his hands together while smacking the sea's surface, he'd managed to keep his head from going under, and kept it so by dog paddling, as fast as he could until he felt his blistered hands touch the security of the shore's bottom.

40

TV executives were first reluctant to hand over videos of Soldier's shooting to detectives without a warrant, not wanting to violate citizens' rights to privacy. However, they acquiesced. A camera editor converted his motel room into a makeshift studio bay, and detectives crammed in to view the footage at different speeds and camera angles. They established that the gunman's first shot narrowly missed Soldier and grazed a bystander positioned fifteen feet behind Soldier. The impact knocked the spectator to the ground. Almost instantaneously after, Soldier was struck. The M.E. doctor reported that one projectile penetrated the left side of Soldier's skull just under his ear, passed left to right and slightly diagonally upward through his brain, then exited above his right ear.

—KCTV, *Overland Park KS*

ENCHANTED WATERS

Merit, panting hard and dripping wet, rolled onto the bank of jagged rocks and pebbles, a brownish volcanic rock that formed wave-cut platform cliffs, rising above his head. He watched the sea as the splintered windsurf board and its rear piece washed onto the rocky beach beside him. Kneeling as he looked at the waves, he could no longer see the sleek man-eater—a great white shark. He'd escaped near-death and landed safely on the golf island.

"Hey, Hubbard!" Merit said as if his words could magically be heard across the continent by the cold case detective. "Ever had to do *that* out on the streets?" Merit wilted to the ground and rested as he caught his breath.

Lugging his battered board behind him, Merit scaled the steep incline of a one-hundred-foot-high cliff. The board was badly damaged, but he might be able to repair it, although he would need materials to do so.

At the top of the cliff, he surveyed the terrain and saw that it was different than that of other islands he'd passed or visited. He limped as he approached an old weather-beaten, twisted metal sign in faded red, white, and blue colors that read:

WARNING

PROPERTY OF THE UNITED STATES GOVERNMENT

TRESPASSING IS PROHIBITED

2027

Unattractive, the island was mostly choppy, with hundreds of gentle rises poking above what seemed to be an endless number of marshes, pools and brackish ponds. The landscape was overgrown with trees, vines, brush, and tall grass interspersed with broad areas of rock and sand. Tall, thin palm trees sprung up randomly, towering high across the rest of the island's lush terrain, like springtime dandelions sprouting up over short blades of grass of a freshly cut lawn.

There were no buildings, homes, or habitants as he'd seen on most of the other islands. The island had an almost prehistoric look but for the fact that Merit could see faded white lines on the remnants of what was once an asphalt parking lot with weeds mushrooming up through the fissures on its uneven surface.

Merit paused on his hike to reflect that somewhere on this island was where the U.S. Open had been played, the very course where Soldier Quinn had been gunned down. Pilgrim seemed a million miles away from the wasteland that spread all around him, but he was where he needed to be to continue his investigation.

No one could have guessed that the island was once the location of a pristine, well-manicured golf course. He removed a map of the course Sgt. Travers put in the folder in his backpack, but he could find no landmarks that corresponded to anything on the piece of paper spread before him.

Merit stowed his wrecked board and sail in a safe place and trekked on. He used a sharp stick to slash through vines and high grass, moving back into the mud and ankle-deep water—sometimes higher—every few yards. Hearing a splash in a shallow pond he crossed, caused him to think there must be an abundance of fish on the island.

He still saw no evidence of a golf course, but he reminded himself that courses had been mostly land and had few identifying features other than fairways, bunkers, and greens. These would no longer be recognizable, with trees and vegetation having overtaken them. He stopped, having heard another splash behind him. He had the unnerving feeling that he was being watched, although he couldn't imagine who would be on such a desolate island this far out in the ocean.

Nightfall was descending, and visibility was poor. Only a waning moon low on the horizon provided any light. He removed the mini flashlight he'd borrowed from a drawer in Starla's kitchen from his pack and aimed it at the nearby ground as he turned in a complete circle. He saw nothing, however, and resumed his forward motion.

He trudged through the muck, now hearing a sloshing sound, not unlike the noise his own legs were producing in the water. He wheeled around sharply. When he'd passed the dark object seconds earlier, he assumed it was a partially submerged log, but having moved forward twenty yards, he noted that a brown elongated form still lurked slightly behind and to his left. He blinked his eyes hard to force his pupils to dilate to make out the threat. Was it the marsh monster Nami described during his windsurfing lesson? If Chief Reed hadn't confiscated his weapon, he could have shot it. He turned his head in both directions and spotted a rusted chain-link fence thirty yards or so to the right, sticking out of the marsh water, leaning at an angle. If he could reach the eight-to-ten-foot-high metal fence before the creature reached him, he calculated, he could scale the cockeyed barrier and escape to the other side.

The croaking chorus of toads intensified with each passing moment to an almost deafening pitch, a possible warning that something bad was about to happen. His eyes looked back at the elusive form one last time, only to see the top of the creature next to his feet. Out of sheer panic— he ran through the bog in the direction of the fence, churning his arms and feet as fast as he could, splashing water, mowing over tall cattails and salt grass. Merit extended his hands in anticipation of his leap onto the fence and, clasping his fingers through the diamond-shaped metal links, he felt something clasp onto his ankle, causing him to splash face-down into the dark, cold ooze.

Merit twisted his body, flailed his arms, and looked above him to see a humanoid creature with shiny black skin, bulbous eyes, and a long horn protruding from its face. He had come face to face with the legendary marsh monster. It towered above him, seaweed draped over its head like some unearthly hair on a Halloween costume.

A distorted voice bellowed. "Stay out of my lake!"

★★★

The slinky swamp creature moved past Merit with surprising speed. It was human, a man, and he was carrying a sack on his back filled with objects that clattered against each other.

"Hey!" Merit said.

The beam from Merit's flashlight revealed an old dark-skinned man with long gray hair and a beard to match, a man who appeared to be in his seventies or eighties. He adjusted the goggles to the top of his head and the snorkel from the side of his mouth.

"I guard these waters." He held out his sack at arm's length and shook it. "So go home."

The man opened his eyes wide, revealing the white orbs, which glowed eerily in the darkness. He struck Merit as perhaps a recluse or maybe some marooned soul.

He heaved the bag over the droopy fence and, spry for his age, easily scaled it and dropped to the other side. Merit followed his lead and crawled up and over the barrier.

The man slogged ahead, Merit following at a distance. They shortly arrived at a camp situated on high ground, where a fire blazed beneath a metal apparatus. Higher up on the metallic skeleton, plywood boards and corrugated tin had been used to enclose part of the scaffolding to form a shelter of sorts. It would, Merit theorized, provide a good vantage point for the man, as well as safety from any animal life on the island, although thus far no fauna had shown itself.

Merit cleared his throat to remind the old man that he was still in the rear. "Uh . . . you live here?"

"Most of the time."

"What is your name, sir?"

"Keeper."

Keeper made his way to the ground directly beneath his home resembling a playground jungle gym where he opened his sack, sat on a dirty lawn chair, and removed round black chunks of mud the size of baseballs. He dipped each one in successive buckets of sun-heated water, chipping away the mud with his long fingernails. After the third rinsing, he held up what was white golf balls with the names Wilson, Titleist, and Top Flite printed on them.

"My pearls." Licking his chops, he examined each one closely in the manner of a jeweler inspecting a cut diamond with a magnifying loupe, searching for the slightest imperfection, before tossing the ball into containers surrounding his seat—plastic wastebaskets, garbage cans, a wheelbarrow, buckets, and an overturned hamster cage that had washed up onshore. He had accumulated thousands of balls, the containers extending for several dozen yards in every direction around the camp.

"How long have you been here, Keeper?"

Each toss he made was accurate, and he didn't miss a shot with any of the twenty-two balls he'd collected that day.

He didn't answer.

"How do you find your pearls?" Merit kept a straight face.

Keeper pointed to a collection of rusty club faces broken off from the shafts of irons. "I dig for'em in these enchanted waters."

Merit picked up three golf balls and turned them over in his hand. He'd never held one before. They weren't smooth on the surface, as he perceived them to be, but after inspecting closer saw they were formed with many tiny craters or dimples that comprised the glossy white hardcover. A logo and name brand printed on it was mostly worn away but still discernable if scrutinized closely.

"Put them back," Keeper was staring him down.

Merit could feel the tension and complied. "What do you do with them?"

There was no answer. Merit now realized anew that he was on the golf course where Soldier had been killed, although most of it was completely submerged. He sat atop a piece of history that had reshaped an entire continent. He glanced up at the scaffolding and recognized that it had been used as one of the many platforms to televise the tournament, with cameras and announcers stationed at its top sixty years earlier. Examining his host, he thought it likely that Keeper was insane, mentally ill, or on drugs. What other explanation could account for living an isolated life on an ugly island to collect used balls that he thought were valuable pearls?

"Why are you here?" Keeper looked at him with sterile eyes.

"Me? Why am I here?" Merit stalled to buy some time to come up with an answer. "I'm uh, I'm here on a research mission. In fact, can I borrow your goggles and snorkel tomorrow?"

"What are you researching?"

"Birds." It was the first thing that popped into Merit's mind.

"What kind of birds?"

Merit hadn't anticipated a grilling from the old man and had to think quickly. "Not just birds, sir. Waterfowl." He would shut down the crazy old inquisitive man from asking any more questions by overwhelming him with big words and slick vernacular he recalled from Starla's description. "Aquatic birds. More specifically, *birds of water.*" He rattled off the book title she referenced. "Marine birds of the Pacific Coast. A species conducive to the olden Southern California coastline, most namely the exquisite trumpeter's swan." He hoped he had stunted the old man's curiosity.

Keeper's stare was unsettling to Merit, who suddenly felt that the old man might be far more cognizant than he originally thought. It was amazing, he reasoned, what a person could learn from talking to people . . . "out in the field," as his father might have put it.

"Why would you need my goggles and snorkel if they swim on top of the water?"

Merit kept his composure. He didn't want to, but he would have to ad-lib, something he had little to no experience of. "Good question." He cleared his throat. "Their droppings. I'm looking for the trumpeter swan's droppings—their stool. I'm collecting the marine bird's feces from the marsh's floors to analyze them. With biological technology, we can dissect a fowl's fecal matter and by comparing it to another's stool sample, we can learn a lot about its diet, health, sex, ancestry, diseases. Even mating habits."

Keeper appeared relatively satisfied at the explanation and reluctantly pointed to meals in plastic bags and cans, including drinks. "Eat something if you want."

Merit had worked up a huge appetite after the most exhaustive windsurfing trip and his eyes lit up at the offer, when the host plainly said, "Yes."

Merit looked at him confused. "Yes what, sir?"

"Yes, you can borrow my snorkel and goggles." He then looked Merit dead in the eye, "But I'll be watching you—bird poop boy." He bit the head of a raw fish off and threw it on the fire.

41

Over the next several days, countless additional media outlets from around the world swarmed to the course. They set up camps in tents, trailers, on hotel balconies, rooftops, in picnic areas, anywhere they could finagle a piece of real estate. It was a circus. Primetime TV anchors aired nightly news from the site and broadcasted Soldier's investigation coverage twenty-four hours a day. The media received daily briefings from the department's homicide lieutenant. The most urgent question of the media, the public, and the U.S. President, "Was the shooting an act of terrorism?" Homeland Security reported, "they had zero intelligence to suggest the killer had foreign or domestic terrorist ties." Reporters peppered the detective lieutenant, "Was the shooter a spectator? —Were there more than one?"— "What kind of gun was used?" The public was still in a state of shock and didn't know what to believe.
—Elisha Blank, *WLS.com/Updated June 21,10:04 AM ET*

RITE OF BAPTISM

Merit awoke early the following morning after arriving on the island. He'd slept on a green blowup kid's raft the old man salvaged along the coast and used a plastic tarp as a blanket to keep warm. Tying makeshift bandages around his blistered feet, Merit waded through several shallow bogs, most of which were only two feet deep. He was traversing the very site where Soldier was shot, and his mind was processing the video footage he'd studied and how it unfolded. He stopped thigh deep and looked around three hundred and sixty degrees.

With all the people in attendance, TV cameras, cell phone cameras and security staff, how did no one see or hear the shooting? He had deduced after the "miracle ball" came to a stop, the crowd's deafening roar could have drowned out the sound of shots, or the gun's muzzle was equipped with a silencer. He figured the hitman likely fired the shot from a substantial distance, using a high-powered rifle, but ruled nothing out— could have been a female. Merit calculated the shot could not have been made from too far, maybe over a mile at best. The tall trees and rising and sloping terrain would have obstructed a clear line of sight for the shooter.

Merit drudged forward.

Given the timing, it became obvious that the gunman's objective was to prevent Soldier from winning. It stood to reason, then, the shooter had to have an unobstructed view of Soldier—or had the information fed by a second party—to know Soldier landed the miracle shot that set him up to putt for the inevitable win. Had Soldier's fairway shot landed in the row of hedges, clearly making him out of contention, he wouldn't have been shot and killed.

Wearing a set of Keeper's goggles and gripping the snorkel uncomfortably between his teeth, he poked only his facemask into the murky water again and again, searching for landmarks that he'd seen on the footage obtained from the evidence building. The holes of many golf courses had wooden plaques on each tee describing the hole and giving its distance, but he didn't see any of the eighteen markers. The wooden signs would have rotted by now from the seawater.

Instead, he saw nothing but mud and seaweed.

In deeper pools, where visibility was better, he saw colorful coral reefs, their intricate patterns spreading out several yards in irregular shapes as small fish fed on the bacteria produced by the underwater habitats.

Merit took a break every half hour since the sun was rising higher in the sky, and it was getting warmer. He noticed Keeper in an adjacent lake as he relentlessly dove for his precious pearls. He grasped what looked like the face of a nine iron to claw at the muddy bottom and scoop up whatever treasure he found. He could hold his breath for over four minutes, an impressive feat, Merit noted, for a man of approximately seventy-five.

It was mid-afternoon when Merit stood erect in a pond that was waist-deep and noticed that Keeper was sitting on a rock next to the pool, motioning for him to come over and talk.

"Open your mouth," Keeper said.

"Huh?"

"You heard me." Keeper demonstrated by opening his mouth.

Merit complied, opening his mouth, baring his teeth, and sticking out his tongue.

"Now pull the pockets out of your shorts." Keeper said next.

Merit tugged on his wet pockets until they were inside out.

"Now drop your trousers."

"Nope. Not unless you want a knee in your mouth."

"Do it—drop your shorts." He flourished a broken club in his hand.

Merit again obeyed Keeper's bizarre request, grabbing and lifting his genitals.

"Okay," the old man said. "Just making sure you're not holding out on me."

The detective finally understood that the sole resident of the island was concerned that Merit had been concealing golf balls and hiked his shorts back up, snapping them shut. Keeper was like old-time cops Merit had heard about, patting down perps while looking for hidden dope.

"Did you find the bird poop you were looking for?" He smiled insincerely.

"No. Not yet."

Keeper laughed unexpectedly. "You're not going to find *anything* unless you learn to swim. You need to go underwater all the way. Most ponds are too dark to explore unless you put your face right next to the bottom, plus there are a lot of deep lakes around here."

"No thanks." Merit crossed his palms back and forth.

"I'll teach you." He dove off the rock into the water and disappeared before he resurfaced unexpectedly, like a mythical mermaid, on a rock behind Merit's back. "The faster you find what you're looking for, the faster you leave my island."

Merit thought of the arduous journey he'd made thus far and the obstacles he'd encountered – a dust storm, adolescents shooting oranges at him, vigilantes, belligerent crowds, chases through the streets, branding, and shark attacks. If he didn't find some landmarks soon, he would have wasted his time and endured a lot of pain for nothing. He supposed he could learn to swim if it were absolutely necessary—and it was. "Let's do it."

Keeper moved next to Merit and dunked a plastic bucket into the lake filling it to the brim. "This is how my dad taught me as a little kid." He took a deep breath and dipped his face into the pail of swamp water, blowing bubbles to the side as he slowly let the air out of his lungs. "Okay. You do it."

Merit looked uneasily from Keeper to the bucket of water. He followed suit, but only for a few seconds.

"Longer." Keeper was a tough teacher.

Merit held his breath underwater, as if bobbing for apples, for ten long seconds,

"Now take three deep breaths and see if you can make it for thirty seconds."

Merit did as he was told. Half a minute later, he lifted his head, wheezing for breath.

"See Bird-Boy, you didn't drown. Now let's try it in the lake. Go under and kick your legs behind you. Spread your arms out and then move them again and again like you're scooping away dirt on a hill."

Merit went under and made a circle in the pond but came up coughing.

"You opened your mouth, dummy—you panicked. Try it again."

After several more attempts, Merit was getting the hang of it.

"What did you do to your neck?"

Merit had forgotten about the PP brand—He reached his hand back, it was still attached, the fresh bandage Starla reapplied with extra tape the day before he left. "I cut it. On a shelf." He told himself to check several times a day to make sure it was attached.

Merit then went to a nearby lake that was ten yards deep in spots and dove to the bottom. He felt fish brush past his body but surfaced spastically after seeing a large oval creature with a shell.

"It's a sea turtle," Keeper laughed. "Gentle as a lamb."

Merit continued diving, and over the course of several hours, for the first time he saw objects that he'd been looking for. He saw the remains of a parking lot, a long section of a chain-link fence that surrounded the entire course, and the remains of the clubhouse, which was covered in green slime. On subsequent dives, he saw the cast-iron drinking fountain and famous *Whales Breach Rock* that aided Soldier with two lucky bounces on his last hit off the fairway.

He was getting his bearings for the layout of the course. He also noticed thousands of divots around and on the 18th green and realized that these were spots where Keeper had been digging for his *magic* pearls. He was excited, feeling as if he were exploring a sunken shipwreck, similar to the rush he got from steering the drone camera from the homiscope into a crime scene, but this was real life.

★★★

Weary, Merit rose and hiked back to Keeper's campsite. It was late evening, and the guardian of the island roasted beheaded halibut over a fire. The detective pulled a few mud balls from his pocket that he'd stumbled on during his search and tossed them in Keeper's direction.

Keeper picked them up excitedly, rinsed them off, and examined each one carefully as if he were interested in the brand of each ball. Merit was still puzzled at the old man's fascination with such ordinary objects, but he'd concluded that his host wasn't crazy. Eccentric, perhaps, but not crazy.

Merit realized how much he missed real, juicy red meat, but devoured the flakey, charred white fish eagerly, as a welcomed change in diet from Starla's bland veggie dishes. "I'm looking for a large lake that once had a big water fountain in it."

Keeper looked up, his eyes wide. "What do you want there?"

"It's where I believe these swans congregated many years ago."

"You should stay out of that lake. There's something down there." Keeper sounded like a teen camp counselor huddled around a fire at night, telling ghost stories and trying to scare little kids. "When there were big storms, the ocean crested and dumped all kinds of creatures in these waters, and they're trapped. I think they've crossbred over the years. I saw something deep in the fountain lake one time, something I never wanted to see again. Looked like a cross between a giant—" He waved his arms in the air and opened his mouth as wide as he could, but couldn't describe it further, as if he was spooked. "Just stay away from the fountain lake."

The next morning, Merit snuck away from camp, knowing that he had to find the forbidden lake that housed the elegant, golden-colored octagon-shaped water fountain.

42

The media got wind that detectives were pursuing their first good lead. The homicide lieutenant requested the media not release it, so as not to jeopardize the case. A concession stands employee described a Hispanic male in his thirties, just after the shooting, concealing something in a long thin bag, then stuffed it in a garbage bin. The contractor who had hired the worker explained to detectives, that three weeks before the tournament, being short on laborers to erect the chain-link fence, they picked up several temp. workers. He described the strip off Laguna Canyon Road where illegals gathered each morning to get day work. Detectives coordinated with the C.H.P. and set up a sting. Two days later, they snatched the person of interest and snuck him into a substation for an interview. The worker lied about his name, denied being at the site on Sunday. The lead detective insinuated he could be deported and would not see his family if he didn't tell the truth.

—National Press, 1 hour ago

SERPENT'S TONGUE

Merit thought that Keeper was merely trying to frighten him away from diving in the lake with the fountain, with his tale of a sea ghoul, which made him more determined than ever to find it.

He was swimming better and could hold his breath for over a minute. He skimmed along the bottom of a deep lake when he spotted something long sticking up from the mud. Peeling away the algae, he saw that it was a hollow metal rod protruding at a steep angle from a concrete bowl sitting on the bottom. The bowl was encrusted with barnacles and seashells.

Seeing other metal rods, he knew that he'd located the octagon-shaped fountain and that he was in the lake next to the 16ᵗʰ fairway. With his fingernails, Merit aggressively peeled off the outer layer of moss exposing a patch of one-by-one square inch, sparkly yellow mosaic tiles, set with pale yellow grout lines. The fountain was larger than he imagined from watching the videos, and he knew that he was in the general area where the swans had been swimming when Soldier had been shot. He didn't know what he was looking for, but his gut told him to check it out.

He started to surface to get a new lung-full of air, but something thick wrapped snugly around his right thigh muscle and pulled him down. Twisting his head to the side, Merit saw that the primal creature with a huge head in the shape of a snake and tiny yellow eyes and a long body had seized him. He had intruded the habitat of a giant, white, leopard-spotted moray eel.

By thriving on a steady diet of large waterfowl, the mammoth-sized fish survived for at least fifty years in the lake. Using its powerful twenty-foot-long tail that split at the end like a noose, the repulsive eel would snag the feathered prey from the surface, yank it underwater before devouring them whole.

Merit instantly knew Keeper hadn't made up the story about the lake monster, it was real, but was too late to escape its grip. The metallic-skinned sea serpent wrapped its slithery tail around Merit's upper torso, squeezing his arms against his body as if he were in a straitjacket. It pulled Merit toward the bottom, attempting to shove him into its devilish grinning mouth. Merit saw his right leg being inserted in the grotesque beast's gaping mouth, lined with long, pointed teeth fashioned like icicles that could sever his extremity with one bite. Merit kicked maniacally with the heel of his one free leg at the moray's snout, and with mud, sand and sediment churning, he temporarily prevented it from devouring his limb.

Just before Merit passed out from lack of air, he saw that Keeper was behind the fish from hell, spearing it madly with the spikes of a rod iron rake used to groom sand traps. The water was bloody, indicating that his efforts were being successful in wounding the creature, and it released Merit from its stranglehold and turned its attention to Keeper.

★★★

Merit awoke as Keeper pushed down on his chest. Lying on a flat rock, he turned his body to the side and snorted out water lodged in his nose and throat leaving a stinging salty taste in his mouth and bringing air into his lungs.

Keeper was furious. "I told you to stay out of that lake!"

"What happened?" Merit appeared as if he'd just awakened from a ten-year coma.

"Tell me what the hell you're really doing on this island!"

"I told you. I'm here to do some research. Reproduction is down, the swan population is declining."

Keeper reached behind him, took hold of a lit torch, and brought it to within a foot of the windsurfing board that Merit had dragged up from the rocky coast and shouted, "Give me the real reason you're here or I'll burn your board and sail!"

"Okay, okay!"

"And don't feed me that you're here researching bird-shit, bullshit." He jutted his jaw.

"I'm what you call a private researcher— investigator. On this piece of land decades ago someone was killed on it. Someone's writing a book about it and is paying me to research it. They asked me to keep it a secret till the book's finished and published."

Keeper looked at Merit with doubting eyes, the torch's searing flame perilously close to the sail of the windsurfer board.

"Seriously. A man was killed on this golf course over sixty years ago here. I watched a lot of old videos of it and saw some swans just south of the water fountain. It looked odd."

"There aren't any swans around here. Some other large birds, seagulls or cranes but no swans."

"That's why I'm here." Merit did his best to sound convincing. "Have you ever heard about the murder?"

Keeper looked in his eyes. "Why did somebody want to kill this golfer?"

43

The detained Hispanic temp worker changed his tune and admitted that during his work stint at the site of the U.S. Open, he befriended a guy to set up a drug deal. The transaction was to take place at the course on that crowded Sunday, so no one would notice. He described how he altered the date on his work-pass to gain entry. He claimed he'd bought a golf umbrella, entered a porta-potty, and stowed a small stash of pills and weed inside. When he went to swap the umbrella for money, the riot broke out, he got scared and hid it in a dumpster. The bomb squad removed it and confirmed it held drugs. His story appeared truthful, except for the fact that the umbrella contained over five hundred thousand dollars' worth of cocaine, fentanyl, and heroin. Not the petty amount he claimed. Detectives reneged on their promise and charged him with several drug counts to get his name in the database. The cops neglected to tell the media they cleared him as a person of interest, to keep them off their backs to buy more time.

—Clarence Young, *London Post*

MAGIC PEARLS

Back at camp, Merit approached Keeper hesitantly. "Earlier you asked why someone wanted to kill this golfer. I don't know. I'm not paid to find out why, I'm only paid to help find out who."

Keeper wasn't sold. "You're not telling me the whole truth."

"Yes, I am. I told you I'm looking for something related to the swans that were swimming in the lake with the water fountain when this golfer was killed. You know the topography like the back of your hand, and I could really use your help searching underwater. I know that doesn't make much sense, but that's what my instinct tells me to do."

"Do it yourself then."

Merit had another instinct, one he chose to verbalize. "You're not telling me the truth about everything either. You said you're here collecting pearls. But Keeper, come on, I'm not dumb, and I know you're not dumb, and we both know there used to be a golf course under these swamps here a long time ago, right?"

Keeper's expression didn't change.

Merit pressed on. "So, if you were only looking to collect the pearls, I began to wonder why most of the thousands of divots I saw underwater from all your digging were around what used to be the 18th green. And so, I asked myself..." Merit gave a dramatic pause. "... if golfers lose balls all the time in water hazards and in the roughs over the span of an *entire* eighteen-hole course, why aren't there very many holes dug elsewhere? Why so few around the 1st hole, the second hole, third hole? I don't know a lot about golf, but I know that people don't usually lose balls just at the last hole, unless ..."

"Unless what?"

Merit recalled that there was pandemonium on the course after Soldier was shot. People no doubt had unknowingly kicked Soldier's golf ball, which had come to rest on the 18th green, as they ran and screamed. He guessed that somebody—maybe a lot of people—eventually stepped on Soldier's ball and trampled it deep into the turf. He'd read the police detective's report, the FBI report about the missing "miracle ball" and figured Keeper had spent a long time trying to find it. "Unless, of course, you're not looking for pearls," Merit said. "We both know these aren't enchanted waters with magical pearls." Merit picked up a golf ball and rolled it between his fingers. "So, what are you really looking for, Keeper?" He stared him down with a pompous smirk.

Looking defeated, Keeper rubbed his beard. "Yeah, I'm looking for golf balls."

"And that's why you put on the swamp monster act. It usually scares most people off, doesn't it?" Merit had to choose his words carefully so as not to let on that he knew the details of Soldier's killing. "You know all these old balls will only fetch you about a buck apiece, and you aren't even trying to sell them. So, there must be one ball you're looking for that must be very special?"

Keeper reluctantly nodded.

Merit, figuring someone had told Keeper about the prized ball asked, "I bet you know exactly what kind of ball it is. It's why you examine each one of your pearls so carefully. It must be very valuable, worth a lot of money. Hundreds? Thousands? Maybe millions?"

"And some people think it holds some kind of charm, and it will grant them a special wish," Keeper said.

"But you don't believe that, do you Keeper? You're hoping to find it so that you can cash it in and get rich."

Keeper was visibly upset and raised his voice. "No! That's not why. It's important to me. Trust me—I'll know it when I see it."

Merit spoke respectfully, trying to diffuse the tension between the two men. "I believe you, and I hope you find it. To clarify, I'm not here to find it. I'm paid by someone else only to find out who killed this golfer, and I'll give you any ball I find. Okay?"

Keeper cautiously nodded his head.

Merit wandered away, proud that he was able to figure out Keeper's real reason for his daily dives and still not expose he was a cop sent there to investigate Soldier's murder and convince Keeper he was conducting his research for a second party. He didn't want to wake up dead in the morning because Keeper hated Pilgrim Pigs and thought he was sent there to capture him, or to have him tip off the vigilantes of his whereabouts.

Merit had concluded that Keeper was there to get Soldier's ball. The miracle ball, the announcer at the U.S. Open coined it, was a one-of-a-kind golf ball and was probably very collectible, a piece of old America's past as well as Frontier's future. He'd gotten Keeper to admit his purpose. A confession of sorts, more of an admission, his first, and Merit was beginning to feel a little bit more like a real cold case detective.

★★★

Merit dove in the deeper water of the lake the next day, the next, and the next exploring what had been the water hazard next to the 16th fairway. He still wasn't sure what he was looking for, but he couldn't get the images of the swans out of his mind.

He'd found the fountain, but that wasn't enough to move the case forward. He concluded, the week he spent there was all a waste of time since there was nothing to connect the swans and understand their significance to the murder. He returned that afternoon to find Keeper cleaning more of his pearls.

"I'm not making any headway." Merit lowered his head. "There's nothing here of value, and I don't know what to make of the swans I saw in the lake. I think I'm gonna head back tomorrow."

"Are you sure? You're not quitting already?"

"Yeah. It's time to quit. I bet you're happy I'm leaving." He looked up and back over the waterscapes with a look of defeat. "But I gotta get back to Pilgrim."

"Pilgrim?"

Merit had let it slip. He didn't want Keeper to know where he was from, the cat was out of the bag, but he was leaving anyway so it was of little consequence telling him. "It's where I live and where I'll report my findings for the book. Do you know how I can get back there?"

Keeper drew a circle in the dirt with his index finger, outlining a map. "You'll need to get to the city of Las Vegas. From there, you catch a sun-tram to the Pilgrim border. It's an all-day ride."

Keeper returned to his daily routine of cleaning balls, remaining silent.

44

Fifteen days after Soldier Quinn's murder, a reporter for the La Hoya Sentinel stumbled upon the Hispanic worker doing janitorial duties in a dingy bodybuilding gym. The worker exaggerated his encounter with the detectives, and the reporter penned a scathing article exposing the police's threats to deport him. The press was furious they were misled by the Lt. Detective for two weeks. In retaliation, they penned stories laced with innuendoes, such as "What else were the police hiding?" They raised questions about the detective unit possibly 'losing key evidence' even though it was not the case. The national media piled on, hinting that the town's detective's bureau was inexperienced, biased in their mistreatment of the illegal immigrant, and posed a misleading "hypothetical" poll question asking viewers, "If Soldier were white, would investigators work the case harder?"
—Cleveland18>entertainment>Open Highlights

BULLS-EYE

The following morning, Merit finished patching his windsurfing board, which he'd hauled to the campsite. He'd been able to reattach the tail of the board to the front by using a strong adhesive that Keeper made by boiling the resin of local plants. He then wrapped the seam in duct tape until it was as strong as it was before the shark had bitten it.

Merit looked over to Keeper. "So, I guess this is goodbye."

"No more swans, huh Bird-Boy? You wanna try one more day?"

"I tried, but, uh, I didn't find anything."

Keeper stood up, grabbing his goggles, eagerly offering his services to Merit's surprise. "Maybe I can help you find what you're looking for?"

"Nah," Merit realized that Keeper probably wanted him to stay and have him look for balls, plus the pathetic old man was lonely.

Very lonely.

Merit continued, "But I learned how to swim underwater and ate some good fish. Thanks." He dug his hand in his back pocket. "Yeah, and I hope *you* find that ball. Oh, here. I found two more."

Merit softball underhand-pitched the balls to Keeper, who quickly scoured them clean, studied them and determined they were of no value before throwing them into a nearby container. One, however, clipped the canister and bounced back to Merit, who took his own shot and made it dead center of the container.

"Bull's-eye," Keeper said.

Merit smiled, but his attention was drawn to the ball container where he'd made the shot, one that was coated with a thick layer of dried mud. He tilted his head, to figure what the ball hopper that was propped up against a rail, would look like right side up. He crouched down on his hands and knees to inspect the oddly shaped drum with two legs of different lengths more carefully.

"Hold on." Merit contorted his body farther and was practically doing a headstand.

"What?" Keeper looked at him like he was nuts.

Merit dumped all the balls from the canister's deep cavity.

"Stop!" Keeper put his hands out in front. "What are you doing?"

Merit began prying away mud from the receptacle, oblivious to what Keeper was saying. Dried grass was thatched with mud, making the process slow and tedious, so he grabbed a rusty five iron and began chipping away at the dirt with the clubface.

He turned the ball holder over, rinsed it off with warm water from several of Keeper's buckets, and stepped back to look at the shape. It was a large plastic decoy swan, slightly larger than a real swan, but it was crafted perfectly into the shape of the waterfowl. Most of the paint was faded except for some light yellow and blue near the tail feathers and black beak. The neck was elongated at a thirty-degree angle, and its beak was slightly open, and the winged tail protruded at about the same degree in the opposite direction.

"Could it be?" Merit put his hand to his forehead. "When did you find this?"

"I don't remember, a long time ago."

"Where?" Merit raised his voice.

"I dug it out of the mud from somewhere."

"From land or underwater?" Merit pressed for more.

"I think it was underwater." Keeper said.

"Do you know what this is Keeper?" There was optimism in his voice.

"Um, it's a plastic bird decoy that floats on the water to attract other birds."

"Right." He flipped the decoy over, exposing the large hole on the bottom. "But it won't float!" The bottom, where the balls were stored, had an opening through which one's upper body could fit. "Do you get it?"

The body of the swan decoy was half the size of a large beachball, enough to cover Merit from the chest up. He grabbed an intact driver, placed the giant decoy over his head and upper torso and pointed the end of the club's handle toward the swan's winged tail until the grip's tip barely protruded. He then lodged the large wooden head of the driver under his armpit, as if it were the stock of a gun, simulating someone holding a rifle inside the slightly oversized decoy. Merit was essentially facing backward inside the shell of the decoy, aiming the long barrel of a rifle to fire out of the rear of the swan's pointed feathered tail.

"How ingenious!" Merit's voice reverberated from inside the hollow chamber. "This is it, Keeper."

"That's the swan you've been looking for?" Keeper appeared confused.

"The Trumpeter Swan. I didn't know it, but this is it, the twelfth trumpeter swan." Merit was as excited as a child opening the exact gift, he'd wished for on Christmas morning.

"Very clever." Merit removed the decoy over his head, set it down, and looked at Keeper. "There were twelve swans on the lake before the golfer was killed. Three flew away at the sound of the gunshot and resulting noise from the gallery. In all the videos I looked at— hundreds—there were only eight swans left after the rifle was fired. One swan was missing. I figured it flew away, but it didn't, and this was it—a decoy. The killer shot Soldier from inside this plastic swan, dove underwater, and probably left this decoy on the bottom of the lake."

Keeper's mouth hung open in disbelief. "Did you say, Soldier?"

"Yeah. Soldier Quinn."

Keeper's friendly eyes went cold, and it was then that Merit realized he had given up his cover, the real reason he was on the island. In his excitement, he'd forgotten the half-truths he'd told Keeper that it was some random guy playing a round of golf, not Soldier Quinn. He needed to come clean quickly, but not all the way.

"Keeper don't get mad." He raised his hands in a defensive gesture. "My employer—my boss is writing a book about the murder of a golfer, but not just any golfer. He was a famous golfer killed on this course over sixty years ago. The research led us to watch video footage of the murder, which showed swans in the lakes. That's who's ball you've been looking for. Soldier Quinn. You've heard of him?"

Keeper held his stare. "What did the shooter do next?"

Merit was taken aback by his question, as he figured Keeper was going to go off and rip him further about his deceitfulness, burn his windsurfer board, or worse, but he didn't. Merit tightened his lips and thought for several seconds. "Good question, Keeper. What did the shooter do after he shot him? After sinking this decoy, he most likely swam away, slipped out, and blended into the crowd stampeding away. But he may have left other clues on the bottom of the lake. Maybe he, at some point either ditched the rifle or took it with him, but I want to find out exactly where the shooter positioned himself in reference to the landmarks on the course. To do that, I need to reenact the murder." He blew out a breath then almost begged, "I could really use your help."

Keeper nodded. "I wanna know who killed him too."

"Awesome! Now, this is crucial, Keeper, I need you to remember exactly where you found this." He held the swan up in front, "Which lake? Think hard . . .It's really important."

Keeper focused his eyes on the faded plastic swan while he appeared to rack his brain, sucking on the tip of his thumb. As the answer came to him, a look of terror crossed his face.

45

The accusations against the detective's mistreatment of the migrant worker put the department on its heels. Its spokesperson presented the facts to set the record straight. Unfortunately, that night, a nationally televised special produced a damaging piece, when it drew comparisons between the mostly Caucasian beach town's police investigation of Soldier, to the 1994's L.A.P.D.'s racially charged investigation of another high-profile athlete, O.J. Simpson. The day after the exposé, the police were stripped off the case. The FBI announced it would be leading the investigation. Its rationale—the course's lakes and ponds, by having had provided a natural habitat for California's large water birds such as stork, geese, pelicans, swans, herons, and osprey, constituted a wildlife refuge, and thus as a technicality, under federal authority they had jurisdiction. The public felt a sense of redemption and renewed hope.

—auth. P.D. Peterson *Soldier's Drive*

SWAN DIVE

Merit and Keeper paddled into the dangerous lake that held the submerged large, golden-yellow mosaic-tiled water fountain, Merit on his repaired wind surfboard, minus the sail, and Keeper on an inflatable rubber raft.

Keeper had warned Merit about the dangers of swimming in the deep section of the lake for fear of a second encounter with the ugly eel, but Merit dismissed the risks for the sake of research and suspected Keeper had stabbed the ghostly creature to death anyway. Keeper wasn't so sure but agreed to assist as long as he could stay a safe distance away from the water fountain, which he believed the monster used as his dwelling.

To create a re-enactment of the murder, they improvised by attaching buoys to heavy rocks using nylon cords and dropped them into several of the lakes, marking the 18th tee box, the clubhouse, *Whale's Breach Rock*, the cast-iron drinking fountain, the 18th green pin placement and other pertinent spots on the day Soldier was murdered. Many locations were only several yards deep.

Utilizing his watchband device, Merit calculated the exact place Soldier would have stood on the 18th fairway and had Keeper mark the spot. Keeper stood in water only knee-deep because the terrain was on an upslope. It took them the entire day and into the late afternoon to measure and mark the course so it could be viewed above water.

Merit positioned himself twenty-five yards south of the water fountain and recalled what he knew from watching the videos and reading the police and FBI reports. The 18th hole was from the tee box to the hole, 570 yards long, and Soldier's tee shot had traveled 270 yards since he had 300 yards to go from his lie on the fairway to the cup.

The great distance left to the pin was why his teen caddy had suggested using a driver instead of an iron. As Merit had already learned, Soldier needed an eagle, or two under par, to pass his young North Korean opponent and win the U.S. Open. Soldier, however, hadn't hit the ball true, but he had received help courtesy of the two lucky ricochets, gaining extra yardage and a double redirection.

Merit sighted an imaginary line straight to his left and then, using binoculars that he'd borrowed from Keeper, measured 300 yards from the pin to the place where Soldier would have stood to make the shot. Keeper was still too far to the north.

"Walk south fifty-two steps," Merit yelled through a washed-up rubber traffic cone he substituted as a megaphone to his partner while motioning left with his outstretched hand.

Keeper slogged through the thick mud, each of his strides roughly equaling a yard.

Merit, standing on a submerged, partially inflated inner tube tire for support, placed the swan decoy over his head and shoulders. He positioned the swan's beak to point northwest, in the opposite direction through which he would simulate firing the shot through a small hole beneath the protrusion that simulated tail feathers. He now had a clear line of sight south-east to the fairway and could easily poke the butt of the golf club through the rear of the swan. But Keeper still wasn't in the right place.

Merit lifted his head from under the decoy, and yelled out louder, "Move twelve more steps!" He gestured for Keeper to stop after he'd counted the last step.

Looking quickly at all the buoys, with pieces of torn, colorful cloths tied to the top of sticks as visual markers, Merit saw that he and Keeper were perfectly situated to triangulate the shooting incident— *A crime scene reconstruction.* They were at precisely the same locations where the shooter and Soldier had been on the fateful day when the game of golf had died. Merit was still impressed with the killer's ingenuity and how he'd blended in with nature, but how did he get there without being seen by all the spectators, security, police and cameras?

"Hit it!" Merit waved a red flag as a signal while simultaneously shouting.

"Now?" Keeper cupped his other hand by his mouth to direct the sound.

"Yes, now!" Merit shouted at the top of his lungs. "Swing! Swing now!"

Keeper, using an old fiberglass driver, positioned himself over the imaginary ball and swung, emulating Soldier's fairway drive, and stuck his follow-through, pretending to watch the ball fly through the air.

Merit situated back inside the decoy's cavity, watched with one eye closed as if he were looking through the scope of the rifle. He steadied the site on the left side of Keeper's head, pointer right finger ready to press the trigger. He calculated that the masses of fans standing hundreds deep wouldn't have blocked the long-distance shot angled upwards at twenty-six degrees. It was the ideal location to shoot just over their heads and not be seen. Merit's left hand, which steadied the rifle forestock was shaking uncontrollably as the intensity rose.

Keeper held out his arms in the classic Y pose, Jesus on the cross, used by Soldier after the successful golf shot.

Merit knew that the rifle had been highly accurate and powerful and, with its scope, shooting Soldier from this range—he approximated *150-200* yards, would have been easy for an accomplished marksman.

Keeper was standing exactly where Soldier had been after the ball had landed off the tee.

"Now!" Merit then released a steady stream of air between his lips, to steady his nerves, then smoothly pressed the imaginary trigger with his pointer finger, just as the original sniper had done. Keeper, after choreographing Soldier's final swing, his Jesus pose and gunshot to the head, dropped into the shallow water, his body collapsing on itself just as Soldier's had, his legs folded beneath him.

Merit dove under the surface filled the swan decoy's cavity with water, and let it sink to the bottom since it seemed logical that the shooter had done the same. He held his breath and waited for thirty seconds, the time he estimated the hordes of frightened spectators would have fled past, allowing the sniper to surface and blend in to make his escape. Merit then rose to the surface to make additional calculations, adjustments, and notes.

He saw Keeper walking up to the peak of the slope of the 18th fairway, peering out to sea. He was pointing with his right index finger, but, having surfaced, Merit saw nothing since his position did not afford him the elevation necessary to see what lay far to the east, beyond the island's elevated rocky coastline.

Merit, in all the excitement and with his single-minded focus on the task at hand, had completely forgotten the paralyzing phobia he'd manifested his entire life of submerging his head beneath the water. He adjusted the goggles over his eyes and plunged into the lake many times with no hesitation hoping to find clues, such as the two shell casings ejected by the rifle. He clutched handfuls of dense mud, made fists squeezing the ooze through his fingers, feeling for the ejected casings or any telling items.

Looking through an old expandable telescope he'd discovered washed up along the coast, Keeper was able to identify the visitors to the island immediately. Five bad-ass vigilantes rode windsurfing boards, knees buckling and elbows jerking the boom back and forth as they bounced over choppy waves like skateboarders jumping over railings and concrete ledges on city sidewalks. Their bright blue and green sails were getting closer, and it was only a matter of time before they arrived on his turf. Keeper climbed to a vantage point on rocks several yards higher than the 18th fairway and saw the five vigilantes land their windsurf boards on the island's sandy shore, a quarter mile from where Merit hit aground below the rocky cliffs. He then jogged to the south and mounted the summit of the ridge he'd been standing on and with one eye, looked through his telescope.

The pro-Frontier bandits dismounted, left their boards, and walked about the shore with noticeable swagger, looking back and forth as they appeared to case the island. They wore long blue cutoff jeans and muscle shirts, and each had his individual style of facial growth.

Keeper watched as the tall leader looked at his comrades. The head Vigilante then signaled with a wave of his right hand that they should move forward. In unison, they tugged up their bandanas, tied loosely around their necks, over their noses to disguise their faces and advanced toward the rocks they needed to climb to reach the level part of the island.

Keeper keenly watched their movements, in the past, he'd always ignored their presence.

★ ★ ★

The tall lead vigilante, Vigilante one, suddenly crumpled onto the sandy beach, clutching his thigh and moaning in pain. "Damn! I've been shot!" A round quarter-sized welt instantly appeared.

The fat vigilante went down next, his soft beer belly exposed to the sky, flabby arms outstretched.

His buddy, the tough-talking one with the Mohican-cut hairstyle dove to his side. He called his comrade by name and shook his lifeless shoulders. "He's been shot!" He checked for a pulse on the side of his neck by his windpipe and shook his head. "Rusty's dead."

His dead friend, who looked nothing like his squared-jawed, buffed, broad-shouldered compadres, had taken a direct hit to the right temple, dropping him instantly.

"We're sitting ducks." The leader frantically waved to the others to move. "Take cover!"

The four muscle-bound men scrambled through the sand, diving for protection behind dunes and rocks.

The man with the Mohawk pleaded his case. "We can't leave him, boss."

"Leave the tub of shit! You wanna die too?" The lead vigilante said as he lay behind a tree stump, rubbing his thigh. "Who the hell is firing at us?"

"I can't tell how many," the stockiest of the four Frontier fighters peaked around a boulder. "We're outgunned."

After one projectile exploded at his feet, sending sand into the air like shrapnel, the leader glanced at the strike zone and realized what the enemy was firing. His jaw dropped. "It's a ball." He picked up the white, dimpled ball, perplexed." Somebody's hitting fucking balls at us."

He peered over the rock to look for the threat but ducked down as another ball ricocheted, like a silver pinball against rubber bumpers, *ding-ding-ding,* between an outcropping of rocks near his face. He considered striking back with a spear gun that was slung over his shoulder but rendered it useless since he couldn't see his enemy.

"I'm going to circle around and find whoever did this to Rusty." The brush-cut Vigilante was irate, hyperventilating while wiping snot from his runny nose. "I'm gonna kill those motherfuckers." He seized a rock the size of a softball to use as a weapon and slithered through the dense foliage.

46

The FBI selected thirty-one of their most qualified special agents based in California to investigate the murder of Soldier. They first solicited surrounding counties' police academy classes and bussed hundreds of cadets to the site. The recruits executed daily exhausting spiral and grid searches over the expansive eighty-five-acre property. They recovered batteries, phones, wallets, coins, credit cards, shoes, lighters, jewelry, etc. lost by fleeing fans. The items were collected, but in the end, had no evidentiary value. Ballistic experts believed the second projectile fired fragmented upon impact after being discharged from a high-powered rifle, and the shooter pocketed the two casings before he escaped. After several weeks of searching with no luck, they abandoned the recruit conducted searches.

—by Nicole Palmer *Arizona Herald*

PURGATORY

Keeper, armed with a three wood, was cracking highly accurate low flying line drive rocket shots at the intruders. "Fore!" He was getting winded, but still, as fast as he could crack one, he snagged another ball from the bucket, placed it atop a tee, and smoked another, "Get off my island, you assholes." As Keeper had finished his backswing and started to pull the club forward, someone from behind grabbed the throat of the three wood and wretched it wickedly from his hands almost breaking his arms. He turned to see the Mohawk-headed Vigilante with fury in his eyes and slobber coming from his mouth. "Where's the PP?"

"Who?" Keeper stood empty-handed.

"The Pilgrim Pig, you old fart!"

Keeper looked startled. "There *isn't* any Pilgrim Pig around here!"

Before Keeper could finish his sentence, the bulked-up man, gripping the softball-sized rock in his other hand, delivered a roundhouse sucker punch and struck the side of Keeper's head. Keeper fell like a stiff board and landed on his back. Surprisingly, with blood spilling from his ear's cavity, he was still conscious and rolled onto his hands and knees and crawled in circles like a deranged dog.

Below, the other three vigilantes, having recovered from the surprise beach attack, turned over several containers of golf balls and rocked over the scaffolding where Keeper had built his lodging, rendering it a twisted heap of metal rods, and lit the rest of his belongings on fire.

Keeper, spying Merit as he surfaced in the distant pond, gathered enough wits to yell out, "Get away Merit! Hurry!" Merit submerged his body as both the short stocky-built vigilante and the bald-headed vigilante ran down the sloping grade to the lake, although their progress was slow because the sludge water became deeper with each stride they took.

Merit surfaced, using the swan decoy as cover, but he was facing the wrong direction. Meanwhile, the lead Vigilante cocked a spear gun he'd been carrying on his back and aimed it at the heart of the swan, now floating seventy-five yards away.

"Shoot him!"

The Mohawk-headed vigilante's sudden outburst startled the leader's concentration. He flinched as he pulled the trigger of his long, slender bow, sending the spear zinging fifty feet over his intended target. "Shut up!" He reacted, stomping one foot.

Merit ducked under the water just as the arrow sprang from the bow. Keeper blew out a quick sigh of relief, but it wasn't over. He watched as Merit pulled the decoy underwater as Vigilante Four, the shiny-headed bald one, sprinted along the shore of the lake to the spot where the fake plastic bird had suddenly disappeared.

A minute later, Merit surfaced inside the decoy to watch Vigilante four unsheathe a long-bladed knife strapped to his leg and dive in after him. Seeing his pursuer swimming freestyle in a line towards him, Merit sucked in a big breath of oxygen and kicked his feet to dive deeper. He regretted letting go of the decoy since it was his sole piece of physical evidence, but if he wanted to live, he needed to have both hands free to fight back if necessary. After only a few frog kicks, a belt loop on the back of Merit's shorts got snagged on a rusty lever attached to a round metal plate, hidden under a coating of algae. He tugged at his pants frantically trying to rip them free, but he was stuck.

The bald vigilante advanced underwater rapidly and was about to strike Merit with his blade, his arm upraised as his hand firmly clutched the dagger, but he was suddenly jolted backward. The demonic-looking sea beast drew him close to its body, its yawning mouth endowed with long pointed, glass-like shards of teeth, ready to clamp down like a giant paper cutter.

The water grew cloudy with blood, but Merit was able to see that the creature had cleanly severed both the vigilante's arms and legs. The limbless torso of the chrome-domed gangster, unable to swim, eyes screaming in a state of horror and mouth bubbling sunk to the bottom like a dud torpedo, the giant eel descending to gorge on the meaty part of his catch.

Recoiling, Merit flailed with all his might to free himself from the rod, figuring he was the second-course meal. In doing so, he somehow forced the lever to the right, and the heavy circular-shaped cover it was attached to slid down clockwise, exposing an open hatch in the wall of the pond.

Merit, his pants freed from ensnarement, and considering that this might very well have been how the killer escaped, squirmed through the narrow drainage aperture. His lungs were ready to burst, but he frantically swam parallel through the pipe, which widened ten yards farther on until he found that the top of the conduit had a few inches of air running its length. He greedily gulped stale air and swam forward again, hoping he would find another exit.

He'd only gone twenty yards in the dark water when he bumped into something slick and large. Was it another creature or eel? A dead seal? He pushed the soggy mass before him hard. With several tremendous rams of his shoulder, the object budged, and both he and whatever he'd run into surged ahead on the slow current of water emptying from the lake. Hunched over at the waist, he spelunked to a junction ahead where he could stand erect as water flowed past his waist, giving him time to rest his spent muscles.

Looking up, he saw blue sky beyond the end of a pipe, which was as wide as a silo, but the cement curved sides were smooth and slimy, and he knew he wouldn't be able to scale the massive structure. Besides, he heard a distant roar and knew that the tide was coming in and would soon pour into the wide intake grate he was looking through, flooding the underground drainage system.

Standing in waist-deep water, he looked at the lumpy black blob he'd encountered—bumping against his hip—and after a double-take made out it was a human inside a black wetsuit. He looked at it for several long seconds then squeamishly rolled the heavy figure over, apprehensive, and yet at the same time excited to learn its identity through the face mask. Was it possible that he was looking at Soldier's killer, who had tried to escape through the underground pipes before becoming trapped? The glass had fogged up and wiping it with his hand didn't help.

It would explain why no one had been able to find the killer for decades. His heart raced, as he saw a diver's watch around the left wrist of the dead man and looked closely at its date, frozen in time. The glass over the watch face was cracked, and the hands above the dial were broken, indicating that the watch had been damaged, causing its internal chronometer to stop on the date displayed. It read November 12, 2026, five months after Soldier's murder, but the *very year* of the last U.S. Open. It couldn't have been a coincidence. Either rushing water slapped the dead man's wrist against the pipe smashing the watch, or a hard object swirling past struck it. It all made too much sense. There were no other plausible explanations for all of the elements to have come together. Merit came to the obvious conclusion, he had stumbled onto Soldier's killer and solved the case. But would anyone ever know it? He was now trapped.

Merit grabbed the flaccid frogman and tugged the heavy load forward as the ground below his feet shook for several seconds. He knew from the videos he'd watched on the history of the area, as well as Starla's talk of earthquakes, that it was a tremor from the tectonic plates beneath what used to be called Southern California.

He looked about hurriedly, wondering if the pipe he was in would be crushed or inundated with water. Bolts and pieces of rust fell about his head. Should he go back and resurface in the lake near the sixteenth fairway where the remaining vigilantes could be waiting or go forward into the direction of the unknown?

The tremor grew with intensity, and Merit clutched the frogman as tightly as Keeper held his sack of pearls. He looked at the sky again and saw that water was spilling down the sides of the intake pipe. A roar sounded in his ears, the sound of rocks grinding together and metal pipes bending and breaking. Suddenly, the blue sky vanished as seawater flooded the underground drainage system.

Merit sucked in one last lungful of air and hoped that an exit point lay ahead. He would let the water carry him forward and hope that the end wasn't far away. Torrents poured down from above, flushing Merit and the scuba man along as if he were on a ride at a water park.

Merit wrapped his arms and legs around the frogman's body, knowing that if he let go of the black wetsuit form that he would have nothing to show for his work, he'd already surrendered the decoy. He body-surfed for several hundred yards or so in the pitch dark, picking up speed as he was tossed violently from side to side against the cast iron pipe. A minute later, without warning he was ejected out from a hole in the side of a high cliff with the pressure of a fireman's hose, the water sending his listless frame hurtling through the air.

47

Three months after Soldier's murder, the FBI requested that anyone who had attended the U.S. Open submit their cell phone footage. It was discouraging to the public's expectations to realize they had no leads. The FBI hoped an onlooker may have inadvertently filmed the shooter at, in, or around the town, airports, restaurants, and bus stations during, prior to, or after the week-long event. Most spectators participated. While FBI agents studied countless hours of received cell video, other agents reviewed Soldier's phone records, bank statements, social media accounts, internet searches, credit card receipts and airline travel. Agents across the country gave interviews, executed search warrants, conducted knock and talks, administered polygraphs, coordinated phone wiretaps and ran surveillance scouring for any red flags, but didn't find one.

—www.NYNYpost.com

BAG OF BONES

Merit had landed from his wild water ride onto a lush bed of green grass and foliage. Gurgling up green seawater, Merit stirred from a state of semi-consciousness to find he was in a place of great beauty, soft light, and warmth. He was surrounded by colorful flowers, bushes, and the singing of brightly colored songbirds and flittering butterflies. Had he died? Was he in paradise, the one he'd read about so many times in the Bible?

Propping himself up, he saw an exposed pipe extending from a cliff towering one hundred feet above him. He figured he came out of it and landed on the sloped dune and rolled to the base of a tiny, dormant volcanic island located on the back-west side of the one on which

Keeper lived. Over several hundred yards of ocean water now separated the two islands, but after traveling through the pipe, he knew the long pipe ran under the sea connecting the two islands, and surmised many years ago, before the quakes, it was one piece of land.

He quickly reasoned that the exposed pipe was connected to the water hazard of the 16th hole and that the diver had accessed the lake by entering the pipe that was thirty yards above him from the ocean shore. When the shooter had retreated, he could have gotten trapped at any number of junctures, the oxygen in his tank running out, then preserved in a time capsule. And, at any point over the past sixty years, his sniper rifle would have traveled through the pipes and been tossed around in the open sea until it and had recently been unearthed by little kids digging sandcastles on some beach.

Merit panicked. Where was the frogman? He'd come to Frontier to solve the murder, and now the dead body in the diving suit was missing.

He army-crawled using his elbows and looked for the remains of the killer that he'd have to bring back to Pilgrim so an identification could be made based on the bones and dental records. He looked through low-lying bushes, tearing away vines and tropical flowers to see if the diver was beneath them. Retracing his steps, he breathed a sigh of relief when he saw the black wetsuit, rolled almost into a ball tucked under green foliage.

Merit knew that he couldn't bring the two-hundred-pound corpse all the way to Pilgrim, so he decided he would have to examine the body to assess how best to transport what was left of the murderer. Indeed, he wouldn't even be able to make it back to the mainland with such a cumbersome load, and even if he could, he would certainly arouse suspicion carrying around a rotten body. Who *was* this killer? He was about to find out what millions of people had wondered about for the past sixty years.

Kneeling, he unsnapped the corroded knife from the sheath attached to the frogman's belt and gingerly sawed the straps that held the oxygen tank and mask. After carefully removing the rubber from the shooter's skull, he made an incision from below the chin to the groin. As a boy, Merit gutted a Green Sunfish he caught in a pond with a pocketknife and as a detective from the homiscope watched the medical examiner perform autopsies, but now he was about to do one of his own.

He peeled the rubber back carefully, anticipating that he'd have to make the suit into a satchel that would hold the remains before him. He then made an incision in the flesh—what was left of it—and turned away, gagging from the putrid odor, and filleted the torso. Taking a deep breath and holding it, he scooped out the squishy viscera with his hand that mostly consisted of dark slippery muck and green slime.

The internal organs had decayed long ago. Mostly the skeleton now remained, and he pulled on the bones—they separated easily—and washed them off in a clear pool in the middle of the vegetation. Having stacked them neatly, like kindling wood, he searched the nearby trees and found a thin, tough vine curling around the tender bark of a spry valley oak tree. He cut a length of the vine and took the wide portions of the wet suit and, using the knife to make holes in them, stitched together what became a black bag. When the bones had sun and air-dried, he carefully arranged them in the sack and sewed it shut.

He slung the black sack containing bones and the skull over his shoulder and hiked up a forty-five-degree sand dune slope until he reached the rim of the tiny island. Merit hustled down the coast until he saw a windsurfer's board with a blue and green sail. It obviously belonged to one of the vigilantes—the tremor had caused it to drift from U.S. Open Island—and picking it up, he apprehensively waded into the choppy surf.

He debated returning to the island to inform Keeper of his huge find but reasoned the vigilantes were after him, not Keeper. They meant business, and he needed to haul ass back to Pilgrim before they caught up to him. His eyes scanned the surface for sightings of the great white's calling card, and when the coast looked clear he nervously straddled the buoyant board and paddled out over the smaller late afternoon waves and headed northeast towards land.

He picked up the speed, with the warm sun setting behind him, soon he would run out of daylight and the temperature would drop.

48

The FBI suffered a credibility crisis when a secretly filmed cell phone video surfaced, captured by a pizza delivery driver. The clip showed four white FBI agents putting on a green. One agent copied Soldier's last miraculous drive. Imitating his Jesus pose, he pretended to take a bullet to the head, then in slow motion collapsed like a puppet. They laughed hysterically, exchanged high fives. An FBI supervisor justified his agents' actions as a technique used to "relieve stress on an intense investigation," but the public didn't buy it. The U.S. President was infuriated. Citizens felt betrayed by law enforcement again. Some media outlets cited an anonymous source's claim that the FBI knew the shooter but were afraid to release his identity because of his suspected ties to law enforcement. "Who else would have access to the course with a gun and go undetected?"

—twitter@hashtag>chicagopolitics

HOLD YOUR HORSES

After catching the electric rail from old L.A., Merit boarded a solar-powered tram that departed the Las Vegas terminal and floated across the salt flats of what had once been the state of Nevada. As it slowly picked up speed, the triangular, flat ship resembled a stingray gracefully skimming the ocean's bottom. Its streamlined exterior, formed of ultra-lightweight aluminum, was only six feet in height and had a narrow center aisle. On either side of which was a series of three horizontal berths stacked one on top of another, each no larger than a coffin. The sun-tram could sleep eighteen people—nine on each side as it levitated inches above the desert floor's rising hot air.

He felt a sense of satisfaction that he had accomplished what many before him—the police, the FBI, the Major Inquiry, Detective Darrins and even his father—had failed to do, namely solve the greatest cold case of all time.

After leaving the U.S. Open Island, he had planned on retrieving Soldier's golf bag he'd left at Starla's place, but after some contemplation, talked himself out of it. He reasoned the bag contained some important items, but he had the killer's skeleton and broken watch, and couldn't take any chances of getting caught.

Well, he had with him *most* of the killer's skeleton. To lighten the load, he kept only one set of leg bones, the femur and humerus, to determine the shooter's height, one arm to include the hand, the skull, and the pelvis bone, which both would be instrumental for the forensic anthropologist in determining the frogman's gender and age.

Merit slept in his cramped cubby for the first thirty minutes of the thirteen-hour trip but woke because his head rested on the uncomfortable pillow of bony cartilage. He looked through the round portal on his left and saw a pack of wild horses running parallel with the ship cruising at a speed he estimated to be thirty-five to forty miles per hour.

The horses were beautiful and reminded Merit of a school of dolphins escorting a schooner through the open ocean. The pack was powerful and elegant, their heads bobbing up and down like racehorses as they ran into the home stretch. They were muscular and kicked up a plume of dust in their wake as they chased the tram, their hooves striking the earth in a steady rhythm for a quarter of a mile.

One caught Merit's attention, a chocolate-colored horse whose eye seemed to be focused on the exact opening from which he peered. Merit was so sure of this almost supernatural gaze that he lifted his head and pressed his nose against the glass to get a better look at his speeding companion. The desert vessel was picking up speed, however, and the captivating pack soon veered northward and headed toward a blue mountain range far in the distance.

He laid the side of his head against the pillow of bones and rested his eyes.

In his dream, Merit was twelve, riding bareback with his father, who glanced over his shoulder as if to urge his son forward. Merit rose to the challenge, spurring his quarter horse and gaining ground as he drew close to his father. He rode hard, not wanting to let his father down. They cantered in formation, like two military jets performing in an aerial show. Suddenly, the dream changed, and Merit was on the more formidable lead horse and twenty-nine years old. As he looked to the rear, he noticed that his father was falling farther and farther behind. Each time Merit looked over his shoulder, his father was older and weaker, motioning with a feeble, outstretched arm for his son to ride ahead. As his father's horse fell hopelessly behind, Merit shifted forward to see they had run out of land. With his eyeless horse galloping blindly out of control at full speed, Merit rode the large thoroughbred off the edge of a cliff, free-falling and consumed by a gray, misty fog.

Merit awakened as he hit the floor with a *thud*, recalling that he was on a tram headed back to Pilgrim. His dad, he remembered, had died, and Merit knew that he was now on the lead horse and had to look ahead so that he wouldn't let his father down. Giving any more thought about the loss of his father and remembering his dad wouldn't be home when he returned fostered feelings he wasn't ready to handle right now.

He made his way to the rear of the coach, where there were public phones, a restroom, and a few feet to stretch. He decided that he had to focus on his future and punched a code into the dial pad below a disposable telephone. He placed a call to Ruth; the reception was poor, and excitedly told her that he'd solved the case and that he would be arriving at the Pilgrim-Frontier border in twelve or so hours.

"I don't care about your cold case." Ruth's voice at first sounded controlled yet stressed. "I have photographs of you and some little blonde slut standing on a cliff, kissing."

Merit was not only caught off guard by Ruth's revelation, but by her crude accusatory tone. He'd never heard that side of her personality and it was ugly; he started to wonder if he knew Ruth as well as he thought, but first, he had to plead his case.

"Kissing? No. No Ruth. I was—I did not kiss that girl. I swear."

"Did you screw her too?" she fumed. "You're just like your dad. I knew you couldn't handle your urges."

Merit was in shock, the hand holding the phone was trembling. How could Ruth possibly have known about him and Starla on the cliff? "No!

I never kissed her. She has sex for money—it's sickening. I could never be with her. I know the way it must look, but I didn't do anything."

The flashing yellow light on the phone indicated that he only had two minutes left before the phone expired.

Merit decided the only way to avoid more conflict and to possibly salvage the relationship was to change the subject. He thought quickly. Out of desperation and being the first thing that popped into his brain that was funny, he told Ruth about was the kooky marsh-monster man, the one who religiously collected golf balls from an underwater course and referred to them as magic pearls.

It worked. Ruth was unable to suppress her anger and laughed at the unusual reference and his clever delivery. Merit was encouraged at her change in tone and to seal the deal, he reiterated what he knew she wanted to hear.

"Remember, Ruth—I told you that when I got home, I would marry you."

"Are you serious, James? Do you really mean it?"

"Yes. And that was an *act* I put on with that girl. I had to do that to get information from her for the investigation. It's crazy here. I realize even more how much we have in common. I want to spend my life with you." As Merit released the words, he felt they sounded robotic and unromantic but hoped she wouldn't pick up on it.

There was a long pause on the other end of the line. "Okay, James. I'll meet you at border station number nine when you—"

The call ended abruptly as Merit's time ran out, but he was relieved that he'd gotten through to Ruth and had convinced her of his sincerity, even though he wasn't completely forthright. His feelings toward Ruth, he was scared to admit, had shifted. He brushed off the slight change as caused by their first time spent apart for so long, fifteen days. He'd committed to her and didn't want to let her down. Following through on one's word was a trait deeply instilled in him, besides his parents, there had been no other persons close to him in his life to test his loyalty. When he returned to Pilgrim, he and Ruth would get back in their routine and he'd feel the way he felt about her before he'd left. He crushed the disposable phone into a ball by making a fist and dropped it in the recycle chute.

He walked back to his horizontal cubby and, looking about him, noticed that the other passengers were neatly dressed and clean-shaven. There were no hippies or people with lurid tattoos. They were folks on their way back to Pilgrim, some possibly returning from visiting a family member or perhaps decided to move out of Frontier—Citizens from both states had the option to move to the other, but most elected to stay put. He was among his own, and by night-time, he'd be among good God-fearing, clean, gun-toting people who went to church and respected the law.

Upon his return, he'd need to file a police report explaining how and why he'd lost his department-issued service firearm, that was policy. And yes, he felt a little bad about fibbing to Ruth. He'd fibbed, deceived, tricked, misled people more in the past two weeks—Starla, Beck, Nami, Keeper, Ruth than he had in his adult life, but that was inconsequential, he had the killer. He'd turned into *Pinocchio,* the naughty wooden boy who lied to get out of trouble and get what he wanted. He touched the tip of his nose to ensure it hadn't grown. Back home, everything would be forgotten, there would be no marijuana tea and no serviles pretending to enforce laws that, in reality, meant nothing—or churches that supplied drugs or kissing girls or stupid *meltings* of guns. Back to where things made sense.

Merit tried to sleep, but his mind was filled with too many thoughts; his wild experiences in Frontier had been a rush of highs and lows. He pulled out the photo of Ruth he kept in a slot of his wallet and studied her features. That was a close one, he thought to himself. As he thought more, he wondered how Ruth obtained a photo of him—and who could have taken the photo of him and Starla on the cliff, baffled him even more. Was he being followed or watched? He'd gotten a taste of his own medicine he conceded to himself, caught in the act on camera, like the criminals he'd prosecuted back in Pilgrim, and he felt violated.

He understood why Ruth was angry at him but didn't appreciate the jab she had made about his father's indiscretions. Reflecting on his time in Frontier, he now understood how even a man he believed as infallible as his father had succumbed to the salacious temptations and had committed adultery on his mother.

He was initially saddened by Ruth's revelation, but quickly came to a place to forgive his dad and had moved on. He was grateful to God and said a quick prayer before returning her photo to his billfold. He'd solved the cold case and most of his life lay before him with Ruth.

★★★

To kill some time and maybe put himself back to sleep, he angled his computer wristband to project a larger image onto the cramped cubby's wall and viewed Soldier play the 12th hole of the U.S. Open.

He'd birdied the eleventh hole, and the crowd had roared to life, cheering the man who they hoped would make a miraculous comeback. He was only four shots back, and it was conceivable that the senior could catch his youthful North Korean opponent. He'd hit a bad tee shot, and his ball had landed in the woods to the left of the fairway.

The voiceover of the TV color commentator explained that golfers in a tournament wrote their initials on their golf balls before each round for just such an instance, a unique mark known only to the golfer and his caddy. It was always possible that an avid fan would drop another ball in a more advantageous spot, giving their favorite player a better lie.

It was working. Merit's eyelids started to get heavy, but the broadcaster's voice echoing "a unique mark known only to the golfer and his caddy" shook him from his drowsiness. He was reminded of how Soldier had put his initials on his golf ball, before the round started, with his teen-caddy looking over his shoulder. His attention now fully engaged, Merit froze the frame and studied it as he thought of what had transpired with Keeper on the island.

Keeper was an old man who said "bull's-eye" when Merit tossed the golf ball into the plastic container, just as some of Soldier's fans had yelled when he made a special shot throughout the rounds. Also, when re-enacting the murder on the 18th fairway, Keeper had collapsed exactly as Soldier had. And most importantly, Keeper said he was looking for a certain ball, and he would know it when he saw it—How would *he* know it if he saw it? Then it hit him—*Hold on a sec.* Keeper was seventy-five years old, and the murder occurred sixty years earlier, making Keeper at the time…Merit did the subtraction in his head… about fifteen years old. Keeper knew how Soldier had collapsed to the ground, and how he could tell it was the special ball if he'd found it— because he was there!

Soldier's fifteen-year-old caddy had been Keeper!

But why hadn't Keeper told him the truth—that he'd been right next to Soldier when the crime had been committed? Surely, he knew more than he was letting on. Way more. Merit had a sick feeling lodged in his throat. Something didn't add up. What else was Keeper hiding about the murder? Merit rolled onto his stomach, propped up on his elbows, his hands under his chin.

Merit didn't want to return to Pilgrim claiming to have solved the famous murder without understanding Keeper's real involvement, and on the flip side, he surely didn't want to return to Frontier and risk losing everything he'd gotten. He'd never second-guessed himself before at home, but there would always be unanswered questions, and if he didn't go back immediately, he knew he would probably never be able to locate that . . . *master fabricator* . . . again.

He had been *played*. He had been played a fool. Merit's heart beat faster, and his ego kicked in.

Swinging his legs out, Merit slid out of his cabin with the bag of bones, ducked his head and shuffled sideways down the narrow aisle to the attendant. "I need you to stop the tram," he said to the attendant.

The male steward frowned. "Stop the tram? That's impossible, sir. It has no brakes. It's calibrated to stop at the Pilgrim border by utilizing just the right amount of solar power."

"Then let me off."

"I'm sorry sir, I told you that it can't stop!"

A female hostess slid between them. "You need to return to your assigned bed, sir."

"Then I'll jump." He'd threatened them to get his way, with no intent on following through.

The hostess looked horrified. "We're going too fast! You'll kill yourself!"

The other passengers torqued their heads from their compartments, looking at the man in the stern of the tram who'd disturbed their peace. Two travelers strained their bodies out of their bays and stood in the aisle, looking angrily at Merit.

"Crazy Frontier fool!" one well-dressed man said.

Merit's hair was messy and oily from swimming in salty marsh waters, his face was unshaven, his skin was blistered, and he reeked of dried sweat.

"Let him jump." Another passenger edged toward Merit. "We don't want him in Pilgrim."

Merit looked through a sliver in the horizontal window out at the salt flats. Every second, he was farther away from Keeper, the man who had answers that he desperately needed.

"He's geeking out on drugs!" A mother clutched her infant child closer to her chest.

Merit didn't have time to explain to the passengers who he was and his mission. He dialed the handle that opened the sealed security door at the very rear of the sun ship and stood on an aluminum platform, the wind blowing his hair straight up as the male attendant reached out his hand to pull him back inside the compartment. Merit knew he was about to do something totally illogical, but he felt compelled to return to Capital City.

"Hold on—Don't do it!" The male attendant's shirttail flapped in the wind.

You're not a real detective. Merit couldn't escape the accusation of Detective Hubbard and his pastor preaching the principle, *avoiding the challenge that we most need to tackle, is laziness* echoing in his mind.

The two cabin staffers were inches away from grabbing hold of Merit's hand and pulling him in. As inherently rational as Merit was, he couldn't stop his impulse. Securing the precious carry-on duffle of bones to his chest, he bent to his knees to get as close to the ground to soften his landing and rolled out from the tram like someone parachuting from a Cessna plane. His body bounced like a rag doll across the crusty hardpan as the desert liner sailed out of sight until it was only a dot on the horizon. Then everything went black.

★★★

By late afternoon, the sun had parched one side of Merit's face when he struggled to open his eyes. In the far distance, Merit saw the pack of wild horses standing atop a flat body of moving water. Was it a hallucination? He felt the gentle nudge of a horse's cold nose against his bare shoulder as if it wanted his attention. The pack of horses had been no mirage.

"Hey, fella." Merit patted the chocolate horse's forehead down to its muzzle. "What's your name?"

The horse neighed, as if making a request, then nudged his arm again with its snout.

Merit didn't know how or why, but the horse had an affinity for this stranger in the baked wasteland. Besides a fist-sized abrasion on his shoulder and skinned knees, he withstood the fall from the tram with no major injuries, and he quickly backtracked barefoot across the scorching surface to recover his flip-flops. They'd flown off his feet when he struck the ground.

Then, to gain the horse's trust, Merit strode ten yards ahead for the first two miles of the twenty-mile trek back to Vegas, breaking off bits of his remaining energy bars and dropping them to lure the wild horse closer until he fed him the last two bites by hand. Merit then walked alongside with his right hand resting atop the stallion's high side to acclimate the spirited mammal to human contact. The way the horse was quickly taking to him indicated it hadn't always been wild. Merit's experience raising horses told him it was more likely raised domesticated and at some later time been set free, probably when Frontier deemed owning animals was *wrong*, as Starla had sternly phrased it.

Being in a horse's presence while carrying on a calming dialog, then working up to physical contact, was a technique his father had taught him when breaking in a new horse.

Merit had never ridden a stallion of this stature. His withers exceeded about sixteen hands tall, over six feet high. With no fence posts to assist him up, and after several tries running and leaping that failed comically, Merit on his seventh attempt tried a different method.

Using an angled approach of a high jumper, he skipped several steps gaining speed then leaped as high as he could, and grabbing a handful of mane, he suspended his body against the sturdy stallion's side. Then swinging his lower body back and forth like a pendulum, he kicked his right foot over its croup, slid forward and finally mounted him.

After catching his breath and wiping the dripping sweat from his face, Merit rode west, bareback, the bag of bones cinched to his waist toward the city of Vegas on the horizon.

★★★

He galloped at a conservative pace across the old Nevada desert, the horse's hooves leaving a trail of white dust in the moonlight, like the contrails coming from jet engines as planes streaked across the sky. After riding hard for an hour and a half, with several breaks along the way, they neared the outskirts of the gambling town.

Merit rode through a new subdivision, some houses still under construction, his horse hurtling a fence separating two properties. Merit and the horse charged into the quiet street and rode down its center, approaching a man sitting on his porch steps in his boxers, savoring a hit from his pipe of crack cocaine.

"Hey, get off that animal, you idiot!" The stoner flipped him the middle finger.

Merit looked at him, flashed a peace sign with two fingers as he passed.

The glassy-eyed man rose from his seat and ran into the street about to give chase, but he stopped dead in his tracks, as he heard a thunderous roar to his rear. He turned and saw the rest of the pack charging down the street, their hooves striking the asphalt. Panicking, the addict streaked between two homes and dove into a swimming pool, his metal pipe extinguished.

To circumvent the downtown congestion of the most populated city in Frontier, and to avoid any more confrontations from extremist animal lovers, Merit traveled southeast along the outskirts of the *Sin City*, when he hit the jackpot. An orchard, with a posted sign that read: ADAM'S APPLE GARDEN, was being doused with misty water from a myriad of commercial sprinklers, a man-made oasis of sorts, to harvest apples for a farm winery.

Dawn was breaking when he trotted into a meadow, dismounted, and the beloved animal fed on green apples and rested. The pack of horses had followed and drunk from the runoff water before their lips plucked tart-tasting apples off low branches and chomped them down.

Merit stroked the horse's neck, moving his hand down the flow of his silky brown hair. "It's time to say goodbye." He patted the chivalrous mammal several more times and pressed his body against the horse's flank, turning him back east in the direction they had come.

Merit slapped the horse's rump, "Yah!' and it rejoined the pack which, as if on cue, trotted back into the arid desert.

49

The tension grew each month when no new information appeared in the Soldier murder case. After a six-month investigation, the FBI stated they would release their findings. A week prior, the FBI director warned the PGA president they had no leads but would continue investigating with a scaled-back staff and slashed resources. The PGA chairman, to head off a public backlash, scrambled to come up with a new idea before all hell broke loose. To take the sting out of the FBI's statement, the PGA gave notice they were creating an independent counsel, spearheaded by highly respected ex-Olympic President Pratt, to investigate Soldier's murder and it was to be funded by the PGA. Unknown if the suspect or suspects were domestic or foreign was the primary rationale behind the choice of Pratt, he had deep international ties; in addition, was previously a state attorney, a taskmaster and enforced the importance of equality in the games. The public's reaction was overwhelmingly positive.

—Andrew Downs, *Newstracker.net 1.6k shares*

ADMITTED

Arriving back in Frontier's Capital City, with assistance from a variety of snail-paced, non-fossil-fueled modes of transportation, Merit headed southwest to Hacienda Heights, where Keeper had mentioned in one of their campfire conversations that he'd maintained an apartment, apartment number *seventy-two*. It was an easy number for Merit to remember; he learned that 72 was the cumulative number of holes played in the four rounds of a golf tournament. When no one answered the knock on his door, a nosey neighbor who lived in an adjoining unit told him she'd heard that Keeper was admitted into a hospital.

215

After quizzing Merit about his purpose for inquiring, she boasted other rumors she'd heard about Keeper from fellow renters.

She said some tenants kept tabs on Keeper after becoming worried about his quirky obsession they referred to as his *Easter egg hunting*, as well as his safety traversing to that *scary* island. One occupant told her that Keeper had been transported into a medical clinic in Diamond Bar, a community located twelve miles south, but didn't know why. When the blabber-mouth lady started to give some *dirt* on some woman who lived three doors down, Meri cut her off — '*Thanks*', but he had to go.

As Merit headed south, he started thinking it possible that the old man's encounter with the vigilantes had not turned out well, but he still felt the need to confront Keeper and ask him why he'd withheld crucial information on Soldier's murder. Keeper was an actual eyewitness to the most famous murder of all time—quite possibly the only living one—and he'd known that Merit was investigating the murder that entire time they were on the island. Merit couldn't let it go—couldn't wait to lay into him.

What was Keeper hiding? It wasn't how he'd solved murders in the homiscope, but Merit decided to let his mind roam. Was it possible that, as a teen caddy, Keeper was in cahoots with the sniper, perhaps relaying information, giving hand signals, feeding him with updated scores during the final round? How else would the shooter have known that the last ball hit by Soldier had ricocheted twice and landed on the green, placing him in a position to win? Because Keeper was right *there*!

And what had happened to the caddy Soldier used on the first three days of the tournament? Out of the blue on the *last* day, this new young caddy replaced him, and Soldier was killed—It wasn't a coincidence. He'd set him up. It was brilliant. The more Merit thought about it, the more it made sense.

That's why Keeper had been on the secluded island all these years. He wasn't the triggerman, but he was an accomplice and had been on the run for sixty years. What a shrewd place to hide, in plain sight at the crime scene. And Keeper had seen where that 'miracle ball' had landed and knew exactly how valuable it was—and that explained why he was so fixated on finding it.

It was a big piece of the puzzle. He was glad he'd decided to come back; now he could get the full story.

Merit used his thumb and hitchhiked the last two miles to the Diamond Bar Hospital and while riding shotgun in a solar-powered three-wheeler had to listen to the driver who couldn't contain his excitement for the upcoming July Fourth *Acopalypse Day* celebration! It reminded Merit that in twelve days they'd be blowing up the evidence warehouse and how stupid it was to celebrate old Independence Day in such a disrespectful way.

★ ★ ★

The medical facility looked more like a rundown mental institution for the insane than the modern, spotless, hospitals Merit was accustomed to in Pilgrim. From a lost and found wicker bin, he snatched a brown scarf and slipped into the lobby restroom. Inside, he peeled the tattered gauze wrap from his neck and cleaned the area. It had been over two weeks since being seared and there was no pain. To conceal the PP imprint, he ripped the scarf in half and wore it around his collar like a cowboy on the plains.

He was taken to the tenth floor by a pear-shaped body nurse. "My God, this place is gross." Merit pinched his nose shut. "And the smell!" He turned right and left as he followed the nurse down the corridors of the ward to Keeper's room.

"Sir, it's free healthcare." The nurse with shortly cut bangs turned sharply. "You may need it one day. And where did you get all those cuts and bruises?"

"He's okay, right?" Merit said, brushing off her presumptuous remark.

"The doctors said when he was brought in that he was lucky to be alive."

Merit walked faster. Keeper was old and maybe had fallen and broken his hip. But that didn't matter, he reminded himself, Keeper was a conspirator of Soldier's killing.

The nurse continued in a loud monotone voice. "He has internal bleeding of his head."

"What did he do—Fall?"

"I'm not at liberty to divulge that, sir."

"You just told me his condition, but you can't tell me how it happened?" He picked up his pace to catch up in stride with hers.

"A group of intoxicated teens on a party barge found him passed out and shivering on a rocky beach." She read the report on her clipboard as if she were doing him a huge favor. "He was admitted several days ago, sir."

"How though? How'd he get hurt?"

She stopped abruptly. "Excuse me, sir. He has rights. If he wants to tell you himself, that's his prerogative." Her tone remained rude. "His room is at the end and to the left."

"Thank you, ma'am," He offered her a half-assed right-handed salute to his forehead.

Merit had prepared himself to verbally confront Keeper, but with Nurse Witch's injury update, he had to take it down a notch, use a softer approach until he knew his condition.

Merit hesitated at Keeper's doorway and looked at the body lying motionless on a cot high off the ground supported by caster wheels. A dingy white blanket covered the patient, and Keeper's entire head was wrapped with a large bandage like an ancient Egyptian mummy. He rested on his left side, facing away toward the window, which was covered by dusty Venetian blinds.

"Keeper?" Merit spoke so as not to wake him in case he was sleeping.

There was no movement from the patient's bed. Merit tentatively circled to the opposite side of the cot, bracing himself for what he might see.

The face of the former guardian of the U.S. Open Island was badly swollen and bruised.

"Keeper?"

"Who is it?" Keeper slurred his words as if he were intoxicated.

Merit was disturbed by the sight of Keeper's face and wanted to look away. He'd seen thousands of images in the homiscope over the years of gruesomely committed murders – men, women, kids, even babies' bodies that had been shot, cut, stabbed, chopped with an ax, beaten with baseball bats, cooked, hung, decayed . . . but this was different.

This trauma had happened to someone he'd come to know, a kind person, and to see his face swollen to being almost unidentifiable, made him angry.

"It's Merit. From the island. The one looking for the swan. What happened? —Did you fall?"

Keeper barely shook his head and made only a weak grunt.

"Did someone do this to you?" Merit tensed, and quickly recalled his last recollection of his stay on the island before he escaped through the underwater pipe, "Did those vigilantes do it?" He was hoping it wasn't the case. At the time it happened, he was justified in not returning to the golf island, he'd rightly assumed the vigilantes had come for him, not Keeper. Keeper had only warned him to *run*, which wouldn't have warranted them hurting him. Even so, a dose of guilt set off through his system, something he was unaccustomed to feeling.

Merit strained to hear him. "What?"

"How's the novel?" Keeper said.

"Novel?" Merit suspected that Keeper was probably on pain medication and was talking illogically. "What novel?"

Keeper's garbled speech came from the side of his lips. "You said you were researching Soldier's murder *for a book*."

Oh shit, Merit thought, caught in his own web of deceit.

"You lied to me," Keeper's voice got stronger. "You're a cop. A Pilgrim pig."

"Is that why they beat you up? Because they thought you were helping me?" Merit clenched his teeth. "Those motherfuckers."

Merit turned to the window, cracked a blind, and looked outside at the courtyard ten stories down. He himself knew what it was like to be savagely attacked by ruthless vigilantes. Merit felt sorry for the man and started second-guessing his conspirator theory. Why would Keeper have helped him solve the crime by teaching him to swim and reenacting the crime if he was trying to get away with the murder? Merit hadn't thought it out. He'd rushed to judgment.

"I was looking for Soldier's killer." Merit said. "That part was true. And I told you I was from Pilgrim. That was true, too. But there's no book, no novel. I'm a police detective from Pilgrim investigating the murder of Soldier Quinn that took place sixty years ago. I didn't tell you that because people here hate the police from Pilgrim and think we're out to get them. I didn't want you thinking I was after you." Merit cleared his throat, clearly uncomfortable since he'd planned on an angry confrontation with the island hermit. "I admit to it. Okay?"

Keeper didn't respond.

"Let's be real Keeper. You weren't so honest-Abe yourself." Merit waited to see if Keeper would come clean about his real reason for being on the island. "Searching for pearls?"

Each of Keeper's words took effort, and his breathing was labored. "No, I told you, I . . . was looking . . . for golf balls."

"Why did you want Soldier's golf ball?" Merit pushed for more. "It's gotta be the money. Why would a normal grown man be diving in a bunch of nasty lakes for golf balls on a forbidden island? It doesn't make sense. When I came up for air, I saw you on the cliff driving those balls. You got a pretty sweet swing, for someone who said he doesn't know anything about golf."

"I never said that." Keeper offered up in his defense. "I might know a little."

"Well, remember that one time when you referred to the lake as a hazard? That's a golf term for water. How did you know that?" He waved his finger in the air. "And remember when I threw that ball in the bucket and you said 'bull's-eye'? That was the phrase yelled by some of Soldier's crazy fans after he crushed a ball or struck a putt," Merit paused, "Sixty years ago!" Merit paced back and forth as if he were a tough guy detective he'd seen in classic police movies, where officers worked the criminal over in stark, dimly lit rooms with flippant questions, teasing, poking, and prodding to extort a confession.

"I asked if you knew about Soldier's murder, and you said no."

"I didn't say that either. I didn't answer you."

Merit thought back, Keeper hadn't answered him, but he wasn't giving up.

Keeper shifted his head to avoid Merit's intense stare. "Your interrogation methods don't scare me."

Merit continued his verbal assault. "You know more than just a *little* about golf. When we re-enacted the murder after Soldier hit his last shot, how did you know how to hold your arms up like Jesus on the cross? And when Soldier got popped, how did you know exactly how to fall?" Merit paused and put one foot up on a chair as he reflected on his questions. "You also said that you'd recognize that ball you'd been searching for if you found it. How would you be able to do that? Huh?" He turned up the heat even more. "I'll tell you how. Because you were there! You were standing next to him when he placed the identifying mark on the golf ball before the start of the last round."

Keeper's emotionless eyes tracked Merit as he paced back and forth.

"You were his caddy." Merit sounded more like a lawyer giving an emotional closing argument than a cop. "You were fifteen or sixteen years old, and you were his caddy. And you were also right there on the 18th fairway and saw his head get blown to smithereens."

Keeper remained silent for several long seconds, seeming to ponder Merit's accusations. "Okay, Mr. Hot Shot Detective," Keeper said, "You got me. I was his caddy. I saw him get shot." He cleared his throat. "So there, I admitted to it. But if you're so smart, maybe you can tell me now, who shot my father?"

... *my father?*

50

Ex-Olympic President Pratt coined his investigation the "Major Murder Inquiry." He handpicked a diverse, one-hundred-person crew consisting of ex-CIA and ATF Agents, NCAA investigators, ex-Secret Service Agents, ex-counterterrorism personnel, military engineers, Army Ranger snipers, forensic science techs, computer espionage specialists and more. He also hired a firm of ex-NASA engineers, based out of Houston, Texas, "Think-Tank," billed as having the 'smartest people' in the world to assist. The trusted, charismatic ex-president vowed to solve the murder mystery within a year. He promised a transparent, non-prejudicial inquiry with the emphasis not only on finding who committed the crime, but just as importantly the motive.

—Marcus Himmler, Time Now, *2 hours ago*

A BOY'S HERO

Merit stood in Keeper's hospital room, wobbly, looking as if he'd withstood a fifteen-round boxing match. He was the first to speak.

"Soldier Quinn was *your* father? *Soldier Quinn* was *your* father."

He repeated the phrase aloud several ways until he could wrap his brain around the concept. "You, *Keeper*, are the son of the great golfer Soldier Quinn?"

"That's right," Keeper then groaned as he rolled his battered body over on the mattress to face away from Merit. "Soldier was my dad."

Merit maneuvered around the bed and looked at Keeper's bloodshot eyes.

Keeper stared back, and each man knew that he'd been guilty of withholding the complete truth. All the pent-up anger, mistrust, accusations, fear, and frustration that had built up between them since Merit's arrival in the hospital room suddenly vanished, *poof*, like the air from a popped balloon.

Shocked by the revelation, Merit took a step back and slowly sunk in the chair several feet from Keeper, then sat back with his shoulders slumped. He could sense that Keeper was in deep thought and was on the brink of divulging more.

"My parents divorced when I was young. I rarely saw my dad much because he was always away on tour. When I was fifteen, I was playing a junior qualifier tourney—up north of here in San Luis Obispo—when he called and asked me to caddy for him on the last day of the U.S. Open. It was the best call I'd ever got." He paused as a tear streaked down his cheek. "He still thought about me."

There was no doubt in Merit's mind that Keeper was telling him the truth, but he nevertheless needed more answers.

Keeper looked at Merit, clearly wishing to change the topic, and cleared his dry throat before addressing him, "Did the murder re-enactment on the island help you find out anything?"

It dawned on Merit. Once Keeper determined he was on the island to solve Soldier's—his father's murder, he helped him. He'd taught him to swim, fed him, re-constructed the murder, but didn't want his identity exposed. Since Keeper had come clean, Merit figured it was his turn. He started to talk then turned, reached over shut the door, pulled the metal folding chair close to the bed, and spoke in a low voice. "I found him." It felt good deep down to let it out. "I found the person that killed your father."

Keeper had a look of astonishment. "Who was it?"

"I don't know his name, but I got him." He flashed a cocky smile.

Keeper shot him an intense look. "Was he white?"

Merit placed his pointer finger on his lips and looked around him, feeling paranoid about discussing the murder case that was responsible for polarizing the old United States. He tiptoed into the hospital hall and appropriated a stray wheelchair, steered it into the room, and helped Keeper swing his feet over the tall bed and half-walk, half-stumble onto its seat. When Miss Snotty vacated the nurses' station, Merit draped a towel over Keeper's head and pushed the rickety chair to an elevator, and the two men rode down to the main floor.

Merit then wheeled him through the lobby into the rear courtyard of rosebushes, where Keeper could breathe fresh air, feel the warm sun, and speak more freely. Merit, still dumbfounded over the idea that Keeper was not only Soldier's caddy but his son, explained his perilous odyssey through the drainage system of the course and how he'd encountered the remains of the scuba diver.

"Is he white?" Keeper turned his head and looked over his shoulder up at Merit.

Merit shrugged. It was only logical the killer was Caucasian, considering all of the facts he heard from the videos. "I'm sure he was, but I couldn't tell, the corpse was mush." He motioned to the black rubber satchel by his side. "All I have are his bones—they're white, but I'm positive he's the killer. When I take him back, they'll do tests on them and determine who he was in a day."

Keeper gave his visitor a half-smile with a blank stare. "On that Sunday morning, my dad told me that he had something to give to me, although I never got it."

"What do you think it was?"

"I don't know. It was in his golf club bag. He said he'd give it to me after the final round." He sighed.

Merit sat on a concrete bench opposite the wheelchair and looked up at the bleak medical structure, which sorely needed a face-lift. Merit told Keeper about hospitals in Pilgrim, as well as the society and how advanced it was compared to that of Frontiers. He spoke of religion, law and order, respect for rules, sports, music, government, and the clean streets.

Keeper spoke with great difficulty, gasping for breath after every few words. "I think I'd like to visit Pilgrim sometime."

"That's a date— Pencil it in." Merit then tried to lighten the moment. "We'll eat some food. *Real* meat. Red meat. Grilled thick steaks." His mouth salivated at the thought of chewing a piece and could see from the way Keeper licked his lips, he craved the taste of one too. Merit waited before broaching the subject. "What happened after your dad was killed?"

Keeper sighed heavily. "Things were never the same. Things just didn't sit well with me as I got older. Then when they couldn't solve it and gave up investigating, I thought about going back to the crime scene and searching the entire course for clues. Then the earthquakes and tsunamis happened, and most of the course was submerged. A couple of years later, before they got rid of gasoline, at first on weekends, I'd take a motorboat over there and started diving in the lakes and ponds, looking for the ball."

"The *miracle* ball." Merit said.

"Yeah. That's right."

"He wrote something on that ball Keeper, that only *you* would know."

"Before the last round, he used a marker to write—" Keeper's voice cracked.

Merit sensed from Keeper's hesitation to answer, it must be sentimental to him.

"You don't have to tell me what he wrote. I understand. It was personal. It was some sort of connection between the two of you."

There was a long pause before Keeper gathered his composure and spoke. "Thanks." He cleared his throat. "It's okay. I can tell you. First, he always wrote his initials—SQ. Everyone knew that. Then he wrote—" It was hard for him to say the rest, and he got choked up.

"Don't tell me." Merit was insistent. "I don't need to know. It's between you and your dad."

Keeper nodded for twenty long seconds in a state of trance.

"I can see now why you wanted it so badly, Keeper. That's why you've been searching for all these years."

Keeper paused and stared at the ground, having bared his soul to Merit. "That, and I thought that by being there I was somehow protecting the course."

"Protecting it from what?" Merit asked.

"I don't know. I guess I've guarded the course for so many years that I hoped somebody would come along one day and try and *really* solve the case." He lowered his voice. "And you're the first person to ever come to the island to do that."

At that moment, Merit felt a strong kinship with Keeper, and the case took on a whole new meaning to him. A deeper meaning.

The moment, however, was interrupted by a rapid series of annoying taps coming from inside the hospital. They both looked up for the source of the knocking. It was the wide-girthed nurse, the one with the permanent look of pain on her face, rapping her stubby knuckles on the third-floor window. She then strictly tapped her wrist, indicating it was *time* to come in.

Keeper held a straight face. "Your girlfriend's here."

Merit cackled and gave him a friendly punch in his shoulder.

51

The Orange Golf Club, which had hosted the U.S. Open, had been in lockdown for over a year. The grass had grown several feet and was infested with weeds. Pratt's Major Murder Inquiry team had collected turf samples from the grounds, sand from the traps, water from the hazards and analyzed them for clues. Thousands of shoe print casts were made to compare against those of a suspect when one was found. Smart drones, sonar and laser equipment, on loan from the military, scanned for the two casings, the second projectile, and any other leads. Scuba-divers scoured the waters as U.C.L.A. archaeology students excavated hillsides for signs of tunneling, while snipers performed hundreds of long-range test firings. The costs were astronomical and public pressure was mounting. Pratt's promised one-year inquiry stretched on for two and a half. But then, he announced they'd found their suspect.

—François Herbert, *Murder on 18*

KUMQUATS

Having taken a little snooze in his hospital bed, Keeper's eyes fluttered open, causing Merit to lean forward and hold out a glass of juice with a straw. Keeper took a long pull and then spoke in a raspy voice from where they'd left off. "After the Major Murder Inquiry and many times since I asked the Frontier P.D. to reopen the investigation, but they said they didn't work cold cases anymore."

Merit nodded while standing in the stark room to stretch his legs.

"When we were in the courtyard, you mentioned the rifle was found," Keeper said.

"Yeah. That's why I came here to Frontier in the first place. Some kids found the rifle while digging on a beach."

"What beach?"

"The chief wouldn't tell me."

"You have the rifle now?"

"It's gone. That idiot chief melted the murder weapon before I could look at it. It's weird, I don't know why he'd call and said they'd found a rifle and wanted me to come here."

Keeper's eyes opened wide in disbelief as he gasped. "Why would he do that?"

"Cuz he's an idiot. It's crazy. You'd think they'd want to solve the murder of someone as important as your dad is here, but no one has given me any help except for a cop named Beck."

"Is that the female cop?" Keeper asked.

"No. Beck's a guy—definitely a guy. He's a servile from Frontier. The female cop I think you're referring to might have been a Pilgrim detective sent here ten or so years ago."

"Yeah. She was good. I thought she might get to the bottom of it."

"Would you remember what she looked like?" Merit punched in a sequence of characters on the face of his watch computer. Pilgrim P.D.'s headshot stock photo of Detective Darrins wearing her class-A patrol uniform appeared on the watch screen. He angled the watch to project a larger image on the wall for the old man to see.

Keeper adjusted his eyes, then nodded up and down. "Yeah, that was her. Darrins. Detective Darrins. She was asking questions and poking around, then just disappeared. I thought she quit and went home."

"No. She never came back."

"That's terrible. Those vigilantes probably killed her, then disposed of her on my island. That's where they get rid of a lot of their bodies they don't want people to know about."

"What other bodies would they be getting rid of?" Merit's head tilted slightly.

Keeper threw him a scowl as to suggest *that it was a good question.*

"Maybe that's why the island is off-limits to the public." Merit bit his bottom lip.

Keeper bobbed his head. "And that marsh monster gobbles up bodies like candy."

Merit recited *corpus delicti.* "No body, no crime."

★★★

Keeper appeared lost in thought for many silent minutes, a look of sadness claiming his face.

Merit was done pressing for answers and asked him simply, "Do you miss it?"

"The island?" Keeper said.

"No. Golf."

"I think about it sometimes." Keeper peered out the window. "It was fun back then. I played a lot growing up. It was a part of my life that's over. But it was a tough sport to play."

"Tough sport?" Merit scowled and raised one eyebrow. "Didn't look like a sport to me."

Keeper shot up in the cot and looked around the room, spouting directions. "Here, kid detective. Hand me my cane." He then reached in a ceramic bowl stacked with kumquats, miniature round oranges the size of a golf ball and tossed one to Merit. "Now pour out my drinking glass and put it in the corner on its side. We'll see if golf is so easy."

For the next several hours, Keeper leaned over the bed and gave Merit private golf lessons, tips instructing him how to hold the club correctly and stroke the ball. Merit made hundreds of attempts at putting the orange kumquats across the tile floor into the tipped glass as if it were a green's hole. When finished, Keeper also illustrated how to use woods and irons. Merit smacked tightly wadded-up balls of aluminum foil against an 'O' drawn on the wall as a target, foil used to wrap peanut butter sandwiches heisted from the cafeteria.

"Keep your left leg locked and your hips even and facing forward. Now bring the club back but point your knee in slightly. That's it. Left arm straight. Now swing in an easy, smooth motion."

Merit hammered the foiled balls against the wall as Keeper laughed. Merit set up one mock ball after another, not one to lose a challenge.

"You sliced it." He shook his head. "That would have landed fifty yards right of the green."

Merit stayed with Keeper the entire day, and when night came the wounded guardian of the island felt strong enough to stand assisted by a walker in the corner of the room.

"Give it to me."

Merit surrendered the cane to Keeper.

"You're doing it wrong." Keeper held the cane in his hands and stood over a tiny orange to demonstrate the subtle craft of putting when the door swung open.

The thick ankled, no-nonsense nurse stepped inside with her supply of medicines. It was past visiting hours, and Keeper had been instructed to stay off his feet—doctor's orders. She glared at Keeper, who was hunched over his cane to tap a putt. Her hawk-like eyes spotted the mini-oranges clustered near the drinking glass in the corner of the room, and she stared icily at the two men. "Who did this?" The nurse placed her other hand on her hip.

Merit and Keeper looked wide-eyed at each other like two schoolboys caught peeking in the girl's bathroom door. They shrugged and snickered mischievously.

She looked at Merit, "You." She then pointed at the stash of kumquats and aluminum foil balls littered about the floor. "Pick those up right now. Visiting hours were up, and you should have left a long time ago—and you mister," her eyes shifted to Keeper, "get back in that bed. I'm telling your doctor." She about-faced and slammed the door.

When it closed and she was gone, Merit mimicked her by placing his hand on his hip and imitating her high and mighty dialect. "I'm telling your doctor."

They exchanged looks and busted out laughing.

52

On the third-year memorial of Soldier's death, people around the globe tuned into their televisions and devices to hear Pratt name the culprit. Atop the clubhouse steps, his team of experts seated below, he praised Soldier's bravery for pursuing the record in a sport laden with a past of inequality. He ensured that his staff had proof that the suspect committed the killing. He described the dangers this sick individual's twisted thinking posed to society. He then reported the killer's motive as "unequivocally race-hate related." He demanded "...that people all over the world must not allow Soldier's blood, sweat and tears to have gone to waste...We must fight the powers who perpetuated this attitude of hate...where Soldier, was not only on the cusp of breaking golf's most prestigious record but breaking down the long-standing racial barriers that golf itself, had erected before he was executed. Executed, not by the hate in one man's heart, but by privileged, powerful people who promote exclusivity and suppress minorities by cowering behind the pearly white gates and ivy-covered walls in country clubs across America, like this one right here." He demonstratively pointed his finger to the ground!

—Brett Silver, *UK-Newsminute.com*

OBSESSED

Merit stayed for another three days in the dumpy hospital, helping Keeper with his meals and talking with him as he lay in bed when the doctors weren't running tests to assess the extent of his injuries. He was finally able to eat some solid food he got from the cafeteria if a drug-free hamburger patty formed out of mashed avocado and pulverized nuts to give it a brown hue, qualified as a substantial and satisfying meal. The rest time was also beneficial to Merit, a chance to heal his inner thighs, still sore from straddling the girth of the wild stallion several days earlier.

The doctors and nurses, whose abilities Merit didn't trust, were worried about the severe head injury the elderly patient had sustained from the vigilante's attack. At night, when visiting hours were over, Merit hopped on the elevator acting to leave, but doubled back up the stairwell dressed in a pair of dirty scrubs snatched from the laundry room, then slept on a makeshift bed of towels and sheets piled on the floor concealed inside a closet in Keeper's room.

Their relationship continued to grow, as they shared stories about their lives and what was important to them. Keeper described what it was like growing up in the 2010s and 20s as a millennial, sports, social media, politics and more of his life on the island, while Merit explained work back home in the homiscope, his life, childhood, dad, and engagement to Ruth.

Keeper was particularly interested in Pilgrim's take on the environment and what supplied its power. Merit explained his state ran on a combination of natural resources, oil from the south, coal out of the Appalachian region, solar from the southeast, and thousands of turbines placed along the Mississippi River that harnessed its current for hydropower. But the source that generated seventy-five percent of the electricity to Merit's state was the economical, nature-friendly energy of fusion technology.

When Keeper nodded off, which he did frequently, it gave Merit time to plan his next move. He decided he wouldn't make the same mistake twice, this time he'd stay and make sure Keeper was *out of the woods* health-wise before returning home. Ruth might not be so happy about it. Ruth, he visualized her waiting for his arrival at the tram station and the look on her face when he didn't de-board, and it wasn't pretty. After hearing her chew his ass about the photo she had of him and Starla *kissing*— which he really didn't, he figured she was probably extra ticked off. But he had to make a quick choice at the time, proceed home with the bones where she would be waiting or, finish the job, and come back to find out Keeper's role in the murder. So far, his decision was paying off.

Merit got up and strolled the empty halls while mulling over the idea of finding a phone and contacting Ruth. She deserved to know.

He rehearsed what he would say to justify his return to Frontier and line of thinking, but ultimately concluded doing so would only make things worse and circled back to the room. He didn't want to admit it, but his feelings towards Ruth were waning, and it caused an unsettling feeling in his gut.

The night nurse had given Merit updates on Keeper's status. She was a hundred times nicer than the day nurse. Keeper had been upgraded to a stable condition. Due to his age, she explained, his recovery could take weeks, but since he was in exceptional physical condition it could be much quicker. Keeper's face was noticeably better, some of the swelling had receded, especially around the eyes. The rock that struck Keeper could have killed him, and doctors planned on conducting more tests.

Keeper had told him after he was hit, the same Mohawk-headed vigilante stomped his chest fracturing three of his ribs, then lit his home on fire. Hearing the details only ratcheted up Merit's hate for the jerk. To beat *him* up, a police officer from Pilgrim, who'd trespassed on *their* grounds was one thing, but to kick an innocent old man who was a Frontier resident, stirred a sense of rage inside him he'd never experienced.

"I'm glad you found the killer." Keeper had stirred from another catnap. "Or at least his bones. They looked underwater, but I guess nobody ever thought to look in the old pipes used to pump water to the hazards."

"I'll admit, I was a little lucky. And I had your help too." Merit cranked a lever that propped Keeper's cot up to forty-five degrees, then stood and paced, "I'm glad they said you're improving, slowly, but improving and uh," Merit paused, looked away and fiddled with the string that drew the blinds. "I have to go back to Pilgrim pretty soon—and I'm sure our forensics lab will be able to quickly identify the killer. Our technology is advanced. The facilities here in Frontier are crap." Merit looked back. "I wish I didn't have to leave before you were discharged from the hospital but knowing the killer's identity might one day give you closure."

Keeper, who'd been staring at the drab beige tiles on the walls, gazed at Merit and shook his head. "Go ahead. Leave." There was callousness in his voice.

"I Iold on." Merit was confused by his response, "What else do you want me to do Keeper? I found the killer, the very person who gunned down your father in front of your eyes." Merit was worked up. "His bones are in this room right now. So what's bugging you?"

A frown crossed Keeper's face. "I'm more interested in *why* he did it."

Merit's shoulders sagged. "Why? You *know* why! Your dad was a minority and was on the cusp of breaking that white guy's record. The Inquiry proved it. I watched clips of it and read articles. The ex-president of the IOC Pratt and his expert crew determined his murder was *unequivocally* race-hate related—I'm not sure what that word *means* or even how to say it but sounds pretty fucking serious." Merit had gotten tongue-tied pronouncing the word.

Keeper appeared dismissive with the response. "That's what people believed ever since that night. But no suspect was ever found. Come on Merit—think about it. You're a detective. How could they have determined it was race-hate-related if they never found a suspect? That seemed to get lost in his message. You even said that was odd."

Merit was getting frustrated. "No. I said it was *weird* about the chief calling me here to investigate after they found the rifle, which he then proceeded to melt. But his murder was clearly, in all probability, race-related."

Keeper continued passionately. "And for my father's legacy to represent the death of golf and the division of America, both of which he loved, is why I want to know the killer's true motive." He snapped at Merit. "And that's what's really bugging me."

"Why are you mad at me?"

Keeper shook his finger at Merit. "Because all you seem to care about is that you've solved the case and your bag of bones." He turned and looked out the window. "If the killer did it because my father was going to break Vic Jackson's record or because of his race, then there's nothing I can do about it. But I want to know for sure. When I know the *true* reason why he was murdered, then I can have peace. Not because *Pratt's* inquiry said so."

"I wouldn't even begin to know how to discover a sixty-year-old motive." Merit walked over, removed the skull from the bag, held it up, and mockingly questioned its hollow-eyed sockets like a mad man. "Why did you do it, Mister?"

Keeper was angry that Merit was making light of his concerns. "Then why'd you bother to come back here?"

"Why? To find out if you were his caddy and to see if you were hiding anything else."

"Well, you found your answer, Detective. Soldier was my dad. So, goodbye."

Keeper flicked his wrist toward the door as if dismissing the detective.

53

Immediately after Ex-IOC Pratt delivered the findings, many viewers were inspired by his speech but perplexed by his message. He assured his crack squad had found the suspect, collected evidence proving he committed the murder and determined his motivation, but neglected at the time to reveal his actual name. News analysts assumed an arrest was imminent or there was a sealed indictment; other pundits interpreted it to mean the suspect was on the run or dead, while most people were relieved it was over. Out of Pratt's twelve-minute speech, one phrase resonated: "Soldier's murder was unequivocally race-hate related." Fearing a backlash of riots, big-city police departments, small municipalities, sheriff's departments braced for an upheaval, businesses boarded up their windows…

—NRP radioprogramming.org

POINT OF VIEW

Merit left the hospital infirmary room feeling empty, knowing he'd let Keeper down. As he walked through the lobby of the main floor, a female receptionist asked Merit if he was Mr. Hubbard.

"Huh?" Merit was caught off guard, still shaken by the heated exchange with Keeper.

"I have a letter for Dick Hubbard," the woman said.

"That's not me."

"I'm sorry, you looked like the gentleman described."

On second thought, Merit figured that maybe somebody from Pilgrim was trying to communicate with him by using secret code words such as the name of the detective who had virtually dared him to make the trip to solve the cold case—Det. Dick Hubbard.

"Yeah, that's me." He returned to take a sealed envelope. "But . . . uh . . . I'm him, I'm Dick Hubbard. Sorry—I just don't like hospitals."

The letter might contain an urgent message—even a map or diagram. When he looked inside, however, he saw a scrap of paper with a crude sketch of a round homiscope with a drawing of a fuzzy caterpillar with a face on it representing Merit—asleep inside it.

Merit wasn't in the mood and figured it was a practical joke from Hubbard and ripped the note in half and dropped the paper into a trash bin before exiting the hospital.

Merit waited at a transportation station outside the hospital for a shuttle to take him back to the Las Vegas solar tram depot. He looked at a video projected onto the wall from his watchband computer, focusing on the moment when Keeper, a fifteen-year-old caddy at the time, handed his father the driver on the 18th fairway. The glance they exchanged was poignant. When the ball bounced from *Whales Breach Rock* to the concrete base of the drinking fountain— to the ball's final resting place on the green, they exchanged glances again.

Keeper had been proud to be a part of his father's shot, and Soldier had been appreciative of his son, who had shown up to caddy for him and had insisted that he *go for it*. Had Soldier lived, Merit thought it likely that it would have been a defining moment in the relationship.

He then fast-forwarded the video to the moments following the murder and saw the young, traumatized, blood-spattered face of Keeper moving toward his slaughtered father, only to be bowled over by the cops then swept away by the crowd—away from the man who had called him at the last minute and asked him for his help at the U.S. Open.

There was confusion in the teenager's eyes, a loss of innocence that would forever change the course of his life. He now understood why Keeper had journeyed back and forth to the island for almost sixty years. It had become a way to be close to his father and honor his memory. He couldn't let it go. Merit realized for the first time that the old man had lived with pain and loneliness as he searched for the one special golf ball that would connect him with his father in a way that nothing else could. Finding the ball had become his life's calling.

And yet finding the ball would only represent partial fulfillment. What Keeper really wanted to know was *why* someone had pulled the trigger of the rifle, even though the motive had been clearly established long ago.

Merit pondered how he would have reacted if his own father had been killed at an early age. Seeing the person that raised you, fed you, and tucked you in bed at night get his head blown off was too difficult for him to comprehend. At least he'd known his father until age twenty-nine, reconnecting with him in the final years of his life as they rode horses together. Keeper, on the other hand, had just begun the process of re-establishing a bond with his dad, and it had lasted only a day.

For the first time in his nine-year law enforcement career, Merit had gotten to know a victim's family member—Keeper, the son of the murder victim—and something had changed. Keeper had taught him to swim, helped him re-enact the murder, protected him on the island, given him golf lessons, made him laugh and bared his soul.

His transportation was arriving, but before he boarded Merit took several steps back from the hospital and looked up at the tenth-floor window, the way a golfer might back away from his shot and look at the fairway from a different perspective before re-addressing the ball. He had convinced Sergeant Traver's that he'd wanted to solve the cold case crime to *prove something to himself.* Maybe there was something more than just the success of solving a crime? He imagined Keeper, with no family, lying in solitude in his tiny, dreary room, staring out the blinds and the nurse who wasn't kind to him.

When I know the true reason why he was murdered, I can have peace.

★★★

Merit strutted past the nurse's station and into Keeper's room, angling his bed on wheels to face the open window and the moon hanging in the night sky like a silver dollar. Before Keeper could say anything, Merit surrendered the satchel of bones to Keeper.

A smile spread across Keeper's contused face, as he realized that Merit had returned to discover the motive behind his father's murder, entrusting him with the bones of the man that had cut down his father in cold blood. The deep agony in his soul had been transformed into a hope that Merit might bring his lifelong quest for justice to an end.

"Do you think your dad would have made that last twelve-foot putt?"

Keeper looked into Merit's eyes.

A trust in the relationship of the two men having grown deeper in the space of a few seconds, Keeper extended his hand, which Merit grasped in a firm handshake. No words or apologies were needed as Merit exited.

54

. . .Several hours following the inquiries' release, which concluded Soldier was killed because he was a minority, law enforcement and government officials were relieved, America's city streets and social media freeways were surprisingly quiet. Then, at 10 P.M., a single tweeted video was the catalyst that lit a fuse that would ignite the golf world. A shaky, eighteen-second phone video, shot at night, showed an unknown car fishtailing down the center of a nondescript golf course's fairway, back tires ripping up the pristine turf, leaving a dual trail of muddy tracks. The video went viral. Many viewers believed the stunt was a protest of Soldier's murder—and some even made the leap to say that people at the lavish clubs also bore some blame for the killer's actions.

—NPR *radioprogramming.org*

JUNE GLOOM

A motive.

Merit kept murmuring the words *a motive* to himself as he searched for a charged scooter. *Why?* Why did this man—or woman want Soldier dead? That was the question he needed to answer. Where would he even begin? He had no idea, and he was starting to second guess his impulsive decision to accept the challenge, but Keeper had made a valid point. How did the inquiry conclude it was a race-hate-related murder without ever finding a suspect?

Beck had offered Merit his services, but where would he find him?

As Merit scratched his scruffy beard, he recalled his first day in Frontier when the two of them were drinking *hey* tea in a café and Beck shared the name of the condos where he lived in case Merit needed his help in the future. With all the distractions—tan-bodied females with cucumber-shaped breasts and all, Merit had neglected to key it into his watch. But by tinkering with his wrist device, his memory about one of the microcomputer's multi-functions was jogged.

Merit's watch, in fact, all Pilgrim P.D. watchband computers, was programmed to activate at the sound of dialog and record *all* conversations. The pinhead-sized drives could store up to thirty days before recording over themselves. It was a nifty gadget but working murders in the homiscope and having never interviewed someone outside of the h-scope, he never needed to access it, up until then.

Using a series of voice commands requesting dates and times, Merit quickly tracked the conversation he'd had with Beck in the café of lazy cats. He listened intently to Beck's recorded voice – *Santa Monica Cliffside Living* was the name of the condos where Beck said he lived.

As Merit steered the two-wheel scooter through the crowded city streets toward Beck's condos, he recognized he didn't feel nearly as conspicuous as when he first arrived in Frontier twenty-four days earlier. He had no further need for a disguise to look like a citizen of the state since he no longer wore a uniform, and his hair and beard allowed him to blend in with the rest of the population even though he'd washed off Starla's temporary tattoos. When he walked down the street, still wearing one of Starla's boyfriend's shirts, shorts, and flip-flops, he made sure not to stare at any pedestrians. To be on the safe side, however, he wore Soldier's green visor tugged down to keep his facial features in shadow.

Back to a motive. He then remembered an article he'd skimmed, a list of persons of interest the FBI had compiled, that at the time he didn't think was relevant to his investigation. Even though it was overcast, he pulled over to the side and under the shady overhang and showed his computer screen onto a wall, maybe reviewing it would provide a jumpstart to a motive he needed.

The FBI's list of potential suspects had been many: Was it a terrorist who shot the U.S. golfer to strike fear among Americans? Perhaps a jealous competitor or someone in Vic Jackson's camp who smuggled a long gun in a club bag and shot Soldier to prevent him from breaking the record? Maybe a lone wolf to garner attention by killing someone famous. A radical individual or anarchist group to bring awareness to a political cause. Some deranged, mentally ill person, who'd heard voices telling him to do it. A family member to collect on his inheritance or life insurance. A racist group, Ku Klux Klan, white supremacists, skinheads to suppress minorities. A thrill-seeking *sicko* attempting to pull off the perfect murder. Someone in the underworld, mafia, organized crime to score a big, wagered bet. Or perhaps it was as simple as a disgruntled ex-employee, ex-girlfriend, accountant, business manager, or someone with a personal grudge. There was even an off-the-wall conspiracy theory that Soldier had staged his own death.

When he arrived at Beck's condo complex atop the Santa Monica cliffs at dawn the next morning, he stood outside the glass lobby, which was locked, and looked at the list of residents who lived at the address. He pressed the buzzer button next to the name "Becker" written on a panel outside the main entrance. Maybe his real name was Becker but went by Beck.

There was no reply. Stepping back, he looked up at the stubby, putty-colored adobe facade to see if he could see any signs of life. Overhead he noticed the fog was very low and watched it quickly drift inland, skimming the rooftop of the three-story structure. He rubbed his exposed arms and hands together to warm them on this chilly, sunless morning.

He pressed the intercom button adjacent to the doorbell button. "Hey, Becker," he said. "Beck, it's me—the guy you met near the Commons and then took to the property building to get that evidence."

There was no response, and he had the uneasy feeling that he was being watched. He casually turned around to see a figure crossing the wide street, heading straight for him. He assumed it was a vigilante—his face was covered by a toboggan-style ski cap with two holes cut out for his eyes—so he decided that it would be wise to leave the area quickly.

Grabbing a small metal trowel from a large stone flowerpot to use as a weapon, he seized the handlebars of a beach cruiser bike that leaned against the side of the building and pedaled with pace to get away from the stranger. He looked over his shoulder and saw that the vigilante had snatched a cruiser from a bike rack and was giving chase at full speed.

Angling between parked vehicles every few feet, Merit zigzagged from the sidewalk to the street and back to the sidewalk several times.

He then flew to the opposite side of the street, his legs cycling hard, but the vigilante was gaining on him. Moving to the center, Merit saw the beach forty yards straight ahead, but moving to the tract of sand would leave him too exposed. A sudden glance back and Merit saw the chaser was practically on his tail.

Spotting an alley past a line of closed storefronts not far from the beach, Merit prepared to make a sharp right, but the vigilante's front wheel clipped his rear tire, and the two men tumbled forward, their bikes flying end over end, and landed in the cool morning sand. They struggled to their knees and wrestled, Merit swinging the trowel wildly, but the vigilante inexplicably deflected all of Merit's thrusts in a defensive posture. Sand flew through the air like a mini-dust storm, concealing the face of Merit's foe.

"Stop!" said the vigilante.

Merit swung again, not trusting his adversary, his fist barely clipping his chin.

"Merit!" The suspect peeled off his ski mask. "What are you doing?" He put his hands up and leaned back.

With sand covering his face, Merit paused in the middle of his next punch to wipe the grit from his eyes. The man he was fighting wasn't a vigilante after all, it was Servile Beck. Merit collapsed, exhausted and bleeding.

"Why didn't you stop?" Beck was panting, trying to catch his breath.

"I thought you were a vigilante." Merit stood and started brushing off the sand that was stuck to his sweaty skin.

"Yeah, well, I was chasing you because I didn't think I'd be able to find you again. Thought you'd gone back to Pilgrim." Beck brushed the sand off himself. "Then somebody told me you hooked up with some dark-skinned babe, so I figured that you were starting to like it here."

"No, not just yet." Merit was still disenchanted with the idea of living in Frontier.

"Well, you look the part." He nodded in approval of Merit's transformation from when he first met him to his current bohemian appearance, "I wasn't sure it was you."

Merit used his fingers like claws and raked the sand particles from his beard, "And the dark-skinned babe—she's just a girl I met."

"Maybe I'll track her down for myself," Beck said.

"Yeah, do that." Merit changed the subject. He didn't like the thought of Beck and Starla hooking up. "Why didn't you answer when I buzzed your apartment?"

"Cuz I actually live across the street. That's in case vigilantes come after me. Like I said, I'm still employed as a servile, at least for a week until the rehab program in Frontier is complete. I have the intercom hooked up electronically to my second apartment. That way I can keep an eye on who's looking for me. When I saw it could be you, you took off." Beck stood and offered a hand to lift Merit up. "How's the investigation going, my Pilgrim friend?"

"It's going okay." Merit moved to the wrecked bikes and began to untangle the handlebars.

"So you haven't cracked the crime of the century. I told you it was unsolvable."

"Actually," Merit said, "I *did* solve it. I even have the bones of the killer."

Beck squinted his eyes and cocked his head. "That's impossible. I mean, I knew you were good, but I didn't really think the case could be solved. Who was it? Who is it?" They each picked up their beach cruiser bike and lugged them back to the cement boardwalk.

"When I get back to Pilgrim, they'll be able to identify the remains and find out who pulled the trigger, but now I need to know *why* the crime was committed."

Beck shook his head in frustration. "The motive? Everybody knows why. That Inquiry determined that it was unequivocally race-hate related. Somebody that was white didn't want Soldier to break the white golfer's record. And you've got his DNA."

"Yup. I think so, too, but I have a source who thinks otherwise. And he wants me to look into it." Merit downplayed the significance. "I'm just doing him a favor."

"Your source is wrong— Let *me* talk to him. It's a waste of time."

"I agree," Merit twirled his finger around his head, to suggest that his source was a bit crazy. He wanted to protect Keeper from more stress.

"Hey, but if you want some help. Sure, I'll help—I got nothin' else to do." He shrugged.

The two of them walked alongside the bikes down the boardwalk as the sun tried to cut through the thick fog on the last days of *June Gloom*, a term he learned locals used to describe unwanted overcast skies during early summer along the coast. Merit looked up as the heavy fog rolled off the coast and hoped the murder motive was hidden like the sun behind the clouds, and in time would become clearer. Time wasn't on his side, July Fourth was a week away and he needed to make things happen. Seven days to figure the motive seemed impossible. He was pleased that he located Beck, it was a gamble coming back, and Merit felt a sense of comradery being back together.

Merit conveyed how the scuba diver entered the course from an open pipe from under the ocean and surfaced in one of the course's lakes and then how he used the decoy as cover while he shot Soldier with a high-powered rifle before he tried to escape.

"I'd like to know how the shooter could have gained so much information about the underground drainage system," Merit said. "Believe me—it's intricate. I have a map of the course, but I want to see *everything*—the sewer lines, landlines, the drainage, the electrical grid— all of it. A guy doesn't just wake up one day and decide that he's going to crawl a couple of miles through underground pipes, surface in a pond, and whack a famous golfer. He had to have known every inch of that course."

"Golf courses required tons of water a day to make all that grass grow," Beck said. "Some of those pipes could have fed water to different areas of the course to water it. Other pipes could have been used for sewage or stormwater runoffs. We can probably find what you're looking for at the Bureau of Public Records. Nothing is confidential here. Records of criminals aren't available to the public because they might judge them. See what a great place this is?"

Merit ignored answering his leading question and asked his own. "How are we gonna get there?"

55

The morning after the Major Murder Inquiries findings were disseminated, many members arrived at their golf clubs across the nation to find their lawns riddled with deep crisscrossing tire tracks. Law enforcement and government officials hoped the vandal's crime spree was a one-night fling. Social justice warriors justified the destruction stating, "If Soldier can't play, neither can you." Some posted clips of their conquests on social sites spurning others. Angry protestors, instead of staging the typical marches on foot, organized secret vehicle parade raids. Cars, trucks, and ATVs assembled in long single-file lines and for the next thirty nights, set out to attack courses. They programmed "private golf clubs, country clubs, golf resorts, golf lodges" in their GPS's, then convoyed like a long train across suburbia, and tore up golf courses.

—AP Podcast, SportNewsEntertainment

THE 91

Merit and Beck rode their bulky beach cruisers along the concrete beach path and exchanged them for two lightweight racing bikes with razor-thin tires designed for speed and distance. As the two helmeted detectives peddled southeast along the 105 Freeway, which was mostly flat and dry for the twenty-five miles, they made good time by drafting behind each other, like road racers in the Tour de France, to their destination.

"The bureau of records is in the Orange County Bay." Beck pointed up at a faded, green freeway sign as they cruised under an overpass. "We take the 605 south past Fullerton Hills and get on the 91 and go east to the Anaheim Hills islands."

"How long will it take us?" Merit shifted to a lower gear to travel more efficiently.

"It's sixty miles. It'll take a couple of hours to get there, and we gotta beat the tide."

As they got farther along, they rode through water rising one inch deep.

"I may not have timed this very well," Beck said. "Moving forward is going to get rough."

Having to stand up on their bikes peddles to generate more power, they passed hundreds of people, soaking wet, returning from the islands using the force of the tide, which began to cover more and more of the city like an enormous sheet of gray satin. It was the exact opposite of what Merit had seen when he and Starla had watched the ocean receding while standing on the cliff at sunset, with people waiting to set off for the islands.

They pedaled into water that was several inches deep, their quad muscles aching as they pushed the streamlined racers through the rising tide.

"See that?" Beck pointed to the south. "That's the Matterhorn."

Merit looked to his right and noticed an odd-shaped, snowcapped mountain sprouting up from the rising water from the middle of nowhere. On it was roller coaster cars on looping tracks caked with barnacles and seaweed.

"The area over there used to be Disneyland."

Merit could still see some of the rusted rides poking out of the water. He chalked the strange allusion up to one more anomaly in the state of Frontier.

"Half of it will be underwater in a few minutes," Beck said.

"Beck, I can't pedal any longer."

The water was a quarter up to the top of the tires, and they were making little progress.

They abandoned the racing bikes, which were swiftly carried east by the surging water. Beck seemed amused.

They exited the 91 and were wading through waist-high waves when Merit grabbed onto a light post to keep from being swept away by an undercurrent, which was gaining strength.

"I could use some help!" Merit's body was almost horizontal. With each passing second, his grip on the post was slipping, his fingers tenuously wrapped around the slimy concrete pole.

"It's not much farther." Beck secured Merit's arm and dragged him through the current until they reached a spot where the water was calmer.

"Anaheim Hills is made up of twenty little islands, and the records bureau is on top of the first one on the right up ahead. Let's go, push it."

56

Local cops, county sheriffs and state troopers could only pull to the shoulder and watch as processions of cars passed, drivers taunting them in route to go trash the lawns of unsuspecting clubs. Police choppers hovered helplessly above as miles-long parades of vehicles snaked along winding rural back roads to snare their prey. State governors instructed the police to "back down" while others demanded "consequences" for the perpetrators. With no fear of retribution, activists veered farther outside city limits to sabotage clubs in rural areas during the day. Naive members playing a round of golf ran for cover as the motorcades stormed entrances, revved their engines and blared music as they destroyed the luscious turfs. They snatched pin hole flag sticks as trophies and flew the flags out their windows on their way to the next unwary club.

—Marc Warren, *digitalracket&clubmag.com*

DEVIANT SEX

Merit and Beck waded fifty yards against the rising tide, the undercurrent stronger with each step until they were able to crawl up the slick algae-covered concrete overpass that led to the Bureau of Public Records.

Having air-dried off, they stood at the rear of a room on the second floor of the Bureau of Public Records and huddled over large ledgers from the former City of Newport Beach, several miles north of where Orange Golf Club course had been located. The thick files contained maps, grids and zoning permits for the decades 1980 to 2030. Merit had difficulty interpreting the map key and the indices for the books, so Beck ran his finger along the yellowed paper and flipped the 17 x

11 inch-sized, dusty pages over until they found the schematics for the back nine holes of the golf course.

Two young interns continued to drop off folders on the table they believed could help in Merit and Beck's search and collected the stack off the floor that was deemed irrelevant. Merit noted a few visitors browsed through journals and periodicals, a few stood in lines to request copies of birth and death certificates, and other vital records. He figured, since the building held pertinent personal information, they'd probably blow it up in the future too.

"This is exactly what I'm looking for." Merit was excited seeing dozens of pages showing hundreds of pipes for the labyrinthine drainage and irrigation system underneath the course. The system of pipes connected beneath each hole, with every other hole having a wider pipe that fed a master drainage pipe. The master was located underneath the 16th hole and ran through the lake, under the length of the course where it emptied into the ocean below.

"This is where the diver tried to escape," Merit indicated with his finger, "and this connecting pipe is what I traveled through, bumping into the frogman before being flushed a long way—then blasted out of the side of the cliff."

"Do you have the bones with you? That'd be cool to see them."

"No, sorry. They're locked away. I'll show you them later." Merit promised him but had no intention of doing so.

"You're lucky you didn't drown," Beck said.

"It was a close call." Merit nodded in agreement while continuing to scrutinize the diagrams.

"Do you see what you're looking for?" Beck pulled up a chair next to him.

"Maybe. According to these records, this wasn't a public course but privately owned. From what I've learned, it was a huge honor for a course to be selected for any tournament on the PGA Tour, let alone one of the four majors."

"Four majors?" Beck asked.

"Yeah. I read where the majors were the four most prestigious golf tournaments played each year. Three were played in the old United

States and one overseas. Vic Jackson and Soldier both won twenty-two majors, and Soldier was trying to break his long-standing record."

Beck leaned back in his chair and balanced it on two legs. "What are you going to do now?"

"I'd like to know who owned this Orange Golf Club at the time Soldier was killed." Merit stood and used his high-tech watch to snap photographs of the relevant pages.

"We'd probably find that information at the Register of Deeds. It's on the island right next to this one. I'll show you."

Beck was genuinely accommodating, but Merit felt deficient in having to depend on someone else for help. He'd been used to handling most aspects of a case by himself, but given his lack of options, he accepted the servile's offer.

Merit toted the unwieldy books back to the counter, his arms full before dropping them in front of the clerk. He turned to address Beck, only to find that the illusive servile had disappeared again. He walked into the hall to see if Beck was waiting for him, but the spacious corridor was empty.

The glass door of the main room opened behind Merit as the clerk rushed into the hall.

"Mr. Darrins, you forgot to sign the books back in." She read from the book's checkout library card that was stored in the front sleeve of the books he'd used, "Derry Darrins."

"I did?" Merit was puzzled by the reference to the missing female Pilgrim Detective Darrins. He took the card from the clerk's hand and pointed to his signature as he stepped back into the room and stood at the desk.

The clerk took the card from Merit and flipped it over. "Sorry, Mr. Merit. My mistake. I was looking at the wrong side of the card." She apologized with a meek smile.

"Can I see that again?" Merit studied Darrin's signature on the flip side of the card and noted that the stamped date she'd checked it out was in 2074. Over ten years prior, she checked out the same ledger book he did.

"Thank you, ma'am."

Merit now knew that Pilgrim Detective Darrins had gotten very far in her investigation before going missing—perhaps too far. Had she uncovered the motive for the murder and been killed because of what she'd learned? He eyed the room of people, some sitting by themselves, others at desks pouring over information from books, periodicals, and maps. One man wearing thick glasses looked up at Merit for a moment and then buried his head in his book again. Was one of them spying on him, he wondered. Was he being followed? Was he in danger too?

He backpedaled into the hall, turned, and walked down the stairs to the lobby and heard groaning noises coming from a janitor's closet to his right.

Merit, suspecting that someone was being harmed, pressed his back to the wall and cautiously opened the door to the closet, ready to help. Next to a stale mop and a yellow bucket, Beck was receiving oral sex from a mostly disrobed, young intern from Public Records. His shorts were down by his knees and his head rested back against the wall as the long-legged, and rich brown-haired apprentice, who worked in the upstairs office pleasured him—Her neck plunging back and forth across his lap, in a smooth hypnotic motion.

Beck gestured by tilting his head to Merit, to join in and take her from behind. Merit wasn't naïve. He was well aware of nontraditional sex practices. He'd come across deviant sex acts gone wrong in a number of his murder cases, but he never imagined that he would be invited to be part of a ménage a trois.

His moral compass was true and pointed to what was right through God's eyes, but he was on foreign ground, a land with no rules, no law and order, no right or wrong, no truth—or consequences. Suddenly, the arrow in his internal compass spun like a top. The visual imagery before him was spellbinding. The young naked girl was perched on all fours; her flawless skin glistened across her arched back, and her long silky hair hid half of her face. While seductively glaring into Merit's eyes, she extended her right hand, encouraging him to partake in the animalistic act.

Merit stared back into the loveless eyes of the vulnerable girl and couldn't look away. A charge of tingling sensation flooded his skin and blood engorged his veins. In that split second, *something* took hold of his brain, and any previous inhibitions he had regarding unfettered pleasure were lifted, allowing him unbridled permission to taste the forbidden fruit.

Merit entered the closet.

57

The rampage of vehicles defacing course lawns continued for thirty days and nights. Like a row of dominoes, courses across the nation began to fall victim. Anti-golf activists labeled all people who belonged to private country clubs as racist and silent supporters of Soldier's killer. Some believed a group of influential club owners knew the shooter's identity and were harboring him, transporting him from club to club. To oust the murderer, they smashed windows, ransacked clubhouses, pillaged pro shops, defecated in pools, even committed arson, setting clubhouses afire. Anyone or anything associated with the game of golf was labeled a racist.

–Henry Simons, *Quest for the Major (BMA books)*

SUICIDE BY

Merit passed into the janitor's closet to engage in the sensual fantasy where Beck was being sexually pleased by the young long-haired intern. Then, from the pit of his soul, *something* triggered, and his knees locked, not allowing him to move. A set of eyes were watching him, barely visible from the back of the dimly lit closet. They caught Merit's long stare—*Eyes* he didn't recognize that were black and full of raging lust. Merit shuddered when he realized the eyes of the *stranger* belonged to *him*. A tiny vanity mirror hung by the custodian to comb his hair each morning, caused Merit to see his own reflection—A glimpse into a demented dark side. It was enough time to muster a morsel of strength to lift the curse of the erotic Medusa-like brunette.

Retracing his steps backward, he shut the door and momentarily closed his eyes, waiting for his heavy breathing to steady and the vision of the youthful, flawless female to be purged from his imagination, then exited the sliding front glass doors.

He hiked up a dirt path to the other side of the island and came to a zip line station on the coast. During his walk, he shook his head violently and took in and expelled big breaths of air trying to erase the picture of the *girl in the closet* from his mind, but he couldn't, and that scared him. He trivially regretted not accepting a couple of those blue *memory loss* pills Starla had offered him. It would have been a perfect time to pop a few.

The island to the north was where the office for the Register of Deeds was located, but the landmass was one hundred yards away. Between the islands was rough water with a dangerous current, a strait of sorts, and jagged rocks lined the coasts of both. Merit saw a man in his thirties stepping into the harness of the first of three ziplines.

"Sir, is there any other way to get to Anaheim Hills Island Number Two?"

The man laughed as if Merit had no common sense.

The man fastened his seatbelt and hooked his carabineer to the pulley spool positioned on top of the heavy-duty metal cable spanning the distance between islands. Gripping the T-rod with his hands, he lifted his feet and pressed the safety to release the brake, sending his body sailing through the air at twenty miles per hour in a downward curve until he reached Anaheim Hills Island Number Two.

Merit approached the zipline to the immediate right with caution. With some of the threads of the metal cable having frayed over the years, it didn't appear to be in perfect operating condition, and Merit stepped back. Glancing over his shoulder, hoping that Beck had caught up, he saw that he had been joined by three bony coyotes. Their teeth bared, they appeared intent on cornering the prey. He'd encountered coyotes back home but never aggressive ones.

Animals of all kinds, according to Frontier's philosophy, were on the same hierarchical rank as man. There was no need or purpose in ever taking a human life and there was no justification in killing an animal. With no controlled animal depopulation programs in place to stop over-propagating, it wasn't uncommon for hungry mountain lions, bears or other wild animals to attack people for food.

Realizing that he had no options if he wanted to get to the other island, keeping one eye on the animals, Merit moved to the third zipline and quickly strapped himself into the harness. He'd observed the actions of the man who'd sailed over the water, and he thought he knew how to operate the controls, including the braking system.

He was ready to swing out over the cliff when one of the mangy wild dogs grabbed his calve and bit down hard, flailing his head left to right as if Merit's leg was a rag doll between its savage teeth. Merit twisted and turned to get away, but the canine's hold on his flesh was firm, and blood oozed over his feet and between his toes. Merit swung the large stick he'd picked up off the ground at the animal's head, but it had no effect.

The pain was severe, and for a moment he considered ziplining with the animal still biting down on his leg, hoping that the sudden swing into the air would cause the animal to fall to its death below. No, he thought. That would be too risky. The coyote didn't weigh a lot, and it was possible that it would make the crossing with Merit to the other side. If it *did* fall, it might even tear away a sizable portion of flesh from Merit's leg.

Taking his large stick in both hands, he brought it down hard on the skull of the creature again and again until he heard the splinter of bone as the coyote limped away, wounded and bleeding. Before the second coyote had a chance to attack, Merit swung out over the precipice and began gliding downwards toward a tiny section of sandy beach.

He was halfway across when his harness slowed and then stopped. He dangled precariously above the white-capped water below and realized that his line had become tangled while he was twisting to escape the jaws of the ferocious coyote.

"Get out of the way, you idiot!" a voice shouted from behind. "What are you doing?"

Merit spun around to see that another zipliner, who must've assumed Merit knew how to operate the high-wire apparatus, had departed from the cliff and was coming at him fast. If they collided, both men would fall to their deaths below.

★★★

To avoid a collision with the oncoming zipliner, Merit twisted his body and rocked to untangle the line and right the pulley spool above him, which had tilted fifteen degrees above the metal cable.

The other zipliner was only ten yards away when Merit's body resumed its course, gaining speed quickly. He hadn't been able to use the brake for full effect since he knew that he had to get out of the way of the rider behind him. Instead, he released his hands from the T-rod, tumbling hard onto the sand. The other zipliner turned and looked at Merit angrily.

"Sorry." Merit released himself from the harness. "My line got snagged."

Bleeding badly, Merit ripped off a strip of fabric from the bottom of his shirt and used it as a bandage by tying it around his calve applying pressure to the set of four burning tooth punctures. He was worried that the wound might get infected or produce rabies, but he had no time to check into a hospital, not that he would have trusted any medical facility in Frontier to treat the bite.

He limped into the building where the Register of Deeds was located and took a seat on a plain bench that looked as if it had once been a church pew. He sat for thirty minutes as others were called before him, and he wondered if he was being ignored. Just then a female clerk called him to her desk. Merit informed her that he was looking for the name of the owner of The Orange Golf Club from back in 2026.

The clerk was a middle-aged woman, and she too he noted had several strikingly provocative tattoos on her arms and neck. Her hair was faux blonde and cut in a fashion that Merit thought was not in keeping with someone her age, but then he didn't think that any of the clothing, jewelry, tattoos, or makeup that people in Frontier wore was tasteful or appropriate. She was, however, accommodating and didn't seem to regard Merit any differently than anyone else she dealt with in her office. The badge on her T-shirt indicated that her name was Spacer.

She pulled several files from a silver metal cabinet behind her and placed them on the desk. The files contained information on previous owners, taxes, mortgages, escrow, liens, insurance, market value, appraisals, selling prices, and deeds of legal ownership. Spacer informed Merit that the owner of the Orange Golf Club had been Sean

Lewis, who had bought the property in 1982. Lewis's wife, Sally Lewis, was listed as co-owner of the eighty-five-acre tract in Orange County and had sold the course two years after the shooting, to an Alex Novak.

"I assume that there's no way any of these people could still be alive," Merit thought aloud. "They'd be well over a hundred years old."

"You're probably correct," Spacer said. "Mrs. Lewis is listed as deceased. I have no information on Mr. Novak other than that he was the last owner of the course. It never changed hands again after that transaction."

With the earthquakes and tsunamis, what would have been the point, Merit realized. "Ma'am, where could I find out more about the club owners Mr. and Mrs. Lewis?"

"Rich and affluent people like them were usually written up in local newspapers and magazines. You might try to find some articles about them."

"What are newspapers?"

The clerk smiled. "They were pieces of thin white paper with news, sports and weather printed on them. They were sold on the street or thrown on people's lawns."

"Hmm. Where could I find these newspapers?"

"They were destroyed long ago."

Merit frowned.

"However, before they were recycled, their stories were transferred to something called microfiche, which is basically video footage of old, still photos."

Merit's eyes lit up when he heard the words "video footage."

The clerk retrieved spools of celluloid tape and handed them to Merit. "You don't have much time though, young man. We close in an hour. It could take you days to look through all of those papers."

Merit formed a confident smile.

★★★

He sat in a cubicle, loaded the tape onto a huge machine, and began to survey newspapers between the years 2015 and 2028. He came across thousands of references to a time and culture that were alien to him.

He recognized almost nothing of the history, entertainment, or politics of the time.

He discovered articles on golf, and the first amazing bit of information he found was a piece that said the course had been selected as the site of the U.S. Open only six months prior to the tournament because the original site, an established course on the east coast, had experienced an infestation of insects around the sand-based greens. Phoenician billbugs and larvae had gone unnoticed by the course superintendent, and it had spread to the fairways, resulting in dying grass on much of the course and some greens.

When PGA officials had inspected the course, and with not enough time to correct the problem, they deemed it unplayable. They turned to the opposite coastline to a course owned by Lewis because it was green, well-kept, and was challenging enough to qualify for one of the major tournaments comprising the Grand Slam.

Spacer's head popped up from behind the cubicle. "Only thirty minutes left till closing."

Merit continued to turn the crank handle of the machine, which looked like an old arcade game he'd seen in a museum. Surprisingly, he saw articles on Soldier's first three rounds at the U.S. Open, and he scanned them quickly since he needed to find information on the owners of the course, not Soldier.

The one new detail he gleaned was that a *bystander* had been shot when Soldier was killed. The bystander was wounded. So, two people had been shot, one died, and one didn't. Why had no one ever told him this? Perhaps, he figured, Soldier was so famous that no one thought of mentioning that one of the people in the gallery, probably a nobody had also been shot, although not fatally.

Ten minutes later, he came across a short back-page article on the suicide of Orange Golf Club owner Sean Lewis a year after Soldier's murder. He sat up straighter in the wooden chair. This wasn't what he had expected to find, Lewis had killed himself. Why? How?

The overhead fluorescent lights dimmed twice, and Merit knew it was his cue to leave.

58

By the end of summer 2028, every one of America's private and public golf clubs, lodges, resorts, driving ranges, par-three and even putt-putt mini-golf courses were demolished. Tens of millions of dollars in damages were reported to insurance companies. While inspecting the damage caused by vandals at a course outside Beaumont, TX, an adjuster found an elderly man stripped nude, posed face up, dead. A metal flagstick pierced through his gut, like an Indian spear, to send a message to any golfer. Members were afraid to go to their clubs and quit paying dues, and with soaring repair costs, many facilities were abandoned. The once posh manicured lawns became desolate plots of land with little value.

—Andrew Hughes, Money and Wealth>download

TWO SHOT LEAD

Using a tiny, round BB as currency, one that the nice-looking couple had tossed him thinking he was homeless, Merit rented a cheap motel room for the night.

Despite having to prop his wounded leg up on two pillows, Merit had one of his better night's sleep. He was awakened the next morning by a tap on the window. Groggy, he rose from the sagging mattress, peaked through a stained curtain to see it was Beck wearing a black handkerchief across his nose and mouth. Merit moved to the door favoring his bad foot and invited him in.

Beck entered offering him a cup of coffee and seaweed donut as if the sex act in the closet the day before had never happened. "Did you find out who the owner of the course was?"

"Yeah. Sean Lewis." Merit said. "And I read he committed suicide, but it didn't say why or how."

"Asphyxiation. He hung himself. I assume this is what you're talking about." Beck handed Merit a manila folder. "Sean Lewis and his wife Sally were the club owners." He flashed a Cheshire Cat grin, knowing that he'd gotten one step ahead of Merit.

Merit looked dumbfounded. "But—wait . . . I mean, how did you . . ."

"After finishing off that long-haired intern in the closet I went to the Police Archives Building, which, by the way, is going to be bulldozed after the property building is destroyed. Why keep statistics on criminals when crime will be a thing of the past? This is the suicide report on Sean Lewis. It's the original case file." He handed the documents to Merit.

"Thanks, but you knew that Lewis killed himself?"

"I thought I'd look further into it since you're so interested in the club. I think you're going down a path that leads nowhere, but hey, you wanted the help. Did you know that Lewis was not only the owner of the course but was the innocent bystander behind Soldier—The one who got shot on the eighteenth fairway? Weird, huh?"

"I read that a spectator had been wounded, but I didn't know it was the Orange Club owner, Lewis." Merit cocked his head slightly while he processed the lowdown. "So the *bystander* that was watching in the crowd and who was shot in the neck— but survived, was the *owner* of the Orange Golf Club, and then later killed himself. Yeah, that *is* weird." Merit rubbed his forehead.

"And he's certainly not a suspect since he also got popped on the last day of the tournament. So what's the big deal about knowing who owned the course?"

"I never said he was a suspect."

Merit was not being entirely candid. He'd hoped that something in the records would link the club owner to the death of Soldier Quinn, but Beck had made a valid point. The club owner could be ruled out as being involved since he, too, had been shot the day Soldier was murdered.

"I skimmed over the suicide file on the way over here," Beck said. "Pretty interesting. The club owner, Mr. Lewis, must have felt pretty unlucky. The poor fat dude was standing right near the guy who was about to break Vic Jackson's record and then *Bam!*—he's shot in the neck. Then Soldier, on *his* course takes a headshot. I can see why he had a massive guilt trip and offed himself. But why is that so important?"

"I don't know, I'm following the leads, or have you forgotten how to work?"

Beck laughed off the barb. "My main occupation is . . . well, hiding my occupation. But I think you're wasting time here, you're going backward."

"Maybe." Merit shared his newly acquired appreciation of the thinking man's game. "But like in golf I'm finding out, sometimes you have to hit back, to layup for a better shot going forward."

"Good tip coach, but the game of golf is long gone."

Beck's sex-craved eye zeroed in on a girl through the window. She was a maid on her way to clean a room at the end of the hall—and not a cute one at that. Beck glanced back at Merit, indicating she was fresh meat for the taking. Merit rolled his eyes.

"Let me borrow some money for her, man," Beck made the universal gesture for money, rubbing two fingers together with his thumb. "I'm good for it."

Merit reluctantly pointed to several pieces of folded paper currency lying on the bureau, also tossed at him by the good-looking couple who thought he was a street person.

"I could use some maid *service* ...if you know what I mean." Beck crudely cupped his crotch, pocketed the currency, and as he exited turned and said, "Hey, can we use your room?"

Merit flashed him a dumb look, '*No'*, then stiff-armed him outside, and closed the door.

After cleaning his lacerated calf in the tub with hot water and soap, then wrapping it with a small towel, Merit sat on the hotel chair and examined the suicide report. He saw corroboration from what he'd read in the microfiche newspaper article.

Next, Merit looked at the crime scene photos. His method of suicide, by hanging. As he looked at the sheet tied around Lewis's neck, much like the feeling he'd gotten when first watching the swans in the pond evidence footage, something looked ...off.

Before leaving, Merit did a cursory search of the property to find Beck. He wanted to thank him for providing the report and ask also how he knew to find him at that hotel. He hadn't told him beforehand and the last time he'd seen him—Beck was having sex in the library closet.

Twenty minutes later with no luck, Merit checked out of the seedy motel and returned to the Capital City. He decided that he would be in Frontier for at least four more days and wanted to stay somewhere safe since vigilantes would no doubt still be searching for him.

As Merit made his way to Starla's home, he recognized the leg wound was feeling surprisingly pain-free, but then became agitated realizing why. The coffee Beck supplied him was spiked with *loose* or *hey*. On second thought figured, maybe this time it wasn't so bad. It numbed the throbbing and allowed him to make it to her house with no discomfort.

He didn't know how Starla would react. When he last saw her, they weren't on the best of terms, he'd slipped out before daybreak without saying goodbye on the surf trip to the island.

He knocked on the door. It was opened, but not by Starla.

59

In anticipation of being the next target, curators at the Golf Hall of Fame located in St. Augustine, Florida—in the cover of night—boxed up a majority of their golf history memorabilia. They sold the collection to a Japanese business tycoon who agreed to preserve it in his privately owned museum in the city of Osaka. They stowed the collectibles in purposely mismarked storage containers that were shipped overseas. The curators intentionally set their building on fire, then falsely stated to authorities' rebel social activists committed the arson and reported that all contents were tragically destroyed by the three-alarm blaze.
— Orlando News, Weather Sports, WESI-TV *Chan. 8*

KINKY GIRL

Instead of Starla opening the door to her home as Merit had anticipated, one of her boyfriends with hundreds of realistic-looking, three-dimensional roaches and houseflies tattooed to his face and neck, brushed past him into the street. "Next," he said, then stuck out his tongue and wiggled the tip of it nastily.

Merit, irked by his glib comment, turned and followed him.

"Hey, something wrong, mister?" The insect-inked boyfriend came to a stop.

"I don't think you should come here anymore." Merit stuck his chest out.

The man laughed loudly. "Really. Who are you—her daddy?"

"Why don't you shut up?"

"Why don't you come and say it to my face?"

Merit advanced, intending to punch the pompous little punk, but a scolding voice behind him stopped him dead in his tracks.

"Merit!"

It was the voice of Starla, who stood in the street, a punitive look on her face.

Merit pivoted to see that she was motioning that he should step inside.

The boyfriend formed a teasing 'Uuuw' sound with puckered lips, then said, "Now go to your mommy."

Merit approached the bug-infested-faced man and threw a hard left jab to his stomach, knocking the wind out of the punk. The boyfriend buckled over, looking over at Starla as if Merit were crazy. He angrily moved his lips, but no words came out as he backed away.

Starla shouted, "Stop it!"

Merit strutted past her.

"The more attention you call to yourself, the more likely it is that you'll attract serviles or vigilantes. I told you, the way I make my living is normal."

She was wearing a tattered blue jean mini-skirt and Merit was again reminded that he was attracted to her. She was tiny and trim, but with unusual proportions, Starla had long legs with a shorter torso and bony wide shoulders.

"What did you come back for?"

The remark jarred Merit's memory, and instantly he switched mental gears. He began to talk fast, pumped with adrenaline. "I solved it. I solved the case."

"No way! That's great!" Starla gave him a big hug. "Come in and tell me what happened."

"First, thanks to you and your friend the windsurfer girl, Nami, I made it to U.S. Open Island and found out who shot Soldier Quinn!"

"I knew you could do it." Her smile was beaming ear to ear.

★★★

Throughout the day, they dipped in her pool and sat on the rooftop terrace. They sipped non-weed tea and he caught Starla up on his adventures. Several times she reached over and playfully rubbed his freshly grown one inch in length beard, as if she were petting a puppy.

He told her about Keeper, the swan decoy, the underground irrigation and pipe system, and how he'd been on his way back to Pilgrim when he felt in his gut that he had to find out who Soldier's caddy was—and that it had indeed been Keeper and how Soldier was his dad. He also spoke of how the old man had convinced him to discover the motive. How he'd found who the owner of the course had been in 2026 and that he had allegedly committed suicide in 2027 and his widow sold the course in 2028.

"Look at these crime scene photos." He produced the suicide case file Beck had scrounged up from the police archives building.

"Oh, I can't, they're yuck." She glanced at the pictures of the club owner Sean Lewis slumped on the floor, his back against his bedroom door, a sheet strung taut around his stumpy neck and the other end around the doorknob. He was a short, bug-eyed, red-faced, purple-lipped, rotund man with a bad comb-over. She dropped the photographs on a table and walked away.

"I'm sorry," Merit said, "but there's something about them that bothers me."

Happy Birthday.

"What are you talking about?"

Merit went into the kitchen and rifled through drawers. "I need a rope or something."

"Here, will this work?"

When Merit returned to the living room empty-handed, he saw that Starla had removed the sash of her beach robe, exposing more of her tanned body and mustard yellow swimsuit.

Merit took a deep breath as he looked at Starla's shapely physique, but he pressed on to make his point. "I want to duplicate the knots. The photo shows that the owner wore a watch on his left wrist, which meant that he was right-handed." He stood behind Starla, circled the sash around her neck, and tied a knot at her throat, right below her jaw.

"Kinky," she said in a husky voice.

Merit ignored her humor and continued in a serious tone. "It's the way my father taught me to tie a tie when I was young." His hands and wrists rubbed gently against her shoulders and neck, and he inhaled the fragrance of her perfume. He'd never been this close to her before except when she'd straddled his body to apply ointment to his wounds the first day he'd stayed in her apartment. Then, however, he'd been in pain and under the influence of marijuana tea. "This is the way the knot should look if you tie it yourself." He undid the knot, walked to the front of her body, and tied the knot again, this time while facing her. "See the difference? Get it? The bulge in the knot is facing in the opposite direction."

"I get it Merit. Lewis didn't tie the knot himself."

"He was probably strangled to death first, then hung to make it look like a suicide."

His lips were inches away from her own. Her breath was sweet from the warm peppermint tea she'd sipped, and he could feel her exhalations on his face. She stared directly into his eyes as she brought her right hand to his, which was still grasping the bottom of the tie. He swallowed hard and backed away, looking down at his feet awkwardly to avoid her gaze.

"Anything else?" She gave a breathy invitation to maintain their intimate moment.

"Yeah. Maybe there's a connection between the two crimes."

Starla offered a plausible explanation. "It could be a coincidence. Maybe. On the other hand, first, you saw something weird with the swans, and now you see something weird with the shape of a knot. Maybe you're onto something—again."

Merit picked up the photo and inspected it closer. Their romantic moment had once again passed because of Merit's timidity.

"What's your next move?" Starla abandoned her attempt to seduce him.

"The suicide report says that Mr. Lewis's body was discovered by their Hispanic maid. She was an illegal immigrant and, at the time, was worried about being deported, so she tried calling Mrs. Lewis rather than the police. The wife, however, didn't answer, so the maid called their seventeen-year-old daughter, who was stuck in traffic. The daughter called 911— the cops responded to their home thirteen minutes later. The maid didn't speak English well, so the daughter, Britney Lewis, arriving shortly after was questioned instead. Her address is different and is listed in the police report."

"I wonder if the daughter is still alive and, if so, lives at the same house that she did back then?" Starla reached for the file. "Seems like a long shot. What's her address?"

Merit showed Starla the location listed in the file.

"That's way up in Steeple Hills; it's a very wealthy area," Starla said.

"I need to get there and canvass."

"What's canvass?"

"It's a police term. It means to get out in the field, the sticks and bricks. Knock on doors, shake the trees, beat the bushes, you know, ask questions. It's how you work a cold case."

Starla smiled. "Steeple Hills is hard to get to. It overlooks the LA Basin Bay. You'd have to get up there from the backside, from the east, the San Fernando Valley Bay. I'll go with you."

"No way. It's too dangerous. If I'm getting close to the answers, you could be in harm's way since a lot of people don't want the case solved. And vigilantes are out there."

Starla drooped her shoulders, batted her puppy eyes at Merit, and pouted her lower lip pleading for him to change his mind.

"Okay Starla, you can tag along." As if he had no other choice, but inside he was pleased she wanted to, and he didn't mind having some company to bounce ideas off.

"Let's go canvassing!" Starla sprung to life and marched out the door with a clenched fist extended in the air in victory, "Shake the bricks and knock out trees."

Merit was amused with her youthful display of exuberance, even though she'd butchered the saying. He then thought about Ruth and remembered how she was so stiff and lady-like. She never acted spontaneously like Starla.

60

One summer evening, a group of activists, still disgruntled over the lack of an arrest, overpowered the gate guard at an upscale resort in the Carolina Keys. Outside Vic Jackson's vacation home, they taunted him and made lewd remarks about his wife. His family was terrified. The pack accused him of orchestrating Soldier's murder to protect his record. When Vic stepped on a balcony and denied the claims, a hurled liquor bottle struck the eighty-eight-year-old and he crawled inside bloodied. One brazen teen scaled a trellis and slipped into a third-story broken window. Minutes later, he emerged modeling one of Vic's Master's green jackets as the mob cheered. Vic's family narrowly escaped. His home was looted and many one-of-a-kind golf collectibles, trophies, photographs were heisted and later sold on the black market. The following day, Vic's pet Labrador dog "Eagle" was found hung on its leash from a porch rafter.
    —G.L. Meeks, *The Autumn Fox Autobiography @www.publishcity.com*

BEAT THE BUSHES

Merit and Starla traveled by a tandem kayak across old Southern California's "The Valley" basin to reach the backside of Steeple Hills. Starla rowed while Merit continued to study the suicide report. Time was critical since only three days remained before the evidence building was destroyed. Although he didn't presently have any reason to return to it, the idea that he'd never be able to retrieve something from it if needed was like a ticking time bomb in the back of his mind. Three days.

    "The police report says that there was no sign of forced entry," Merit didn't look up from the folder in his lap. "The wife and daughter showed up at the suicide crime scene a short time later—the Lewis residence in Irvine."

Starla's strokes were steady and even, propelling the canoe through the water. Although she was thin, Merit noticed that her arms appeared slender and strong. She had not protested when Merit asked her to paddle while he studied the report.

"Why would somebody want to kill Mr. Lewis?" Starla moved the paddle from the left side of the kayak to the right side to steer it left.

"I'm not sure, but since he was the owner of the course and got accidentally shot when Soldier did, I think that's odd, and it's a lead I have to follow."

"His wife could have killed him," she said.

"Yeah. Maybe his wife was having an affair and she had her husband killed."

"Or maybe *he* was having an affair and she wanted him dead?"

"Touché," he said. "Or she wanted him dead to collect the insurance money. Then again, maybe Mr. Lewis owed someone money and couldn't pay it back."

"Money's not a motivator in Frontier," she said back.

"Remember, this happened before Frontier existed. He could have been murdered for any number of reasons." Merit fell into a deep stare and looked philosophically at the ripples her paddle was creating in the water. "I never had to worry about motives."

"It's nice that you're doing it for this gentleman, Keeper."

The kayak bumped into a gently sloping hill on which weeping willows and sycamores grew. Merit dragged the craft onto the bank and hid the oars under a bush before he and Starla trudged up the incline and began hiking the steep winding road named Cold Water Canyon Drive.

"It's pretty nice here," Merit glanced around. "These homes look very high-end."

"It was—and is—it's a very wealthy area. A long time ago it used to be called Beverly Hills, but they changed the name to Steeple Hills. Beverly Hills was known for where rich movie stars and celebrities lived. The name had connotations of privilege and luxury, so it was changed because it hurt the will and feelings of people who struggle with less."

"I'm sure the name change made a big difference." Either she didn't hear him or chose to ignore him because she didn't react to his wisecrack.

Two hours later they cut up a side street, Steeple Crest Drive— formally named Beverly Crest Drive that twisted around magnificently designed homes perched precariously over cliffs that came to look over the L.A. Bay below.

Having arrived at the right address, Merit knocked on the door, waited, and then knocked again. They could make out a deep rhythmic musical beat pulsating from inside and figured the homeowner couldn't hear the doorbell ring or knocks. Suddenly the door was opened by a large mid-sectioned, middle-aged woman who was perspiring and wearing an unflattering tight-fitting spandex suit. It appeared as if she'd been working out.

"We're looking for a Ms. Britney Lewis." Merit smiled. "Does she live here?"

"No, I'm afraid not." She closed the door behind her to drown out the workout music.

"Have you ever heard of her? Or could she have lived here before you?"

"I've never heard the name, Britney Lewis. My parents bought this home many years ago, and I don't recall who they bought it from. I'm sorry."

She was very congenial, but Merit was dejected. He'd spent a great deal of time tracking down information on the owner of the course after aborting his return trip to Pilgrim. He'd followed leads from the Bureau of Public Records and the Register of Deeds, but his efforts had been in vain.

"Thanks anyway." Merit was ready to return to the kayak.

"Hold on." Starla pressed her hand on Merit's chest, preventing him from leaving. She extracted an old California State driver's license photocopy of Britney Lewis from the suicide case file and showed it to the homeowner. "Have you ever seen anyone who looks like this?"

The homeowner in the full-bodied leotard took the picture and studied it briefly, squinting in the bright sun. "Yes. I think I have." She smiled. "She favors Rebecca. I don't know her last name. This looks like the person who used to live here— the same person my parents purchased the home from. Rebecca's her name, not Brittany. She lives up the road." She stepped barefooted out onto the narrow lane, pointed practically straight up at a home hanging dubiously, high overhead. "She looks quite young for her age, and I'm pretty certain that this is the same person, even though the photo appears to be very old."

"Thanks." Starla made a broad grin. "That's a big help."

"Good luck." The woman said before she closed the front door.

Merit slapped Starla a high-five. "Maybe you should become a detective." Merit said. "You know, me and you. Good cop, bad cop."

Starla put her hands on her hips and stared at him with narrowed eyes reminding him, "They're all bad," but her look was good-natured rather than admonishing.

"So, we have to keep hiking," he said. "This is the steepest road I've climbed."

"There's a shortcut." Starla stopped and pointed to a steep hill. "You're an athlete and work out." She flexed her thin long biceps over her head and gritted her teeth, like a bodybuilder competing in a Mr. Olympia pose.

"Let's workout." Merit was reminded of how different she was from Ruth.

Starla turned off the road and began climbing a shrub and ivy-covered rise with a sharp grade of what felt like ninety degrees. They clawed their way up for the next ten minutes, grabbing onto bushes and using large rocks as handholds, with the expansive bay glimmering to their backs. They cut up the side of the home and emerged onto the lane again after it had made a hairpin jog to the right and brushed off the dirt and leaves. In front of them was the house they were looking for.

"Nice pad," Merit said. "The place has a four-car garage." Peering through vertical slits in the doors, with very little natural light, he observed several antique cars, including two matching '68 Porsche Targas, one signal yellow and one pearl white, a '72 racing green MG Triumph Spitfire and a black 1980s Fiat Soldier. All convertibles in pristine "show car" condition but coated with a sheet of dust. "Wow. Look at this. A '68 Porsche 911." Besides raising horses, Merit's father's other passion was old cars. Whenever his dad got the itch to purchase one, he always talked himself out of it, claiming that collecting antique cars was a bad investment or took a great deal of work and money to keep them running, but did take Merit to car shows and auctions. Merit wished he was alive and could see these sports cars and chomped at the bit of driving one.

Uninterested, Starla walked on the road along the front of the windowless, white-painted stucco and wood-framed constructed home. It had a flat roof and sat on tall stilts propping up back half of the house that was suspended over the cliff and she rang the unusual-sounding doorbell of church chimes. Merit crossed his fingers on both hands.

The summons was finally answered by a woman with hair that was a tasteful mixture of gray and blonde. She had hazel blue eyes and high cheekbones. She was, Merit thought, a woman who was up in years but had stayed in good shape, just as the homeowner below had implied. She looked at her visitors through a slat in a tall wooden security gate that protected the front door, a gentle dispositioned Golden Labrador retriever by her side.

"May I help you?" The woman had a sophisticated way about her.

"I'm Merit, and we're looking for Britney Lewis. Are you her?"

She shook her head. "No, I'm not. There's no one here by that name." The lady spoke impatiently as if she wanted them to leave her property.

"He's here to look into the murder of Soldier Quinn." Starla flashed the photocopy of a young Brittany Lewis's driver's license, the likeness was uncanny. "He was a golfer who was killed a long time ago on a course owned by Brittany Lewis's father."

The woman shifted her eyes from the picture to Starla and Merit. "Please don't use the G-word out here." She delicately placed her pointer finger over her lips, indicating quiet, "And meet me by the side entrance." She retreated into her home.

★★★

Starla sat on the curb. Merit paced outside the tall white painted wooden gate situated on the home's left side for several minutes, questioning if they were going to be stood up by the pretty lady.

"How's your leg?" Starla asked. "Did that climbing bother it?"

273

"No. It feels good." Merit rubbed the fresh bandage that Starla applied daily. "Your ointment treatment is working."

The latch on the gate opened with a tug on a string by the cultured woman on the other side wearing a red floppy hat. "I was doing some gardening when you rang the bell. Please come in." The entry led to a quaint garden. "I go by the name of Rebecca now. Not Brittany, but Rebecca Smith."

They followed Rebecca down a steep concrete and brick path bordered by topiary, potted plants, and row after row of terraced gardens, where flowers of every variety and color grew.

"So Rebecca, Sean Lewis was your father, can you tell me about him?" Merit floated the question. "I know that he owned the Orange Golf Club."

Picking up a metal gardening fork and working the dirt in a large, round container holding a rainbow of colorful perennial flowers, Smith looked ruefully at the detective.

"The O.G.C. I believe was built in the 1920s, and my father bought it as an investment in 1982, during a recession. His plan was to sell it to make a profit. Only about a hundred-yard stretch of the course's property bordered the Pacific Coast, that stretch was situated high on the cliffs and the rest of the course grounds rose even higher up along the canyon to a large plateau. Any land near the ocean was considered prime real estate then. When the market recovered eight years later, he liked it so much, and the attention it brought him, that he decided not to sell. Over the years, he made a lot of modifications to it."

"Like what?" Merit asked.

Starla stroked the lab's shiny coat as Rebecca spoke. "During those times there were a lot of droughts, and the state was strict in rationing water, so my father installed a unique irrigation system to water the grounds. Instead of tapping the local water supply, however, a desalination pump siphoned water directly from under the ocean. The unit extracted the salt and then fed the freshwater up through underground pipes and used it to irrigate the entire course. It saved a lot of money and kept the club in the black."

Merit immediately knew the pipe she had described—the passage through which the killer frogman had most likely accessed from under the ocean before making his way and surfacing at the sixteenth hole water hazard, then having fired the coup de grace. It was the same pipe Merit's belt loop got hung up on the portal latch under the lake, "And?"

Rebecca continued, "Then in the 1990s, with an emphasis on protecting the environment, the city council voted to make him stop siphoning from the sea, they claimed it could upset the coastline's coral reef ecosystem and shut it down. He had to dig up and install another irrigation system to keep the vegetation green. The new sprinkler system was costly and drew from uncertain water levels stored in the Orange County Groundwater basin, supplied from unreliable sources like rainfall, snowmelt and treated wastewater from the Santa Ana River."

She sat on a stool and poured water out of the spout of a watering bucket onto the soil. "And, as my parents got older, my mom urged my dad to sell the course to free up some liquid cash. But he loved golf. He was no good at it, but he liked owning the club and rubbing elbows with some local pros and celebrities, singers, actors and professional athletes."

"Keep going."

"As much as he loved the club, he agreed on a handshake to sell it to a land developer. He did it for my mother since they were getting older in their mid-sixties."

This was exactly the detailed kind of information he'd been searching for.

"That's when out of the blue, the PGA contacted my father and told him how beautiful his course was." She bent down on a knee, reached into a bag, and sprinkled handfuls of potting soil around the flora. "They told him that the original site for the U.S. Open that year, a course somewhere out east, wasn't playable for some reason. They wanted to hold the tourney at his club. Not just any tournament, but a major. He couldn't resist the offer."

"What happened to the real estate deal?" Starla said.

"I don't know, but I assume it broke off." Rebecca Smith patted the dirt with the back of the trowel and looked up using her other hand to block the sun from her eyes, "Why do you ask?"

61

A popular sports magazine depicted a demolished country club on its cover. In the foreground, golf carts were dumped in a pond like beached whale carcasses. The fairway was viciously slashed and mutilated, bleeding brown soil, the flags were shredded, and poles snapped. In the background laid the remnants of a historic clubhouse, burnt black to its stone foundation, smoldered with orange embers of fire, and spewed gray smoke that blanketed the blue skies with soot. It looked like the aftermath of a violent battle scene from a war. The headline read, "Golf, Sudden Death."

—Gary Lyons, *The Lyon Interviews[pc #2202*

REVELATIONS

After rinsing off her hands with a garden hose, Ms. Smith led Starla and Merit into her 1959 mid-modern century residence. She showed them the magnificent view from a panoramic window that ran the full length of the house. They looked out in awe at the palatial homes in Steeple Hill's valley below. According to Ms. Smith, where many movie stars, actors, producers, directors, and famous singers had once lived. She then prepared hot cocoa for her surprise guests.

Merit fished for more particulars. "So, your mother never really liked the club or golf?"

Smith tilted her head as she thought about the question. "I wouldn't say that. She was a tree-hugger well before it became fashionable. Mother was the creative type. She'd stop at yard sales and collected smoothed broken glass and shells that washed up on the beach for a mosaic art project she envisioned doing in the future. She majored in art at Redlands College in the late 1970s and loved gardening—loved to paint, sketch and do pottery also."

Rebecca motioned to the walls and display cases in the den, pointing out some of her mother's paintings and smaller sculptures. "When pops first bought the club, she got bored. She convinced him to let her landscape a couple of the holes on the back nine because she didn't like regular golf courses, which she thought all looked alike—Too perfect. She envisioned the course as one large canvas on which she could make her mark by creating unusual features into the green, tees and fairways. She incorporated a lot of distinctive artistic designs to make the holes more aesthetically pleasing. I'm sure that's what caught the eye of the tour officials. My father was the one who worked one-on-one with the course's land engineer to make it a playable, challenging course, but it was mother who was written large over most of it."

Ms. Smith preceded them to a room next to the den where more of her mother's work was displayed on the walls. Her home resembled more of a well-lit, modern art gallery.

"You can see it in some of her sketches. Some holes exhibited a Japanese theme, where she used pebbles and plants common to the botanical gardens. Another hole was a cowboy theme where she incorporated different breeds of cacti and large boulders indigenous to the southwest. She even had the fossilized remains of an old wooden covered wagon helicoptered in."

Ms. Smith politely smiled, as she straightened a crooked painting and removed her red sunbonnet. Merit could have sworn that from certain angles, the old woman was forty-seven instead of seventy-seven.

Rebecca Smith breathed heavily and looked at her guests. "After my dad was shot and Soldier was killed, people started making threats against him. Many claimed he was responsible. It was a difficult time, and mom became even more insistent that he sell the course. The entire club was designated a crime scene while the Major Murder Inquiry investigated Soldier's death, and the course was closed to everyone. A year after my dad died, my mom sold it."

"I'm very sorry," Starla looked sincerely in her eyes. "It must have been a difficult time."

Merit recognized an eighteen-inch-tall clay sculpture on one of the shelves. "That's Soldier, isn't it?"

The sculpture was of Soldier striking his famous, Jesus on the cross, *Y-pose*, seconds before he was struck down.

"Yes, detective. You are a detective?"

Merit nodded and sipped the hot chocolate. He hadn't told her, but she deduced so and assumed he was from Pilgrim.

"You've got a good eye, detective. Mother commissioned a well-respected sculptor from up in Marin County to make a statue of Soldier as a memorial. This is her original miniature." She gingerly removed it from the glass-fronted cabinet, blew one soft puff of air to remove surface dust and showed it to Starla and Merit. "They later made a giant bronze statue exactly like it."

"Where did they put it?" Starla intently listened too.

"They laid it on its side and built a wooden crate around it—it was a bronze likeness over thirty feet high—and lugged it from Northern California on a flatbed semi to the course. It was supposed to be placed somewhere on the grounds—I'm not exactly sure where—and it was to be unveiled on an anniversary of Soldier's death."

Merit thought back to his days on the island. He recalled nothing, neither on land nor in the many lakes, that remotely resembled a statue of Soldier.

"What happened to it?" Starla followed up.

"A week before the unveiling in the early two-thousand and thirties, earthquakes and tsunamis destroyed most of Southern Cal., and the course has been underwater ever since. From what I understood, the wide load semi-truck hauling the statute sadly never made it to the club."

After treating them to a platter of homemade butter cookies, Rebecca and her retriever, loyally following her two steps behind, led them on a tour of the rest of her elegant home, including the rooftop balcony with a spectacular view of Los Angeles Bay. At the southwestern base of Steeple Hills was the shoreline, much like Orange Bay. The greater L.A. area was a submerged basin. In the distance lay a sprawl of thirty or more abandoned skyscrapers of various designs and heights. The historic downtown business district of L.A. rose ghostly above the waterline, resembling the fabled city of Atlantis.

Rebeca turned to Starla. "Earlier when we were outside, you asked what happened to the real estate deal?"

Starla looked at Merit.

Merit broached the taboo topic cautiously. "Ms. Smith, do you believe your dad killed himself?"

Smith's features changed, becoming downcast as she spoke. "It's what the Orange County sheriff's investigator concluded. My dad was distraught that Soldier was killed on *his* course, but it was still difficult for us to fathom he took his own life."

Merit considered whether he should tell Rebecca Smith the truth. "Ms. Smith, your father didn't take his own life."

She shifted her weight to the back foot.

"I think he was murdered," he said, "In fact, I know he was."

Her mouth dropped open.

Merit detailed what he'd learned from the case file, including the text her mother had received from her father, alerting her that she should sell the course just before he *supposedly* committed suicide. He also related what the crime photos showed did not tally with a suicide.

"Did you ever hear your parents mention a man named, Alex Novak?" Merit over-enunciated his name. "He was the land developer who bought the course from your mother?"

"I was in my late teens when all this took place. I wasn't privy to the details."

Merit could see that Rebecca was upset and didn't want to dredge up more painful memories, but he needed to find answers. He realized that this was the very reason he'd thrived working in the homiscope— his cocoon—insulated from the real-life drama and pain of the people who'd lost their loved ones to murder.

"Do you know of anyone who would have wanted to see your father dead?"

"Yes. Most of the people who blamed him—the people who hated golf after Soldier was killed and eventually tore up the golf courses and burned down the clubhouses."

"That's a lot of people." Merit grimaced. "I wish I could access your father's communications between him and that land developer Novak regarding the sale of the club, but the phone records are long gone."

Rebecca's head twitched slightly, then again in the other direction, as if she were retrieving bits of fragmented data deeply stored in her long-term memory. Then, with a look of enlightenment, she tipped her head back and pointed her left hand to the ceiling.

★★★

Minutes later, Merit, sprawled out on his stomach flat across her attic floor, carefully handed down two shoeboxes through the open trap door to Starla reaching up from below. "Are these it?" The boxes were filled with old phones, electronics, pins, pens, and golf memorabilia.

"I've had to keep all of this hidden for obvious reasons." Rebecca peered in the boxes. "The mere mention of the name of the game can cause some people to become suspicious and angry." Starla untangled input and output cords and Merit, after climbing down on a step ladder, plugged the phones into the chargers as Rebecca elaborated, "Anyway, I hid all things related to golf when my parents began receiving death threats because so many people blamed them. For my safety, they bought me the house down the lane. Later, they bought me the house we're in now as a precaution and changed my name from Brittany to Rebecca. Anything, anyone related to the g-word was racist and had to be hidden. It was a dangerous time."

Starla was sitting cross-legged on the floor pillow and looked up. "Are you still in hiding?"

"No dear, that was many years ago. But I watch what I say out in public."

Merit, who had been absorbed in rooting through the contents of the boxes as he listened to Smith, looked over and said, "The text to your mom, the one instructing her to sell the course, I'm figuring was from the person who strangled your dad to death and then faked his hanging. Whoever sent the text really wanted the club. The only way to get it was by killing him."

"That's plausible," Smith placed her pointer finger over her lips thinking about it.

While waiting for the phones to hopefully take a charge, Merit lightened the heavy conversation. "I couldn't help notice your old cars—they're beautiful." There was a twinkle in Merit's eye. "The two 911's."

"Yes, aren't they lovely. They were my pop's babies, besides me." She guided them through an interior sliding glass door, to the right several steps down a hall, then propped open an interior wooden door, leading them into the dark garage. She flipped the light switches on.

The four-car garage was mostly barren except for the dust-covered vehicles, one circa 1980's Schwinn Varsity Sport woman's bicycle, and a wooden-handled broom. Stacked on the bottom shelf of a wall rack, were two rectangular-shaped plastic gas tanks and several quarts of 10W-60 motor oil. "Mom drove the white Targa and dad had the yellow. The Fiat he bought for me on my sixteenth birthday."

As they orbited the antique sportscars, Merit purposely inhaled through his nose, as the smell of gasoline grounded him, reminding him of home—Fumes of petroleum pumped from the ground by steel-framed rigs that resembled dinosaurs roaming old Oklahoma's oil fields. "I see the keys in their ignition. Do they still run?"

"Yes. Like daddy instructed me, I make sure to always keep a little fuel in the tank, and I start them up once a month. I'll lend them out to show them off at some big special events. They'll pull them along with cables or ropes, but I can't drive them."

"Why?" Merit asked.

"—They're *gas*-powered." Starla glared at him.

Merit brushed off her statement, "I'd give anything to drive that white one." He then used his right hand and acted as if he were shifting a gear stick from into third to fourth gear.

"No one is supposed to drive them," Starla shook her head. "They ruined the atmosphere."

★★★

Thirty minutes later, several beeps came from in the house, indicating that the phones had been charged. Smith ushered them back inside and showed Merit how to navigate the menus on the phone's small screens to find emails, texts, voicemails, contacts, and a list of incoming and outgoing calls.

Merit punched a number on the keypad and triggered a saved voice message from Sean Lewis to his daughter: "Hang in there little princess," the gargled recording said. "I know you'll do your best in your interview. If it's meant to be, it's meant to be." Rebecca shed silent tears at the sound of her father's voice offering encouragement before a first waitressing job interview.

"But aren't things better in Frontier?" Starla persuasively nodded her head. "I mean, you live up here in this gorgeous home, Ms. Smith."

Ms. Smith had a guarded expression on her face. "You mustn't tell anyone, but no—it isn't. The wealthy pay ninety-five percent of the cost to feed, house and clothe the rest of society. And then there's the crime rate."

Merit's ears perked up. "Crime rate? I thought crime was almost completely eliminated."

"Very few know this..." She used a hushed tone. "...but the very wealthy also secretly pay the Pilgrim police to cross the border into Frontier and find rapists, murderers, and other violent criminals and make them *disappear*. If you get my gist?"

Starla had a look of doubt on her face.

"I'm so sorry honey to break this to you..." She took Starla's hands and spoke to her with kid gloves. "...but here's how it works. The super-rich people of Frontier pay the Pilgrim police *and* Frontier vigilantes lots of *under the table* money to capture these violent criminals and eliminate them. It's not pretty, but it keeps us safe and makes the rehab program look successful, but it's smoke and mirrors."

She released Starla's hands and addressed the two of them. "These poor citizens think it's true, and believe their theory is valid and want it to work so badly, it makes them feel good about others and about themselves, but it's not real."

Starla shook her head back and forth, she wasn't buying it. "How are you so sure?"

Rebecca responded in a definitive tone, "Because I'm one of those people who pay."

Merit could tell she'd been holding the fact in for a long time. She was scared and it exposed her vulnerability, but she entrusted the two of them by divulging the *real* truth. He recalled that the vigilantes had asked him who he was there to *get,* and Keeper had told him about bodies being disposed of on the U.S. Open island marshes, now he was getting an understanding of what it all had really meant. Merit figured there must be some clandestine, word-of-mouth *arrangements* for Pilgrim cops to make extra cash on the side. He'd never heard of any officers' partaking, but that didn't mean it hadn't been happening. He admittedly was out of the loop at his workplace, and since Pilgrim made up half of the country's territory, that meant thousands of P.P.D. cops had the opportunity to take advantage of the crooked, moonlighting gig.

"I thought the citizens of Frontier policed themselves," he said, "Organically."

"It doesn't work." Smith looked at them. "The truth is that there's a lot of crime here, and when the remaining prisoners are set free, a lot of more dangerous criminals will roam the land."

Merit gave a severe look at Starla then he reengaged with Ms. Smith. "I just learned recently that your dad was shot also. I didn't know that *He* was the innocent bystander that was wounded while watching Soldier. Where were you when it happened?"

"I was seventeen and was helping in the club's pro shop—it was so busy. I'll never forget, it was a delightful, sunny morning." She walked over to the floor-to-ceiling windows and looked far out across the hills and water below. "And just before noon, a tournament official rushed up to me with some kid about my age and said the kid needed long white pants. He said the boy was caddying, and the shorts he was wearing weren't regulation. I didn't know at the time, but the kid was Soldier's son. Keeper, I still remember his name. So I had him try on several pairs of long white pants and sent him out. He was sweet." Her blushing cheeks flashed pink. "I had a little crush on him."

Merit smiled without letting on that he knew Keeper. "Interesting."

She turned to them. "So later that day, I was in the lady's locker room replacing paper towels in the dispenser when someone rushed in and said that someone was shot. It was a madhouse. There were thousands of fans running in all directions. I hid in a bin. A lady threw used towels over me to hide me. Later, SWAT officers found me and took me to the hospital where my dad was. A detective told me that the first shot missed Soldier and accidentally wounded my dad, and the second bullet killed Soldier. Doctors said my dad, who was close to being classified as obese, was lucky that the bullet went through the fleshy part of his neck and only knocked him over. It was terrifying."

62

By 2029, due to the mass ravaging, there were few golf courses left to play on American soil and all PGA events were canceled. The PGA's sponsors dried up and with golf no longer televised, so did their stream of revenue. High school golf teams were dropped. Athletes on university golf scholarships were ostracized, bullied by fellow students and forced to transfer to other schools. The NCAA invoked the death penalty on collegiate golf. Professional golfers, to make a living and stay safe, moved overseas, and competed on the European or Asian tours, but for much less money. Within two years, the game of golf in America was abolished.

—Wikipedia, *query>History of Golf*

A BIG DEAL

Merit and Starla plodded back down the steep, twisting road of what used to be Beverly Hills.

"I knew it, Starla. Now, do you believe me when I say that Frontier is not a crime-free society? This is all a façade. Paid for by the rich. There are bad people out here."

"No! I feel sorry for her, but she's just old and scared of change." Starla walked with her arms crossed.

"Why would she make that up?"

"Frontier is a society that's working. She's wrong. She shouldn't have told us that."

"You gonna tell on her?" Merit poked fun at her. "You gonna tell on her because she made cookies with *real* sugar, or had a can of gas, or owned a dog? — I saw you petting it."

Not for the first time, Starla gave Merit the silent treatment, as they trudged down the incline.

Merit didn't only question Frontier's criminal justice program, but after listening to Rebecca, he was beginning to wonder about their financial system. Pilgrim's economy was based on old America's form of capitalism, an industry run by private ownership and flourished under the supply and demand model. Healthy competition and consumerism drove the prices and profit, the better or cheaper product would rise to the top. If one rested on their laurels, the next harder working person would overtake them— it worked just like it did in sports. The better the athlete got, their value rose and was compensated.

Merit couldn't make heads or tails out of Frontier's currency system. The rich paying *ninety percent* of their income to feed and house others, guns when melted into the shape of doves increased astronomically in value, tiny metal B-Bs, giving *free* money to people so they wouldn't need to steal, rob or rape, and women being wealthier than men through the sale of sex didn't add up. However, he wasn't there to figure that out. He was there to solve the murder, and it wasn't worth any more thought.

★★★

Attempting to move past their little spat, Starla asked as she paddled the kayak, "Who would have wanted to kill Mr. Lewis? Any thoughts now that you've spoken to his daughter?"

"Rebecca said her dad had a lot of enemies, so it could have been almost anyone."

"True," Starla said, "but Rebecca painted a picture of a loving family. I can't imagine the wife harming her husband."

"It seems unlikely that the wife would have staged her husband's suicide." Merit said.

As they glided along in the kayak, Merit studied the phone's saved messages and call history. Rebecca was kind enough to surrender the phones over to Merit to analyze them for clues. He viewed the many correspondences between the land developer, Alex Novak, and club owner Mr. Lewis. Fortunately for Merit, Mr. Lewis didn't delete his texts, voicemails, or videos. He was either too lazy or kept them on purpose, and a lot of information remained on the phone's flash memory. "I see that they'd been communicating frequently for a long time before the U.S. Open."

Merit looked up and saw that Starla was still listening attentively.

"Alex Novak is the name I saw at the Bureau of Public Records," Merit continued, "and he's eventually the person who bought the course from Rebecca's mom. According to the article I read, Mr. Lewis and Novak agreed on the business deal to sell his club, and this confirms it. Her dad backed out of their verbal contract at the last minute when he was contacted by the PGA to host the U.S. Open. I see Novak sent Mr. Lewis tons of texts trying to close the contract they'd settled on. He was waiting for an answer from Lewis, who had obviously changed his mind and decided to keep the club and host the major instead. It looks like Mr. Lewis stopped texting Novak back, which probably aggravated Novak even more."

Merit hunted through more texts, emails, and the photo library where video files were kept and found one that caught his eye.

"Here," he said, "Novak sent Lewis a five-minute video project he was working on."

"What's it about?"

"It looks like data in the form of slides. You know what I'm thinking? Novak wanted that land badly. He probably had a lot riding on purchasing that club, and for Mr. Lewis to pull out of their arrangement at the last second sent Novak over the edge. I'm thinking somehow Novak suffocated Mr. Lewis, then hung him, and then used his phone and texted Lewis's wife instructing her to sell the club should anything happen to him."

Merit loosened the knot of the scarf from around his neck and dipped it in the moving water. He wrung it dry and while retying it he looked again at Starla. She was concentrating on the evening her strokes.

"You're a good *canvasser,*" he said.

She returned a cute smile. "When we get back, do you wanna get some dinner in the city?"

Merit nodded, and at the same time something—a sparkle of light, had garnered their attention high above them. The late afternoon sun was catching the reflection of a silver-colored balloon, one used to signify the melting of a gun, shimmering as it floated across the blue sky.

"Hope it wasn't yours," Starla said with a tone of ambiguity referencing the seizure of his handgun by Chief Reed.

"Better not be." Merit gave it the evil eye as it passed overhead, then aimed his pointer finger and pretended to shoot it down—*Pow*, just before it vanished.

★★★

As they sat on an outside balcony of a downtown restaurant eating a zucchini casserole, Starla became quite animated with her facial expressions as she discussed her acting career. Seated across from each other under a canopy, she told Merit that after seeing the homes where old movie stars lived, it reminded her of how she'd dreamed of being on television or in the movies ever since she was a girl when she would stage short scenes for friends and relatives. It didn't make much difference what kind of job she got, she said if it was in front of the camera.

"Do some acting right now." Merit leaned forward in his chair to encourage her.

"Here? —Now?" She looked around.

"Sure! Why not?" He pushed his chair back and crossed his legs at the ankles.

Starla wasn't the bashful type and began to imitate her favorite actress, impressing Merit with a skill he'd not seen in her before. She was able to transform herself as she re-enacted a part from a film that he'd never heard of. She had thrown herself into the part when, having looked away from their outside table, she grew suddenly quiet and halted her performance.

"What's the matter?" Merit sat upright. "Why'd you stop? Is it part of the act?"

He twisted around in his chair, looked across the street, and saw that ten prisoners were being given free time outside the local jail to help them acclimate to civilian life in anticipation of their imminent release from prison. They stood on the street in orange jumpsuits, drawing the applause of many pedestrians as well as those at the restaurant, while they stretched their legs. They were guarded by serviles wearing disguises, all of whom were heckled by nearby citizens who regarded the incarceration of the inmates cruel and undeserved punishment.

Merit noticed three of the prisoners were glaring up at Starla: a white man with dirty blond hair and a double ponytail, a fat black man with a bald head, and a skinny dark-skinned man with a long goatee. The white inmate pointed at Starla and drew *something* in the air with his finger.

Merit attempted to comfort his dinner companion, "Just ignore them."

She grabbed her belongings and stormed out.

63

The PGA's honorable intention to fund Ex-IOC President Pratt's Major Murder Inquiry in hopes of nabbing Soldier's killer and saving golf's reputation, backfired. A motive was determined but a suspect was never specifically named, the PGA went under, and the gentleman's sport was killed. People speculated which sport would next fall prey to society's moral wrath. Would it be baseball, with the steep decline in African American participation, ice hockey, with its mostly Euro-Canadian Caucasian players, NASCAR's good ol' boy network, the white-powdered privileged sport of snowboarding, or golf's white attired kissin' cousin, tennis?

—By Ronald Gonzales, CMN Updated 11:51 AM Feb. 22

X-RATED

At Starla's place, Merit downloaded all communications from the club owner's cell phones onto a computer—videos, photographs, and blueprints that Lewis and Novak had swapped during their negotiations about the course, including the developer's short video presentation.

"You should see this, Star!" Merit said after a cursory examination of the video. Alex Novak, speaking with a slight Eastern Bloc accent, could be seen giving a private presentation to a group of wealthy investors on the mini city he proposed to construct on the site of the Orange Golf Club. A well-dressed, highly motivated man of thirty-two, Novak pointed to an artist's rendering of his city built within a clear cube of immense proportions, inside of which were restaurants, high-rises, shops, theaters, and ten thousand condominium units.

It was an impressive three-dimensional plastic molded mockup of the condo community that included miniature people, vehicles, and palm trees. Only a limited amount of the condo units bordered the cliffs overlooking the one-hundred-yard ocean view property, but every location within the city would be constructed, he articulated, to afford a breathtaking view of the Pacific. How? By using mirrored glass windows in the construction, "every condo's view would be precisely engineered at an angle to catch a reflection from a surrounding condo's glass guaranteeing a seascape of the Pacific Ocean."

"This is amazing," Merit looked over his shoulder in Starla's direction. "A year before Soldier was murdered, Novak wanted to build a self-contained city that was green. *Green* meant environmentally safe back then."

Merit muted the music to the ending credits of the progressive-minded land developers' presentation and flipped on the lights. Starla had left the living area and gone to her bedroom. He rose and knocked gently on the door. "Star, you alright? Can I come in?"

"Go away."

Merit turned the knob and entered the room, which was completely dark. The opened door created enough light for him to make out Starla lying face-down on her bed, crying. An open bottle of her guilt-free pills was near her arm on the bedspread. The blue pills designed to erase her memory from the previous two hours. "You're not still upset about those dumb shit prisoners we saw at dinner, are you?"

She didn't reply. Merit began to think her silence was cause for concern.

"Do you know them?"

She shook her head, which was buried in the bedspread.

"Starla, tell me." He gently shook her shoulders. "Do you know them?"

"I was providing pleasure with the white guy one time, and the two others joined in and gang-raped me. And that's who did it."

Merit didn't want to know the answer but asked out of obligation. "Did what?"

She sat up and apprehensively unbuttoned her loose-fitting blouse, exposing her multi-colored tattooed chest with a salad plate-sized design of a moth. An iridescent lime-green tattoo of a Luna Moth had been inked by a master artist. Merit looked closer. He noted two eight-inch-long, crisscross scars between her tiny, cupped breasts. The expert tattooist cleverly disguised the two disfiguring lacerations within the insect's fanned wings—permanent wounds to the flat-chested woman that had been inflicted by the sharp blade of a box cutter.

"Which one cut you?" Merit wasn't unaccustomed to comforting people since he'd been such a loner, but he reached out and tenderly traced the outline of her scars with his finger.

"The white guy." She began refastening her buttons.

"With the fruity ponytails?" Merit recalled the design the white inmate drew in the air with his finger, an X, he'd been taunting her while they at the restaurant. "Fuckin' criminal! You need to stay away from there—When did this happen?"

"Seven years ago."

"How much time did they get?"

"Twenty years each." Starla stared at Merit like he was dumb. "Haven't you understood anything, or have you been so absorbed in your case that you can't remember what's going on here?' She completed buttoning her blouse, one buttonhole higher than normal. 'Like Rebecca said, all prisoners are being released on July Fourth. *Everyone*, Merit!"

Merit retreated a step, taken aback by Starla's accusatory tone.

"You're the one who said this place was supposed to be crime-free." Merit went on the offensive. "Those freaks committed a crime, and they need to be punished—it's that simple. This whole crime reduction forgiveness and no victims program—is total bullshit."

"No. It *will* work Merit. It's not their fault. It's all of our fault—society's fault." Starla got up and wiped the tears from her face. "Forget I told you. I'll put the whole incident behind me. Frontier's forgiveness program *will* work." She downed two blue pills. "It's taken a lot of time to get where it is. They didn't do anything wrong. Sometimes here, one has the duty to suffer for the greater good, and I'm willing to do that."

Starla's body trembled despite her renewed argument for the culture of Frontier. Her rhetoric, Merit thought, was a vain attempt to convince herself that she was correct.

"So, it's your duty to get raped?" he said. "That's warped. It's sick for you to think you're indirectly to blame for someone cutting you up like a piece of meat. That's stupid."

"So I'm stupid now? —Is that it?"

64

By 2030, there was only one golf course still intact in America, but it was not actively used. It was the Orange Golf Club where Soldier was slain. The overgrown course looked like a jungle. The PGA's funds to guard the course had dried up. The course was sold to a land developer to build an enviro-friendly, luxury condo community, but the future of the construction was in limbo. Every so often, some curious kid scaled the fence and snapped a selfie to document where Soldier was shot. Or some devout fans passing through left flowers, but all in all, the course was left alone. The incumbent U.S. President, to avoid more civil strife, deemed the land a federal crime scene and ordered the gates closed indefinitely. The land developer's file for bankruptcy was later rejected.

—Howie Ardman, *FollowTheOShow@Twitter*

THE BLOW MOLD

Because all records in Frontier were indeed accessible to the public, Merit followed his instincts and tracked down the storage facility where the young real estate land developer, Novak, had rented a unit decades earlier, Unit W-1031. It was in a section of Capital City called Pasadena, which was partially submerged depending on the tide. He'd read deeper about Novak's history and found documents showing where the aspiring builder had investor groups lined up to finance constructing two strip malls on separate occasions, but when too much time passed the funders got cold feet and they nixed the deals. He wasn't going to let that happen again, Merit believed.

Using a slim solar-powered flashlight that was low on a charge,

Merit dove beneath the surface of the salty water and found the unit he was looking for. After prying off the corroded combination lock, he pulled on its handle, but it was sealed tightly by rust. He rose to the surface, and thanks to Keeper's swim lessons, he took fresh air into his lungs and dove again. This time, the garage door slowly opened upward as he jerked on the handle, but Merit recoiled as a school of a thousand tiny blue and white fish, like stardust, shimmied past his face. Recovering, he scissor-kicked under the door and swam up into the unit and saw that a pocket of air existed four feet above the waterline and the metal ceiling.

Many objects floated on the small waves he'd produced, but one item instantly caught his attention: a plastic model of the proposed *green city by the sea* project he'd seen in Novak's PowerPoint presentation. Near it was a large bowl-shaped mold made of a plastic polymer from which the plastic swan decoy had been fashioned.

He couldn't believe it. There were two identical halves, one stacked inside the other, like a set of bowls. While treading water and gripping the flashlight between his teeth, he peeled the two halves apart. He flipped one half around and lined up the edges of the two halves and deduced that hot liquid plastic had been poured into the mold. When removed, the cast would have resulted in the swan decoy. The original blow mold cast of the swan decoy he discovered on the U.S. Open Island. The decoy Keeper had found and turned upside down to be used as a golf ball bucket holder.

Paint would have been applied later to color the swan's feathers, eyes, and black bill to give details and add authenticity. He couldn't believe he found it so quickly, "Yes!" he said. This was concrete evidence tying Novak to the killing of Soldier and further validation of his theory to how the murder was committed. Just then, his flashlight died, and he had to make his way out of the dark by feel.

As he surfaced and walked atop the long row of units with the cast of the swan blow mold, he felt a sense of panic, as if he needed to share his findings quickly in case someone was on his tail. Was someone going to eliminate him before he exposed the truth? Detective Darrins had gotten deep into solving the case but hadn't made it this far to find the plastic decoy cast. He needed to explain his theory to someone he could trust.

★★★

With only three days remaining, Merit was ecstatic to return to Beck's secret second apartment in Santa Monica to tell the servile of his breakthrough. Once admitted to the small, unsurprisingly dirty, and sparsely furnished apartment—just what Merit had envisioned for the horn-dog detective—he used photographs, documents, and hand-sketched diagrams to illustrate his points. He even laid out a large map of the course with seashells labeled to represent Soldier, Keeper, Mr. Lewis and the shooter's locations and movements.

Merit ignored the fact that Beck was puffing a weed-filled stogie and spoke with devotion as he acted out the crime, adopting the bodily postures of the shooter and Soldier. "I'm going to confirm this theory and expose it." He explained that Novak had intended to use Soldier as a smokescreen to cover the crime lest his investors pull out of the land deal.

Merit spoke distinctly as if he were testifying in court while describing what he'd learned about the negotiations between Novak and Mr. Lewis and the reluctance of the club owner to sell the property to the ambitious land developer. It was, Merit outlined, the motive that he'd been searching for. He explained why Novak had hired the scuba diver to swim through the irrigation pipe system to murder *both* Soldier and Mr. Lewis.

Merit presented the polyurethane cast of the swan decoy above his head like the winner's cup. "The scuba diver-sharpshooter first shot the club owner with the intent to kill him, but *unknowingly* only injured him. He then fired a second shot that killed Soldier Quinn, all under the guise that the public, the media, and law enforcement would make the obvious assumption that the shooter meant to shoot Soldier first, but missed and *accidentally* shot some unlucky bystander, being the owner. Novak arranged to have Soldier shot to make it seem as if the shooter's motive was to prevent a minority from breaking Vic Jackson's record, thus deflecting attention from the business deal, which was the sale and purchase of the course." He blew out a big breath of air as if he were exhausted before extending a finger in the air and accentuating the word, "But!"

"But what?" Beck was keenly attuned to Merit's every word.

"But the shooter, when he fled underwater, didn't realize he'd only wounded the club owner in the neck, and then he got stuck in the abandoned irrigation pipe and died. A year later, the developer Novak, who'd hired the shooter—even more desperate to buy the club since the murder attempt of Mr. Lewis failed, snuck into the club owner's home and staged his death. He didn't die of hanging himself—I saw from the crime scene photos of the hanging that the knot that tied the noose around Lewis's neck faced the wrong way. It was tied by someone standing in front of him, proving it wasn't a suicide. He was suffocated first, then impersonating the dead club owner Lewis, Novak texted the owner's wife, stating how guilty he felt about Soldier being killed on his course, urging her to sell the club. The distraught wife, following her dead husband's last texted *wish*, sold the cursed course to the land developer, Novak."

"That's pretty good, Merit. I followed all of it." Beck nodded in approval. "No, *real* good."

He clapped three times. "You've been a busy bee."

"It wasn't a race-hate-related murder." Merit shook his head. "Soldier was killed over the greed of money—good old-fashioned American greed." He smiled showing his teeth.

"Capitalism." Beck had contempt in his voice.

"Good greed, Beck. Capitalism isn't perfect—but the crime was. It was the perfect murder. Even the frogman getting stuck in the tunnel helped Novak. There were no loose ends. You know, loose lips sink ships—*assassinate the assassin*. But there was one thing Novak couldn't have anticipated."

"What was that?"

"He didn't think it would lead to such a lengthy investigation and the course being declared a federal crime scene, forcing it to be closed indefinitely. The developer was never able to build his dream green city on the course. I read that Novak later went bankrupt after the earthquakes and flooding." Merit was thrilled that Beck agreed with his findings and clenched both fists in triumph.

Beck picked up and studied the halves of the plastic swan molds and fit them together. "I like it, but . . ."

"But what?" Merit was pumped and wanted some feedback. "— Tell me."

"To be honest, and I don't want to hurt your feelings Merit, but it sounds a little ... convoluted. It's an awful lot to take in, don't you think?" Beck reeled it off fast, rehashing it in a whimsical discrediting way, "A Pilgrim Pig— you, Detective Merit, claim that sixty years ago, some hotdog real estate agent hired a frogman to swim through a secret tunnel and surface above a pond inside a duck suit and shoot a fat golf club man in the neck. This foreigner, Novak, later lynched the chubby club owner using an upside-down knot, so he could send a text to finagle a golf course sale out of the hands of his dead widow. All, to build a magical green city of mirrors."

Merit faked a smile. "Said like a nursery rhyme doesn't make it sound so good. But I've assembled all the pieces to the puzzle!" Merit pointed to the evidence. "It's all right here!"

Beck shook his head. "The people are dead. You have no one who can corroborate any of this. What you've got barely rises to circumstantial evidence, indirect proof that no one today really cares about. What are you going to do with all this? Go back to Pilgrim and file a report that will be never seen? You can't arrest anybody."

"It's a sixty-year-old murder of a famous, influential golfer." Merit said.

Beck shook his head. "Best case scenario? You'd need someone in the media, like a writer or someone, to help you lay it all out, and that's not going to happen here in Frontier." Beck paused and rubbed his chin as he eyed the detective. "You did great work, but it was a waste of time. I told you when you first arrived, you should have gone through the motions and enjoyed yourself, you know soaked up some sun, man, get some ass." He offered him a hit off the reefer stick.

Merit was stung by Beck's cavalier attitude and shook off his passing of the peace pipe.

"You don't get it, Beck."

"—No Merit, *you* don't get it. It's good police work, but let's be honest, do you have the murder weapon? Do you know the name of the scuba diver? Even if the bones get identified, they'll be linked to a guy who got stuck in a pipe with a broken watch. And if he was the killer, then what? Stand up that skeleton you found in front of Pilgrim's firing squad and shoot it to death? It won't matter anyway, especially after tomorrow."

"Why? What's tomorrow?"

"Your old Fourth of July, man—*Acopalypse* Day. Remember? A parade. Fireworks. They blow up the Property and Evidence Building, kaboom." He blew out a plume of smoke, "And free the last one hundred prisoners."

"You seem to be happy about it." Merit fanned the smoke from his face.

Beck shrugged, "There's nothing I can do about it."

Merit looked at the evidence strewn across the room. His enthusiasm had waned, and Beck had a point. Despite everything he'd learned, he didn't have what he needed to bring the case to court. What he had were maps, texts, architectural plans, chunks of plastic, and a bag of bones. It wasn't enough. Beck, he concluded, was correct.

"What the people believe happened here is false," Merit said.

"I guess, but think of it this way, it led us to a better way of life."

"I wish I could've read that Major Murder Inquiry." Merit bowed his head in defeat.

"You can. It's still in the Evidence Room. That big book? I looked at it that first day we went there. Remember, the cover was *MMI* and I thought it was a rule book, but I'm sure it was the Inquiry. The Major Murder Inquiry. We can go get it."

Merit shook his head, thinking that it would be a waste of time.

"You did a good job, Merit. I couldn't have done that. I'll still lend a hand if you want—really—or else I can help you settle down in Frontier."

"No thanks. This entire state needs to be blown up." Merit manufactured his own explosion sound, then chucked the evidence into a box.

"Hey, at least you got some skirt from that skanky Chiquita before you go back and get hitched for life."

65

With no suspect ever named or determined, people referred to Soldier's killer as the guy who committed the "unequivocal race-hate crime." Besides the three-year-old little blonde beauty pageant contestant JonBenet Ramsey, who was strangled to death in her Colorado home in the 1990s, and the bizarre sexual circumstances surrounding the slashing death of 1960s television sitcom actor Robert Crane of "Hogan's Heroes," Soldier's death was the most famous unsolved murder of all time.

—Timothy Rands, *Biography of Soldier Quinn*

LUNA MOTH

Merit hated Beck's vulgar sexual innuendos about Starla when he called her *skanky*, and it ate away at him the whole way walking back to her home. He wished he would have said something, Beck was the *sex freak*, but he was done debating.

Merit returned to Starla's house to find that she wasn't home. She'd left a note saying that she had another tryout for a small part in a video pilot and had a good feeling about it. She apologized for getting mad at him and thanked him for comforting her. She thought Merit was an awesome detective for solving the case and that she'd be home soon, at which time they'd celebrate. Below her name she'd drawn the tiny outline of a handgun, then in a series of three sketches, left to right, creatively transformed the gun into the silhouette of a dove.

Merit wasn't in a good mood and tossed the note and all of his evidence into a garbage can in the kitchen and started to pack for his journey home. He'd given the case his all, but he'd come up short.

As he stuffed his belongings into Soldier's golf bag, Starla arrived in a decidedly bad mood also.

Merit called to Starla who was in the other room. "How'd it go?"

"I didn't get the part." She sounded sullen, before noticing Merit was moving about with a purpose. "What are you doing?"

"I'm packing." He glanced up at her. "I showed it to Beck, and he was right. The whole case as I've outlined is complicated. No one out here would buy it, and nobody wants to hear it."

"But I understood it," Starla said. "The decoy, the shooter, the motive—everything. I'll admit that it's a lot of information to take in, but I got it. It just needs someone to present it in a certain way."

"People here, like you, want their lifestyle, not the truth about an old murder they don't care about." Merit said.

"Well, some people *like me* do care!"

Merit wasn't in the mindset to discuss the case any longer since Starla didn't fully understand the odds he was up against. "What happened at the audition?"

"Not good. I could tell they didn't like me as soon as I walked in."

"Bummer. What's next then?

"They posted for a gig as a reveal reporter."

"Are you gonna try out?"

"I'd love to." Her eyes lit up. "Revealers here get to research a topic and then go on TV and reveal stuff—like people mistreating animals or exposing prejudiced cops and judges in Pilgrim and other countries and how they shoot innocent people or force little kids to wear guns or make prisoners live cooped up like chickens on some prison ships."

"You mean catching rapists and murders and making them pay for their crimes."

"Well, that's what I'd really like to do. It would be more fulfilling as opposed to just acting, and you still get to be in front of a camera."

"So you're gonna try out?"

"Nah. I wouldn't have a chance." She shook her head as she described the broadcasting industry. "Male producers and directors are biased too—the whole lot of them. I give up."

"You shouldn't. You're good. And stop blaming others for your troubles."

Starla's voice was filled with indignation. "Well, *you're* giving up too, Merit!"

Merit saw Starla's lip quiver at the mention of his departure, and her efforts to conceal her emotions weren't working.

"What's her name?" Starla raised her upper lip with a snarl.

"Who? —What name?"

"You never said it. Your *girlfriend*. You never told me her name." She crossed her arms.

Merit wondered why he hadn't, but knew deep inside why, talking about her would personalize things and make him vulnerable, and Starla didn't *really* want to know. "Ruth." He said looking her square in eyes. It was followed by several seconds of silence.

Her face turned stoic. "It's good that you're leaving. You're just too different."

"Me? *I'm* too different. Don't you have that backwards?"

"We could never live together. Look at you." She popped the lid off her pill bottle. "You're the strangest guy I've ever met. You don't have tattoos, your skin is—plain, your hair's . . . brown, and the way you talk, sound, and think is all wrong." She downed a pill with a glass of juice she poured with a shaky hand.

Merit kept a stiff lip as she belittled him, then retorted. "And that's *your* problem—taking all those pills to forget things you choose to do or say."

"Did I choose to be raped and cut open?" Her tone was angry, challenging, as she ripped open her blouse exposing her 'X' scarred Luna Moth tattoo on her chest.

"That's bullshit!" Merit wished he could take it back, but he'd been holding everything in and couldn't stop himself. "You allow yourself to be raped every day!"

She appeared deeply wounded at the accusation.

"Forget everything. Just go home to your God, guns, drones, and *Little Goody Two-Shoes* girlfriend. You just wanted a place to stay while you worked on your case. I shouldn't have let you stay here. You used me!" Starla chucked her pill bottle at Merit's face, and hundreds of blue tablets scattered across the floor. She opened the front door, went outside, and screamed. "Hey! There's a PP in here! Help. A Pilgrim Pig is in my home!"

Merit hurriedly scooped up the rest of his belongings into Soldier's golf bag, and looping the strap over his shoulder, escaped out the deck side door. There was no way to calm her fiery temperament.

"By the way." She spit the words at Merit before he was out of earshot, "some rude nurse from some hospital sent a message saying your swamp friend isn't doing so well."

Merit hurried away before vigilantes had time to respond to Starla's tirade.

With tears streaming down her face, Starla slammed the door.

66

Soldier's senseless death was not only synonymous with hate crimes but became linked to a political cause. Democrats used his murder as a platform to demand a nationwide ban on all firearms. Spurned by a proliferation of conservative podcast show-hosts, Republicans historically considered the "silent majority," out of fear of losing their right to bear arms, vocally pushed back. Politics, once considered to be poor taste to be mentioned in public, were freely discussed. People hurled insults in stores, malls, schools, workplaces, even in churches, which devolved into spitting and fistfights.
—source unk., *Title: The AmericanDream?/YouTube 56k views*

GO FOR IT

Keeper had been transferred to another ward, 11 North. A different nurse on Keeper's floor told Merit that the latest scans indicated that the old man's condition was worsening. When Merit entered Keeper's new windowless room, Keeper's eyes came to life. Merit removed the cumbersome golf bag that weighed heavy on his shoulder and leaned it against the wall.

"Was my dad's murder racially motivated?" Keeper leaned forward in his bed.

"No, it wasn't." Merit pulled up a chair and sat back. "But it's a complicated story, and I doubt anyone would believe me."

Keeper tried to get out of bed, but he didn't have the strength.

Merit spent the next fifteen minutes explaining the motive in exacting detail, much as he'd outlined it in chapter and verse for Beck and Starla. He tried to hide the anxiousness he was experiencing while presenting his findings, but Keeper was too astute and detected a change in his demeanor.

"You alright?"

"Yeah, I'm fine." Merit was still bothered by his tumultuous departure from Starla. She was unpredictable and he'd never associated with people on drugs. He worried that some of the things he said weren't very nice and could have pushed her over the edge causing her to do something desperate, like overdosing on the pills.

"Girl problems." Keeper muttered.

Merit indecisively shrugged his shoulders. He knew Keeper wasn't looking to discuss his personal matters but was rather acknowledging the age-old dilemma, man to man.

"Take a look at a two-minute timeline I made." Merit unclasped his watchband computer and positioned it on the table next to Keeper's bed to cast the video clip onto the ceiling, allowing Keeper to recline and view it on a much bigger screen. "It explains everything in more detail. It includes everything from the swans on the lake to the recreation of the crime to what I learned about the owner of the course and his refusal to sell the land."

After tinkering with the focus and volume, Merit dimmed the lights and tapped the PLAY button.

Keeper intensely scrutinized the short video, then looked at Merit. "It's a lot to digest, but it's the truth. The whole thing was done for money, and my dad was a red herring."

"Beck said it's too convoluted." Merit looked up at the ceiling as the video continuously replayed on a loop and muted the sound. "It's overwhelming, and even includes Pratt reading his Major Murder Inquiry findings. Nobody is going to take my word over a renowned ex-Olympic president and his team of one hundred experts."

Merit produced a thin rectangular box he'd discovered in the bottom of a side pouch of Soldier's club bag. "I got something for you though." He passed it to him.

"Super." Keeper shook the box and smirked, "Just what I needed, a box of golf tees."

"Look inside it."

Keeper opened the end flap to discover about twenty stamp-sized mini-cassette tapes, each stored inside plastic jewel cases. He spilled some onto the bed next to his pillow.

"They're personal audio recordings your dad made the year he died," Merit picked up one mini-cassette. "He discussed his childhood, his mother and father, the game of golf, and all of the things he went through in his golfing and personal life—setbacks and other personal revelations about his marriage and a lot about you, Keeper. How he felt about you."

Choked with emotion, Keeper swallowed hard. "Thanks, Merit. You're a good man."

"They've been in this bag since you last caddied him at the U.S. Open. That's where I found them. Nobody's ever heard them."

"I bet these are what he said he was going to give me after the round," Keeper said.

"I bet you're right. There are hours and hours of recordings."

Merit's smile faded and changed the topic to his inevitable departure. "I wish I had some easy way to say this, but I have to get going soon."

Keeper nodded. "You did what you said you'd do. You got the killer and figured out the *real* motive. And that's all that mattered to me. I have peace now." Keeper inhaled, and his eyes got glassy. "You have a safe trip back home, okay." He pulled out the knapsack of bones he'd stowed under the covers for safekeeping and returned them to Merit.

Both men figured it was probably best to make their goodbyes short and sweet. Merit firmly shook the hand of Keeper, with the bag of bones over one shoulder, he grabbed the golf bag and walked out the door and halfway down the hall when he heard Keeper call out for him.

"Wait!"

Merit wheeled sharply and returned to see Keeper looking up with great interest. His two-minute video was still playing on a loop, and he assumed Keeper was calling him back to retrieve the watch device he'd forgotten on the stand, but he was wrong.

"You have to see this!" Keeper pointed up at the ceiling. He was viewing the raw footage that followed Merit's two-minute video. "Quick! Rewind it!"

★★★

Lengthy segments of miscellaneous video that Merit had used to cut and paste snippets for his two-minute clip were still displayed on the ceiling. The segment Keeper asked Merit to rewind was of then ex-President Pratt *after* he'd presented the Inquiry's findings. Pratt, holding the official Major Murder Inquiry in his hands while he stood atop the steps of the Orange Golf Clubhouse, was flanked by the one hundred investigators who had comprised his team.

The two men in the hospital room watched the scene several times.

"I don't see anything," Merit's head cocked back, looking up at the ceiling.

"Rewind it again and look with the sound on."

Merit complied, and they viewed the scene again, this time listening to ex-IOC President Pratt declare emphatically that the murder of Soldier Quinn was "unequivocally race-hate related." Just as Pratt made his pronouncement, one that would go down in history and be repeated by millions of people for sixty years, two investigators on his team, one male and one female, subtly glanced back in his direction, a troubled look claiming their features.

"Freeze it! Did you see that?" Keeper used his cane as a pointer and indicated the investigators seated at opposite ends of the steps. "Rewind twenty seconds and play it again."

Merit kept his eyes fixed on the investigators' movements as the speech concluded and everyone disbanded, the two agents hurriedly approached Pratt in the crowd and appeared to confront him while they pointed at the inquiry book he was holding. "Yeah. I see it. They look confused as if he wasn't relating what the inquiry report really said."

"Exactly. I wonder if Pratt went off-script, and these two agents picked up on it?"

"Good eye, Keeper." Merit assessed the actions and reactions in the footage of the three subjects involved, over and over. "How did I miss that?" Merit scolded himself for the oversight. "I liked Pratt, but I wonder if he made up the race motive, or if someone made him say it? You were around back then Keeper—was golf racist?"

"No." Merit shook his head. "Golf was *not* racist. In fact, the *game* of golf was the most objective sport there probably ever was. It took you either one, two, three, four or however-many strokes to hit the ball into the hole. There was nothing left to subjectivity or opinion. Your ethnicity or gender or age or height or weight or how much money you made, had no effect on the game—your ball either went in the hole, or it didn't. That's what my dad loved about it. Now joining some of the private clubs where golf was played, that was a different story. It was very subjective. Your ethnicity, gender, age, background, occupation, politics, connections, marital status and wealth could've had a *big* influence on being selected as a member or not. But the actual *game* of golf was pure as snow."

"How did you get to play?"

"Golf was expensive. I was fortunate. My dad paid for it. Not everyone could afford to play. Most individual sports like swimming, snowboarding, tennis, equestrian, race car driving, were costly and your parents had to pay *all* the expenses. But even team sports, which had traditionally been paid for by the schools and taxpayers were getting pricey for the athletes. If adults wanted their kids to compete at a higher level, they had to foot more of the bill.

"That's the way it is back in Pilgrim now. Not everyone can afford the same things." Merit looked up at the ceiling and paused the video with Pratt's face in frame. "Why do you think Pratt made it up?"

"It seemed logical at the time—you know. All of the *indicators* pointed to a race-related crime." Keeper put a finger on his chin, then tapped it several times. "Maybe Pratt felt the pressure to supply an answer to satisfy the people? His team exhausted every lead and had run out of time. Maybe he was scared to say it— Or, since it looked like no one would ever solve it, he thought he could get away with saying it? —To keep the peace." He shook his head and snickered, "It worked. He said it, and they believed it. *No one* questioned it—*not* even the media—for all these years." Keeper looked out the window for several seconds, "And look what it led to."

Merit's head sunk forward as he looked down at the floor.

Keeper then looked back at Merit. "If we had that book, the Major Murder Inquiry, we could see what it really read. It could clarify if my dad was killed because of prejudice or not—*for the record.*" Keeper suddenly looked dejected. "I'm sure it's long gone by now."

Merit looked up with a gleam in his eye and moved close to Keeper. "I know where it is." His smile vanished. "Oh shit—what's today's date?"

Keeper glanced at the nurses' paperwork attached to his cot. "It's, uh, the fourth."

Merit stood up and slapped his forehead. "No. — Acopalypse Day! The evidence building."

The intense conversation of the two men was interrupted when three doctors dressed in white and four nurses barged into the room, a concerned look bore their faces. The mean nurse ordered Merit to exit immediately.

"No. It's okay nurse, he can stay." Keeper shot her a stern glare. "He's my friend."

The doctor sounded grave. "I'm afraid sir, you need emergency surgery," He looked at scans on a clipboard, "You're hemorrhaging in the brain and are at serious risk for a stroke. We have to operate immediately to repair a blood vessel."

Several nurses were already prepping Keeper for surgery with a sense of urgency, inserting a plastic oxygen tube in his nose and electrocardiogram leads to his chest. Three orderlies entered the room and swiftly transferred Keeper to a gurney.

"I'll wait here for you Keeper."

As they wheeled Keeper out of the room, he lifted his head, "No! Don't wait. Go get it!" There was an extra look of determination on his face when his mouth formed the words, "*Go for it.*"

Merit shook his head defiantly, realizing they were the same words he uttered to his father to hit the miracle shot off the fairway to the 18th green with the driver. He watched as the stretcher holding Keeper was steered down a hall by a mob of staff, pierced through two swinging red doors, and disappeared. He presumed it was the last time he'd see Keeper.

67

Failure to display one's party affiliation would mean being publicly outed. It was common for people to tattoo their bodies with social cause slogans or the face of the candidate they endorsed. Parents indoctrinated their children to side with their chosen party instead of letting them grow up to develop their own beliefs. Kids sported backpacks, lunch boxes, and hats with political phrases. Restaurants, bars, stores chains, sports franchises and automakers were pressured to make an alliance with one party or stood to lose their customer base. Some suffered from PD "political depression," for which psychiatrists provided therapy or prescribed medication. Marriage counselors urged new couples to choose a mate with the same party affiliation to avoid divorce down the line, and families with opposing views stopped communicating and became fractured.
—Dr. R Price *M.D., Religion, Psychology and Politics in the New World*

A GOOD LIE

By late afternoon, Merit tracked down Beck standing a block from his apartment, sharing a white powdered substance through a straw, which he assumed to be cocaine, chatting it up with two hot girls in French-cut bikinis who were much younger than he. Merit motioned for him to step aside.

"You're back! I thought you went home, my friend." Beck had a big grin and trotted over to give Merit an embrace. "You changed your mind—you're staying?"

"No." Merit stiffly endured the man-hug. "I need to go back to the evidence room."

"Yeah, they're blowin' it up tonight—and you wanna watch? Excellent!"

"No. I need to get the Major Murder Inquiry book. You said it was there."

"Sure. Okay. Why do you need it?" Beck gestured to the girls to standby, then turned to Merit. "Let's do these double-trouble babes first?"

Merit looked over at the two thin-thighed, bullet-breasted Barbie-doll like girls, paused for three long testosterone-boosted seconds, then nodded no.

"Okay." Beck said, "You don't mind if I knock out these *bookends* before we go?"

"Yeah, I do mind." He grabbed Beck's elbow and pulled him away. "I gotta hurry."

The sun-kissed, blonde-streaked twinsies got the hint and walked away holding hands, glancing back, giggling over their shoulder at Merit.

Merit proceeded to relate what he and Keeper had seen on his computer watch while viewing footage of ex-Olympic President Pratt after delivering the commission's findings.

"I don't think you should go. If someone sees you, there'll be trouble, man."

"You coming or not Beck?"

"There have been no problems for years in Frontier," Beck's tone changing to one of contention. "You could jeopardize race relations."

"Then I'm going without you." Merit started to turn to walk.

In resignation, Beck ran his fingers through his hair. "Merit! Stop. The book's not there. I took it when we were being chased by vigilantes. Remember? You didn't have room in the golf bag. I was going to give it to you later, but I forgot. Don't panic, I hid it somewhere safe."

"Good." Merit breathed a sigh of relief, time was running out. "Let's go get it."

Beck hesitated, a pained expression on his face. "Look, Merit, I don't think we should go. I told you before, I wouldn't mess with history. Besides man, I think deep down you like it here." A sinister grin crossed Beck's face. "You looked so happy in those pics up on that cliff, kissing Starla."

"How do you know her name?" Merit stood looking confused, "And how'd you know about the pictures?" The photos he hadn't seen that Ruth had confronted him with on the phone.

"Because I took them," Beck chuckled. "I had to doctor them a bit before sending them to Ruth. Remember your fiancée, *Ruth*?"

"Shit, Beck! Why did you do that? That was *you* up there?"

Merit remembered the rustling of bushes and the sound of a branch snapping on the cliff where he'd stood with Starla during the orange sunset. "And I didn't kiss her."

The Frontier servile shrugged. "I know. I was hoping it would make you wanna stay. Ruth would see you cheating and would break off your engagement and you'd stay here."

Merit stared at him speechlessly, his mouth slightly open in a state of bewilderment, Beck had crossed the line.

Then, without warning, Beck leaned in to kiss him on the mouth.

Merit flinched his head in time and managed to evade the unwanted advance but couldn't contain his anger. His first punch caught Beck under the jaw and stunned him, sending him flat on his back. Merit dropped and straddled his waist and was about to deliver a knockout punch, but spotted two faint initials on the servile's neck, under his mane of hair when he turned away to avoid the blow.

"PP?" Merit said, holding his fist cocked in the air. "You're a Pilgrim Pig?"

68

By the year 2031, every day brought some new political debate that overshadowed Soldier's murder, which receded from the public consciousness. Still, every year the media ran specials around the time he was killed, highlighting his accomplishments, and rehashing the same unanswered questions. Even though interest in Soldier's murder diminished, the manner of his death—by firearm—ramped up a public furor. Pro-and anti-gun rights groups debated and had fistfights. NRA members and second amendment followers egged on the anti-gun demonstrators by parading with their sidearms in plain view. In retaliation, anti-gun activists organized large sit-ins at gun shows and disrupted business transactions, leading to violent standoffs. There was an unsettling feeling that either side would go to drastic measures to make their point.

—Fox and Allen Live, *Podcast News Commentary hour*

KISS GOODBYE

Walking with pace, Beck used a flashlight as he led Merit to a distant cabin house near the northeastern part of Orange Bay. "I should've told you I used to be a cop from Pilgrim. I'm real sorry." He'd been rambling. "And I apologize again, man, I shouldn't have taken those pictures of you and Starla. That was selfish. And I shouldn't have tried to kiss you. I just wanted you to like Frontier, man." He glanced over his shoulder at Merit who held an intense stare. "But aren't you glad I saved the Inquiry book? I had a feeling you might need it one day. We still friends?"

Merit felt violated and looked flustered. First, men didn't interfere with other men's relationships, another rule his father had taught him, and second, even though many gay people lived in Pilgrim, he had never been propositioned by a man. He needed the Inquiry and restrained from voicing his disgust and changed the topic. "You were right, my evidence was too complicated. But later I looked up the two investigators who confronted ex-President on the night he delivered the inquiry's findings, and both died two weeks later, *he* in a one-vehicle car accident, and *she* from carbon monoxide poisoning. She *accidentally* left her car running in her attached garage. The exhaust fumes seeped under the door into her house." Merit shook his head. "That wasn't a coincidence."

"Really? I agree, and you'll become the greatest detective of all time if you're right."

"That's not why I'm doing it. And where'd you hide this inquiry book?"

"We're almost there. This is my mom's fishing cabin. Keep following me down the garden path. It's in the tool shed to the right of the cabin house."

Beck opened a creaky metal door and spun around with no warning and pistol-whipped Merit in the jaw—*Whack*, knocking him woozy into a bed of flowers and mulch.

"Put your hands on your head." Beck aimed the gun down at Merit's chest.

Merit slowly sat up as blood leaked from his inner lip, "That's my gun." He recognized it instantly. A matt black Beretta double-action-only semi-auto handgun.

Beck flashed a wicked smile. "You should've gone home Merit."

Merit squinted his eyes and looked up at Beck's smooth skin and his facial complexion, which had no hint of any stubble or five o'clock shadow. He examined his blue eyes, slender nose, and thick, lustrous hair. It was then that he had his epiphany.

"No way. . . No way. I know who you are. You're not only a Pilgrim cop, you were a Pilgrim detective. You're Detective Derry Darrins. You're him, or you used to be her." He shook his head confused.

"You solved another mystery." Beck was unhappy that his identity had been exposed but held off from showing his displeasure.

"Everyone thinks you're dead." Merit was about to comment on the undetectable gender change Beck had undergone, but a loaded gun pointed at him and unsure of Beck's intentions had prevented further commentary. "Did you know the land developer had the course owner killed—and all the rest I told you about?"

"No, but I was getting closer," Beck said. "I never connected all of the dots like you."

"Why'd you quit?"

Beck didn't answer.

"The Inquiry book isn't here, is it?" Merit knew the answer to his question; it was back in the evidence warehouse, Beck had lured him away to the remote spot. Beck looked at Merit pathetically. Merit now understood why Beck had been so interested in whether he could solve the case. Beck was a product of Pilgrim's upbringing, and he'd also wanted to make sure that Merit didn't solve the homicide so that Frontier's culture could be preserved. The stakes were raised even higher when he noticed Vigilantes One and Two emerging from the shadows behind the former Pilgrim detective.

Beck seemed pleased. "Good timing, guys."

The Mohawk-headed Vigilante pushed Merit back to the ground and kicked him in the ribs. "That's for your golf partner killing Rusty." He then stomped Merit in the gut, temporarily knocking the wind out of him. "And that's for my buddy who drowned trying to catch you."

"You're real tough—roughing up an old man," Merit said when he got his breath back. He didn't want to enlighten him to the fact that his buddy who drowned *technically* was devoured by the devil sea-snake.

Under Beck's direction, the vigilantes dragged Merit by his feet down to the bay's shore and handcuffed him to the dock's light pole as night descended.

"You gonna shoot me? Thought you didn't believe in guns and killing?"

"Don't flatter yourself." Beck without looking, ejected the magazine, then the one round from the chamber of Merit's handgun and laid it and the key to the handcuffs on a nearby rock. "In an hour, the evidence building will be destroyed and all its contents, including Pratt's Inquiry report book. I'm doing you a favor, in the morning, some drifter or boater will come along and set you free. Then you can work your way back to Pilgrim with your trusty gun and bag of bones. It's over Merit. We could have been friends."

"You're going to let the truth remain hidden so you can live in a society you *feel* is better? You're still a cop. Our job is to find the facts and present them. It's not for us to decide whether we like them. *You* know that. I saw your police photo back when you were first sworn in. The uniform, badge, the Pilgrim flag behind you—what happened?"

"I moved forward." The renegade servile paused for a second. "And after tonight's celebration, I'm going to pay a *pleasure* call on your acting friend."

"What acting friend?"

"You're smart, but you're naïve Merit." Beck snickered. "Starla is *already* an actress."

"What do you mean?"

"I paid for her to go to the market that first day you landed here and seduce you. She's been watching you for me the entire time. That way I could know what you were always doing. It's an act."

"You're full of it, Beck!"

"How else would I have known you'd be on the cliff so I could take that picture? She's a pretty good actress, eh? Her act is over, and so are you. Old-time cops are a thing of the past. So, bye-bye, Miss American pie."

"You're the real *miss*—*Miss* Beck or *Miss* Darrins or *Mis-fit* whatever you are."

Vigilante One handed Beck a V-shaped folded aluminum-framed kite attached with a lightweight electric charged motor. "First, I'm gonna watch the firework's explosions and then enjoy the building implosion. He stuck his finger in his mouth, pressed it against the inside of his cheek, and pulled it out, creating a popping *whoop-de-do* sound effect, mocking old America's treasured Independence Day. "Happy Fourth of July." With a snide smile, Beck took a knee next to him.

Merit sensed what was coming but had no choice, with his hands shackled, he shied his face to the right, closed his eyes, and cringed as Beck kissed his other cheek.

Beck grabbed the sleekly fashioned kite's crossbar and began running along the sand toward the shore's edge, taking a couple of steps in the shallow waves before the warm breeze gathered beneath the extended wings and lifted him from the water. He was airborne and skimming over the waves of the moonlit sea. Gradually, aided by the small engine's propulsion, he gained height and soared high above the peaceful bay, passing through gauze-like clouds until he was out of sight.

Vigilante Two stooped over and picked up Merit's gun, a crazed look in his eye. Merit realized with the rarity of guns in Frontier, it was probably the first time the Mohawk-headed vigilante had ever held a firearm. The way the contoured grip fits in the palm of one's hand, the way fingers naturally wrapped around the cold metal could provide a sense of power that was intoxicating. Merit could see from the Vigilante's increased breathing that his emotions had been seized and were being overtaken by an innate impulse to squeeze the trigger. He approached Merit, bloodlust in his eyes.

"Easy partner," the head Vigilante cautioned his itchy trigger-finger subordinate. "Beck wanted us here to make sure there were no problems, nothing more."

"You killed Rusty. My best friend," Vigilante Two fumed while using his free hand to stroke the bristly ends of his low-cut hairdo. "Tell me, Pilgrim Pig—who are you here for?"

"No one. I told you. I was here on an investigation."

He steadied the muzzle directly between Merit's eyes and slowly squeezed the trigger.

Merit stared down the barrel, knowing there was no talking to the dumb ox, so he closed his eyes.

★★★

The chamber clicked, but the weapon didn't discharge. Merit grimaced, then opened one eye.

Vigilante One looked exasperated. "Give me the gun, dumb shit."

"No. I'm gonna kill this PP." The Mohawk-headed brute ripped the handgun back, pointing it at Merit's forehead. With a big smile, he pressed the trigger a second time, but there was still only a click of the chamber. "Shit."

Merit flinched each time he heard the ominous sound of the trigger being squeezed. It would be bitter irony, he thought, if he were killed by his own weapon after everything he'd endured in Frontier and where guns were practically nonexistent. Where was justice? Maybe there wasn't a God.

Vigilante One picked up the loaded magazine from the rock and stripped the gun from the hands of Vigilante Two. He shook his head as if his fellow vigilante were ignorant.

"You gotta load it." He fumbled with the clip at first, as if unsure how the ammunition was loaded. "The bullets go in—" but then inserted the magazine into the gun's handle smoothly. "The bullets go in this, and this thing goes in here." He then ran the action, gripping the top of the gun's barrel and shoving it back toward him, loading a .40 Caliber round into the chamber. "Then you do this. I think."

The head honcho Vigilante aimed the loaded weapon at Merit's temple, a look of satisfaction in his eyes. At the last second, however, he pointed the gun to the side and shot Vigilante Two in the forehead—Dead center. The Mohawk-headed vigilante, the one that had taken the most pleasure in torturing Merit and Keeper, collapsed on the beach, blood pooling like syrup in a depression in the sand.

Vigilante One then walked up to Merit, the gun at his side.

Merit winced at what he thought was going to be certain death. He bowed his head, calmly asserting, "Keep the gun. I know it's worth a lot. Just don't shoot me! I'll return to Pilgrim and won't say a thing."

Instead, the boss-man removed the cuffs off his prisoner, and Merit stood defenseless with his hands up. The vigilante speedily ejected the magazine containing fourteen bullets, then the round from the chamber and handed the gun, magazine and projectile to Merit, the harsh look on his face fading. He was suddenly, surprisingly adept at handling a firearm.

"I'm a Pilgrim cop too." He was matter of fact saying it.

"Another defector?" Merit walked backward into the shallow edge of the bay.

"No. I'm here on special assignment. Trust me."

"I don't believe you."

"Before you left Pilgrim—when you were with Sergeant Travers on your last night—you saw an *informant* being led into the interrogation room by the Fraud Unit. Remember?"

"The guy with the towel over his head?" Merit hesitantly nodded. "Yeah, I remember."

"That was me. They brought me back from Frontier and were briefing me about your investigation. I infiltrated this band of vigilantes two years ago."

Merit was suspicious. Was he being set up? How could he believe anyone in Frontier? His eyes shifted down to the dead vigilante, a fine thread of smoke wafted up from the bullet hole in his forehead, the hot projectile had singed the outer layer of skin before penetrating his skull. Merit's eyes darted back. "Prove it." He aimed the gun at the lead vigilante's chest after swiftly reloading the magazine and chambering a round.

The unshakable undercover cop answered calmly. "When we first confronted you in the market and you shoved that fruit in my face, do you think peach juice would've blinded me? And when we captured you at the market, did *I* kick or hit you? No. When you were taking your windsurfing lesson, did I see you hiding under the board? —Yes. Did I expose you? —No. When you were in the lake and that arrow I shot passed high over you, way high, did you think that was by accident? And I just gave you back your standard-issued loaded gun."

A figure came out from the shadows, barely visible in the moonlight.

"Hubbard?" Merit squinted to confirm his identity. "Is that you?"

"Yes, Merit. And he's Pilgrim PD." An unlit cigarette was situated loosely between his lips.

The old cold case Detective Hubbard removed a body bag from the inner pocket of his tweed jacket, unfolded it, then laid it out next to the dead vigilante, and with the aid of the undercover cop's help, rolled the cumbersome load onto his side and into the bag before zipping it shut.

"Ruth contacted us when you didn't show up at the Frontier-Pilgrim border." Hubbard stopped, removed the cigarette from his lips, and tucked it above his ear, much like one would do with a pencil. "The attendants told her you were high on drugs and jumped from the tram and were probably dead. We've spent the last two weeks trying to find you." He produced a folded piece of stationery paper and read from it. "This is from Ruth." He slipped on his crooked reading glasses. "Merit. If you are still alive, I'm sorry for what I said. Your dad *didn't* cheat on your mom. I made that up because I was scared. I met someone else and am moving on. I hope you can forgive me. Ruth." He passed Merit the note.

Merit read the brief note trying to assimilate the information. Ruth was a good fit on paper, but there was no real emotional connection, and he had to admit he was relieved it was over.

"I followed you the best I could without hurting you." The undercover officer shrugged.

With no holster, Merit tucked the gun in the back of his waistband. Having his sidearm back felt good. "But you let them brand me," as he rubbed the back of his neck.

"I couldn't stop them without blowing my cover." The undercover officer removed two extra sets of drones from his pack as he spoke. "Your sergeant says your time is up. You and I gotta fly out of here now. They'll be after us." Using the side of his foot, he nonchalantly bulldozed several layers of sand onto the vigilante's coagulated puddle of blood until it was blanketed.

Merit, sitting on the dock, couldn't believe what he was hearing. "I need to get the Major Murder Inquiry book. It's in the basement of the Evidence Building, which is going to be destroyed in one hour! It holds proof about Soldier's murder."

Hubbard looked at the conflicted detective. "There's not enough time, Merit." He powered on an extra cell phone and handed it to Merit.

Merit slid the phone in his back pocket and gazed at the distant city lights far across the bay. Hubbard was right. By the time he flew to the city, it might be too late.

"I was so close." Merit snapped the drones onto his feet and elbows.

The Pilgrim undercover detective checked his digital compass and pointed out the direction in which he and Merit needed to fly.

Hubbard rolled the heavy body bag like a log to the end of the dock, then unzipped it several inches to allow water to flood it. It was almost laughable—a riddle of sorts. He'd spent his entire career *uncovering* murders, the ultimate injustice inflicted on mankind and here *he* was, covering *up* a murder. This was how it would end—a week away from retiring? *So cliché* he thought. Like a cop on his last day on the beat that is killed—But *he* wasn't being killed, *he* was doing the killing. Either way, it was the worst thing that could happen.

With the heel of one foot, he directed the heavy sack into the bay, *Plunk*. "It's legal here, right?" he said with an air of condescending double-talk while lighting a cigarette. The typically outspoken Detective Hubbard, however, was torn on the inside. He knew murder was morally wrong. But even stranger, he *knew* he'd get away with it— There was no longer crime in their world—No one to investigate him. No worries about a knock on the door in the wee hours of the night, like killers in the past *heard* in their sleep.

Hubbard watched as the bag securing the dead thug slowly took in water, capsized, and began to drop out of sight. As the normally overly cautious investigator took a drag, he realized the odd predicament he was in, and how he could've anticipated or avoided it. For his unblemished law enforcement profession to end in this manner would haunt him for the rest of his life. He smirked to himself, *Shit*, then flicked his cigarette into the water as the last air bubbles escaping the sinking cadaver bag popped on the surface. He informed the two detectives he would be leaving the area in the next several minutes. He'd catch the Las Vegas tram back to Pilgrim, being he wasn't fond of flying.

Merit rose into the air and spoke to his comrades below. "Sorry guys, I gotta get that book." The two looked at him like he was out of his mind. "Officer. Go to Starla's house and make sure she's okay——tell her where I'm headed, The Property Room. And Hubbard, take that bag—It contains the killer's bones. And go to Diamond Bar Hospital and check on Keeper Quinn. He's Soldier's son."

"No, Merit!" Hubbard waved wildly as if his gestures could stop the Pilgrim detective.

"Don't be stupid. You can't do it!"

Merit ascended into the sky and yelled down. "Now Hubbard, that's passion!"

69

The pro-and anti-gun forces in America were at a stalemate. There was no resolution, making gun rights America's most polarizing political issue. Other historically divisive matters such as abortion, civil rights, religious freedom, and the death penalty took a backseat to the gun issue and law enforcement's misuse of power. Decades of school shootings, mass shootings and soaring homicide rates, which previously drew national debate but never resulted in any changes, finally reached a tipping point. Soldier's murder by firearm was the straw that broke the camel's back, and an anti-gun campaign that claimed to own a firearm, in and of itself was racist, pushed voters to pick a side. When it came to casting ballots, citizens put all their stock in a politician's line on guns. Individuals and families, fearing their liberties would be stripped, began to migrate to states that embraced their stance on gun rights and the use of law enforcement.
—Roman Johansen, Quebec Gazette (10/2032)

ACOPALYPSE DAY!

The soon-to-be ex-Servile Beck soared through the night sky like a huge condor, feeling gratified that he had preserved Frontier from the clever, yet pesky detective from Pilgrim without resorting to gun violence. He genuinely liked Merit, although he was jealous of his tenacity and the relationship he'd developed with Starla.

Riding the updrafts on his kite, which had a wingspan of twelve feet, he had a literal birds-eye view of the celebration he was approaching, which was growing in size and intensity. The Fourth of July fireworks show had started with exactly one hour left before the bells in the clock towers around the city struck midnight.

The state of Frontier's Fourth of July festival was designed to poke fun at the old America's Fourth of July celebration, where parades and fireworks acknowledged its independence from the grips of England in 1776 and embraced a new capitalist society based on greed by the wealthy and punishment of the poor.

The people of Frontier would commemorate not only its physical separation from Pilgrim back in 2035, but also a philosophical divorce from Pilgrim's ultra-conservative laws, greedy capitalistic system, over-aggressive policing, and unfair punishment of the breakers of such pointless laws.

Beck was reared under Pilgrim's strict doctrines, convinced he was a victim of their shortsightedness, and it stunted his brain development as a child. At the age of seven, all Pilgrim State residents were instructed on how to shoot a gun and wear a holstered pistol to protect themselves, and he believed by being mandated to do so, restricted a child's innate proclivity to trust others and instilled them with a distorted sense of power. When Beck was a teen, his parents, teachers, and role models taught him to follow a specific line of thinking and how it corresponded to money, success, relationships, and religion. He felt being raised without the leeway to explore and express his inner thoughts, act on his emotions and sexual carnalities––without the fear of judgment or punishment, grossly misshaped his outlook on life and his mental maturation.

Detective Darrins had proved to be a respected detective on Pilgrim's Police Department, and it was only when she traveled to Frontier to work Soldier Quinn's cold case did she begin to discover the truth about herself. Her experimentation with drugs and sex broadened her thinking and unlocked something deep inside of her, a *masculine* side, allowing her to have a complete gender change operation.

It gnawed at Beck that Merit exposed him as an ex-Pilgrim cop and had figured he used to be a female. Feelings of insecurities he hadn't felt since he had the procedure years earlier, were stirred. He was hurt when Merit made fun of him, calling him *Miss Whatever you are*. It made him even angrier because he'd helped with the Soldier case and also had feelings for him. Merit was the repressed sexual misfit, not him. He clearly suffered from the Madonna-whore complex, Ruth and Starla, the two women who fit the bill but was too uptight to ever own up to it.

He felt sorry for Pilgrim cops like Merit, who lived their lives under the unnatural notion that ideas and people had to be fit into a certain box, a right and wrong way, and it was their job to enforce it on non-conformists. He'd hoped once Merit had tasted the fruits of Frontier, he would break the chains that bound him and reach his true potential, but Merit was too focused on solving the stupid case.

Whether Soldier's murder was committed because of a race-hate crime or capitalistic greed didn't matter to Beck now. Frontier's philosophy was the future, and Beck saw himself as a trailblazer, not a defector as Merit probably fingered him out to be, for saving Frontier from Merit and all the stifling of progress Pilgrim represented.

Hundreds of thousands of citizens had gathered in the main town plaza below, which Beck circled as colorful floats and marching bands assembled for a parade that would travel twenty blocks to the Property and Evidence Building. Spontaneous cheers erupted as the crowd, packed together, took up chants such as "No more laws!" and "No more crime!" and "No more serviles!"

A longhaired hipster type with a headband and beard stood on a riser and addressed the scores of onlookers with a megaphone, denouncing all serviles and praising the decriminalization program, which would reach fruition at midnight.

★★★

The last one hundred prisoners in Frontier, serious violent criminals, stood dressed in blue jumpsuits outside the city slammer, overjoyed, jumping up and down in anticipation of their imminent release and ready to join the parade. Citizens praised them for their patience in the face of injustice since they had endured oppression at the hands of serviles, who had been the final instruments and symbols of a police state that had thankfully eroded over the decades. The members of the great gathering gifted the prisoners with flowers, food, and necklaces with dove pendants while glaring at the handful of serviles still charged with guarding the oppressed inmates.

Finished with his rant on the complete liberation from the tyranny of rules, the hippie speaker hopped off the platform and slipped through the crowd as people congratulated him on his extemporaneous speech.

When he reached the perimeter of the square, he ducked behind a dumpster and tore off his clothes and fake beard and threw them into the receptacle, setting the trash on fire.

He then donned the hood of his official office, for he was Chief Reed, the police chief of Capital City.

70

Patriotism was threatened in the Sixties by hippies objecting to the Vietnam War, in the seventies with public flag burnings in protest of the Kent State shootings, and in the 2010s when pro-athletes refused to stand during the national anthem. But nothing compared to the outrage that erupted in 2032. Government employees arrived at work to discover eagle carcasses strewn on the steps. Notes tied to the majestic bird's necks threatened that more would be butchered unless all gun sales were banned. People from both parties were repulsed by the protected bird of prey's genocide, but neither was willing to compromise. When the radical group's unrealistic demands went unmet, more eagles were found decapitated, skewed with arrows, eaglets clubbed to death, or lit on fire. The bald eagle, once the proud symbol of what was best about America, over the next year, was exterminated.

—Thomas Poster, *Washington D.C.@Esquire.com*

FINAL HOLE

Powered by a set of fresh drones, Merit leaned forward, aiming his body like a rocket at the lights of Capital City, now just several hundred yards ahead. Glancing at his watchband, he noted that he had little time to retrieve the Major Murder Inquiry report. If he was lucky, he would be able to get in and out of the Property and Evidence warehouse with a few minutes to spare.

Merit could now see the festivities below, and the beast-like silhouette of the evidence structure looming to the sky far on his left. He saw an object in his peripheral vision. Examining it more closely, he saw that it was Beck, speeding through the air straight for him, wings pinned back on his kite, like a hawk dive-bombing for a field mouse. He tried to maneuver away, but it was too late. The former Pilgrim detective clipped Merit, sending him spinning out of control, but he recovered by changing the controls of his drones.

Deafening fireworks exploded around the pair as Beck circled back and scissored Merit's waist with his legs. They quickly lost altitude, diving for the earth with their bodies twisted together, but they disengaged three hundred feet above the crowd, shielded from view by the reds, blues and greens of fireworks.

Streaks, flares, and bursts of hot color nearly blinded the two men until they regained altitude. Beck dove at Merit a second time, and the dogfighters, dancing on the wind, exchanged wild blows as they desperately tried to maintain balance and equilibrium. Each landed a few punches, but most swings were fists flailing in the air, missing the other man by several inches as their positions constantly shifted in aerial combat.

★★★

Beck sailed in close enough to strip the handgun from Merit's waistband before veering right and putting distance between himself and his foe. He was now armed, but it was difficult to see his target as the fireworks continued to light up the sky, illuminating it and then leaving it in darkness before the next salvo of colorful explosions were fired from the pyrotechnic crew below.

As Merit's body appeared and disappeared a dozen times, Beck fired wildly at a moving target that vanished every few seconds. He would commit a violent act for the greater good of preventing future violence. After several failed attempts, Beck got off a lucky shot that grazed Merit in the shoulder. He saved three shots in case they should become necessary. Merit was a tenacious fighter, and if he recovered, Beck wanted more ammo to use against him.

In point of fact, he wanted to kill Merit outright and end his meddlesome investigation for good.

★★★

Merit accelerated toward his target but suddenly veered to the right, clearly having trouble controlling his flight. His maneuverability was further compromised when a firework exploded directly below his feet, taking out one foot drone and burning his ankle. He spiraled into an uncontrolled accelerating descent to the north, ironically comparable to how Soldier's last shot off the fairway started straight for the green, but inexplicably peeled off right and down toward the thickets.

Flames ignited the bottom of Merit's short trousers as he continued his rapid descent.

Whoop-whoop. "Pull up. Pull up." The drone's ground proximity system sounded. He quickly surveyed his options and saw a tiny glowing body of aqua blue in a residential section to the right, a lighted swimming pool, and by angling his body sideways, he had barely enough control to steer for the backyard pool, splashing into the deeper end of the water twenty seconds later.

His plummet to the earth had not gone unnoticed, however, by people on the fringe of the crowd who had seen a man wearing drones and knew that he was not from Frontier. *A drone-man!* They'd broken away from the hoopla, running at full speed for the pool while cursing the Pilgrim Pig and his technology. They scaled a backyard fence enclosing the swimming pool as Merit hauled his dripping body out of the deep end.

Merit climbed a white trellis on the side of the home and scampered across the flat roof. With a half dozen citizens in pursuit, he hopped from roof to roof, his speed impeded by his soaking wet clothes. He jumped off the last house in the subdivision and ran as fast as his legs could carry him.

Turning a corner, he ran into the parade plodding in the direction of the property building. With his pursuers only a block to the rear, he stripped off his wet shirt and tied it around his head to wear like a turban, then blended in with the parade and marched at a steady pace, fake smiling and waving a mini-Frontier pennant on a stick. But the crowd was catching up with him and hurling barbs in his direction, pointing to the Pilgrim Pig who was threatening to disrupt their long-awaited Frontier celebration.

The shrieks of his pursuers attracted the attention of the prisoner leading his fellow army of inmates along the parade route. He was the incarcerated creep with the double ponytail, the very white male shitbag who had not only participated in the violent rape of Starla, but the one who mutilated her chest with the letter X, and he made direct stone-cold eye contact with Merit.

The prisoners in front surged forward, with inmates and rowdy citizens chasing the policeman who had fallen like a comet. Desperate, Merit turned his head left and right to look for a means of escape. He spotted a procession of antique show cars being pulled by ropes as part of the festivities and instantly recognized one vehicle from the garage of Rebecca's father's collection, the pearl white '68 Porsche Targa.

Remembering she'd kept the key in the ignition and her father had taught her to keep a little gas in the tank to start it once a month, he forced his way through the participants.

Would he be as fortunate as Soldier's last drive where the "miracle ball" had provided him *two* lucky bounces? The first bounce struck *Whales Breach Rock* redirecting away from the thickets, and the second bounce off the drinking fountain that deflected the ball toward the green and saved him from a disastrous round.

Merit had been granted his first *stroke of luck* when he dodged death by splash landing his flaming drone into the residential pool, but could lighting strike twice? He urgently needed out of his situation, and that second charmed bounce would have to come in the form of a vintage Porsche. If the key was in the ignition and a smidgen of gas was left in the tank, as Rebecca had said there was, he could use the roadster to escape major trouble and propel him closer to the Evidence building.

He made a running leap over the driver's door of the opened convertible and landed on the leather bucket seat of the rare sports car. *Phew*, the key was there. He squeezed his eyes shut and turned it clockwise, the coup cranked on the first turn, "Thank you, Lord," and he roared it down the street, revving the engine, shifting gears quickly putting distance between himself and the chasers. Once again, he was taunted by angry shouts.

"Hey, stop, you asshole!"

Others weren't quite sure if the gas-guzzling, foreign German two-seater was part of the entertainment.

"Look Mommy, man in a race car!" a few little toddlers tugging on their parents' pants, pointed out.

Merit was ahead of the parade and raised his head to see the beams of great spotlights crisscrossing the front of the old evidence building just as lights had long ago played across the sky for Hollywood premiers. He accelerated for the lights, knowing that there was precious little time left. He knew exactly where the book was—if only he could get inside.

Directly in front of him were hard hat workers inside a chain-link fence setting the final charges for the controlled implosion of the building. Hundreds of people sat in temporary bleachers and lawn chairs on three sides at a safe distance, and the back row held up a large banner that read PRISONERS, FORGIVE US and ACOPALYPSE DAY! Merit could go no farther and braked to a stop.

The engine purring, obstructed from the view of the people, Merit sat motionless for several seconds, staring ahead at his lie. If the white Targa was Soldier's golf ball resting on the 18th green, trying to make it into the final hole for a win, and the dungeon of the evidence warehouse being the bottom of the cup, he was now one putt away from triumph.

He'd been kicked in the ribs at the beach house, had been grazed in the shoulder by Beck and had fallen from the sky, but he knew that he had to force his muscles to move, for he could hear the parade drawing close as a demolition worker announced through a bullhorn "T-minus ten minutes and counting!"

Merit slipped unnoticed into the unguarded evidence warehouse—demolition workers were coming and going through the front door every few seconds—

★★★

The mayor, who would shortly voluntarily abandon his position of political power, had started delivering his final speech on a stage outside LAPD's Property and Evidence building. He was still holding forth with just minutes left before the scheduled implosion, reciting the benefits of doing away with the police and the very concept of criminals.

"We first outgrew parents, lifeguards, then matured past teachers, professors, mentors and politicians—like me," he spoke through an electronic bullhorn. "And we've finally succeeded the worst rank of society that ever existed, namely the law enforcement.'

The word "law enforcement" drew booing and hissing from the crowd, which began shouting, "No more serviles!"

"The serviles and police tried to control our behavior for generations!" the mayor said. "They told us how to act, but all they did was perpetuate repression and force their outdated values on a population that doesn't need their guidance any longer. There's no need for the police to abuse their power and watch over our shoulders! This Fourth of July, we are truly independent."

The crowd grew rambunctious with each word of the mayor's diatribe as the demolition crew hurried to a safe place outside of the fence. The foreman called out "T-minus five minutes!" The prisoners, seated on rows of benches on a raised platform under a colorfully striped canopy, sensing that their confinement was almost at an end, were shedding their jail jumpsuits, donning new clothes and money thrown to them by the crowd.

★★★

Amid the chaos, Chief Reed approached one of his servile guards near the prisoners and told him what a great job he'd done in the face of such opposition. "You'd better get out of here. It's no longer safe. The days of police work are over."

After midnight, it wouldn't be safe to be known as the servile who had once headed the city's entire law enforcement division. Wearing medallions and putting a different fake beard on his face, he sifted in with the crowd and grabbed a bullhorn, condemning the forces of law and order that had plagued Capital City for so long. He decided he would retain his new persona indefinitely, allowing his natural beard and hair to grow out in the weeks ahead. He would change his name, take injections to have his skin pigment altered, and never again be associated with his former job.

He knew, of course, that crime really existed in Frontier and would continue to flourish. He'd meltdown two of the three 9mm pistols he'd secretly confiscated years earlier for a plentiful reward, keep the other for protection, find a home somewhere in the desert or travel the world with his wife and get the good life that they'd denied themselves for so many years.

71

In 2033, a controversial law was passed that gave federal agents authority to randomly search citizens' homes to conduct a 'gun inventory'. But when the folks of a tiny town in Arkansas refused to comply by barricading their streets and taking up small arms, the Army was called in to enforce the order. The televised standoff that pitted a handful of rural American citizens against U.S. troops equipped with tanks and high-powered weapons inspired neighboring towns and states to back the Ozark hillbillies' revolt. Under the cover of night, a growing number of gun-rights supporters tactfully surrounded the military and pinned the troops from both sides. Three months of nightly skirmishes killed eleven resisters and fourteen soldiers, placing the U.S. President in a precarious position. Allied leaders, concerned about the "superpower's" stability and a genuine threat of civil war, consulted with the President. With the nation teetering on anarchy, he beckoned all former presidents and vice presidents to converge at Camp David for an emergency summit.

—by Armous, Barga and Scully, *American History textbook/level 9*

FIREWORKS FINALE

Detective Merit descended into the guts of the property warehouse where Soldier's evidence had been stored. Five minutes until the demolition was the last announcement he'd heard from the demo unit. Using the light from the cell phone Hubbard had provided him, he shone the light ahead, its beam illuminating the dusty gray metal shelves holding precious evidence from thousands of cases, cases that would never be solved after the cartons were destroyed in a matter of minutes.

There was nothing Merit could do about the grave injustice that was about to transpire, but he could at least solve one case—maybe the most important in history—if he could get the Major Murder Inquiry book. He aimed his beam in every direction of the inner caves, trying to get his bearings since every row looked the same. He paused when he saw what looked like the outline of a man standing on the other side of the room. Beck.

Both men froze as the sound of the parade circling the block reached their ears, the mayor of Capital City making a grandiose speech about the decriminalization of Frontier and the new era that would be ushered in when the building fell, and evidence was destroyed. The crowd was in a frenzy, believing that Frontier would now attain new heights.

Merit's attention was jarred back to his enemy at the far end of the aisle. He charged at the former female detective traitor, who dropped his light when he saw his nemesis running toward him.

Beck looked shocked to see a man who he'd written off as dead. "Jesus Christ! You don't go away."

Beck wrapped his fingers around the handle of a hatchet coated in dried blood that had been sealed in a paper evidence bag. "You're out of time." He waved it back and forth as if getting a feel for its grip and weight, all the while keeping his eyes steadily fixed on Merit.

In response, Merit ransacked several evidence cartons at random and took hold of the first solid object he found, which was a steering wheel from an automobile. As Beck advanced, swinging his hatchet at the Pilgrim cop, Merit, grasping the wheel with both hands, deflected the sharp blade time after time, like a knight warding off the blows of a sword with his shield. Beck drove ahead with hatred in his eyes and pushed Merit backward, causing him to fall.

Dazed, he recovered quickly and threw the steering wheel sideways, causing it to spin forward like a discus, whacking Beck in the knee. The servile howled in pain as he lost his balance, pulling boxes from shelves as he searched for any object to use as a weapon. Merit did the same, and the two men heaved arbitrary pieces of evidence at each other. Beck tossed a bronze lamp at Merit, who pitched a wind-up clock, like a fastball, at his opponent's head which missed.

Having run out of objects to throw, Merit retreated down the center aisle and when he looked back saw through a gap in the shelves that Beck had wasted no time in locating the inquiry book and was setting it on fire with a lighter.

★★★

The inquiry book rested on the floor, with Beck kneeling over it and blowing on the small flame to get the entire volume to ignite and turn into a heap of ashes.

There was no time left. Merit circled the shelves and approached Beck from the rear. He surprised Beck from behind and scooped up the flaming inquiry book, which was as thick as a dictionary, and ran, hurtling cartons every few feet. He clutched the smoldering manual to his chest, having managed to put out the fire by covering it against his chest, depriving the flame of oxygen. Seeing that he was trapped at the end of a long, dark aisle, he took out the phone Det. Hubbard had provided him. He naturally wouldn't be able to call for help or get any service, but he hectically punched a few numbers on the keypad and crouched, hands around his knees.

Moments later, he could see the beam from Beck's flashlight panning left and right like a tank's turret as he made his way down the center aisle looking for him. At row 51D, the second to last one on that sector of the floor, Beck turned left and looked to the end. Merit sat helplessly, cornered with his back to the wall and his knees tucked up his chest.

"Give me the fucking book!" Beck was done horsing around.

Merit didn't make the slightest move and stared back with petrified eyes. He was defeated, for there was no place left to run. Beck raised the gun and aimed carefully. He squeezed the trigger, the gun recoiled in his hand, but the bullet ricocheted off the wall, producing a loud *ping* as it hit a nearby metal shelf. Merit remained seated as if the bullet had passed cleanly through his body.

"What's going on?" Beck approached the investigator with the barrel's site aimed at Merit's forehead.

The hologram of Merit dissolved into thin air, and Merit's phone lay on the ground with a tiny purple dot flashing.

Merit had taken a photo of himself seated in the crouched position, then programmed the phone to call itself generating his image.

The *actual* Merit, by sucking in his stomach and getting as thin and tall as he could have wedged his body sideways into the narrowest of gaps at the end of the row and hid between a shelf and the wall. His unintended weight-loss of fourteen pounds since crossing the border, unlike Soldier's self-imposed diet that provided his arthritic ankles enough temporary relief to compete in one last major, allowed a slimmer Merit to slip through the crease to other side and provided him one last chance to get the inquiry. He made a mad dash up row 52D for the center aisle running past his startled opponent. Beck turned and squeezed off a hurried round, missing Merit by several feet.

Seeing the servile making his way down the aisle as he leaped over cartons of evidence, Merit reached for a slender metal rod on the shelf behind him as a weapon—Soldier's driver he'd taken from Beck's hands-on their original trip into the building and placed on the shelf. He slipped around the corner and pressed his back against the shelf at the end of the center aisle, the thin bar clasped in both of his hands.

He heard Beck's steps, and when he deemed that the servile was two feet from him, Merit spun around and swung the bar, catching Beck in the windpipe with the metal shaft and clothes-lined him to the floor. Merit stood over the body to see that his gun, which had one round left in the chamber, was within Beck's arm's length—It was a draw. Acting as he was coached, Merit gripped Soldier's club and brought it behind his shoulder, hips locked and his left arm straight, just as Keeper had taught him in the hospital room. Beck looked up at Merit then glanced over at the gun, and in a split-second reaction uncoiled his body and extended his hand for the pistol.

At that moment, Merit brought down the end of the driver against Beck's head. The clubface cracked open Beck's skull, blood and bone spraying in all directions, like one of the cherry-red fireworks that were exploding outside. *Bull's-eye!* The blow killed him instantly.

Merit dropped the driver and ran up to the lobby with the inquiry but saw that the door was padlocked from the outside by the workmen. Moving upstairs to the second-floor window, he tried to break the glass, but it was too thick. "You can't blow it up! There's someone in here!"

The demolition crew was too far away to hear his cries, and even if they'd been closer, the crowd noise was deafening.

"T-minus two minutes!" the foreman broadcasted and blared an air horn as a warning.

Still clutching the smoking inquiry, he sprinted to the stairwell and bounded up the stairs, taking steps three at a time. When he reached the black tarred roof, he ran to the four corners of the building to see the frenzied spectators cheering and doing *the wave.*

Fireworks were blasting into the sky, and far below, he spied the foreman standing above the detonator, ready to flip the switch and begin a series of controlled explosions caused by charges that had been placed strategically on every floor so that the building would fall vertically and not onto the crowd.

"T-minus thirty seconds!"

Merit thought of jumping, but he saw no safe landing spot below. There were no swimming pools or patches of shrubbery, only a sea of people filling the concrete streets surrounding the building and the Commons in front of it.

Merit felt the building shake slightly as the foreman began his final countdown.

"Twenty, nineteen..."

Merit was confused. The charges hadn't been detonated yet. What had caused the building to shake?

"Sixteen, fifteen..."

Merit decided that he needed to prepare for his death and sank to his knees. "I'm sorry, God. Forgive me for anything I've done wrong in my life. And Mom and Dad, I love you. I gave it my best, and I hope you're proud."

"Thirteen, twelve..."

Merit saw to the west in the distance that city lights were rapidly going dark on successive blocks. Entire buildings toppled like a deck of cards. The warehouse building shook again, and Merit, having been in Frontier for a month, knew what was happening. An earthquake was striking the area, and not a small one. The building he was on would fall shortly too, but not because of any controlled demolition. The earthquake was going to wipe out the city.

Some citizens scurried in every direction since they, too, realized what was happening, while many others oblivious, continued to party. The prisoners, so close to personal freedom, became helpless like moths caught in a spider's web when the ropes holding the tent above them snapped causing the canopy to plunge entangling them beneath.

Pandemonium filled the air, turning the carnival atmosphere into a disaster in progress. In an instant, Merit thought of the footage he'd viewed of the U.S. Golf Open and how the panicked crowd had scattered in every direction, trampling others in the gallery in the immediate aftermath of the frogman's rifle shot that had killed Soldier and wounded Mr. Lewis. It was playing out again, although this was happening on a much larger scale. He presumed that thousands of the city's innocent inhabitants would be killed in the next several minutes, people on the higher ground like Ms. Rebecca Smith he hoped would be spared, but not her classic white Targa. Out of instinct, he clutched the smoky inquiry book to his chest. If he was going to fall to his death, maybe his body would one day be discovered, and someone, by the grace of God, would read the book in his hands, and set history straight.

"Hey!" A faint voice harkened him. "Over here."

Merit looked around. Was he already dead? Was he hearing the voice of an angel?

The building was now leaning sharply, and his body was sliding to the southwest corner of the roof.

"Merit. It's me."

Merit gazed up to see the young Hispanic angel elevating above the roof. Starla was operating a drone, a drone furnished to her by the Pilgrim undercover cop.

She held out her left arm, allowing Merit to leap off the roof's edge into her embrace. Despite the added weight, the newly powered drone easily supported the two of them, her small frame having very little impact, and Merit took over the controls.

The skinny white punk with the double ponytail, who'd managed to have shimmied free from under the giant tent, looked into the sky to see his *victim* and the Pilgrim cop hovering safely ten stories above the chaos and trampled bodies.

"Help!" He was jumping up and down waving his arms over his head. "Come get me!"

Starla watched, emotionless, as the oldest structure remaining in Frontier, the massive ugly building that stomached the paramount evidence to convict the lawbreakers toppled sideways, and in an instant pulverized the last hundred dangerous felons and the man who'd savagely violated her, into obliteration.

The drone's many rotors spun faster, and the downward thrust rose the pair into the sky.

Soon, Merit and Starla were a thousand feet up, allowing them to see the tsunami that was forming behind the earthquake further west in the Pacific Ocean. The land was undergoing a major shift for the first time in decades, the earth's crust buckling as fault lines appeared throughout the city. Some areas tilted toward the sky, while others dipped toward the bowels of the earth. The entire landmass would soon be flooded.

Merit looked in Starla's eyes, whose face was just inches from his as they raced east towards the safety of the foothills on higher ground—the San Bernardino Mountain Range. He leaned forward, both closing their eyes, and kissed her lovingly on the lips.

72

Seven tense days later, the Presidential leaders emerged from Camp David with a strategy to bring Arkansas 'gun inventory' revolt to an end and save the country. The plan was radical and violated the principles on which the nation was founded. Desperate to make his point, the presiding President compared America's political "right" and the "lefts" relentless pursuit to create their "perfect" society, to artists with opposing visions of beauty. He likened two sculptors with an obsession for perfection, who couldn't stop chiseling away at the same statue until there was no marble left to carve. He proposed that the people vote to replace the "U.S. Constitution" with the "U.S. Resolution," dividing The United States into two giant states, a left and a right, before "America the beautiful" crumbled to dust.
—Jaden Swift, *LIVEmag.com* May 9, 2033, 2:14 pm PST

SECOND COMING

After months of additional aftershocks and tremors, a portion of the land of Frontier that had been referred to in history as Southern California had shifted, and the eighty-five-acre golf course island, the one that had hosted the *last* U.S. Open, righted itself.

Water drained off the sides of its cliffs, and the muddy flats, swamps, and lakes began to show signs of supple green vegetation. Trees and shrubbery were healthy, and deer and other wildlife emerged from thickets to nibble the new growth. Also visible were the drinking fountain and *Whale's Breach Rock* near the eighteenth hole, both near the clubhouse. The clubhouse itself was an empty shell of a building, and like most other features of the course, was covered in algae and barnacles. The aluminum stadium bleachers surrounding the eighteenth green looked like a coral reef amphitheater, and the towers used by television crews were green, bent, and, in most cases, lying on the ground.

Against this backdrop of both failure and hope, Starla, a clean and sober reporter who was professionally dressed, stood on the steps of the clubhouse, the very spot where ex-Olympic Games President Pratt had delivered the findings of the Major Murder Inquiry. With two hands she held up the fifty-six-year-old Major Murder Inquiry book that detailed the report of its one hundred investigators.

Starla spoke into her microphone as a cameraman focused on a headshot of the lovely, glowing reporter. "...and I will begin a ten-part series of reports on what actually happened to bring about the Divided States of America back in the 2020s."

"The hallowed grounds where I'm standing today are an expansive piece of real estate where sixty years ago visionary land developer, Alex Novak, intended to purchase and build his eco-friendly condo city. When the owner of the eighty-five-acre golf course, Mr. Sean Lewis, refused to sell the seaside property, the overzealous developer plotted to have him killed and procure the valuable land. In 2026, golf legend, Soldier Quinn, was attempting to win The U.S. Open and break the record for the most major titles when he and the course owner, Lewis, were gunned down. A hitman, hired by Novak, shot both men, banking on Soldier's high-profile assassination and the optics surrounding his death to cover up the motive for the *accidental* murder of Mr. Lewis."

"This is the story of a crime that was almost perfect in its execution, even the staging of a suicide after the assassin botched the shooting of Orange Golf Club owner Sean Lewis."

"As you'll learn, this Inquiry reads that all the *indicators* pointed to the *certainty* that Soldier was killed to prevent him from surpassing Jackson's record, thus leading any reasonable person to deduce that Soldier, a person of color, and Jackson, being of Caucasian descent, the perpetrator's motivation to kill was based on ethnicity. However, after exhausting every possible lead the inquiry failed to uncover one shred of physical, circumstantial, or trace evidence to support the theory."

She opened the Inquiry to a bookmarked section, "The *M.M.I.*— Major Murder Inquiry concluded the status of Soldier Quinn's death was to remain classified as *Undetermined.*" She pointed to the exact word, "*UNDETERMINED*", on the last page of the Inquiry." She looked sternly into the camera. "There was *no* mention of an *unequivocally race-hate-related* homicide."

As you will hear with each broadcast, the homicide of Soldier Quinn was *not* motivated by the color of skin but by simple, old-fangled American greed."

Starla closed the book. "Finally, the tragedy I will be reporting is that of a cold case that remained hidden for decades if not for the courage, intelligence, and heroism of a certain detective who uncovered the facts I have related. A detective who found the many pieces of evidence that explain the assassination and staged suicide-murder that led to the division of the *old* United States."

Over Starla's shoulder, in the distance, the shape and silhouette of a humongous human figure emerged up out from the water's womb, the bronze statue of Soldier striking his Jesus *on the cross*-pose after hitting the miracle shot—the sculpture Ms. Rebecca Lewis's mother had commissioned and assumed to be lost in transit was being unearthed.

Time and saltwater had rotted the wooden crate exposing the likeness of the golfer, his arms extended out to the side, a driver in his hand, and the receding water line created the eerie illusion that he was rising from water's surface. The stunning appearance of the statue symbolized the rebirth of the man and his true legacy.

In her televised remarks, Starla spontaneously alluded that the sculpture was a symbol of redemption, a powerful sign that golf would no longer be a dirty word. She turned profile to the magnificent bronze statue, which was mostly a patina of green and gray from years of tarnish, oxidation and mold, and continued her report. His outstretched arms and humbly bowed head represented a rising from the dead, and resurrection of the banished game of golf and perhaps a new beginning for the entire country."

Starla lowered her microphone as the camera stopped rolling. She looked back at the course and recalled how Merit and Keeper had combed the mysterious island when it was still underwater. It had been an unbelievably hard task, and the two men had risked their lives to explore the marshy terrain to uncover clues. In their quest, they had kindled a special relationship neither had sought but which both needed.

She held up her jadeite engagement ring and looked at it in the lemon light rays of the setting sun. Her tattooed chest and scars remained, but she, too, would have a new beginning. She was inwardly clean and healed, and for that, she was thankful to her soon-to-be husband, James Merit.

Her anticipated marriage to the detective would be a big step in Starla's journey to trust men again, but to have faith in the God and guns that Merit believed, was too big of a leap this early in their relationship.

***

Merit walked through dense thickets and emerged in a cluster of azalea bushes. With the eyes of a trained hot *and* cold case homicide detective, he was sleuthing for something very important. A few feet farther on, he found it, a white-dimpled golf ball.

He'd hit a poor shot off the 18th fairway, and the ball had landed in the deep rough on the right side of the fairway. Merit wore a pullover shirt, white slacks, and golf shoes. He'd been practicing and playing every day on the first course built in Pilgrim since the eradication of golf, a most basic course designed and maintained by the retired cold case Detective Hubbard, and Merit had gotten quite proficient at the game in a short amount of time.

Since Merit's return home to Pilgrim, he'd picked up on his regular exercise regime where he'd left off, kept his investigative skills sharp by solving hot homicides in the homiscope, and was focusing on his new courtship with Starla, which he knew would be demanding, but would handle each challenge one day a time, one shot at a time.

Other than that, everything was back to normal in Merit's life, except for a small comment Sgt. Travers had made in passing over a steak dinner that struck a tiny nerve. His triple-shoulder-striped supervisor had mentioned a new piece of evidence that had surfaced surrounding the murder of another famous person that Merit might have found of interest if he ever felt the urge again to tackle a second cold case.

The questionable killing involved the shooting of a highly influential individual in old America's *Golden Age,* but Merit being ignorant to the old United States' past, once again wasn't familiar with the historical figure who was known by the initials J.F.K.

As for Merit's immediate future, he was concentrating on something more important, his short game, which on this late Sunday afternoon was proving to be his weakness. Merit looked at his golf bag, carefully selecting the right iron for his next shot. He positioned himself, drew the nine-iron back, and struck the ball, which lobbed high onto the front side of the green a hundred and ten feet away. His form was fluid, and he had clearly received some instruction. The ball rolled past the pin and came to rest thirty feet from the 18th pin on the fringe, not exactly what he visioned, but he would hopefully be able to two-putt to save par.

He had a tan and walked with flair across the fairway. His hair was longer than it had been in many years, styled similarly in the way the deceased servile, whom he still had conflicted feelings for, had worn his. Merit had killed Beck, and even though he could come to terms that he was pushed to do so, Beck was a policeman and that would never go away. He kept the P.P. *tattoo* on his neck, one he shared with Beck, as a reminder of his fallen comrade and the challenges he endured across the border. He strode tactfully across the kidney bean–shaped green, and, spotting Keeper approaching the green, he motioned for his pal to putt first.

Keeper, sporting his vintage digs from the 2010s, selected the putter from his dad's old bag. He stood three feet away from the ball and swung his arms gently to simulate the putt he wanted to make. It was a twelve-foot putt. He then stepped forward and stood over the ball lying on the freshly shaved green grass before doing a double-take. Looking closer, he recognized it wasn't the ball he'd launched from the fairway. "That's it," he said under his breath.

He twisted his torso toward Merit, hands trembling, his eyes staring in disbelief, "That's the ball." Moments earlier, when Merit had strolled past Keeper's ball, he had swapped it, replacing it with a Titleist ball. The ball had the distinct markings Keeper's father had written, characters that only Soldier and Keeper could have positively identified on the miracle ball:

SQKQ4VR
Soldier Quinn, Keeper Quinn, forever.

Keeper looked at Merit with wonderment. "Where did you find it?"

Merit, leaning on his putter, had been waiting for the right place and time to show Keeper his find, and this was the moment. "Make this putt and I'll tell you."

There was complete silence, for even the swallows and crickets were auspiciously absent at dusk, as Keeper released the air from his upper chest, then calmly stepped forward to address the ball. He composed himself, read the green, and just as his father would have attempted to win golf's U.S. Open decades earlier, he tapped the left to right breaking twelve-foot putt . . .

police man *USA*

written in 2015

R. ANDERSON

policemanUSA.com

The SHOT that Split America

Made in United States
North Haven, CT
18 February 2024